rosebud
wallpaper

a novel

r.K. Sachdev

Library of Congress Control Number: 2023915732

ISBN 979-8-9887268-1-4 (hardcover)

ISBN 979-8-9887268-2-1 (paperback)

ISBN 979-8-9887268-0-7 (ebook)

Edited By: Sherri Shackelford

First edition 2023.

Published by r. K. Sachdev; San Jose (CA).

*To Mom and Dad, I owe
you everything
&
To those that knew I could do it
and supported me along
the way.*

Thank you.

prologue

Gerald Lambino

One, two, three. Sharp exhale. *One, two, three.*

My habit of repeating this in my head whenever I go on a run has never left me. Since childhood. It comes from my father. Or at least I think it does.

I never actually met him. I never met my mom, either. She died from medical complications when I was born, and I was raised by her sister and her sister's husband. Apparently, my father skipped out on my mom when he found out she was pregnant. Kind of cliché, but what can you do? Nonetheless, I like to imagine what he may have been like. Personify the bastard.

In my head, he ran a lot. Maybe because he figuratively ran when he found out my mom was pregnant. As an avid runner, I approach it as a form of competition with the man who's likely the source of my passion for running. To prove to myself that I am better than him.

One, two, three. Sharper exhale. *One, two, three.* I recite to myself, frustrated, and bring myself back to a constant and steady pace following a sudden quickening of my heartbeat.

Thinking about that man does that to me. He pops into my head every now and then, but only on my runs. The irony doesn't escape me. Neither does he.

I prefer to go on my runs early in the morning. The birds are sleeping and haven't begun their peaceful morning chirping ritual. The only sound I hear is the rippling of the ocean waves from the beach in the distance, making their inevitable contact with the shore.

If I wait to go on my run until later in the day, the streets of Baker Beach will invariably be busy, swarming with people and incessant chatter. Especially in this part of San Francisco, where tourists frequent. Plus, I have to be at school later for a lecture, and a morning run is a good start to the day.

Being a teaching assistant for a prestigious law school is no easy task. I always have to bring my A-game. I *want* to bring my A-game. My aunt and uncle raised me and gave me every opportunity. I owe it to them. For all intents and purposes, they're my parents. They've nourished me with love just the same.

But there's always something or someone to worry about. Running gives me the opportunity to relieve the stress that comes with the high expectations I'm held to. The quiet of the streets calms my nerves, and the darkness of the morning strangely enlightens my thoughts.

I ran twice a day when I actively practiced criminal defense, whenever I could manage the time. I'd have lost my mind if I didn't.

The firm I worked at belonged to a Bheaurmiss School of Law professor. He no longer practices criminal defense law, or any law for that matter, but he teaches criminal law. I, on the other hand, somewhat shifted gears.

The cases he worked on were emotionally taxing. They were the type of cases that left me with gut-wrenching nausea, ranging from robbery, rape, kidnapping, assault, attempted murder, and murder. Actually, many murders. I shiver simply at the thought of them.

It comes with the territory of being a criminal defense attorney, but I didn't have as thick a skin as he did. He was brilliant in his defense of his clients. Some would say he was flawless.

One case in particular was *the* case for me. I was a case analyst and was privy to many details.

That one case was when I decided that I'd had enough. I wasn't cut out for this work.

Despite leaving that type of work behind, the long-lasting feeling of remorse I still felt afterward, however, was not always easy to deal with. I felt the regret down to the very core of my being. I feel it to this day.

A sudden, intermittent flicker of light blares in front of me, interrupting my reflection of my previous life, which would've inevitably led me down a road of self-loathing. The light is blinding and elicits the onset of a pounding headache.

It's an oncoming car. Certainly nothing I haven't seen before at this time of the morning. Then, the driver of the car switches off their headlights.

This—I haven't seen before. My vision momentarily blurs as my eyes adjust to the sudden and unexpected loss of light.

Something isn't right. My heart rate quickens again.

A few seconds later, the driver revs the engine, increasing the speed—the engine roar is powerfully loud at this time of the morning. My legs feel unbearably heavy with each movement on the strong, level pavement. Each step feels as if I'm running in slow motion.

I maintain my running pace, hoping not to be affected by the intimidation of the car, but my heart is exploding inside of my chest. I think it has fallen into the pit of my stomach.

There's no way this car is here for me, I console myself. *I'm okay. I'm okay*, I repeat over and over.

When I see the car veer toward me, I panic.

With fear-induced adrenaline bursting through me, I attempt to move aside, but there's nowhere for me to go. I'm on a narrow road, and there isn't that much space on this part of the street.

This car must be mistaken, but I know I'm falsely assuring myself. *It's going to hit me.*

The car strikes me head-on with immense power that the initial pain does not fully register. The world is spinning, but I think the only thing that's spinning is me.

The immediate impact of the car smashing into my body resonates with me when I hit the cold, hard concrete pavement. I was tossed around as if I were roadkill.

Pain and soreness strike throughout my body. The metallic taste of blood in my saliva makes me not want to swallow. I can feel the strong sting of open wounds all over me.

Normally, I'd ask myself what I'd done to deserve this, but I can't help but wonder whether this moment was predestined.

The car that hit me didn't stop; it kept going faster and faster.

A good start to the day.

Then, everything goes dark.

I hope I wake up.

chapter 1

Bani
Later that day.

Innocent until proven guilty, the presumption of innocence. It's easier said than done.

Whenever I listen to the news, specifically during the crime report, I analyze the crime to see if the district attorney will be able to prosecute the arrested individual and prove guilt. When you're studying law, it's easier to pick up on legal terms and analyze them. Of course, the news doesn't relay all of the information about a crime, as some parts are confidential, but I base my analysis on the presentation of the facts provided. As limited as they might be.

It's nerdy, but it helps with studying, and I need all the help I can get. I'm in my first semester of my second year of law school at Bheaurmiss School of Law, commonly known as "Bheau Law School" or simply "Bheau," and criminal law is both the most interesting and terrifying course thus far. Interesting in the sense that some of the crimes in the cases are ludicrous and read like a story. Terrifying because I always wonder how the convicted individual mustered the courage to commit the crime they were found guilty of. Some people must be completely deranged to be able to commit such violent acts against other people, even children.

The class is additionally terrifying because the professor teaching it is known to be absolutely brilliant but also incredibly tough. He was an extremely well-known criminal defense attorney. Before he went into teaching, he was notorious for working only on serious felony cases. Bheau snatched him up as a professor once he dissolved his practice.

California hasn't implemented the death penalty in years, but Professor Erikson has worked on numerous high-profile death penalty cases. Some of his cases were stomach-twirling, nauseating, truly atrocious crimes. I can't fathom how he maintained his sanity while working on them.

Then again, he's a lawyer, and that's his job.

Aman thinks Professor Erikson is a heartless sociopath and that it's impossible for someone to work on those kinds of cases and continue living unbothered. Aman has been my companion in law school, my confidante, and my best friend. With him, I have the kind of relationship that you rely on to get you through law school. He's also my roommate.

Living with a single, twenty-nine-year-old Punjabi guy as a single, twenty-five-year-old Punjabi girl could be considered appalling to the majority of the Punjabi community. Thankfully, my parents adore Aman and trust him completely. I'm certain they believe Aman and I are perfect for each other and that it's only a matter of time before we realize it.

They especially enjoyed learning that Aman and I frequently speak to each other in Punjabi. I don't know what it is with Punjabi people and being able to speak Punjabi, but they love it. That they speak the language well is one of the highest compliments a parent can receive about their child.

Little do my parents know, Aman is promiscuous as hell. Still, he treats me with so much respect and love that I feel absolutely safe and protected around him.

He's sitting on a couch, watching the news in our living room when I walk in. In between intermittent sips, he rests an overly-filled coffee cup between his palms.

"You're going to spill coffee on the couch," I say. Punjabi, again.

"I'm in my element—coffee and the news. Bani, this guy was found on the street because he was drenched in blood with no visible injuries to identify the blood's source. *Drenched*. What the hell was he doing that he was drenched in blood?"

"With you watching this every day, I've been having nightmares." I blankly stare at him, fully expecting what he'll say next.

"Didn't you say only yesterday that putting on the news helps you study?" A smirk grows on his handsome face. "If you're having nightmares, Ban, you know you can always come to me when you're scared. I'll protect you." His charming smirk is accompanied by a quick wink.

I laughingly throw a pillow at him. "No, I'm okay. When was the last time you even washed your sheets?"

"I'll get around to it after I finish reading the cases for crim-law."

I poke fun at Aman, but he's actually one of the cleanest people I know. In fact, he's particularly anal about it.

"Do some of my laundry too, please."

"Sure, does madam need anything else?" he asks in Punjabi.

"Mmm, that should do it."

Aman realizes we have an evidence lecture in less than a half-hour when the news reporter announces the time on the TV. "Shit! Ban, can you wait for me, please?"

"This is why I tell you to get ready and then get in 'your element.'"

Aman makes a silly face at me before he rushes into his bedroom. Minutes later, a fountain of high-pressured water droplets hit the walls of our modern walk-in shower.

Although I'm a Palo Alto native, I'm quickly transitioning to a San Francisco citizen. I went to college in San Francisco and am now in San Francisco for law school too.

Before law school, I worked as a legal assistant at a small software company in downtown San Francisco called Stardunning, Inc. for nearly two years. My dad was well acquainted with the CEO and helped me secure the position. He felt it was imperative for me to see what working in a legal environment entailed before I invested the time and energy on law school.

My parents bought an apartment in a pseudo-traditional San Francisco building because my dad thought it would be a smart real estate investment. I live in the city because the idea of commuting to and from Palo Alto while in law school is daunting. Since I don't have to pay the high San Francisco rent, and I saved up while working, I can afford to do the simple things that make me happy.

"Don't worry about the money. Your mom makes plenty," my dad playfully and frequently jokes with my mom. I tease that it's their way of modestly flirting with each other in front of their kids.

Between the two of them, my parents are very well off financially. My mom is an accounting partner and director at a major international accounting firm, and my dad is a tenured professor of political science at Jandsin University in Palo Alto.

Aman moved in with me right before the second semester of our first year. Our apartment is small but elegant and chic. I decorated and styled it long before Aman moved in, but I always encouraged him to add things according to his taste, so naturally, it feels like a joint apartment versus just mine.

He's added abstract art pieces along the walls, light gray stools for the kitchen island that contrast well with the royal-blue wooden sides and black countertop of the island, and a vintage entry table he found while we were rummaging through an antique store one random Saturday afternoon. Aman likes unique things and has great taste. Well, with most things.

As a personal favor from my dad, Aman pays a fair but subsidized amount in rent. My dad is well aware of Aman's background and empathizes with him. Aman was born in Punjab and moved to L.A. when he was ten.

He was essentially raised by his mom because, throughout his childhood, Aman's dad was in L.A., earning a living to bring his family to California from Punjab. He chose L.A. because he had a dream to keep his boys close to Disneyland and the beach so he could take them every weekend. My heart breaks for his family every time I hear that.

Aman's dad was a social drinker, but shortly after he came to L.A., the social drinking quickly escalated to alcoholism. Aman came home from school one day and found his dad lying in the garage, lifeless. He passed away when Aman was only fourteen years old.

Aman prefers to keep this aspect of his history to himself. He only shares it once he feels a certain level of comfort with someone, which doesn't happen frequently with him. He's only ever given me a reader's digest version of his father's passing. I don't believe many others know.

As silly as it may sound, I thought Aman was gorgeous when I first met him. And he is—he's very handsome. But when I got to know more about him and his past, my respect and admiration for him skyrocketed.

Given the circumstances he's had to face, he's done very well for himself. I can't imagine experiencing something as traumatizing as that at such an early age. He was shaken up for a while, but he took care of his mom, worked while studying, and went to a local university to stay near his family. Despite being distressed by the experience of his father's passing, he derived strength and incredible maturity from it.

Eventually, his mom remarried. His younger brother, Raman, is still in L.A., working in marketing and living with his girlfriend.

Aman started off his career by working for several years as an engineer. A few years into that profession, he realized how much he disliked it and decided to pursue a career in law. He wanted to go to Bheau specifically, but he also needed to know that his mom and brother were content and comfortable before he could physically move away.

With a few minutes left before we have to be in our respective seats, Aman emerges into the living room, freshly showered. We live within walking distance from school, but I accept that we'll be late. Luckily, it's not the norm for us.

I predict that Professor Gatlin's eyes will follow us to our assigned seats while her face sports a stern look.

"Ms. Sethi, Mr. Wajla, how nice of you to join us," she sarcastically comments in front of the whole class. My cheeks grow warm and spotty as the rest of the class snickers.

Her physical look is the stereotype of a law school professor. She always wears either a pantsuit or skirt suit, black-frame glasses, red lipstick, and her hair in a bun. In fact, I've never seen her hair when it's not in a bun. I don't even know if it's long or short.

She has lovely, sharp features and is one of the younger tenured professors at the law school, if not the youngest. She looks to be in her late thirties.

Professor Gatlin is, in fact, an amiable and approachable professor, especially during office hours. That's the great thing about this school—they have high expectations of their students, but the professors are generally approachable and willing to help, absent a few. But her pet peeve is when students are late, and she doesn't hesitate to vocalize it.

Luckily, Aman and I have assigned seats at the end of the fourth row, and we don't have to disrupt the class further by asking other students to move for us to walk by.

"Aman, I wanted to go to her office hours after class, and now it's going to be awkward. She's going to call me out for being late," I'm careful to whisper quietly.

"Ban, relax. If she says something, and I know she won't, I'll make it up to you."

Professor Gatlin resumes lecturing after flipping through the evidence coursebook, free of any further interruptions during the remainder of class.

chapter 2

Our section's schedule includes evidence on Mondays, Wednesdays, and Fridays, criminal law on Mondays and Wednesdays, and a legal writing class on Tuesdays and Thursdays. In between classes, the professors and teaching assistants, or TAs, hold office hours.

At the beginning of 1L year, Bheau law school puts students in assigned sections that take all the core classes together. There are two sections in our year, and this is the last semester we'll take all of our classes with our sections. Starting next semester, we'll take two to three electives and one core class.

Each core class has two TAs: one that holds office hours for students with last names A-M, and one for N-Z. I prefer going to the professor's office hours, supplemented by the TA's.

Unsurprisingly, the professor's office hours are never as packed as the TA's, likely due to the intimidation factor.

Professor Gatlin's office hours start shortly after the evidence lecture. I sit in the student café on the second floor of the law school, reviewing my notes from the last two lectures in preparation for the discussion with Professor Gatlin.

Evidence is one of the few classes that doesn't revolve around learning the law through cases. Instead, it's a rule-based class with very little case law. It's refreshing, but something I'm not accustomed to.

Professor Gatlin passes by with a coffee and snack in her hand, and I'm relieved when she smiles at me. As she disappears down the corridor, her heels prominently clacking with each step, Mark walks toward me from the opposite direction.

Mark is my other closest friend from the 1L year. He was the first person I met at orientation, and we connected instantly, bonding over how much we both love dogs. I was also intrigued by his last name, Namora, neatly displayed on the sticker nametag on his shirt, and politely asked the origin. Turns out he's Portuguese.

"Hey, Bunny!" Mark playfully calls me by my nickname. I was a bunny for Halloween last year, and Mark has called me Bunny ever since. It also happens to be a lovely play off my name. "I'm going to buy a coffee, and then you want to head up to Professor G's office?"

"Yes, sounds good."

"Do you want anything?"

"No, thank you."

In addition to taking a part-time law school curriculum, Mark externs with a law firm downtown, where he earns credit toward his semester allowance instead of taking the legal writing class. Because of his externship, I rarely see him outside of class during the week. He usually sits with us during the lecture, but he didn't come today because of an urgent work meeting.

I frequently joke that Mark and Aman have a bromance. At first, they were not nearly as close as they are now—because Mark is naturally a quiet person, he limits his interactions to his comfort zone. Aman is the opposite. He's an extrovert and naturally social. Aman was initially put off, but he soon realized how sweet Mark is.

Once Mark returns with his coffee, we journey up to Professor Gatlin's office. He looks upset and finally admits it's because of a recent work incident.

"One of the junior partners came into the conference room my supervising associate attorney and I were in and started grilling him about a case. Chris had literally just gotten back from a vacation and had no idea what was going on. I sat there powerless. I don't understand why partners think they can treat their associates *however* they want."

"It sucks how normal that is."

I'm constantly worried that after I graduate from law school and pass the bar, I'll end up with a job I hate, which will make me wonder why I wanted to be a lawyer to begin with. Stardunning was a wonderful experience, but every workplace is inevitably different.

"Aman said he wants to go out to get a drink tonight. Do you want to come?" I'm hoping a night out will serve as both a distraction and a mood-lifter for Mark.

"Let's do it!" he says. I could use a drink after this week."

Just as I expected.

"Let's go to the new bar on Divis—Magnicifying Glass. I heard it's opening today."

"Isn't that the investigator-themed bar? If it opens today, won't it be packed?" Mark asks.

"I don't think so. This is a soft opening, so it's word-of-mouth versus the publicized grand opening date. If it's too packed, we can go to Suite 22."

Mark gives me a curious look. "I don't get why you still like that bar. It's the most basic bar on Divis."

"Basic or not, I've had some great memories there." I laugh, but I'm certain it sounds inauthentic.

Mark knows exactly what I'm referring to. I met my ex there, and I would be lying if I said that I don't still think about him. That night we met was honestly a great night. Even before I met him.

Things didn't end well between us. When I met him, I thought, *"This guy has got to be different."* He wasn't. He turned out to be someone completely different than who I thought he was—one of the biggest pricks I've ever met.

Dating in San Francisco is a hopeless task. Especially with the vast number of dating apps out there, guys feel like they have infinite options. Girls and guys alike, in fact.

Mark has a girlfriend who lives in his hometown, Portland. They'd been dating for years before he started law school and have been long-distance since he moved. She comes down every now and then, and he goes up to visit her and his family. But I know that with his hours and workload, the long-distance relationship is taxing.

"Bunny, you have to stop thinking about him."

"I'm not," I lie, yet my voice is solemn.

"Professor Gatlin's office is closed." I notice as we approach her office door. "What time is it?"

"Just after eleven."

"Strange, I just saw her downstairs right before you showed up."

chapter 3

Nearly halfway into her scheduled office hours, Professor Gatlin sends an email formally canceling. The email is vague and cryptic.

"Students, I apologize for the late notice, but unfortunately, office hours are canceled due to an urgent matter that I must attend to immediately. There will be make-up office hours next week, and timings will be provided shortly."

Professor Gatlin has canceled office hours before, but she usually provides notice ahead of time. This is the first time she's canceled after the fact.

Prior to receiving her email, Mark and I waited a few minutes but left once we guessed she wasn't coming. Aman seemed completely unbothered when I told him about Professor Gatlin's abrupt and uncharacteristic cancellation. Not surprising for him.

That Friday evening, Aman and Mark are already pregaming at home in preparation for our night out to Magnicifying Glass.

Aman refuses to understand that girls take longer to get ready because there's more to the process. All he does is shower, briefly fix his hair, and put his clothes on. Sometimes, if he looks like a caveman, he trims his beard. I have to shower, put my clothes on, do my hair, and put on makeup. My hair takes me at least fifteen minutes, and my makeup takes me at least thirty.

Tonight, I decide on jeans and a flowy tan and gold top, which shows a bit of tasteful cleavage. I complete my outfit with a modest pair of heels. Using a hair straightener, I add loose curls to my long hair, and I keep my makeup elegant but neutral.

"*Hurry up!* Why does it take such a tiny person so long to get ready?" Aman yells in Punjabi. He's exaggerating. I'm neither skinny nor overweight. I'm curvy, and I'm pretty short, about five-four.

"I'm almost ready! Give me five more minutes."

"Do you believe her?" Aman whispers to Mark, yet loud enough for me to hear.

"I heard that, smart ass!" I yell back.

Aman's chuckle is so low that I almost don't hear it this time. "You look cute anyway. Just come on!"

"I want a drink before we leave, Aman."

"Why didn't you tell me that before? I would've made you one, and you could have finished it while getting ready." There's a hint of annoyance in his voice.

"No one will be at Magnicifying Glass before nine. We have plenty of time."

He's only eager to get there because he told his friends to meet us there, and this group of friends includes a lady friend. That's all I know.

"What time did you tell your friends you were going to be there?" My makeup brush is still in my hands as I leisurely stroll into the living room and spot Aman typing on his phone.

"Eight-thirty."

"Just text them and say you're running late."

"Hm." He pauses before rising from the couch to make my drink. "What do you want?"

"My usual. You look nice!" I add to soften his mood. It works—he happily grins back at me.

He's wearing gray slacks and a black sweater. He trimmed his beard, and his hair is gelled with a slight part to the side. The slight part makes him look dashing and handsome, like a sophisticated young man.

Mark checks his work email on his laptop, fully focused. "Bro, do you want me to make you another drink?" Aman asks.

"No, I'm good. Thanks," Mark replies distractedly. He's wearing a white sweater with jeans and looks adorable.

When I'm at home, my usual drink is rum and soda. When we go out, I prefer an old-fashioned. It's actually how Aman and I first became friends.

Every Thursday, our school has a bar night hosted by a student organization at different bars around the city. First-year students are strongly encouraged to go to these events to socialize with classmates. Since there's a division between the two sections, it's an opportunity for the students in one section to meet and interact with students in the other. Aman and I were in the same section as 1Ls, but we didn't talk until that night, during the second or third week of school.

I was standing with Mark and talking to another girl in our section, Mona. She's a nice person, but I think she stopped liking me because Aman and I grew close. I strongly suspect that what he said to me when I first met him contributed to this dislike because

I'm certain that she and Aman were already hooking up when I first met him.

He approached the three of us, clearly buzzed, as we discussed our torts class. He asked us what we wanted to drink and to join him for another round. When I shared my preferred drink—an old-fashioned—he held a surprised expression and said, "Now, that's my kind of girl!"

He repeatedly said that he hadn't met any girls who liked to drink old-fashioneds, and I could tell by Mona's reaction that she was not pleased. Aman was a bit clueless to say that to me right in front of her when they were hooking up.

Then, since we had it in common, we talked about where in Punjab our families were from, and that led to discussing *bhangra*, fast-paced Punjabi folk music.

"I'm more about the new generation music, or *paindu* songs with the proper instrumental background." I wholeheartedly agreed with him. *Paindu* songs, *paindu* meaning "traditional village type" in Punjabi, are a true treasure.

While Mona and Aman were dating, which was for about two months and not seriously, of course, the four of us were the bar night crew. After that, Mona branched off and stopped coming with us. A few weeks later, she showed up with some of the people that were in the first section. That night, she came up to me, clearly drunk, and said that she was over Aman. She insinuated something between the two of us, but Aman and I only had a friendly relationship then. Mona, surprisingly, alluded to that despite experiencing and witnessing our relationship firsthand.

During winter break and shortly before the start of our second semester, Aman was looking for a new place to live, and I suggested he move in with me. He was reluctant because he didn't want to burden me or my family. Ultimately, I was able to convince him by highlighting the many positive aspects of where I lived. And there are many.

Aman interrupts my reminiscing when he hounds me to quickly finish my drink so that we can leave. I'm lightweight enough that finishing the rest of my drink in ten minutes makes me buzzed already. Plus, Aman was generous with the alcohol.

Mark closes his laptop and calls for a cab. He frequently stays at our apartment, especially on nights we go out. He lives in Oakland, and by the time we get home, public transportation isn't running. Rather than have him leave the bar or restaurant early, we encourage him to stay the night.

"Mark, send a Weevee request to me and Aman." Weevee is a common app in the Bay Area used for transferring money between family and friends.

"Seriously, Bunny, it's all good. You guys let me crash here all the time, and don't ask me to pay rent."

I chortle loudly, then instinctively cover my mouth with my hand out of embarrassment. The hit from the alcohol is strong. "Maybe we should, so that you don't always use that excuse when I ask you to send us a Weevee!"

Once the car arrives and we're situated in the back, we request the driver to play *bhangra* while en route to the bar.

When he's around Aman and me, Mark listens to *bhangra* and sincerely enjoys it. He likes the beat, which is the general consensus when non-Punjabi people hear *bhangra* for the first time. Sometimes he asks us to translate the lyrics, and he marvels at the English translation.

As we near Magnicifying Glass, we pass by Suite 22, the bar. I get a frog-like sensation in my throat, and my stomach ties into knots. Reminding myself that it's the alcohol that's eliciting this reaction, I transfer my focus to my friends as a necessary distraction.

When I see the decent-sized line in front of Magnicifying Glass, I giggle because I know that Aman will complain. He's looking outside the window in the opposite direction, toward Suite 22, deep in thought, and hasn't seen the line outside of Magnicifying Glass yet. I wonder what he's thinking about.

Once he hears me giggle, he appears to lose his pensive train of thought. Bewildered, he looks at me and asks, "What happened?" in Punjabi.

Mark has learned some of the simpler Punjabi words and phrases, and he understands what Aman said. "I think she's giggling at the line."

Aman gazes outside, his eyes eventually landing on the line in front of Magnicifying Glass.

He laughs mockingly. "Not so funny, because my friends are already in line."

chapter 4

I don't recognize the group of friends as we approach them near the front of the line. There are two girls and one guy.

Aman hugs one of the girls. I assume she's the one he came to the bar for, but wait for a confirmation of some sort. Meanwhile, the other guy and girl stand cozily next to each other. They must be dating.

"This is my roommate, Bani, and this is Mark," Aman introduces us.

Mark and I, on cue, say "Hi" and smile back.

"This is Noor, Jules, and Jermaine. I met Noor and Jules at the school gym last week," Aman says.

"I usually prefer going on runs outdoors, but Jules dragged me along with her that day," Noor adds, cycing Aman with a brief but intense look of desire. *That's good enough confirmation for me*, I think to myself.

"Jules had no idea what she was doing on one of the machines," Aman jokes nonchalantly, and we all laugh. His ability to be charming when he's poking fun is astonishing.

"How long have you been waiting?" I ask.

"Not too long." Noor scans the rest of the line, which has gotten longer since our arrival. "About ten minutes."

I'm not surprised that Aman didn't give me any details about Noor. He rarely discusses details of his personal life with me. Instead, he lets me find out through in-person introductions such as these. Although, these introductions are not frequent, which makes me wonder if this is a special occurrence.

One thing that Aman and I have in common is that we both have a type, and we date within that type. He likes tall, skinny girls with hefty makeup, and I like tall, skinny guys with beards. The guy I met at Suite 22, whom I also refer to as Suite 22 because I don't like to say his name, was typical of my type.

Similarly, Noor fits the description of Aman's type. Although she's slightly shorter than what he typically gravitates toward, she's still taller than me. She has medium-length, straight hair, and sharp facial features. Her makeup is heavy around the eyes, and her lipstick is a dark, statement color.

After five minutes of standard introductory chit-chat, we finally arrive at the entrance and the bouncer checks our IDs.

Magnicifying Glass is fantastic. I was expecting the space to be slightly bigger, but it's decently sized. The actual bar forms a horseshoe extending from the back wall. A patterned red fabric runs all along the sides of the horseshoe-shaped bar.

Various investigative and detective props hang on the walls around the room. There's a giant magnifying glass hanging from the ceiling that slowly rocks back and forth, amplifying the writing on the back wall. The handwritten text is blood-red, and the droplets beneath the letters emphasize the mystical and creepy aesthetic.

The spooky writing on the dark gray rosebud wallpaper reads, "Behind every mystery lies a secret, and it's always what you least expect."

Around the perimeter of the room are ten tall, dark wooden booths, each with the same rustic and dimly lit wall sconce protruding from the side. It's dim inside since the sconces are the only main source of light in the room. The three walls, other than the back wall with the writing, are dark green with a red-and-black design that's consistent with the bar's patterned red fabric. Toward the far side of the bar is a dimly lit hallway that leads to the restroom, which I see Aman disappear into.

For Aman's sake, I try to engage with Noor and her friends while he is momentarily absent.

"Are you also law students?" I'm curious, as they must be students from the university if they have access to the gym facilities.

"What was that?" Noor asks as the blaring music in the background is loud enough for us to make our ears vibrate.

I lean in a little closer and repeat, "Are you also law students?"

"No, Jules and I are grad students at the School of Psychology. Jermaine works in finance downtown and is getting his master's."

"How do you like law school?" Jermaine joins in on the conversation. I like that he does that. He makes an effort despite not having an incentive.

"I like it! It definitely lives up to its reputation and can be emotionally taxing, but having a support system helps."

"Are you second-year students?" Jermaine asks.

Mark answers this time. "Yes. Almost over the hump!"

This term is unfamiliar to non-law students. "What?" Jules chuckles, with a brief moment of judgment in her laugh.

"It's a saying law students use when we're halfway done. Since it's three years long, the halfway point is completing a year and a half."

They nod in understanding of our innocent explanation of the phrase.

"Are you talking about the hump?" Aman interjects as he returns to the group. Contrary to the understood meaning, he's using the word in a promiscuous way.

"Aman!" I'm not surprised by his blunt question.

"Ban, you have a dirty mind!" He laughs mischievously, knowing full well what he intended to imply. Noor looks back and forth at us, eyeing us cautiously.

"Let's go to the bar and get a drink," I suggest when I turn toward Mark, knowing that Aman won't join us. He's going to mingle and flirt before he buys a drink for himself and Noor. Neither Mark nor I want to wait.

New bars around here are notorious for having creative names for their specialty drinks. Usually, they're related to the theme of the bar. Mark braves the increasingly crowded bar to get us both a menu. I glance over it and see exactly what I expect—themed names for specialty drinks. Unsurprisingly, there are two that look good to me. One is made with bourbon and the other with rum.

"Should I get the Bold and Fashioned Crime or the Dead Man's Estate?" I contemplate the vast number of options on the menu while fixating on my likely favorites.

"I knew you'd choose between those two," Mark says. "Get both! Just start with one. I think I'll get the Criminal's High."

The Criminal's High is a mix of whiskey, lemon-lime soda, orange hibiscus extract, and other specialty ingredients. Amidst the plethora of patrons, Mark miraculously gets the bartender's attention to order our drinks.

Being surrounded by couples reminds me that I haven't checked in on how Mark and his girlfriend are doing.

"How's Natalia? When is she coming to visit?" I ask while we wait for the bartender to make our drinks.

I like Natalia. She's really nice and understands that guys and girls can be friends without getting involved. In fact, I think she likes me because I'm one of the few people Mark feels comfortable around. She feels similarly toward Aman. Since Mark is far away from home, she appreciates that he has two good friends he can rely on.

"She's good, busy helping her dad. Did I tell you that she's applying to law school this year? She's coming next month to meet with the Bheau admissions committee. Hopefully, she'll move out here too."

"That's great! That would be awesome if she moved here. How long is she staying next month?"

"She'll be here for a week. She's going to visit a few law schools around the Bay Area!" He sounds excited. Depending on which school in the Bay Area she attends, since there are a few, she and Mark will likely live together.

"How are you both doing though?"

He sighs audibly, even with the upbeat music that surrounds us. "Long distance is hard, but we both know that we want to be with each other. It's easier to see each other this year than it was last year. School is more manageable now."

I nod quietly, although my thoughts are filled with melancholy. I understand his sentiment and feel for the two of them. It's a tough situation, but I'm impressed that they have made their relationship work. I can't even make a relationship work while in the same city.

Suite 22, the guy, moved out of San Francisco to San Diego. He told me he was going to move when we first started dating, but he also said he wanted to try and make it work with me. I thought that even after he moved, we'd make it work. I thought he liked me enough. But his actions following his move showed that his intentions weren't serious.

I was more invested than he was, and he was being a typical, single twenty-six-year-old guy. He used moving to San Diego as an excuse to end things with me. I noticed him showing attention to other girls while dating me, but I just thought it was his friendly and flirtatious nature. Somewhat like Aman. In retrospect, I was oblivious to the truth. I was naïve.

Even to this day, I am amazed by how he easily acted like he cared about and liked me. The last thing he said to me was, "Hopefully you'll find a deserving person who can take care of you and keep you happy."

To distract me from my thoughts, the bartender brings us our drinks at the perfect time. Mark's is in a martini glass with a coiled lemon, and mine is in an old-fashioned lowball glass with a tri-angular-shaped ice cube. The glass is see-through but black-tinted. Ironically, it's a novel and interesting look for an old-fashioned.

Mark notices a group getting ready to leave one of the booths and calls me to follow him in that direction. Mark politely thanks the group once they leave, and we scoot into the booth, making ourselves comfortable.

Aman, Noor, Jermaine, and Jules are still talking near the bar. They don't notice us securing the booth until Jermaine looks around for us to see where we went and informs them. Noor indicates that she doesn't want to sit at the table. She looks nervous. Inevitably, Aman stays with her even though it seems like he wants to join us.

I think that with Jermaine and Jules there, she felt more pressure. Now that Jermaine and Jules have left, it looks like she's loosened up a lot more since she has Aman to herself.

Jermaine and Jules thought Mark and I were a couple and that this was a triple-date situation. Mark and I laugh it off because we hear that often—but not more often than the comment about me and Aman being a couple.

I can't help but notice the phenomenal selection of songs by the DJ. Every single song is currently a top-hit or was a top-hit in the past. He's playing my favorites, '90s hip-hop and rap. Every now and then, on cue with the lyrics, Aman and I mouth them to each other from across the room.

I love him. He truly is my best friend.

I recognize two people from our section, Kristen and Ronaldo, during our stationary dancing and singing and call them over. From what I understand and have heard, Kristen and Ronaldo are also roommates.

Kristen is intrigued by Jules' master's in psychology and what she wants to pursue with it. Kristen received her bachelor's in psychology and shares that her favorite class was child development.

"Our professor showed us pictures and videos of her own kids to illustrate the stage of life we were studying. It was adorable." Kristen abruptly turns to me and Mark. "Oh! I wanted to ask. Did you hear why Professor Gatlin canceled her office hours today?"

"No," I reply, leaning further over the table. "We both showed up at her office on time today, and I literally saw her minutes before. It's so weird and unlike her." I'm curious if Kristen has any information on the subject. It sounds like she might.

Kristen talks in a hushed tone, but loud enough for us to hear, considering we're in a noisy environment. "I heard that her evidence TA, Gerald, got into a serious accident and was hospitalized."

Gerald is mine, Aman's, and Mark's TA.

chapter 5

"Ugh," I murmur, waking up with a hangover. My head feels heavy as it rests on my pillow. After two specialty cocktails, I had a third and a fourth one. Probably not my smartest idea.

At that point, I didn't hesitate to drag Aman and Mark along with me to the dancing area of the bar. Immediately, I could tell Noor was not pleased. But I was enjoying myself, and Aman's my friend. If she plans on spending more time with him, she needs to get used to me being there. After all, we're roommates.

Aman danced with both Mark and me for about ten minutes before he diverted his attention back toward Noor. "I'll catch up with you guys in a bit," he said, leaving us on the dance floor.

I vaguely remember the DJ announcing last call, but I don't remember seeing Aman anywhere before Mark ordered us a cab back home.

I stumble into the living room and find Mark texting on his phone.

"Well good morning, drunken beauty." He stopped drinking well before I did last night.

I rub my eyes and respond with a husky, "Good morning." I don't even recognize my voice.

He chuckles. "Bunny, you're a hit when you're drunk."

I laugh lazily with the minimal energy I currently have. "I need to eat something. Want to go get some brunch?"

"Yes! I've been craving eggs benedict for weeks but haven't had time to go," he says excitedly.

"Great, let me shower quickly, and we can walk over to Zuza's." I'm equally excited but am unable to vocally express it the same way.

I first encountered Zuza's while walking home from Ocean Beach on a street with many mom-and-pop restaurants. I was hungry after my three-mile run and went in to get food. The restaurant cooks different cuisines during lunch and dinner but always keeps breakfast continental. Part of the appeal during lunch and dinner is that the meal becomes a game. Patrons get whatever the restaurant is serving without knowing beforehand. Thus far, Zuza's has yet to disappoint us.

I'm eager to help promote the restaurant, especially among law students, so they can see its high quality. My efforts have not been fruitless. Traffic to the restaurant has increased since our first visit. Actually, I think Aman has taken a date there for dinner once or twice. I only know this because the owners mentioned to me that they saw Aman there with a girl. They're used to me being the girl that's with Aman.

On my way to my room, I knock on Aman's closed door. "We're going to eat at Zuza's. Do you want to come?" I ask in Punjabi.

I don't hear a response, nor do I hear any movement coming from his room.

"I don't think he came home last night." Mark sees me waiting outside Aman's door. "At least I didn't hear him. He may have left the bar before we did."

"Okay. We can leave in fifteen minutes then."

"Sure." Mark shrugs. "I'm going to call Natalia while you get ready."

The last text message with Aman was from me to him last night asking where he was when I clearly was drunk. He neglected to let me know that he wasn't coming home, despite knowing that I'd be worried. I suppose, in this instance, he thought I didn't need to worry because there was only one place he would be—Noor's apartment. Regardless, he could have responded.

Since I have a hangover, I'm not in the mood to dress up for brunch. I select a casual outfit comprised of black tights and a loose sweater. It's a chilly but pleasant Saturday in San Francisco as Mark, and I walk to Zuza's.

Once we arrive, we wait for Maryanne or Cyrus, the elderly couple who own Zuza's, to seat us. The restaurant has a homey and unique feel to it—it looks more like a living room and dining room inside an empty-nesters' home than a traditional restaurant. There's a couch on the left part of the restaurant with side tables and lamps on each side, where I like to study or read sometimes.

We take a seat at a table for two, and a newly hired server, Larson, brings us both water glasses. I didn't realize how thirsty I was until I gulped the water down within seconds.

When Larson positions his pencil on his notepad to take our order, Mark requests a regular eggs benedict, and I order crab cakes benedict.

My phone buzzes in my pocket, indicating that I have a text message.

AMAN: WHERE ARE YOU?

I ignore his text and dramatically shove my phone back into my pocket.

"Was that Aman?" Mark guesses correctly.

I nod.

"Are you annoyed with him?"

"Yes, I am. He didn't respond to my message when I asked where he was last night, but he texts me whenever he wants, expecting a response. He didn't even say, 'Sorry, I just saw this.' He just asked me where I was." I intentionally make no effort to hide the irritation in my voice.

"Bunny, relax. You know how he is."

"Yeah, but I'm not going to encourage his behavior if it's wrong."

"That's fair. You know he's going to text me if he doesn't get a response from you in the next few minutes," he says laughingly to lighten the mood.

I feel extra petty. "Don't respond to him either." I laugh with him.

My phone buzzes again.

AMAN: ????

I ignore him again.

Mark and I reflect on our night, specifically what we thought of Magnicifying Glass, Jermaine, Jules, and Noor. Overall, we had a relatively good impression of everyone. We especially loved the bar. I almost forgot what Kristen told us last night—about our evidence TA, Gerald.

"What happened to Gerald is insane," I say.

"Oh yeah! I completely forgot about that. Almost feels like I dreamt it."

"I hope he's okay. She said that he got into a car accident and was hospitalized?"

"Yeah. Let me try searching his name online to see if anything comes up in the news." Mark pulls out his phone, diligently scrolling for any details or updates on the accident.

"Bun, someone slammed into him near Baker Beach and then fled the scene. It was around five in the morning. Isn't it usually still dark around then? There weren't any witnesses. The police think he was outside running in a remote area before someone ran him over. He was found at least a half-hour later by a couple walking their dog. Police are requesting that anyone who may have information about the incident to please come forward. Fuck, that's crazy." Mark flips through various news reports on Gerald's incident to see if any other channel reported anything more or different.

I sit there, shocked. You hear about this stuff all the time, but you never think it will happen to someone you know. Gerald is a sweetheart, too. Whoever hit him and fled will probably get jail time. We learned about this in criminal law—he or she will likely be charged with felony hit-and-run. That is, if the police catch whoever did it.

There was a similar occurrence when I worked at Stardunning. In a building next to ours, one of their employees was getting out of his car, and someone driving a big SUV hit him. The driver fled the scene, and an employee from Stardunning, who usually comes to work early, saw a body on the floor. Once the police reviewed the security cameras, they saw the driver had hit the guy only minutes before the Stardunning employee arrived. The police got the make and model of the SUV from the surveillance footage.

The victim was rushed to the hospital and ended up being okay. Later that day, the person who hit him turned herself into the police, but despite turning herself in, she faced criminal liability.

Here, I can't imagine the police having many leads. Where Gerald was hit, it's primarily all nature. The area is poorly lit, and there aren't any cameras. Plus, no one has turned themselves in thus far. I've gone running in that area, just not that early. From the sounds of it, Gerald was in the wrong place at the wrong time.

"Kristen said it was a car accident. I thought it was something minor." I'm still shocked, with an escalating feeling of uneasiness.

"The article says that he's in critical condition," Mark continues. "The article mentions that he's a TA at our law school. I wouldn't be surprised if there are news trucks at school on Monday."

"That is so sad," I repeat in disbelief. "I hope he stabilizes soon."

"Yeah, me too. It definitely explains why Professor Gatlin canceled her office hours on such late notice yesterday."

"I'm sure she'll mention it on Monday. I guess all we can do is wait."

The arrival of our food interrupts our conversation, and we initially eat quietly. But Gerald's accident and his current condition fully consume my mind. His poor family must be terrified.

To alter the mood, Mark tells me a story about how he went to a brunch place in the South Bay where he ordered chicken and waffles, and the chicken was not fully cooked. He didn't even notice until Natalia pointed it out because he'd had so many mimosas.

Thankful for Mark's presence, my thoughts start to slowly drift away from Gerald's accident as he continues to distract me.

chapter 6

As soon as we finish paying for our food, Mark's phone buzzes energetically on the table top, flashing Aman's name on the screen. "Wow, he actually took thirty minutes this time to call or text me. Bun, you never responded to his text?"

"Nope. I should have made that bet with you." I titter, feeling residual anger toward Aman's carelessness.

He answers Aman's call. "Yo, man. What's up?" He is quiet for a few seconds as he listens to Aman.

"Yeah, just finished brunch at Zuza's." Mark is quiet again. "I don't know, man. You gotta ask her."

I'm certain Aman is either asking Mark if I got his text message or why I didn't respond to it.

"We're paying now. Bunny wants to go grocery shopping. I'll go with her to help her carry the groceries. Bun, are we heading back after that?" he asks me.

I defiantly nod to Mark, not saying a word on purpose so Aman doesn't hear me.

"Yeah, we're coming back after that," Mark tells Aman.

Mark listens again and responds to Aman, saying, "For sure. See ya." Then Mark disconnects the phone. "He told me to tell you to text him back."

"I'll be home soon enough. He can talk to me then."

"Damn, Bun. That much tough love?"

"Yes! It's not cool. Mark, why don't you stay over again tonight? We can order in and watch movies, or we can go out again." I have a strong hunch that he doesn't want to go home to an empty apartment just as much as I want him to stay another day.

"Ah, I should get home, Bun. I have an early meeting on Monday and a lot of work to do." He doesn't sound convinced of himself.

"I do too! But it would be nice if you stayed. Come on, please."

He's quiet for a few seconds before he surrenders. "Okay. We'll play it by ear tonight."

Mark knows I love having him around. He has a great aura about him. Plus, he's a nice buffer when Aman annoys me like he did today. He takes on the role of being the neutral arbitrator to diffuse any lingering tension.

Mark and I say our goodbyes to Maryanne and Cyrus and leave Zuza's for the grocery store, which is less than a block away.

"What do you need to get?" Mark asks.

"I need a lot of stuff, honestly. I'm glad you're here to take groceries home with me. I feel weird taking my trolley. Aman always laughs at me when I have it."

"Do you shop for both you and Aman or just yourself?"

"Usually, just myself. Unless we go together. He's too particular about his diet."

As I unfold my grocery list, I see that Aman scribbled all over it, adding his groceries too. I roll my eyes and show Mark. "I guess I do shop for both Aman and me."

He laughs. "I can't tell if you're mad or not. That guy is hilarious."

"I'll admit that this is cute." Sometimes he can be such a kid. My anger toward Aman slowly subsides when I see his funny antics. I usually don't stay mad at him for too long, but that's not going to stop me from calling him out.

On our walk back from the grocery store, Mark and I plan the remainder of our day. I'm yearning to be surrounded by the peacefulness at Marina Green. The walk around the park is lovely as well.

"Yeah, that sounds like a chill plan. I don't know how much I'm up for going out again." Mark is on board with my suggestion to get dinner around there and then watch a movie at home.

"Me either. Something low-key sounds more appealing."

"Same. Do you think Aman will join?"

"I'm not sure. He might if he thinks I'm still mad at him." I may joke with Mark now, but I know full well that Aman would go just because of me.

Mark chuckles. "Where do you want to eat? Are you craving something in particular?"

I take a moment to consider his question. "Burgers?" Mark finds a place I haven't heard of before named Burger Call that has high ratings.

As we approach home, Aman is already outside, taking the garbage out. He looks like he hasn't showered yet. His fluffy hair is scruffy, and he's wearing his bedtime light-gray sweatpants with his olive-green t-shirt.

When he spots us walking toward him, he runs in our direction, his smile a tad exaggerated. "Hey!" I imagine his tone is purposely, maybe even mischievously, energetic as he senses I'm not speaking to him.

Mark greets him, but I ignore him. Aman grabs the bags I'm carrying, and I dart inside the building.

He talks to Mark as if I'm not there. "She's pissed at me, isn't she?" I can hear the smile in his voice.

Mark laughs. "Lucky for you, she was more pissed about an hour ago."

The three of us maneuver up the stairs to the fourth floor, although I'm far ahead of them. We have an elevator, but it is out of service until next week.

Aman is tall, about six-three, and has long legs. He climbs every other step and quickly catches up to me despite holding the hefty grocery bags he took from me. He is fit, whereas I don't go to the gym as often and would be struggling to breathe at his pace.

"Ban, why are you mad at me?" he asks.

"If you don't know why, you're even dumber than I thought."

Mark, who isn't as far behind us, hears my cheeky statement and yells, "Damnnnnnn. You thought he was dumb?"

Aman and I chuckle. I know Mark says this to ease the tension, taking on his role. He hates it when Aman and I argue.

"Seriously, tell me," Aman presses for an answer as he closes our apartment door behind us.

"Aman, you didn't even tell me that you weren't coming home last night. On top of that, I don't understand why you can't respond to a text message. I asked you where you were, and you didn't respond! Then, when I didn't text you back, you sent me twenty question marks and then called Mark to ask where we were. You expect me to text you back whenever you message, but you don't respond to me." I'm nearly out of breath as I finish ranting.

"Girl, breathe," he says in Punjabi, although he's listening intently.

"No, be consistent. You left early and didn't tell us, despite knowing that I worry."

"I left with Noor," he says matter-of-factly.

"Yes, I know that. But you can't tell either me or Mark when you're leaving?"

"My bad, Ban. I was feeling it a little bit and didn't realize you would be this mad."

"You've done it before, Aman. This happens every time."

"Yeah, so by now, you should know that I'm not going to change, and you're still going to love me." He's trying to be cute to calm me down. His charm is hard to resist sometimes.

"Seriously, you have to be better about it. I worry."

"Yes, ma'am. You worry for no reason," he jokes in Punjabi.

"No, I don't!" He's right, but I refuse to admit it to him.

"Okay, okay. I'm sorry. I will be better. Now, come here." He stretches his arms out for a hug.

"You're such a brat." I suppress a laugh and hug him, relieved that we're no longer bickering. I hate arguing with Aman, no matter how small the argument may be.

"Look at you. All feisty today."

Mark clears his throat to get our attention. "Yo, man. Bunny and I were thinking of walking around the marina today and then going for dinner. Do you have plans tonight?"

Aman looks at me, and I can tell he's gauging my mood.

"If you already have plans, go. We just planned this. Neither of us feels like going out again," I say before he can respond.

"No, I don't have any solid plans. I'm down. When are we going to go?" He is lying. He wouldn't look at me first if he didn't have plans.

"Are you sure? Really, it's fine."

"No, if something comes up, it would be late anyway. Big boy's gotta eat." He rubs his belly and grins playfully.

"Oh yeah, how was your night?" I ask.

"Good." He laughs coyly without elaborating any further.

He never tells me about his nights and hookups, although I know he tells Mark when I'm not there. I presume it's because he feels it's disrespectful to divulge details about his sex life around girls.

"What time are we going to go?" Aman repeats.

"Six?" I ask Mark.

"I think that's good. Aman, I looked up a good burger spot called Burger Call. You good with that?"

"I've been there." He nods. "It's good."

"If you've already been there, we can go somewhere else," I suggest.

"No, I'll go again. I didn't get a burger last time. Only beer and wings."

"Okay. What're you going to do now?" I ask Aman.

"Shower, do some work, and then hit the gym. How much do I owe you for the groceries?" He has a sheepish smirk as he glances at the shopping list with his scribbles.

I chuckle. "Don't worry about it."

He's different when he's with me and Mark. When he's around us, he's silly. When he's around people that he doesn't really know, especially a girl he's interested in, he's chatty but not silly. Last night, he had the smooth and suave Aman channeled. He's naturally very friendly and flirty, which is what makes him so charming, but he's still serious and mature. He even flirts with me, but I don't mind. He channels his behavior based on who he's around. I think everyone does that to some degree. I know I do.

"Do you guys want to go over crim-law?" I ask.

"I haven't read the cases for Monday yet," Aman says.

"Me neither," Mark adds. "Dude, did you hear about Professor G's TA? Gerald?"

"No. What happened?" Aman is intrigued.

"He was the victim of a hit-and-run yesterday. He was running near Baker Beach when he was hit by a speeding car."

"Fuck." He pauses and seems concerned. "I hope he's okay. Ban, you were telling me something yesterday, weren't you?"

"Yeah. How I thought her sudden cancellation of office hours was weird. You thought I was crazy."

Aman ignores my last remark. "Do they have any leads on who it is?"

"No," Mark says. "It happened when it was still dark out, and there weren't a lot of people around."

"Once the police find them, they're screwed. I'm going to shower." Aman is very familiar with the law on the subject as well.

"I think I'll shower after him," Mark says. "Bunny, can I have a towel, please?"

"Of course." I grab Mark's usual towel from the linen closet.

On the way back, I stop at my room to get my criminal law book and course materials so that I can commence reading. Currently, we're learning about specific-intent crimes and general-intent crimes. Professor Erikson mentioned beforehand that the difference between the two could be confusing, and we should discuss the cases with other students.

While Aman showers, I ask Mark to explain the difference between general-intent and specific-intent crimes as he understands it. After his explanation, it seems that the understanding is within my grasp for a moment, but I ultimately lose it.

"Maybe you'll have a better understanding after you finish reading the cases, and you can see actual examples between the two," he reassures me once he sees my frustration.

"Yeah, I hope so. I'm nervous about this class."

"Aman can explain it to you too."

"He always explains it so well."

Mark gestures toward himself.

"No offense to you!" I burst out laughing.

"I hear you guys talking about how smart I am. Please continue." Aman's towel is still around his neck, and his hair is damp from his shower when he re-joins us in the living room.

Mark grins encouragingly. "Are you done with the bathroom? I was going to take a quick shower."

"It's all yours, man."

"Aman, can you explain specific and general intent to me after I finish reading the cases?"

"Hmm. It's going to cost you," he teases in Punjabi.

"Shut up."

"That attitude is not going to help."

"Thank you!" I yell behind him as he goes toward his room.

In the meantime, I open up my books and begin reading the case assignments for criminal law. Specific-intent crimes versus general-intent crimes are not getting any clearer for me.

chapter 7

Aman provides many examples of specific and general intent crimes in order to explain the difference between the two types to me and test my knowledge of the subject. After a long hour of discussion, the difference between general-intent and specific-intent crimes finally seems to make sense.

"Thank you!" I exhale enthusiastically and rush over to hug him. "Please give me your brain. How do you always understand this as soon as you learn it?"

He's naturally very smart and easily comprehends what he learns for the first time.

"Because I actually pay attention in lectures and don't slack off like you." Aman's eyes twinkle when he winks at me.

I raise my eyebrows and stare at him, knowing he's joking. He knows very well that I constantly scribble down notes during lectures.

I'm pleasantly surprised with my progress, given that I was hungover this morning and wasn't expecting to get much done this fast. The cases for crim-law aren't too long, which is surprising for Professor Erikson.

Aman is an exception, but most students will have trouble understanding this topic. My 3L mentor, Sophia, shared that this is generally a difficult area for most students, and criminal law students tend to feel overwhelmed at this point in the semester.

We put a pause on our studies and take a well-deserved break for the evening. The three of us get ready for our marina and dinner night. As usual, I take longer because my routine when dressing up is naturally longer than both Aman's and Mark's.

Tonight, I'm wearing a tank top, strappy sandals, and loose pants that look like sweatpants but are fashionable. I apply dry shampoo to my hair and tie it up because I didn't wash it earlier, then add neutral but light makeup. My look is appropriate for the night we have planned. Simple, but cute.

I return to the living room, and both Aman and Mark are whispering about something at the counter in the kitchen. The conversation they're having comes to a halt when Aman spots me, and I'm almost certain that Aman was telling Mark about his night.

"Why did you guys stop talking?" I ask.

"We didn't. By the way, my plans for tonight are confirmed, so I'll leave after dinner. Get a jacket. You're going to get cold," Aman orders me in Punjabi.

"It's not even cold outside."

"You're telling me that you're not going to feel cold, wearing a tank top, walking next to the water in the marina? I don't want to hear you ask either me or Mark for our jackets," he scolds sarcastic-ally, but maintains a level tone.

"Then cover your ears." I return the sarcasm, but his stern expression speaks louder.

"Fine." I opt for a matching sweater I can tie around my waist. Once I'm back outside, both guys are waiting outside with the front door open.

The marina is about fifteen minutes away from our apartment by car. Frankly, anywhere in the city is about fifteen minutes from our apartment. It's actually a very small city, and our apartment is centrally located.

Since Aman sits in the front passenger seat, he sparks a conver-sation with the driver and learns that she recently moved to San Francisco from Seattle. Aman recommends a few popular places around the city that are wonderful to visit. Mark and I chime in every now and then, but Aman leads the conversation and names plenty of places he knows are my favorite. Any suggestions from me would be redundant.

As we approach the marina, I request that the driver drop us off by the park near Marina Green. It is indeed a beautiful evening. It's on the cooler side, but it isn't unbearably cold. The sun is still up, which helps keep it warm, but wind in this part of the city is inevitable. I won't say it out loud, but Aman was right.

There are plenty of people walking, kids running around on the grass, and couples walking their dogs along the main street.

The scent of the ocean, salty water, and seafood all mixed together is overwhelming yet oddly comforting. The scent is paired with the marvelous crashing of waves against the rocks along the bay. There are spurts of gentle waves intermingled with energetic waves. We can faintly hear the rocking of the boats teth-ered to the dock close by. Meanwhile, the seagulls chirp nearby is loud and clear. A San Francisco classic.

"We should go on an Alcatraz night tour." Mark looks across the water at Alcatraz Island, which stands tall in the middle of the bay. He's wanted to go for a while, but we've never gotten around to it. I've heard that the view of the city from the island during the night tour is enchanting.

"Last I checked, we have to book tickets for the night tour a month in advance," I say.

"Let's try to go around Halloween," Aman suggests excitedly. "It will be spooky and themed."

"That would be sick." Mark sounds equally enthralled with the suggestion.

"I'll look when we get back tonight." I set a reminder on my phone to check tickets once we return home. Once I'm done setting the reminder, Mark's phone rings, and he decreases his walking speed.

Aman and I stroll by the water on a long pathway while Mark stays slightly behind us on his phone.

Within a few minutes of our arrival at the park, the weather cools, and a chill strikes my body. While I untie my sweater from my waist, I notice Aman observing me out of the corner of his eye.

He snickers with victory, predicting this would happen. "I know you so well. I bet you're still cold."

I hug myself to keep warm. Aman takes his jacket off and hands it to me without saying anything.

"You don't have to do that." I appreciate his gesture.

"No, no. I'm good, you keep it," he says simply, illustrating that his warning to me at home not to ask for either his or Mark's jacket was merely a quip.

"Thank you." His jacket looks ridiculously oversized on me, but it keeps me warm and toasty, all while allowing me to enjoy the delicious lingering scent of Aman. It's actually kind of sexy.

Bani, whoa.

"How are your parents? I haven't seen them since the BBQ at their house in June."

"They're, they're..." I scramble for words, thankful that Aman brought my not-so-platonic thoughts about him to a halt, but confused about why they came to mind to begin with. "They're good."

He eyes me with curiosity. "You have my jacket, but you're still shivering and stuttering?" he asks in Punjabi.

"No, I was just remembering what they've been up to," I lie. The man smells incredible. *That's all it is, Bani.* "They've been busy getting ready for Devan's wedding."

My older brother, Devan, is getting married next month. Alina, Devan's fiancée, and Devan met in college at a house party and have been together ever since. I also have a younger sister, Ari, who's still in college.

Devan is five years older than me and nine years older than Ari. He is an older brother and a friend at the same time, and it's because of the way our parents raised us. We're a Punjabi family, but my parents are more toward the modern and liberal end than the conservative end. Both of my parents moved to California when they were a lot younger. The majority of their upbringing was in the United States, and this helped break them out of the conservative shell common among Punjabi parents.

By trade, Devan is a venture capitalist, and Alina is a doctor. Alina enjoys crafts and ceramics recreationally. As part of his proposal, Devan arranged for a private pottery class for the two of them. While he was decorating the vase he'd sculpted, he kept the design hidden from her. When he was ready to show her, he'd written out, "Will you marry me?"

I didn't think he had it in him to come up with something as romantic as that, but he surprised all of us. Alina keeps the finished piece on their fireplace mantel.

My parents invited both Aman and Mark to the wedding, but Mark can't come since Natalia's sister's baby shower is the same weekend.

"You're still coming to that, right?" I ask.

"Wouldn't miss it." Aman grins at me. "Let's rent a car that week. We'll be able to easily drive to and from our place for each of the functions."

"You're going to each of the functions? *Mayian, mehndi,* and *jaggo* too?" I ask him.

"Of course."

"Aman, that's very sweet of you."

He chuckles at my tone. "Why do you sound so surprised?"

I, unintentionally, did sound surprised.

"I know you're busy, and trekking down to Palo Alto every day for the whole week is going to be a lot."

"That's okay. Close weddings don't happen all the time."

I smile to myself. I'm touched that he considers my brother's wedding a priority, a *close* wedding.

Punjabi weddings can easily last a whole week. In the Punjabi culture, there are many rituals, but there are three main pre-wedding events held separately for the bride and groom: *mehndi, jaggo,* and *mayian.*

The *mehndi* ceremony is where family members get henna done. For the bride, the *mehndi* ceremony revolves around the application of her bridal henna, which is traditionally much more elaborate in design, in addition to the henna for family members. For the groom, the *mehndi* is mainly for the female family members, but some guys also like a simple design.

The *jaggo* is a Punjabi ceremony where the family celebrates the wedding with a specific, traditional dance. Traditionally in Punjab, it's held to alert fellow villagers of the upcoming celebrations. During this dance, family members hold a lit, decorated steel vessel and dance while holding the vessel on their heads.

The *mayian* is where family members of the bride and groom rub turmeric paste on the bride or groom in preparation for the wedding. The ritual and ceremony signify cleaning the skin before married life.

"How are your mom, Charan, and Raman?" I ask. Charan is Aman's stepfather.

"Good. I miss my mom. I may go home for a weekend soon."

"You should! When did you go home last?"

"I went for a few days for the Fourth of July."

"Aman! It's September!"

"No, really?" he mocks. "I think I'll surprise my mom in two weeks for her birthday."

"She's going to love that." I daydream of her reaction, sad I won't be able to see it. "I want to get her a birthday present. Can you take it with you?"

He nods.

Aman doesn't go home often since it gets tough with school. During the summer, our school encourages students to get externships at companies or law firms if we're not taking summer school. This past summer, I took summer school, and Aman worked for a law firm downtown.

I'm fortunate that my family is close by. If I'm not able to go home for many weekends in a row, my parents will try to visit me. Recently, they've been so preoccupied with work and my brother's wedding preparations that they haven't had time.

Mark catches up with us and rejoins us on our walk. It's nearing the time for our dinner reservation. We stroll for a few minutes before Mark decides that he can't wait more to eat, and then we make our way to Burger Call. I'm pleased to see that there's a crowd of people outside, attesting to the popularity of the restaurant.

The restaurant has vibrant lighting and colorful decorations. On one wall, there are medium-sized surfboards with each of the fifty states' names on them and a picture that represents that specific state. California's is the only big surfboard, placed in the center of the wall. On California's surfboard, there is a single picture of the sun. Rather appropriate. Washington has a single picture of a tree. Also, rather appropriate.

"Do you want a drink?" Aman asks both me and Mark.

"I'll wait to get one with the burger." We had wine at home before we left, and I want to avoid having another hangover tomorrow morning.

"Yeah, me too." Mark gives it a bit more thought than I do before he decides.

"You go ahead. You have an actual night ahead of you. We're going home," I assure Aman.

Mark and I wait for our table to be ready while Aman orders his drink at the bar. As he's waiting for the bartender to make it, there's a group of girls also at the bar. They look like they're in their early twenties and are already having a good time at this point of the evening.

From my viewpoint, one of them keeps looking in Aman's direction. He's on his phone the entire time he's waiting for the bartender to finish his drink and is oblivious to his close-by admirer.

She walks toward him, and right before she taps his shoulder, she fidgets with a strand of her hair. At first, he looks perplexed, looking at her as if he's trying to place her. She doesn't look familiar to me, at least, but who knows with Aman?

When she says something to him with a seductive grin, he smiles and then also says something. Based on the development of their interaction as I shamelessly observe them, it looks to be a new meeting. They continue talking, with occasional arm touching—on her end—when Mark distracts me to tell me what he's thinking of ordering.

"I want the lamb burger." Mark seems fully captivated by the menu.

"I was thinking that too. I want to order the poutine, but that plus the lamb burger will be too heavy." I run through the menu a second time to make sure I didn't miss anything.

"I'll have some, and I'm sure Aman will too. Have you had the poutine at His Majesty?" The bar night event where Mark and I officially met Aman was at His Majesty. "They revived their menu and dropped the unpopular dishes," Mark adds.

"No! Let's go there this week for dinner."

"I'm in. Let's go on Wednesday, and then we can go to their happy hour as well."

It's not hard to convince Mark to go out. He's very willing to spend time with friends if he's available. The hard part is coordinating a time with his busy schedule, and I snatch any slot I can find with him. School can be overwhelming, and it's enjoyable to have someone who engages in spontaneous activities with me from time to time. I need that.

The hostess calls Mark's name, indicating that our table is ready. I turn my attention back toward Aman and see him still talking to the girl. I really don't want to go there, and instead, I text him to let him know our table is ready. Once he checks his incoming text from me, he looks in my direction and nods to acknowledge it.

The girl he's talking to follows his glance and peers at me in the process, likely wondering who I am to Aman.

Ignorant of this, Aman takes advantage of the fact that his phone is out to exchange phone numbers with her. Before he walks back toward me and Mark, he half hugs her and grabs his drink. I swear she smiles at me defiantly once Aman's back is toward her.

"Enjoy your call!" the hostess says after she sets down the menus at our booth, a funny play off of the name of the restaurant. I laugh in response, and both Mark and Aman look at me incredulously.

"It's not a surprise that I'm a sucker for jokes like that." I giggle. Aman shakes his head at me. "What do you want to order?"

"Alcohol!" I declare. The effect of the wine we had at home before we left for dinner has diminished, and I now consider it safe to have a drink.

We order our food and drinks simultaneously, my stomach rumbling as I place my food order.

For drinks, Mark decides on a whiskey sour, and Aman and I on old-fashioneds. We're pleasantly surprised when they appear at the table rather quickly. Aman is still nursing the one he got from the bar earlier, when he was chatting with the girl.

While we wait for our food to arrive, Mark takes the opportunity to ask Aman about her.

"Honestly, she was plastered. She came up to me and said that I was 'insanely hot.' She's celebrating her friend's twenty-first birthday, and she's the only one who's twenty-two."

"She may have been plastered, but I saw you exchange numbers at the tail end of the conversation," I add when I notice he conveniently left that part out.

"Ban, if a cute girl comes up to me, I'm not going to look away."

Just as I'm about to speak, a belligerently drunk guy comes to our table out of nowhere and says to me, "You are the most beautiful girl I have ever seen."

I'm caught off guard, and all I manage in response is a "Thank you" along with a dry laugh. The guy darts outside of the restaurant immediately after. I'm so flustered, I barely catch a glimpse of him.

"Who the *hell* was that guy?" Aman asks suspiciously, seeming to forget he received a similar compliment earlier.

I shrug. "Dunno."

"Bunny is a hot commodity," Mark says to Aman. "Remember when she met Suite 22?"

chapter 8

It's obvious from Mark's expression that he regrets mentioning Suite 22, not only because of me but because of Aman as well. Aman is not a fan of Suite 22. Whenever I ask him why he strongly dislikes him, Aman always gives a generic response: "He's a jackass," without specifying why.

"Well, Aman, how is what he did to me any different than what you do when you're dating?" This time I probe a bit more, but then immediately regret my choice of words. I came across harsher than I intended. Aman is absolutely nothing like Suite 22. For a second, I glimpse hurt in his expression.

"Those women are not you, and he hurt you. I'm honest with whoever I talk to from the beginning. I don't give anyone false hope that we can progress into something serious. This guy did the opposite. He gave you false hope," he responds solemnly but passionately. His protectiveness over me has never faltered. I'm flattered by it.

"It happens when you date. I'll find a good guy, but it takes experiencing jackasses to get there," I reassure him, consoling myself as well.

"Okay. You asked me why I don't like him, and that's why. I know you still miss him."

"I wouldn't say that I miss him, but he does cross my mind every now and then if there are emotional triggers. With time, I'll forget about him."

Mark doesn't like Suite 22 either. "Let's not talk about him. No one likes him. End of story. We're having a great dinner. Let's continue to enjoy it."

Aman remains solemn. "Agreed."

Despite the consensus to change the subject, an awkward silence lingers for several minutes until we finish our meals, and our waitress asks us if we want dessert. The three of us always share one.

"Do you have to go?" I ask Aman when I notice him frequently checking his phone.

"In a bit."

"Leave after dessert," I say.

"Are you sure you don't want to come?" I can tell that Aman wants us to join him, but neither Mark nor I am up for it. Mark and I plan to head straight home.

"Honestly, I just want to watch a movie at home in my pajamas. I'm kind of in the mood to watch a scary one. Plus, I want to check the tickets for Alcatraz. The sooner we get those, the better."

"If you decide to cut your night short, come home and watch a movie with us," Mark says.

Aman nods in response, seriously considering it. After we annihilate our dessert, he leaves.

Once Mark and I are home, I see that Aman posted a video of himself taking tequila shots with friends. Well, he reposted the video. Someone whose account I don't recognize tagged him in it first. I can't tell who he's with, but I can guess. He seems to be having a good time.

We're nearing the end of *Family Visitor*, the first of two horror movies we selected for tonight when Mark and I hear the front door open. My heart churns, and I can feel each rapid heartbeat throughout my body. To enhance the viewing experience, we turned the lights off before we started the movie, resulting in us being a bit more startled.

In walks Aman. It's before midnight, and we weren't expecting him to come home this early. He didn't text either of us to let us know that he was on his way home.

"Holy shit, man! You scared us!" Mark exclaims.

Aman chuckles. "Sorry."

"Why are you home this early?" I ask.

"I wasn't feeling it, so I left." Based on his demeanor, I can tell something is on his mind.

"You looked like you were having a good time from the post," I add, sincerely surprised by Aman's early arrival. He seemed eager for this night out when we were at dinner. Perhaps he was just eager to go and get it over it.

"That's the thing about social media, Ban. I was bored out of my mind."

"Who all was there?" Mark asks.

"It was me, Noor, Jermaine, Jules, and another one of Noor's friends."

"Noor was cool with you leaving early?" Mark asks again.

Aman shrugs and seems unconcerned. "She's been blowing up my phone, telling me how fucked up I am for leaving early. She wanted me to come back to her place again tonight, but I wanted to sleep in my own bed. I told her when we first met that I'm not looking for anything serious."

Mark hoists an eyebrow. "Girls," and then laughs and looks at me. "What is with y'all?"

"Girls think they can change a guy when he says that he doesn't want something serious," I reply.

Aman did the right thing and made it clear what he was not looking for. If she decided to continue talking to him despite knowing that, she can't blame him if he doesn't pursue it further.

"How's your movie night?" Aman asks, opening a cold-water bottle from the refrigerator.

"We're finishing up the first one—*Family Visitor*," I say.

"I've seen that. It's good." He thirstily chugs the water within seconds.

"Get changed and watch *Fairgrounds* with us. We'll finish this movie by then." I gesture toward the TV.

He disappears into his room to get comfortable before we start the second movie. *Family Visitor* has about five more minutes left by the time Aman returns to the living room.

He plops himself right next to me and takes some of my blanket. "Hey! There's a couch right there." I motion to my left.

"I get scared and need to sit with you." He pouts and snuggles closer to me, hoping I won't make him get up.

"Fine." I succumb, laughing at my adorable roommate. Our arms are side by side, close enough for me to directly feel his chest rise and dip as he breathes, but neither of us moves to increase the distance. I welcome the extra warmth coming from him.

Aman doesn't shy away from startling me each time a scary scene comes on at the beginning of *Fairgrounds*. He, thankfully, eventually stops when he becomes fully fascinated with the plotline himself.

Before we get halfway through the movie, Aman's phone rings, and he ignores the call. It rings again, and he ignores it again. Both times, he holds his phone at an angle, and I'm unable to see who it is.

It rings a third time. He begrudgingly asks Mark to pause the movie and goes into his room, closing the door behind him.

The walls in our apartment are not thin, but Aman is talking loudly enough for us to decipher the irritation in his voice. Based on what he's saying—and we can hear most everything—I think it's Noor.

"I can't talk right now...hanging out with my friends...I told you I was tired...I'm at home, not out...No. I'm not coming... Because I said, I'm busy...Look, you're drunk. We can talk tomorrow...We'll talk tomorrow." He's no longer speaking, and shortly after, he returns to the living room.

Aman runs his hands through his hair as he sits back down next to me, except now, to my disappointment, there is space between us. The additional warmth felt nice, but I don't dwell on it.

He looks exasperated. "Okay, go ahead," he says to Mark, sighing, but both Mark and I stare at Aman quizzically with a "What was that?" look.

"What?" he asks.

"What was that all about?" Mark voices my thoughts.

"Noor is acting crazy." Aman appears nonchalant, but I know Noor threw a wrench in his mood.

"Damn, you must be that good, huh?" Mark laughs at his own joke.

Aman laughs too and then looks at me. "What happened?" he asks in Punjabi.

"You need to stop hooking up with girls before you know if they're crazy or not."

"Ban, all girls are crazy," he jokes.

Mark snorts at that. "Even Natalia has her moments."

"*How am I crazy?*" I ask defensively.

"Do I need to remind you of the tirade you delivered to me earlier this afternoon?"

"That's because you were in the wrong!" He can't seriously be holding that against me.

"That doesn't mean you didn't sound crazy. It's okay. You're cute and crazy." He grins at me and pokes my nose with humor in his voice.

"Ha, ha," I mock as I wave his hand away from my face.

Mark turns the movie back on, and about an hour and a half later, it's over. After I watch a scary movie and before I go to sleep, I watch something comical to distract myself. Aman, of course, is unbothered.

"Let me know if you get scared," Aman says mid-yawn as he turns in for the night. "I'll protect you." Confident, even when he's half asleep.

"I'm good, big guy. You get some rest. Don't run into the door on your way in."

He laughs sleepily. "Night, Ban. Night, Mark."

"Good night," Mark and I say in unison.

I aimlessly flip through the TV channels and look for something that appeals to me and Mark, landing on a popular comedy show.

Twenty minutes later, I look over at Mark—he's asleep. By now, both movies are in a distant part of my mind, and I will be able to easily fall asleep without feeling afraid. I am careful to be as quiet as possible so I don't wake Mark.

My only source of light is from the streetlight outside of our living room window. I can barely see, and I turn my phone flashlight on the dimmest setting to carefully navigate my way back to my room.

Once I lie down on my bed, I drift into deep sleep nearly immediately.

chapter 9

The next day, Sunday, dread fills me. Fortunately, the majority of my day can be spent lounging around the apartment and doing whatever I like. I have some schoolwork remaining, but the bulk of it was completed the day before. Since a leisurely Sunday like today is hard to come by, I use some of my free time to video-call my sister.

The day passes quickly, and just as I'm getting ready to go to bed, a knock at the door startles me back into the living room.

"Are you expecting someone?" I look at Aman, confused.

"Yeah, I told Noor to come over today so we can talk. Don't worry. She's not staying."

"Aman, you know I don't mind if she stays." He's weird about bringing women home. During the entire time we've lived together, no one he's dated has ever stayed over.

"No, Bani. She's not staying," he says sternly. I know he means it because he rarely uses my first name.

He opens the door, and it is indeed Noor. He bends down slightly to hug her, but I can't fully see her because his body is blocking her. When he moves to the side, she nearly smiles at me. I respond with a wave.

There's an uncomfortable coldness in the air, which came with Noor's arrival. Something about her demeanor doesn't sit well with me.

She looks different from when I saw her on Friday night. Her makeup is light, not nearly as dramatic as Friday, and she's wearing laid-back clothes.

I notice a surprised look on her face when he says, "Let me get my keys, and we can head out." She wasn't expecting him to lead her back outside. I wonder how she'll react when she learns she won't be staying the night.

"Be back in a bit, Ban," he says and then closes the door behind them.

It's late. I woke up earlier than usual for a Sunday morning, but I am unable to sleep when I climb into bed. I turn my light back on and grab a novel from my bedside drawer. Within fifteen minutes of reading my novel, I fall asleep with my light on.

I jerk up in my bed with heart-sinking anxiety, and my clothes are moist from lingering sweat. I had a nightmare.

In my nightmare, I was running outside and was being followed by an unknown person. Just as I felt the person was closing in on me, I woke up.

Earlier Sunday morning, when Aman, Mark, and I ate breakfast, we watched the news. I figure the nightmare was a result of the crime report and the scary movies we watched the night before.

But it could also very well be because of Gerald. The themes certainly align, and there was brief coverage of his accident. Details we already knew.

It's half past midnight. I got a text from Aman around midnight saying he's still with Noor and will be up shortly. He probably isn't back yet, because if he was, he would've seen my light on and knocked on my door. Unable to find my water bottle, I reluctantly go to the kitchen to look for it.

My nerves haven't settled because as soon as I hear movement at the front door, my heart sinks once again. It's only Aman.

He's surprised to see me awake. "Aw, are you waiting for me?" he asks in Punjabi.

"I had a bad dream."

It's one of the many reasons I appreciate having Aman as my roommate. He ensures my safety. I don't feel actual fear for my safety, knowing he's down the hall from me.

"You're getting in late." I glance at the time on the microwave clock.

"Yeah, we were hanging out in her car."

"Aman! In public? You're a lawyer in training!"

"Relax, Ban." He chuckles. As usual, he neither confirms nor denies what I implied. "Are you okay? Do you want me to stay up with you and watch some TV?" He purposely deviates from the topic.

I still feel uncomfortable fluttering in my chest, but I don't want him to sacrifice any more sleep because of me. It's late, and we have an early class. If I ask him to stay, he unfailingly would.

"I'm okay. You get some rest. You must be exhausted with both workouts."

He looks confused for a second and then laughs. Again, he doesn't confirm or deny my remark. He walks over to me, gives me a tight hug to calm me, and disappears into his room.

Since he moved in, I haven't invited anyone over to our apartment either, but that's primarily because of my nonexistent dating life. When I was dating Suite 22, I lived with Aman, but the topic of coming back to my apartment never came up.

The next time I date someone, I will invite him home.

chapter 10

Aman and I are in our assigned seats for our evidence lecture on time today. From the edge of the desktop, our seating order is Aman, me, and then Mark. Mark is already in his seat when we take ours.

On our way to school, we saw various news channels outside of the law school and knew they were here regarding Gerald's accident, as Mark predicted.

From what I could see, there were about three different channel trucks. Gerald's accident has become a city-wide news report, given the status and reputation of the Bheaurmiss School of Law.

The media's primary concern is how the police will incriminate the perpetrator without having any witnesses, hard evidence, or even clues as to who committed the crime. The reporters also attempted to discern whether Gerald has a history of violence or has been involved with active aggressors. Gerald's family declined to comment. Their primary concern is, understandably, Gerald's recovery.

The law school, alternatively, is expected to respond to the journalists' queries as long as they are reasonable. The dean and Professor Gatlin are the central individuals at the law school to interact with the press.

The dean because he's the leader of the law school, and Professor Gatlin because the only relation Gerald has to the law school is as her TA. The dean comments that such an incident has never occurred in the history of the law school, let alone involving a specific faculty representative.

There is no precedent on how to handle this situation, but the dean announces that the authorities will receive full cooperation from the university to bring the attacker or attackers of Gerald, a Bheaurmiss School of Law member, to justice.

Professor Gatlin is ten minutes late to lecture, held up by reporters pressing her for details. Appearing physically distressed, she sets her possessions down on the podium and apologizes to the class for her tardiness.

By now, everyone has heard, and the tension in the room is palpable. The lecture hall is pin-drop silent. Students are eagerly waiting to receive an update from Professor Gatlin regarding Gerald's incident and his health. Amelia, the other TA and Gerald's counterpart, is present and standing against the side wall.

Professor Gatlin takes a deep breath and looks up at her students. "I'm sure you all know about Gerald's unfortunate incident, which occurred early Friday morning. Especially with the media outside." She pauses, searching for words.

"Because he wasn't found immediately after he was hit, Gerald lost a lot of blood. He had to undergo emergency surgery as soon as the EMTs brought him to the hospital. His doctors are unable to comment on whether he will regain consciousness or if he'll remember the accident. He's in serious condition."

The students murmur amongst themselves.

"As for the actual accident," she continues. "The police are unwilling to comment on that in order to maintain the integrity of the investigation. Consequently, I don't have any additional information, other than what you may have heard via the news coverage."

Through the extensive recruitment process, professors build close relationships with their TAs to ensure they're making the right selection. Accordingly, I imagine that Professor Gatlin is close to all of her TAs, including Gerald. He's been her TA for years.

The process for appointing a TA takes a few months, and the professors hand-pick them from an ocean of resumes of qualified candidates. At this point in the semester, Professor Gatlin does not have the bandwidth nor the time to appoint a new TA via the established recruitment process. Each semester is only four months long.

"I'm aware that students with last names N through Z are all wondering who will cover Gerald as your TA. The university and I are diligently working to find a suitable replacement within the week to be sure your exam preparation is not compromised. In the meantime, I've requested Amelia make herself available to students with last names N through Z." She gestures toward Amelia, and Amelia gives an encouraging smile.

Professor Gatlin thanks the class for our understanding and patience and begins her scheduled lecture.

No one expects a law school lecture hall to be vibrant and lively, but the atmosphere in this room is several notches below the normal level of uneasiness. It's considerably unpleasant. Gerald is generally a well-liked TA.

I shift in my seat, hoping to shake off the uncomfortable feeling, but it doesn't leave me. Gerald's accident feels much more real now after seeing Professor Gatlin's physical response to the stress.

As soon as class ends, students rush out of the lecture hall like a herd of sheep, Aman, Mark, and me included. We don't go too far because we have criminal law soon.

We quietly review our notes in preparation for any potential cold-calling by Professor Erikson. Law professors are fond of the archaic practice of cold-calling, formally known as the Socratic method, where they'll randomly call on a student in class to present the case or answer a question. But my ability to concentrate is immensely affected by the somber mood following our evidence class.

"What time are you going to the gym today?" Going to the gym with Aman will stimulate me physically, and I could use the uplift in emotional energy.

"Probably around five. I want to get more reading done after class and then take the night off afterward."

"Drag me with you today, please."

He says, "Hmm," and then returns to his books.

We have several minutes remaining before criminal law begins, but we make an early start for the lecture hall. Aman and Mark distractedly chat with each other and don't notice a man, probably in his early thirties, approaching us from the same direction we're heading.

He's in a suit and has a bag hanging from his shoulder, which isn't absurd, but it is unusual since the only individuals at the law school who wear suits are the professors. The man is not a professor.

He has a slight stubble, green eyes, black curly hair, and is wearing black-rimmed glasses. He blatantly stares at me, and I instinctively half-smile at him. He returns the gesture.

I lower my head, and in my peripheral vision, I see him walking past us. I can feel his eyes still on me even though I am no longer looking directly at him. *How forward.*

Like Professor Gatlin, Professor Erikson is one of the younger professors. He's in his early to mid-forties, wears glasses, and has salt-and-pepper hair with a consistent stubble to match. He always wears a coat, a button-up shirt, and slacks. Other professors wear ties, but he doesn't.

A student once nonchalantly asked him why he doesn't wear a tie, and his answer was, "I've worked on death penalty cases for so long that I can't tie things around my neck." It's an example of how intimidating Professor Erikson can be.

On the contrary, Aman thought that was a twisted and morbid response.

As Professor Erikson writes the case names on the board for today's discussion, the student in front of me hurriedly reaches for the syllabus inside his folder and flips through its pages, panicking. He whispers to his friend next to him, "Shit, I read the cases for Wednesday." For his sake, I hope he doesn't get called on. Professor Erikson shows no mercy.

Thanks to Aman and Mark, the class discussion on the difference between specific and general intent crimes contributes to my established understanding of the distinction. He doesn't cold-call anyone and chooses from among the students who raise their hands to answer his questions. The guy in front of me is saved.

Professor Erikson is only lenient at times because he has to be. If it were up to him, he would be as stringent as he felt was appropriate.

There was a particular incident a few years ago with Professor Erikson that prompted a three-way meeting with the dean. From what I've heard, the class was left speechless.

Apparently, Professor Erikson asked a student to leave the lecture hall for some reason, as he felt it was appropriate, to which the student responded, "I am paying to be here. I think I'll stay."

Professor Erikson looked consumed with fury and rage.

No one talks to Professor Erikson like that. Ever.

chapter 11

As the sun sets, the streetlights flicker on, illuminating our quickly darkening pathway as Aman and I traipse to the university gym.

"Don't use your phone when you're walking at night. It's distracting, and you need to be aware," I reprimand Aman.

He manages a simple "Hm" before I attempt to take his phone away to get his attention.

"Aman, I'm serious! It's not safe. Especially when you walk alone," I say in Punjabi.

"Ban, no one is going to mess with me." He flexes his muscular arms and pats his bulging biceps. His black workout tank top really emphasizes the indentation of his muscles.

"What if someone has a gun?"

"I got a gun show right here!" Again, referring to his muscles.

I laugh, but I remain worried that he's not taking me seriously.

"I like it when you come with me to the gym. You should come with me more often, fatty." He chuckles after he calls me "fatty." He only ever calls me "fatty" in Punjabi. It sounds less offensive and more playful that way.

I haven't been to the gym in a few weeks, and we don't usually go together. He likes to go any time of day that he's available. I like to go after completing all my schoolwork, usually in the evening. That's also when it's busiest, and when Aman avoids going.

The massive university gym is two stories high with a basement. It practically takes up a whole San Francisco block. The first floor has a basketball court, an Olympic-sized pool, and a spa. The second floor has an abundance of cardio machines. The basement has all the weight and resistance training machines and free weights. There are a few group exercise rooms in the basement as well, but I've never used them.

Aman proceeds to the basement as I ascend to the second floor. His workouts usually consist of weight and resistance training with one or two days of cardio workouts. I'm the opposite. I start with cardio, usually on the treadmill or a stair-climbing machine, and then end up in the basement to do weights and resistance.

As I expected, there aren't any treadmills or stair-climbing machines available. While I wait for one to free up, I pace back and forth rather than stand still. It makes time go by faster.

I notice a guy stop climbing on a stair machine and leisurely stand for a few minutes while fidgeting with the buttons on the machine. He finally descends from it, prompting me to walk over.

"Were you done?" I ask politely.

"Yeah, I'm going to wipe it down." I appreciate that because I see he's sweating profusely now that I'm closer.

I consider twenty minutes of cardio enough given my recent weeks-long hiatus from the gym. Another person is waiting, and she walks over as I get off.

I'm taken aback when I realize that it's actually Noor in rather skimpy clothing. I didn't recognize her at first.

"Hi, Noor," I say, slightly surprised, as I wasn't expecting to run into her.

"Hey." She purses her lips, the one word dripping with disinterest.

"Let me just clean the machine, and then it's all yours." Our interaction is awkward, almost forced. I wasn't expecting to be best friends, but mild chit-chat isn't absurd.

"Thanks. Is Aman here too?" She scans the room.

"Yeah." I've caught her interest now. "He's downstairs in the basement."

"Cool." She doesn't make much of an effort to talk to me beyond that now that she's seemingly gotten the information she wanted.

I climb back up on the machine to thoroughly clean it before descending back down. "All right, see ya."

"Bye."

I can't tell if Noor is disinterested in talking to anyone, or if it's specifically with me. She seems generally quiet, except maybe when she is alone with Aman.

Feeling marvelous due to a shift in my energy from the cardio exercise, I enter the weight room to commence the second part of my workout with the expectation that my mood will only improve. I spot Aman working on a rowing machine. He's so immersed in his set and doesn't see me initially.

"Hey, Ban." He stops once he sees me approach, panting heavily.

"Look at you." I smile at him.

He laughs and then snatches the water bottle out of my hands, taking heaping gulps of water from it.

"Leave some for me, too!"

"Thanks." He hands the water bottle back to me.

"What are you hitting today?" he asks me, still panting.

"I'm thinking of doing legs and abs."

"Okay, let me know if you need help with any equipment." He grins, looking surprisingly more handsome than usual. It must be how his hair is slightly disheveled.

"How long are you planning on staying?"

"You let me know whenever you're ready, and we'll go."

"That's okay. I can head home if you're not done."

"No. We came together, and we will leave together." Perhaps he was taking me seriously earlier during our walk to the gym.

As I'm speaking to Aman, Noor walks into the weight room. Did she even work out at all? I've been here for less than five minutes. Well, I *did* tell her exactly where she could find Aman.

"Ban, what do you want to have for dinner?" he asks distractedly as he fidgets with the resistance on the machine. He hasn't seen her yet.

"Hmm?" I'm similarly distracted. "Oh, we already have meals prepped, Aman." We prepared our meals for the week the night before.

"I know. But I feel like eating something fatty tonight. Want to get Thai fried rice?"

"Sure." I don't fight it much because the restaurant we get Thai fried rice from is delectable. "Do you—"

Noor interrupts our conversation with an overly enthusiastic "Hey" to Aman, essentially ignoring me. Her tone is blatantly different from how she spoke to me less than ten minutes ago.

"Oh, hey." His tone is the polar opposite of hers. Something tells me that he was not expecting to see her either.

"I'm going to get back to working out. Let me know when you're ready to leave," I say to Aman.

"Okay. I'll order dinner, and we can pick it up on our way home." The Thai restaurant is on the walk back.

Noor clears her throat, but Aman doesn't notice. Or perhaps he does and ignores it. *I hope that's it.* I'm being unnecessarily spiteful.

"Thank you. Bye, Noor."

She smug smiles at me. No words at all.

This bitch.

I'm annoyed with her behavior. I understand that she's uncertain about my and Aman's relationship because *she just met him*, but it doesn't warrant rude behavior when I've been polite to her.

Shaking off Noor's attitude, I do several sets of a few different leg exercises before I complete my workout. Thirty minutes later, I find Aman doing pull-ups on a high bar with uninterrupted ease. He makes it look so seamless.

"I'm ready when you are," I say to him.

He's panting again and nods to acknowledge me. Perhaps it wasn't as effortless for him as I thought.

He grabs my water bottle from me again and gulps down the remaining water more eagerly than before.

I briefly see Noor on an arm machine a few feet away, not-so-discreetly observing me and Aman. She's visibly uncomfortable. For someone who's only known Aman for a short while, her behavior is very insecure.

He finishes up and gestures for me to leave. "Aren't you going to say bye to Noor?" I ask. The gym rush has calmed down by the time we're leaving, making Noor easier to spot amongst the smaller crowd.

"No, I already did earlier."

"Hey, I want to ask you something," I say to Aman once we're out of the building. We're taking the shortest route to the restaurant to pick up our dinner.

"Then ask. Don't preface it with anything." He always says this to me.

"Does Noor not like me?"

"Who wouldn't like you?" He sincerely looks puzzled.

"Girls you date, Aman."

"Oh." He understands what I mean now. "I don't know. Why?"

"Because she's kind of rude to me when I see her. She gives me a vibe that she's territorial over you." My sentiments are strong enough for me to voice them to Aman.

"Shit, really?" He seems pensive. "She always wants to hang out, and there are only so many times I can say 'no.' She asked me to come over earlier, and when I said I couldn't, she looked pissed."

"Exactly what I mean."

He's quiet until we reach the restaurant, and for a few moments after, we collect our dinner before he decides it's time to talk about something other than Noor.

"I forgot to tell you. I booked my ticket to go to L.A. next weekend," Aman says when we're nearly home.

"That's great! To surprise your mom?"

"Yes."

"What's something I can get her that she'll like?"

"You really don't have to." He says it as a formality, but we're beyond formality. He knows that she'll be elated, and what kid wouldn't want to see their parent happy? Especially Aman.

"I know, but I want to." My words are light but convincing.

He grins back at me with admiration. "Raman said she's been into baking recently. She's really feeling the holiday spirit this year."

Aman has mentioned before that his mom is an Anglophile. A British dessert or baking cookbook might be a great present. I'm sure I can find something online that she'll like.

Once we get home, I hurriedly search for a British baking cookbook while Aman showers. The best seller I purchase will arrive early next week, just in time.

chapter 12

Tuesday's legal writing class is nothing out of the ordinary, but our professor gives us an in-class assignment for our upcoming exam. Our legal writing exam is less than a month away, and luckily, Aman and I are in the same class.

Mark is not on campus today, and Aman leaves campus after class. I go to the law library alone and station myself in a cubby in the basement section of the library.

Just as I set my belongings down in the cubicle, I overhear a few girls from my section whispering to each other. I consider asking them to speak softly, but I'm intrigued by their current discussion topic.

"I heard that there were a few interviews for Gerald's replacement yesterday and today," one whispers. She quickly glances around her surroundings but doesn't see me. "They feel pretty comfortable with the options and are almost ready to select one."

"How did you find out about this?" the other asks, mimicking her volume.

"I overheard Professor Gatlin talking to another professor when she asked about Gerald."

I wonder who this new TA will be.

The next day during criminal law, Professor Erikson seems agitated and cold-calls on tons of students, including Aman. Most of the students don't get the answer right, but unsurprisingly, Aman does.

Aman believes Professor Erikson isn't objective because his mood affects his teaching methods, furthering Aman's dislike. "I don't know how Bheau made him a professor here," he once said to me in Punjabi.

He overheard a student comment on his experience at Professor Erikson's office hours once, and the student sounded very peeved.

"He seemed to be in a pissy mood, but I needed clarification on the syllabus." The student had relayed. *"He declared that coming to his office hours to ask my question was a waste of my time and of other students' time who were there to ask substantive questions. I wasn't the only one with that question, and now no one wants to approach him to ask. He's such an ass."*

Aman's not home when I get there that Wednesday evening. He didn't tell me where he was going, but I figured he was going out or hanging out with another mystery girl he started seeing. He hasn't given me any details about the mystery girl, and knowing him, she could be anyone.

Following a burst of desire to speak to my parents, I ring them as I apply light makeup for my happy hour outing with Mark. Granted, I had a rum and soda while getting ready, so it may be the alcohol. And I haven't spoken to them for a few days—maybe even since last week.

"Hi, Banu. What are you doing?" my dad asks in Punjabi when he answers my call.

"Hi, Daddy. I'm going to happy hour with Mark. Getting ready for that. What are you doing?" I reply in Punjabi.

"Your mom and I are at the Indian store. How's school?"

"Good, it's hard. My evidence TA got into an accident last week, and it's been tense on campus."

"I heard. So sad. No updates on who did it?"

"Nope, the police haven't said anything."

"Is this Aman's TA, too?"

"Yes."

"How is he? He's not going with you kids to happy hour?" My dad always changes the subject when bad news comes up.

"No, I'm not sure where he is right now, but he's good. He's going to L.A. next weekend to visit his family."

"That's good. Why don't you also come home next weekend? I don't want you to be alone in the apartment."

"I'll think about it." In fact, that might be a good idea.

"Is he coming to Devan's wedding?"

"Yes, he told me this past weekend that he's coming to all of the events."

"Wonderful. Such a good boy." Dad takes a major interest when it comes to Aman. "Why don't you guys rent a car for that week? It will be easier to come here."

"He suggested that too. I think he's already looked into it. Can I talk to Mom?"

"Yes, let me walk over to the aisle she's in."

"Hun, Banu is on the phone," he says as he finds my mom. I vaguely hear her tell my dad to get something from the next aisle, and then her voice is much clearer.

"Hi sweetheart. How are you?"

"Hi Mom. I'm okay. Busy with school but also trying to have fun. How are you?"

"I'm good, baby. We're busy with Devan's wedding preparations. Is Aman coming to that?"

I smile to myself. My parents really do love him. I make a mental note to tell him about this conversation. It will make him happy.

"Yes, he's coming to all the functions."

"That's wonderful to hear. Bring him home with you one of these days. We haven't seen him for a while."

"I will. He's going home next weekend."

"You come home too."

Again, I smile to myself. My parents are adorable with their similar thought processes. I wonder if that's something that couples develop after years of being together.

"I may just."

I talk to my mom for a few more minutes and then disconnect the phone when I realize it's almost time to leave. Talking to them made me miss them more. I will definitely try to go home next weekend, especially since Ari is visiting as well. It's much better than being in my and Aman's apartment alone for the weekend. And I miss our golden retriever, Nala.

My phone haphazardly buzzes on my dresser, startling me. Mark texts me to update me on his ETA to my apartment. He should be here any minute now.

Out of curiosity, I text Aman to see why he's not home.

> ME: WHERE ARE YOU?

He responds after a few minutes.

> AMAN: I'M AT DINNER. YOU ALL GOOD?

ME: YES, I'M GOING TO HAPPY HOUR WITH MARK.

AMAN: HAVE FUN.

He must be distracted, given the shorter responses. Well, at least he responded. I shrug, tossing my phone onto my bed.

I hear a determined knock on the door, expecting it to be an eager Mark who's excited for tonight. I open the door, smiling, and to my surprise, I see Noor. My smile slowly fades. Aman didn't mention she'd be stopping by. Why would she just show up here? This girl is so weird.

"Hey," she says flatly.

"Hey." I mirror her tone, not being polite this time after her behavior at the gym.

"Is Aman here?"

"No, he's not."

She looks behind me as if she doesn't believe me.

Mark approaches our front door from behind Noor, and I am grateful for his opportune timing. He has a confused and bewildered look on his face, rightfully aimed at Noor.

The vibe between me and Noor is once again uncomfortable.

"Do you want me to let him know you stopped by?" Irrespective of her response, I fully intend to tell him.

"No, it's okay." She abruptly turns around to leave.

She briefly bumps into Mark, excuses herself, and then takes the elevator down to the first floor.

Once she's no longer visible, Mark asks, "Is she officially stalking Aman now?" He's joking, but I'm seriously concerned.

"Dude, honestly. I don't know."

I text Aman to let him know she stopped by, ignoring Noor's answer when I asked her. He needs to know so he can understand exactly what she wants from him. I think he's aware that this behavior is unusual, and I wonder how he'll react to my message. But he doesn't respond.

Even though we're about ready to leave, I invite Mark inside while I quickly gather my belongings. I continue to wonder why Noor is behaving the way she is. I'm not surprised that she's taken such a liking to Aman, but this is not normal behavior.

"Wallet, lipstick, gum, keys. What else am I missing?" I ask Mark, somewhat distracted.

"Phone?"

Oh, right. I left it on my bed.

I notice they've slightly redecorated His Majesty once we arrive. Their main icon is a blue jay with a gold crown on its head. The majestic crown has red, yellow, and green jewels spaced across the outer circumference.

The remainder of the restaurant is decorated like a castle in the forest, with tall trees to mimic redwood trees and tons of other magnificent leafy trees. Since my last visit, they've added more accent colors to the interior to complement the blue jay's crown.

Mark and I snatch up two open seats at the bar, our feet dangling from our chairs. It's not our preference, but it does give us a good vantage point of the others in the restaurant. We could be sitting at the top of King Jay's Tower, people-watching.

We place an order for the poutine, as planned, and I update Mark on the conversation I overheard at the library the day before—about Professor Gatlin's prospective TA. Mark is concerned about the quality of this TA since he or she wasn't subject to the thorough hiring process. However, we trust that the law school has done its best in selecting a competent TA. Its best is all we can ask for.

During round two of our happy hour, I see a peculiar thing near the entrance of the restaurant. Mark doesn't immediately spot the peculiar thing since he's focused on what he wants to order next. To make sure that the drinks are not enabling my imagination, I draw his attention to it—Professor Gatlin and Professor Erikson are leaving the restaurant together. This is an unconventional location for two colleagues to be together at this time of day.

"Is there something going on between them?" Mark asks.

"I know as much as you do. Maybe they're friends?"

At first, I only recognized Professor Erikson. I had to do a double take when I realized the woman with him was Professor Gatlin.

I'm not sure what to think, but one thing I know for certain is that tonight is the first time I've seen Professor Gatlin wearing something other than a suit and without her hair in a bun.

chapter 13

The way that Professor Gatlin and Professor Erikson were walking certainly implied something more than a mere professional relationship. They were fairly close to each other, and I think I saw Professor Gatlin briefly hold Professor Erikson's hand as they left. I can't be certain, though, because it was crowded at the entrance to the restaurant.

I hope to catch Aman before I go to bed, but I'm dozing off. As I get up to go to my room, Aman walks through the front door. I can tell that he's a little buzzed.

He doesn't notice me at first, but when he does, he flashes one of his captivating smiles. "Heyyyy!" His voice is hazy.

"Hi," I say sleepily, but I'm more awake than I was before Aman returned.

"How was the King?" he asks, referring to King Jay from His Majesty.

"It was great. Mark and I saw Professor Erikson and Professor Gatlin there. They looked pretty cozy." I aim to imply that the sighting seemed to be more than a professional one.

"Oh yeah? Get it, Professor E." Now I know for certain that he's buzzed because even on a personal level, there's no way that he would root for Professor Erikson.

I giggle and consider whether to bring up Noor. He seems to be okay enough to have a conversation. It's not that he's incoherent, just feeling good.

"Aman."

"Bani." He mocks me with a serious tone. I giggle again.

"What's going on with you and Noor?"

"She's crazy."

"Yeah, I got that. But what happened? It's weird as hell that she just stopped by today."

"Nothing. She wants something serious, and I don't. She's being clingy, that's all."

"I get that too, but what are you going to do now?"

"I already ended things with her." He straightens his back as if he's lost an extra weight he was carrying on his shoulders and exhales sharply in relief. "After we saw her at the gym on Monday, she blew my phone up because I didn't say goodbye, and then yesterday, she blew my phone up to come see her. I don't want to deal with that drama."

"Wow." It's bizarre that she came over uninvited, knowing Aman had ended their relationship, or whatever it was. How is he nonchalant about this? "I don't think she likes me," I test.

"Oh yeah. In one of her texts, she said something about you, and that's when I ended it. That was the last straw." He fervently shakes his head, convinced there was no other plausible outcome.

"What did she say?" I'm curious to hear this, but don't think I'll get an answer.

"Let's not talk about her now." *Knew it.*

"Where did you go tonight, then?" I intentionally change the subject.

"I had dinner with Sophia."

"*Sophia*, my 3L mentor?" I must look as surprised as I sound.

"Yeah. I ran into her on campus on Monday." He pauses. "No, yesterday. She asked me if I wanted to get dinner today, and I agreed since I wasn't doing anything." He almost makes it sound like he did her a favor.

"I didn't know that you were into her. Or that she was into you."

"Really? I always knew she was." But he doesn't say it in a cocky way. "And I'm not into her. Just hanging out," he adds.

I'm surprised to hear of this development and don't really know what to make of the sudden bomb that Aman just dropped on me. Sophia and I are close, and it never occurred to me that she was interested in Aman.

Next thing I know, Aman gives me a tight side hug with a gentle squeeze. I became so preoccupied with my thoughts that I didn't even notice him approach me.

I lift my arms to cradle his, which are resting on my shoulders, and return the sweet gesture.

"I'm going to go to bed, Ban. See you tomorrow. Don't think so much."

I can hear the teasing in his voice. "Goodnight."

I wonder what it takes to be serious in Aman's mind and how he acts when he's around someone he's truly interested in. Since I met him, he's gone from fling to fling—nothing substantial.

I know that since he's nearing his thirties, he gets tons of questions from his mom, who, despite her leniency in most respects, is still a Punjabi parent.

Granted, he's still in law school and has a few years ahead of him before he solidifies his career, but there's no doubt in my mind that he will do so. He will likely graduate law school with the highest honors. He's that smart.

I go to bed shortly after Aman and fall asleep rather quickly following an influx of exhaustion.

In the middle of the night, I wake up sweating profusely after a terrible nightmare. I dreamt that Noor showed up at our apartment unexpectedly again, barged inside, and threw a vase at Aman's head, knocking him unconscious.

It felt very real, and the recent frequency of my bad dreams is disconcerting. My mind races, and I wonder if Noor is capable of doing something like that. She certainly exhibits possessive and erratic behavior. But I don't think she's capable of intentionally and physically harming anyone.

Because of my difficulty sleeping, I'm awake well before Aman, ready to go by the time he wakes up.

I'm at the counter eating cereal when he enters the living room. He's surprised to see me, but I'm grateful to see him safe and sound.

"How are you awake so early?" he asks in Punjabi.

"Couldn't sleep. Do you want some coffee?" I run faucet water into a mug to pour into our high-tech coffee machine.

"Sure." He searches for the TV remote to turn on the news as per his morning ritual.

"Aman, I had a nightmare again." I point to the TV, although my nightmare was not the result of any news report. At least, I don't think it was.

"You should've come to me then." He winks at me without asking me to divulge any details.

I actually wanted to go into his room and see that he was okay since my nightmare was about him, but I didn't want to alarm or disturb him.

We leave for campus once he's showered and ready to go. Since our class on Thursday isn't as early as it is on Mondays, Wednesdays, and Fridays, we usually spend the downtime in the law library.

During our walk to school, I contemplate whether to broach the Noor and Sophia conversation with him. I choose to discuss Sophia.

"Tell me again how this whole thing with Sophia started?"

"Ban, nothing started. It was a meal," he says resolutely. "But I don't know how you couldn't tell that she's into me. She blatantly flirts with me."

"I guess I never noticed." Or maybe I never paid attention.

"That's why you're so cute." He looks at me with a sidelong glance and smiles. "The other day, I ran into her when I was at the student café, and she asked me how my semester was shaping up. I didn't expect her to forwardly ask me, but she did."

"Hmm."

On our way to the law library, we conveniently run into Sophia and discuss our upcoming legal writing exam with her. She gives us a few tips but assures us that it won't be as difficult as we think.

Throughout our conversation, which lasts around ten minutes, both Sophia and Aman act as if they hadn't gotten dinner together last night.

Come that following Monday morning, it's nearly time for the evidence lecture to begin.

The British baking book that I ordered for Aman's mom arrived over the weekend. Thankfully, Aman was at the gym when it was delivered. I successfully wrapped the book, tied a bow, and placed it on my bedroom dresser table to hand to Aman without him finding out what I got her.

From how it's wrapped and its weight, he'll easily discern that it's a book, but I hope he won't be able to guess the type. I want him to be as surprised as she will be. It means more that way.

The media frenzy outside of the law school has subsided since Gerald's news first broke. Bheau's input has been limited to protect the school, and the news channels soon realized that they were unlikely to get any more information.

A few minutes before class begins, Professor Gatlin walks into the lecture hall. But she's not alone.

A younger, familiar-looking man walks behind her. I rack my brain to recall why he looks familiar, but it doesn't strike me until I find him eyeing me.

Then it hits me. This is the same man that I saw in the hallway a week ago when I was walking to the criminal law lecture. The man who stood out because he wore a suit. He was staring at me then too, and I found that strange as well.

Aman notices his stare. "Do you know who that is?" he whispers.

I frown and shake my head.

Aman diverts his attention back toward the front while sporting a serious expression. Meanwhile, Professor Gatlin speaks to the man in hushed tones.

"Good morning, everyone." Her voice shakes. She looks distraught, and I can immediately sense that she's not about to share good news.

The room is quiet.

"On behalf of myself and the law school faculty, we'd like to thank the students for your patience." She pauses and slowly looks up at the class in the enormous lecture hall. "I received some very unfortunate news a few minutes ago."

Oh, no. I swallow hard.

Clearing her throat, she delivers news that sends the entire room into shock. "Gerald succumbed to his injuries and died late last night."

chapter 14

My stomach sinks in a way I have never felt before. There is an eerie silence in the lecture hall despite there being nearly one hundred students in it. It's difficult to understand that someone I used to see walking the halls and immersed in his notes is dead.

No, he was *killed*. That is the reality. Gerald was killed.

"The law school welcomes you to attend a memorial that will be held Wednesday evening to honor his memory," Professor Gatlin adds.

"The law school also requests all students to respect the privacy of Gerald's family as they mourn this senseless loss."

It sounds like this is something that Professor Gatlin has never experienced firsthand either. I've never seen her this way. Contrary to her usual poised demeanor, she looks broken and angry.

"I understand that there are many lingering questions revolving around this incident, but we're not in a position to answer them." I can't imagine how difficult it must be for her to speak right now, let alone announce something this heartbreaking to a lecture hall full of frightened students.

She abruptly changes the subject, as if in a hurry to talk about anything other than Gerald's death. "In the meantime, I'd like to share that the Bheau faculty has appointed a substitute TA to cover last names N through Z."

She gestures toward the strange man, who walks a little closer to Professor Gatlin as she introduces him.

"This is Marcus Hendricks. Amelia will remain the designated TA for last names A through L and will provide Marcus with support until he is up to speed. Does anyone have any questions?"

There is complete silence, not even a murmur, but understood acknowledgement. "I'll ask Marcus to briefly introduce himself to the class. Marcus?" Professor Gatlin steps aside.

Marcus walks toward the center of the room, repositioning his black-frame glasses on his face and clearing his throat.

"Hi." His voice is slightly scratchy at first. "Very unfortunate circumstances, but I'd like to thank the Bheaurmiss faculty for providing me with this opportunity." He clears his throat again.

"A little about me. I'm a licensed attorney in California but haven't entered the law practice in a firm setting per se. With my judicial clerkship experience, I believe I offer a unique perspective on evidence matters, specifically ones in the eyes of the court." He pauses. "I'm here under unfortunate circumstances, but nonetheless, I'm looking forward to working with you. I've written my email address on the board. Please feel free to reach out to me with any questions. For the first few lectures, I'll sit in on lectures to build familiarity with Professor Gatlin's style. Now, I'll let Professor Gatlin begin her lecture. Otherwise, I'll be completely useless to you all."

He attempts to lighten the mood with a touch of humor, but there's no response from the students. I can't help but notice that he is good-looking in a nerdy sort of way.

As he walks down the aisle toward the back of the lecture hall, I feel his eyes on me again, but I avoid looking at him.

Aman notices this too. *"What the fuck?"* I hear him say quietly under his breath. I don't think I was meant to hear that, but I did. Aman didn't flinch when Professor Gatlin announced Gerald's death, but he sounded mad just now for some reason.

Aman looks back toward where Marcus is sitting and shifts in his seat. I briefly glance at him, and he doesn't look pleased at all. His hands cover his mouth as if he's in deep thought and restraining himself from saying something.

Professor Gatlin's voice strengthens as her lecture progresses, but students hesitate to answer any questions she asks. Well, almost all. Aman remains confident in his delivery, like we hadn't just received such devastating news. His ability to compartmentalize is astounding to me.

Once class is over, I approach Professor Gatlin to ask a brief clarification question regarding a point she made during lecture. Aman and Mark both leave the lecture hall to kill time in the library before our next class.

Professor Gatlin is about to begin her explanation when I suddenly feel someone approach from behind. I instinctively turn around, mid-conversation, and find the new TA, Marcus, listening in on the conversation that I'm having with Professor Gatlin.

"Don't mind me," he says. "I'm observing to build familiarity. Nice to meet you, by the way." He extends his hand for a handshake. "What's your name?"

I slowly extend my hand out as well and say, "Bani. Nice to meet you." He makes me feel nervous.

He frowns slightly before he smiles.

Turning my attention back toward Professor Gatlin, I exit the lecture hall once she's done with her explanation without looking back at Marcus. He says something to Professor Gatlin as the door closes behind me, but I don't hear what.

His behavior toward me is unusual, and he's blatant about it. It is almost like he doesn't care that I notice.

chapter 15

Since I learned of Gerald's death, I've had a persistent headache. In the evening, I go to the gym by myself, hoping it will relieve the intense pressure in my head.

Aman went earlier because he wanted to avoid any possibility of running into Noor and having an in-person, public confrontation. She has been consistently reaching out to him, and he hasn't responded. I hope I don't see her either.

The gym, surprisingly, is not busy for a weekday. I overheard a few undergraduate students discuss a notable football game and assume that's why there isn't as much hustle and bustle as usual.

In between my training sets, my phone vibrates in my pocket.

AMAN: NOOR IS AT THE GYM. SHE TEXTED ME SAYING SHE SAW YOU AND ASKED WHY I'M NOT THERE. I HAVEN'T EVEN BEEN RESPONDING TO HER CRAZY ASS.

ME: SHE'LL GET THE PICTURE EVENTUALLY. WHY DON'T YOU JUST BLOCK HER?

I wait a few minutes before I make a quick scan throughout the weight room for Noor, preventing any obvious disclosure that I'm looking for her. She must've arrived after I did because when I first entered, there were only about ten people in the room, none of whom were her.

Eventually, I spot her a few machines away, and her back is toward me. I have a new message from Aman.

AMAN: I JUST BLOCKED HER. I DON'T LIKE BLOCKING, BUT SHE'S SERIOUSLY ON ANOTHER LEVEL. I DON'T WANT TO DEAL WITH THIS WHEN I'M AT HOME THIS WEEKEND.

Noor will be able to tell that he blocked her—this does not bode well.

Amidst my workout and high-volume music, I momentarily forget about Noor. But a few minutes later, I'm unfortunately reminded of her when she walks over to me to get my attention.

"Hey," she mouths. I pause my music.

"Hey," I respond rather simply at that and wait for what she's going to say next.

"Do you know why Aman is ignoring me?" She cuts straight to the chase.

"Listen, Noor. I don't get in the middle of his personal life."

"But *how* do you not know? I'm sure he tells you stuff." Her tone reeks with disdain.

"No, he doesn't."

"Are you guys a thing?" She asks like she already knows the answer, giving my already growing anger and annoyance an instant boost.

"Excuse me?" There is immense attitude in my voice. I attempted to be patient at first, but her accusatory tone is getting under my skin. This girl is very audacious.

Frankly, she pisses me off and deserves more than an attitude from me, but I refrain from saying anything out of line. "I'm not continuing this conversation. Enjoy your workout. I'm going to get back to mine."

It looks like she's going to respond, but before she has the opportunity to, I turn around and walk away. If she attempts to follow me, she'll draw a lot of attention to herself. I can't fathom that she's that thick.

When I tell Aman that she approached me, his anger is palpable from a mere text.

> **AMAN:** I'M GOING TO GO THERE AND TELL HER ONCE AND FOR ALL THAT SHE NEEDS TO STOP. COMING UP TO YOU IS BULLSHIT.
>
> **ME:** NO, DON'T DO THAT. SHE'S TRYING TO GET YOU TO TALK TO HER. DON'T GIVE HER EXACTLY WHAT SHE WANTS. PLUS, I HANDLED IT LIKE A PRO.

I add a winking face to lighten his mood, but he just responds with 'lol,' and that's it. He's upset.

I opt to jog home once I'm ready to leave the gym. There's a group of students further ahead of me who I assume are undergraduates since I'm on the undergraduate side of campus.

I focus on my breathing with each step I take on the hard pavement.

Amidst my steady breathing, I think I hear footsteps approaching and closing in behind me, similar to the nightmare I had the other night. My anxiety builds rapidly, and my heart thumps inside my chest, but I'm too frightened to turn around.

I transition from jogging to running to reach the group of students ahead of me as fast as I can. They're the only ones I see in my immediate surroundings. It's deserted.

Paranoia strikes. I wonder if Noor went too far and decided to follow me to finish harassing me after my abrupt exodus earlier. But I recall seeing her swimming in the pool right before I left. It's highly unlikely that she cleaned up and left the gym within five minutes.

As I near the group of students, I'm slightly more at ease but still too fretful to look back. If someone was following me, I can no longer sense their presence.

I regret not having Aman come with me to the gym. This group isn't exactly going to drop me off at home. Instead, I make a pit stop at the undergraduate library and text Aman once inside.

> **ME:** CAN YOU PLEASE PICK ME UP FROM THE UNDER-GRADUATE LIBRARY?

He doesn't respond to my text, but immediately calls me instead. "What happened? Are you okay?" he asks in Punjabi.

"Yes, I'm okay." My voice is slightly hushed. "Just got a little spooked. Can you come here and we can walk home together? I'll explain once you get here."

"I'm already walking outside. Be there in less than ten minutes."

"Thank you."

I wait in the lounge area of the library until Aman arrives. The library isn't as packed as it usually is, but there are plenty of people around. Aman doesn't text or call me to ask me where I am because he knows exactly where to find me. He knows that I like the part of the undergraduate library that has fireplaces and cozy couches. During a typical San Francisco evening, the fireplace is comforting to be around.

I don't see him walk up to me, but I immediately recognize a waft of his cologne. "Hey," he says as he sits down next to me. He looks serious.

"Hi."

He frowns. "What happened?"

"I don't know. I left the gym, and midway through my jog home, it felt like someone was following me. I was too scared to turn around and look, scared I'd trip or something, and instead ran faster toward a group of students who were luckily right near the library. Then I texted you." I chuckle half-heartedly.

"What made you feel like someone was following you?" He's still serious.

"I got a weird feeling and thought I heard footsteps behind me. The person was close enough for me to hear his or her breathing, and that's not normal. No one runs that closely."

"Was it Noor?" I was waiting for him to ask that.

"Honestly, at first my paranoia got the best of me, and I thought it was her. But I saw her in the pool right when I left. I think I'm psyching myself out."

"Hmm." Aman is quiet for a moment. "Ready?"

I nod, and we both get up to go home.

The continued anxiety and paranoia I'm feeling must be a combined result of school-related stress, the school atmosphere because of Gerald's death, and the nature of the cases that we're briefing this semester.

I ask Alina for any coping strategies she may know of. She recommends I keep my activity level high at the gym as a form of stress relief.

I felt that effect after my workout today—until I felt that I was being followed on my way home.

chapter 16

That Friday

Aman's flight to L.A. leaves at the end of class today. He'll be skipping evidence lecture since it was unrealistic for him to attend today's lecture and make his flight on time.

Fortunately, lectures are recorded, and he'll have the video available to him shortly after class is dismissed and before the start of the weekend. Plus, he asked me to take thorough notes and share them with him. Being the silent nerd that he is, he asked Mark for a copy of his notes too.

My parents check in to see if I'm coming home this weekend as well. It's a good time to go, before school gets busier.

I plan to go home tomorrow since Sophia invited me to her birthday celebration tonight. I assume she hasn't spoken to Aman much because she insists I bring him as well. When I tell her that he went home for the weekend, she looks surprised.

Wondering if Sophia mentioned her birthday celebration to Aman, I text him to ask.

> **AMAN:** SHE MENTIONED HER BIRTHDAY WAS COMING UP AND THAT SHE MIGHT DO SOMETHING. WHY?
> **ME:** SHE TOLD ME TO BRING YOU TONIGHT TOO.
> **AMAN:** OH OKAY. SHE DIDN'T TELL ME ABOUT ANY SOLID PLANS.
> **ME:** ARE YOU GUYS NOT TALKING?
> **AMAN:** SHE MESSAGES ME BUT I DON'T ENGAGE MUCH. I'M TAKING A BREAK FROM ALL THAT.
> **ME:** ALL THAT?
> **AMAN:** GIRLS AND HANGING.

In all the time I've known him, he's never said he wants to take a break from hanging, or hooking up, or whatever it is he does. It's unusual for him to say that now. Did something happen?

Even though he doesn't give me details, I can usually tell he's hanging or hooking up with someone when he doesn't come home for a night or takes a few hours extra when he's out.

I convinced Mark to come with me to Sophia's birthday celebration so I have a familiar face around. Since Sophia is a 3L, most of her friends are also 3Ls, which means I don't know many of them.

But before I take the rest of the weekend off, I promise myself that I will finish my work for the upcoming week and fully enjoy the time at home.

As I expected, the library is pretty much empty. There's rarely anyone in the library on a Friday afternoon. I prefer it this way, as there are fewer distractions. I'm confident I will be able to complete my readings for the upcoming week well before I have to head out for Sophia's birthday celebration.

The quiet of the library amplifies the buzzing of my phone as it vibrates furiously against the desktop. I didn't realize how loudly I gasped. Thankfully, there aren't many students around to witness the embarrassing moment. I switch my phone to silent to avoid a similar surprise from happening again.

AMAN: MOM LOVES YOUR GIFT.

I smile to myself, relieved that she likes it—loves it.

AMAN: SHE GOT SO HAPPY. YOU DIDN'T HAVE TO.
ME: EXACTLY WHY I WANTED TO.
AMAN: THANK YOU.

I send a smiling emoji back to him.

ME: GLAD YOU TOUCHED DOWN SAFELY.
AMAN: CRAP, FORGOT TO MESSAGE YOU.
ME: NOTHING I'M NOT USED TO.

Ironically, he replies back with an eye-rolling emoji.

I quickly text my family group chat to let them know I'm coming home tomorrow before I place my phone aside and focus. My mom is the first to respond with a series of smiley faces in the chat. My dad sends a thumbs up, Devan sends a "Nice," and Ari sends a "YAY!"

DAD: CAN AMAN ALSO COME?

He must've forgotten that I told him Aman isn't here this weekend.

ME: HE'S IN L.A. FOR THE WEEKEND.

Dad sends a thumbs down.

I screenshot the conversation and send it to Aman. He always gets giddy when I show or tell him how much my dad adores him.

> AMAN: I'M GOING TO HAVE A DRINK WITH HIM AT THE WEDDING.
> ME: I'M SURE HE'D LIKE THAT.
> AMAN: YOU CAN JOIN US IF YOU WANT TO.

Aman adds a winking face.

> ME: WHY THANK YOU FOR THAT HONOR.

He sends another winking face.

I instinctively look up when I hear someone walking around in my immediate vicinity. I am surprised to see our new evidence TA, Marcus, walking in my direction. He's initially so engrossed in the book he's holding that he doesn't realize I'm here. A few seconds later, he looks up at me and does a double-take when he sees me. He does that a lot.

He slowly and dramatically closes his book, squinting inquisitively at me. I smile faintly, hoping that's enough, and turn my attention back toward my books. I have my headphones in my ears and hope that that will deter him from approaching me. I'm not in the mood to have a conversation at the moment. I'm entirely in study mode.

In my peripheral vision, I see him standing very close to me, and I look back up. I remove my headphones and stare at him blankly, slightly annoyed. He's gazing at me, his eyes filled with curiosity.

"You're in Professor Gatlin's evidence class, right?" he asks despite knowing the answer. I met him only a few days ago.

"Yeah." I hope he catches my curt tone and leaves me alone.

"You're very studious. Didn't think that anyone would be here on a Friday afternoon at this time of the school year." He smiles as he speaks.

"This is around the time the workload usually picks up. But not many students stay on campus on a Friday."

"Ah." He pauses. "I see."

I give Marcus a half-smirk, hoping that he'll go about his day and I can resume studying. I really want to go home worry-free tomorrow.

Incidentally, he sees my evidence book on the table and gestures toward it. "Looks like you're diving right into that evidence reading. Is there anything I can help you with?"

"No questions at the moment. I'm just getting started. Thank you, though." I don't think I can make it more painfully obvious that I don't want to engage in a conversation with him. He's not taking the hint.

He looks behind him and grabs a chair to pull up near where I'm sitting. While his back is turned toward me, I roll my eyes, frustrated that he won't leave. I don't know how I should tell him to leave me alone without sounding like a bitch at this point.

He sits a little too close and doesn't do anything to increase the distance between us. It's odd sitting this close to someone I barely know and who is also my TA.

"I finished the reading and made a detailed outline of the topics we're going to cover next week. Do you want to take a look? I think it'll be helpful. The reading isn't long at all, but the topics are complex," he says before I'm able to convey that I want to study alone.

I look at the outline in his hand, and he puts his hand out for me to grab it.

I reluctantly take it. "Thank you."

He briefly explains his organization of the outline to ensure I follow.

"I'll be sitting over there if you need anything." He gestures toward a corner of the library. "I was a law student once. You have the 'I mean business' look right now, and I can tell you're determined to study." He smiles at me. I return the smile since he's actually being thoughtful.

Marcus walks over to the table slightly further away from me, and I peruse through the outline that he gave me in detail. I instantly feel bad when I find out how helpful it is. The outline will minimize my workload tremendously.

This topic for Monday is confusing, and I was planning on reading it twice, maybe even three times, before I could comprehend the content. With Marcus' outline, I will likely only have to read the text once and read his outline to feel the same level of comfort with the topic.

He doesn't bother me the remainder of the time I'm in the library. I do, however, notice him look in my direction or feel his eyes on me several times. We even make eye contact once or twice.

When he's not paying attention, I take a second to study him and realize how good-looking he really is. The sun sets on his profile, making his hair seem lighter than it actually is. His green eyes, paired with his pretty long eyelashes, are exotic.

The setting sun reminds me that I've completely lost track of time. Sophia's birthday celebration starts in a few hours, and I still have to return home to shower and get ready. Mark is meeting me at home and should be on his way any time now.

My time at the library was productive primarily because of Marcus' outline. Now I can truly enjoy the rest of the weekend, both out and at home.

Marcus is working intently and doesn't notice me getting ready to leave. The entire time that we were there, not a single person came to the library. Or at least the floor that we are on.

Once I'm packed, I walk over to Marcus to sincerely thank him for his outline. He must have noticed someone approaching him because he looks up at me and takes his headphones off before I'm at the table, grinning pleasantly.

My voice is lower but not exactly a whisper. "Hey, I'm going to head out. I wanted to thank you for the outline. It was really, really helpful. I didn't think I would be able to finish this early."

His grin broadens. "You're welcome. Glad to know I'm off to a good start." Is he talking about the school or about me?

I reach over to hand it back to him. "Keep it, if it's that helpful," he says.

"Are you sure?"

"Oh yeah. The amazing thing about technology these days is that I can print my own outline as many times as I want." I hear the laughter in his voice. He's teasing me.

I chuckle quietly and thank him again.

"I'm actually heading out as well," he adds.

"I'll wait for you." I try to be as polite as possible to make up for my poor behavior from earlier. If this guy is going to be my TA for the next few months, it's a good idea to at least remain on friendly terms with him.

He tucks his laptop and headphones away, and we both climb the stairs toward the exit.

"Do you have any fun Friday plans?" he asks me once we are outside of the library's quiet area.

"My friend is celebrating her birthday tonight. That's about it. What about you?"

"Nothing, really. I'm adjusting to the city and trying to explore as much as I can during my free time. It's hard since I don't know a lot of people. I've been wanting to see the nightlife, but I think I'd be the 'creeper at the bar' if I went somewhere alone. Know what I mean?"

Would it be strange to ask him if he wants to join Sophia's birthday celebration? I suppose that since Mark will also be there with me, it's not a huge deal.

"Do you want to come to the bar tonight? I don't know a lot of people myself, but I asked one of my friends to come. You can join us."

"I didn't intend to solicit an invitation out of you when I said that." He snickers, but I can tell he's willing.

"I know. But I think it would be fun. I'll buy you a drink as a 'thank you' for giving me your outline and making my weekend."

"My outline made your weekend? I thought you were a bit nerdy for being in the library on a Friday, but it's something else if an outline is making your weekend." He's teasing me again. "I would be thrilled to accompany you, though. Thank you for the invite!"

"You're welcome. It's going to be in North Beach. The bar's name is Red Light, Green Light."

"I think I've heard of that place. The concept is to either wear green, red, or yellow depending on your relationship status, right?"

"Yes, that's the one."

"Is the friend who's coming the guy that sits next to you in class?"

I wonder who he's talking about since I sit next to two guys, Aman and Mark.

I'm with Aman more than I'm with Mark and assume he means him. "The Indian one?" I ask.

"Yes."

"No. It's the other guy that I sit with. The one you're talking about is my roommate. But he's not here this weekend."

"He's your roommate?"

"Yes."

"And who's the other guy?"

"That's Mark. He's in our section. You probably haven't seen him as much. He externs during the week and isn't on campus as often."

"Nice! I'm looking forward to chatting with him about his work experience. What time are you heading over?"

"Probably around nine."

"Sounds good. I'll meet up with you then. Definitely don't

want to be the first one there and have the other students wondering why the new TA is at a law student gig." We both laugh. He's funny.

We awkwardly exchange goodbyes when we are outside of the law library with the understanding he will join us later.

On my walk home, I reflect on how I misjudged Marcus. I do think his behavior was a bit strange every other time I interacted with him before today, but maybe I was reading too much into it.

He seems like a nice, funny guy. I shouldn't be hard on him since he was thrown into the academic schedule at such an unusual time. He didn't have the advantage that all the other TAs had of receiving proper training long before the semester actually began or building relationships with students.

I did note, however, how much of an interest he took in Aman and how surprised he seemed when I told him that Aman is my roommate.

Objectively and definitively, I can say one thing: the entire time we were together, Gerald or his death didn't come up once.

chapter 17

It's likely that Mark is already waiting outside of our apartment building. I haven't seen him much this week, nor have I spoken to him. There's a major trial happening at his firm, and he's been busy helping the partners with the document preparation. I'm excited to have some one-on-one time with him. Well, at least until Marcus shows up.

I wonder if inviting Marcus was a smart idea. I haven't told Mark yet, but I plan to discuss it with him as soon as I see him. He's waiting outside of my apartment building as I approach it, but he's on the phone and looks upset.

As I get closer, I can hear his conversation and assume he's talking to Natalia. They're arguing.

"—work has been crazy, babe. You know I have a trial going on." He pauses. "And I'm sorry…"

I get the impulse to turn away to give Mark some privacy. The conversation doesn't sound like it's ending.

I beeline toward the local market that is about forty feet away from my apartment building. Mark loves tequila. It may not cheer him up, but I know he'll appreciate it if I buy some. I gesture to Mark, and he briefly nods in understanding.

I point to a bottle of tequila on a shelf behind the counter that's positioned in an organized line. As the clerk at the market reaches for it, he asks, "How is your boyfriend?"

I toss him a confused look.

"My boyfriend?"

"Yes. You live with him, no? The tall, muscular guy with the beard?" He slightly flexes his arms to aid in my identification of who he's referring to.

I laugh when I realize he's talking about Aman. I should have known. "He's not my boyfriend. He's my friend and my room-mate. That's why we're always together when we come here."

"I see," he says distractedly as he rings me up. "Nice guy," he adds.

"Yes, he is." I smile and hand him my credit card.

Mark is still on the phone when I leave the store, but I hear him say, "I'll call you tonight when I'm back." He pauses. "I will. Love you."

He ends the call and turns his attention to me. "Sorry about that, Bunny. This trial has been rough, and Natalia is not having it. She's been stressed with law school applications. She's asked me to look over her essay, but I haven't had the time."

"I'm happy to look at it. You have so much more going on, and I'm a better writer than you." I wink to lighten his mood.

He sighs in agreement. "That you are. Are you sure you have the time? With the wedding and everything?"

"Yes! Tell Natalia to send it to me. I can review it tomorrow night when I'm at home."

"Thank you so much."

"Happy to help! I, for one, would not want long distance to get the best of the two of you."

He knows I'm speaking from my own personal experience. And he, again, knows exactly who I'm talking about.

"Bunny, I'm mentally exhausted." He gives me a hug. "Glad you convinced me to come out tonight. I needed a night out." I'm sure he intentionally changed the subject.

"Me too! You're staying over, right?"

"Yeah. I'll leave at the same time as you in the morning."

"Sounds good."

I take the silence as an opportunity to tell him that Marcus will be joining us tonight. "You know the new evidence TA?"

"Yes, what about him? Is he any good?"

"Actually, yes, he is. He was at the library too and gave me his outline. I ended up saving a lot of time because of him. I'll scan a copy of the outline he shared with me to you and Aman."

"That's great, thank you."

I think Mark thought that was the extent of my mention of Marcus. Why would he think there was something in addition to that? It's natural to presume that that was it.

"I, uh, invited him out tonight." My hesitation is prominent.

"To the bar?" He understandably sounds surprised.

"Yeah. Do you think that's weird? He was talking about how he doesn't go out much because he doesn't know anyone. I thought it would be polite to invite him."

"Is this guy interested in you?" Mark asks plainly.

I turn to him, even more surprised. "What?"

"He got you to invite him to the bar outside of school. He knows he's a TA, and you're a student. Yet he did that."

"I don't think that necessarily means he's interested in me." Mark doesn't know about the curious encounters I've had with Marcus before this one. Aman does to a certain degree.

"Bunny, there's some other level here, not just that of a TA and student. And you'll know when you see how he acts with you after he's had a few drinks."

"Well, that's why I have you here." I giggle at the thought.

He laughs. "Would you be interested in him at all?"

"Whoa, Mark. I'm literally looking at this for the first time. I haven't even considered anything like that."

He nods in understanding.

"But he's our TA. That would be weird and unprofessional. I think he's being nice and helpful since he's new."

"Could be, but I've seen weirder." He laughs again.

By now, we're in my apartment, and Mark sets his belongings down near his bed, which is actually the couch.

"Would Aman ever find out if I slept in his bed?" he jokes.

I'm almost to my room and turn around to face him, laughing loudly. "I have no idea, but please do that. It'll be our little secret."

"No way. He's huge and can definitely kick my ass."

I'm still laughing as I walk into my room.

We're supposed to be at Red Light, Green Light soon, but we still have some time, and my stomach is rumbling.

"Have you eaten?" I call out to Mark.

"No. I thought I'd let you feed me!"

"Lucky for you, I went grocery shopping yesterday. How about tacos? We can make margaritas with the tequila I just bought."

"Hell yeah. Tacos and margs. Perfect combo."

"Great. I'm picking out my clothes for tonight and will be right out."

I panic because I remember that I didn't take my phone off silent once I left the library. I have two texts from Aman and five texts from Ari.

111

Ari asks me what time I'm coming home tomorrow for the twentieth time and if she can borrow my blue sweater. Then, she sends about ten question marks and a text that finally says she borrowed my blue sweater despite my lack of response. The last message is of her wearing my blue sweater with a mischievous smile on her face. I snicker at my baby sister's shenanigans.

> **ME:** Looks cute, brat. I'm coming early tomorrow morning. Hopefully I'll catch the 9 am train.

Aman must be missing me because he asks me what I'm up to and how my night is going. Like Ari, he also asks me what time I'm going home tomorrow. He doesn't normally do that. Especially when he's at home with his family.

> **ME:** Night is okay. Just got home from the library and about to make dinner for me and Mark before we go out.
> **ME:** I'm going to catch the 9 am train tomorrow.
> **ME:** How's home?
> **AMAN:** Are you going to do wedding stuff?

The wedding is only a few weeks away.

> **AMAN:** Home is great. We're at dinner for mom's birthday and going to San Diego tomorrow for the day. Taking mom to brunch and walking around the La Jolla cove.
> **AMAN:** Have fun and be safe tonight. I won't be there to protect you.

He adds a winking face.

> **ME:** Okay, big guy lol. If you're at dinner then focus on that. Why are you on your phone?

AMAN: WE'RE STILL WAITING FOR OUR TABLE. WHAT ARE YOU MAKING FOR DINNER?
ME: TACOS.
AMAN: OF COURSE YOU MAKE SOMETHING WHEN I'M NOT THERE.
ME: EXACTLY.

I send a winking face and then put my phone on charge before going outside, taking it off silent mode this time.

My phone vibrates on my bedside table, indicating that I have another text message, but I decide that it can wait. It must be either Aman or Ari.

Mark has taken out and placed the taco ingredients on the counter and has already made a batch of margaritas.

"Thanks for the tequila, by the way, Bunny."

"Thanks for making margaritas." We cheer.

Mark's margaritas are delicious. It's his preferred drink, and he has skillfully concocted the best recipe to make them. They're a bit tangier and have a refreshing taste to them to help avoid a hangover. Something about the extra lime in the drink makes me less nauseated.

"So good." I exhale after I take my first sip. Mark nods in gratitude and subtle agreement.

"Mark, can you make sure I don't segue away from tequila tonight?"

"Why? Don't want to embarrass yourself in front of the new guy?"

"No!" I lightly nudge him. "I don't want to be hungover tomorrow since I'm going home."

"Ah, convenient excuse." He smiles.

I relish my margarita as I prepare the tacos. Mark turns the TV on and situates himself in front of me on one of the stools we have at the counter.

"Aman texted me," he says as he checks his phone.

"Yeah?" I respond distractedly. "What did he say?"

I don't know why he's so intrigued by our weekend. I rarely ever get his attention when he's in L.A.

"Bunny, he told me about the other day. Frankly, I'm a little upset that you didn't tell me yourself."

I don't immediately comprehend what he's referring to. "What do you mean?" I look at him with a somewhat bewildered expression.

"The night of the gym."

Then it comes back to me.

"Especially with what happened with Gerald, it's worrisome. This is unknown territory. We don't know why that happened to him," he adds.

This is why Aman has been much more attentive than usual. I don't why I didn't put those pieces together. I suppose I chose to hide both experiences from my mind. Perhaps that was deliberate.

"Trying not to think about it has been effective. It all feels like a bad dream."

Mark is quiet. He, like Aman, worries about me. However, he, unlike Aman, is less vocal about it.

A sudden surge of love for both of my closest friends washes over me. They're both concerning themselves over me to the point that they're both visibly troubled by it.

Aman is texting to check up on me when he's with his family for his mom's birthday, something he rarely does. Mark agreed to come out with me despite the huge trial at work. I know he's exhausted. It never dawned on me until now that fear of me being alone was what really motivated him to join me tonight versus a pocket of free time or the desire to go out. I wonder if Aman separately urged Mark to stay the night since he wasn't going to be here this weekend.

With the music playing in the background, alternating between Punjabi and hip-hop, Mark asks me about the outline Marcus sent me.

"You know what I was thinking? The school hired him and all, but we don't know anything about him. I'm sure the school knows about his background, education, etc. But we, as students, know nothing about him. At least with Gerald, we had the opportunity to talk to him during the back-to-school events." He pauses, then adds, "I guess that will change tonight. But only for us."

"That's true." The thought had crossed my mind earlier. "He seems like a cool person, though."

"Oh, I bet you do think that." Mark winks at me.

"Shut up!" I laugh. "That's not what I meant." A warm feeling expands in my stomach. Maybe it's a combination of the alcohol and Mark's joke.

Mark is absolutely right about us not knowing about Marcus, though. *I'm going to change that tonight*, I tell myself. I think I want to get to know him.

chapter 18

"Do you know you're known as the Hot Tea?" I loudly proclaim to Marcus. We've been at the bar for about an hour and are loosening up quite a bit. The only reason I'm this forthcoming with Marcus is because I'm tipsy.

Introductions with Mark were hilarious because he was discreetly teasing me. I couldn't stop laughing. Marcus probably thought I was having a fit, but I think he chalked it up to me having a good time.

He ended up taking the concept of Red Light, Green Light very seriously and wore a bright green button-up shirt. No subtlety in his attire whatsoever.

"Are you trying to scream to all the ladies in here that you're single?" Mark teases him.

Marcus bursts out laughing. "It's the square in me. I take things literally. A lot of people are dressed for the cause," he responds as he looks around the bar. "But it seems like she's trying to confuse every single guy in here." Marcus points toward me.

Mark takes the opportunity to speak on my behalf. "Bun, I didn't notice that before we left! You're wearing red, yellow, *and* green. Why don't you want guys to know that you're single?" He does this on purpose.

Even I notice Marcus eagerly waiting for me to confirm my relationship status and answer Mark. "I, uh, don't know." I'm slightly flustered. "Probably because I'm not looking to meet someone at a bar."

Mark understands what I mean by that—Suite 22.

"You're right. A bar is not the best place to meet someone substantial," Marcus agrees. I smile at him with a slight nod.

"Sophia has a big group of friends. This place is swarming with law students," Marcus observes.

I suppose that explains why we haven't interacted with Sophia much at all, especially since it's her birthday. Incidentally, Sophia is making her rounds and coming straight for us.

"I hear that every 2L can't stop gushing over how hot they think you are," she yells across the table to Marcus. Her friends have been buying her drinks nonstop for her birthday. There's no doubt that she is *at least* tipsy.

Marcus chuckles. "Yeah, I just found out myself." He's blushing. He looks cute blushing.

"Where's Aman?" Sophia asks, even though we had a conversation on the topic earlier in the day. Her speech is on the verge of slurring.

"He went home for the weekend. Spending time with his family before things get crazy busy here."

She pulls out her phone and messily dabs on the screen—I wonder if she's texting Aman. Likely yes, but I'm sure I will receive some indication from Aman shortly.

"Are you also a 2L?" Marcus asks her.

"No, thank God for that." She exhales dramatically in relief. "No offense to these guys."

"You did your time." Mark raises both his hands in understanding.

I'm an anomaly in the cohort. I thoroughly enjoy law school and have never really agreed with the majority opinion about it. The fact that my grade in a class is determined by one exam at the end of the quarter for 90% of my classes is surely daunting, but studying for an exam I prepare for is not. I have an entire semester to do that.

"I'm a 3L. But I work with a lot of 2Ls, and the consensus is that you are the hot new TA," Sophia explains to Marcus.

After a quick chortle and without saying anything further, he diverts the conversation toward his experience with the bar exam. He must not be accustomed to receiving compliments on his looks.

My phone vibrates in my purse.

> AMAN: HOW DRUNK IS SOPHIA RIGHT NOW?
> ME: SHE'S DEFINITELY DRUNK. SO AM I. HEHEHEHE.

He disregards the text about Sophia.

> AMAN: BAN, TEXT ME WHEN YOU'RE HOME. MARK IS WITH YOU, RIGHT? I'M GOING TO TEXT HIM.
> ME: OMG. CAN YOU RELAX? I'M FINE. MARK IS WITH ME. MARCUS IS ALSO HERE.

I didn't tell Aman about Marcus joining us tonight. His response takes less than a few seconds.

AMAN: WHO'S MARCUS?

Fuck.

ME: YOU KNOW THE NEW TA FOR EVIDENCE? HIM.

Aman was responding rather quickly to my messages up until now. To gauge his mood, I change the subject.

ME: WHAT ARE YOU GOING TO SAY TO SOPHIA?

Sophia is chatting with Marcus, and I'm not entirely sure whether Aman has responded to her yet. I haven't noticed her check her phone. I'm nervous about Aman's reaction to Marcus being here. I get the impression that he doesn't like Marcus for some "Aman" reason.

The first day Aman saw Marcus staring at me in the lecture hall creeps into my mind. He's protective of me, even more so after the breakup with Suite 22. He witnessed how hard it was for me and doesn't want me to go through that heartbreaking experience again.

Sophia reaches for her phone, and she's smiling. A moment later, my phone vibrates.

AMAN: TEXT ME WHEN YOU'RE HOME.

That's all he says, and Sophia leaves to continue her rounds with her other friends.

Aman is annoyed. I'm not entirely sure why, but I know him well enough to know that he is. He rarely consciously disregards my messages when he's already messaging me unless he's annoyed.

I contemplate whether to poke him and stimulate his thoughts. I want to know what he's thinking.

ME: AMAN, IS SOMETHING WRONG?

The chat box bubbles appear and disappear multiple times.

He finally texts me, ignoring my last question and responding to my previous text—what he was going to say to Sophia.

> **AMAN:** I MADE PLANS TO TAKE HER OUT FOR HER BIRTHDAY SINCE I COULDN'T MAKE IT TONIGHT.
> **ME:** THAT LASTED LONG.

I refer to his earlier decision of wanting to "take a break" from girls and hanging.

Now I'm annoyed. It's highly likely that the alcohol in my system is influencing my rapid mood swings, but it's typical of Aman to swing back and forth so easily. I shouldn't be surprised.

I put my phone away bitterly and find Marcus looking at me, puzzled. I smile at him—Aman pissing me off isn't his fault.

"Are you okay?" Mark asks me.

"Yeah." My response is brief.

"Did you know that Professor Gatlin and Professor Erikson are a thing?" Mark says, probably referring to the night we saw them when we went to His Majesty. I'm a little surprised by his overtness. It's out of character.

Both Marcus and I are more attentive toward Mark.

"Bunny, remember when we saw them out when we went to dinner? A few days ago, I went out with friends from work and saw something that made it obvious there's definitely something going on between them."

"What did you see?" I ask curiously.

"I was leaving the restaurant with my team, and they were waiting to be seated. Professor Gatlin had her hand on Professor Erikson's thigh. Then Professor Erikson grazed her hair and kissed her."

I exclaim an inarticulate sound.

"I already knew that." Marcus must have seen them out as well.

"Well, good for them. Neither of them is married, so who cares? I wonder if the school is okay with it," I add. They don't seem to be keen on hiding it outside of school.

"They must be. I don't think either of them would risk their careers and reputations for something that wasn't allowed," Mark states.

Suddenly, Marcus excuses himself to use the restroom, leaving only me and Mark.

"Soooo." Mark teases.

I chuckle. "What?"

"How's it going with the Hot Tea?"

"Mark, you've been here the entire time. What do you think?"

"I think homeboy is into you. Without a doubt. When you were on your phone, he kept glancing at you even when Sophia was talking to him."

"Really? I didn't realize."

"Yes. Probably because you've had a few. Hell, Sophia didn't notice, and she was talking directly to him." Mark chuckles.

"Mark, I'm definitely feeling a nice buzz."

He laughs. "I think I am too. Who were you texting, by the way?"

"Aman."

Marcus rejoins us after what seems like a very long while. "Where have you been?" Mark asks.

"Sophia grabbed me for a shot with her other friends when I was coming back from the restroom." He looks at me with a huge grin on his face.

"Hey, our name starts with the same sound. Mark, Marcus!" he exclaims, clearly intoxicated. Mark goes on to have a laughing fit.

It's interesting, almost refreshing, to see a TA comfortably buzzed. TAs usually maintain a cordial and professional relationship with their students. However, Marcus seems to have established himself within the group as a casual, friendly TA, different from the norm.

I have to admit, he's charismatic and is winning over many Bheau students currently in the building.

"I wish you were my TA when I was taking evidence. Mine had an off-putting obsession with character evidence and impeachment," I heard a 3L say to him.

Marcus shares that he also has "evidence obsessions," and it's not unusual for TAs to be drawn to specific subject matters. His evidence obsessions are the destruction of evidence and false testimony and how an individual can get away with, first, destroying incriminating evidence and, second, falsely testifying despite the threat of penalty of perjury.

"It happens when you see it a lot. You'd be surprised," is his reasoning.

"Why are you smiling?" Marcus shifts his attention to me.

I didn't realize I was. "You're such a nerd," I say, rolling my eyes, albeit a tad flirtatiously.

"Is that a bad thing?" Marcus is smiling at me now, also a tad flirtatiously.

My skin feels blotchy and warm as my face turns red. "No," I say. The shyness is overpowering. I'm suddenly paranoid that the entire room is watching.

Mark gazes back and forth between me and Marcus with an observant look on his face. Marcus' attention is on the bar, and Mark smirks at me. I shake my head, but I'm grinning. I'm relishing the newness and excitement of it all. I haven't felt it for a while.

"Do you want another drink?" Marcus asks me.

"Sure, an old-fashioned would be nice."

"Okay. You want anything?" he asks Mark.

"Scratch her old-fashioned, and we'll both have a margarita. Only tequila for me and Bunny. She made me promise not to let her deviate from tequila tonight." I'm about to be teased endlessly by Mark as soon as Marcus is no longer within earshot.

"Be right back." Marcus heads toward the bar and stations himself in a spot that's less crowded.

"What?" I ask Mark as he's smiling ear-to-ear at me.

"This is cute."

"What is?" I ask innocently, despite knowing exactly what he's referring to.

"When the Hot Tea is into the Bunny, things get steamier."

I laugh at Mark's clever but corny sense of humor.

At this point, I can also sense that Mark may be right about Marcus' interest in me. He's received a lot of attention throughout the course of the evening but has primarily been focused on me.

I used to be more forthcoming and vocal when approaching a guy. After Suite 22, I toned down my approach.

Suite 22 and I had noticed each other earlier in the evening that day, but we didn't interact. As the night progressed, his friend initiated a conversation with me while Suite 22 stood to the side. I found Suite 22 attractive as soon as I saw him, and I wanted to make this fact known. At that point, I loudly said, "Why is your friend standing by himself?" Suite 22 was so enthralled with his surroundings that he didn't hear at first.

His friend, with whom I had been speaking, got his attention for me by calling him over. We exchanged details about our backgrounds and learned that Suite 22, his friend, and I had gone to the same undergraduate school. Our time there had overlapped, but since it was a public university with a big campus, it wasn't unusual that our paths had never crossed. We did name a few individuals that we had in common, though, which made it a bit surprising that we never met before.

"Marcus, do you know anything about Gerald's death?" Mark asks him as he hands both Mark and me our drinks. He's very bold tonight.

"Who?" Marcus seems confused, perplexing both me and Mark.

"The TA you replaced. The one who was killed," I say.

"Oh. Sorry, Bani's old-fashioneds are getting the best of me. No, I haven't heard anything."

"It's very sad," Mark and I say at the same time.

"Hm," he responds simply, turning toward me. "Bani, are you busy tomorrow night?"

chapter 19

I disembark from the train near the waiting area of the Palo Alto train station. Ari texts me to ask how far I am and how much longer I'll be. As I approach the entrance of the station, I look over a sea of on-coming cars for my mom's car and spot it on the street. Ari is driving.

"Why don't you walk yourself over here so that I don't have to wait in all this traffic?" she says with a playful, sassy tone when I answer her phone call.

"Okay, I'm coming, brat."

I haven't seen my sister in almost two months—probably the longest we've ever gone, and the first thing I see is her huge grin as I approach the car.

I'm itching to tell her about the recent developments with Marcus, particularly after last night. She'll be upset that I didn't mention anything to her sooner, but there honestly wasn't anything worth mentioning until last night.

I hop into the car and quickly hug my sister, being cognizant not to hold up traffic behind us.

"Tell me everything," Ari demands as she focuses on getting out of the train station traffic.

I dive right into the Marcus topic. "I think I may have met someone."

"*What*?" Ari exclaims. She knows that once Suite 22 and I ended, I essentially withdrew myself from dating.

I giggle. "Well, I think so. It's very early stages, if even that. He asked me out last night, and I would've accepted if I wasn't coming home."

"Who is this guy?"

"That's the other thing. He's the new TA for my evidence class."

"Bub! I didn't know that you had it in you to talk to someone who works at your school. What's his name?" she asks excitedly, still focused on driving.

"His name is Marcus." I pause. "It's weird. Definitely not typical of my type, but he's smooth in a unique way."

"*Why didn't you tell me before*?" Ari asks the inevitable question I predicted she would ask.

"Babe, everything literally happened yesterday. I hadn't talked to him much until then. First, I ran into him at the library when I was studying, and he really helped me out by giving me his outline. Then, as a thank you, I invited him out to a birthday party with me and Mark. Things escalated at the bar."

"What happened when he asked you out? What did he say?"

"He asked me if I was busy tonight, and I told him I was heading down the peninsula for the day. He seemed bummed, but I suggested that we coordinate something during the week."

"How did the night end then?"

"We were all pretty buzzed. At one point, when Marcus and I were alone, he was kind of stroking the back of my hand."

"Very, very interesting!" Ari sounds exhilarated. "What does Mark think of him? Has Aman met him?" she asks.

"Mark thinks that he's completely and obviously interested in me, but I'm not entirely convinced. I *think* I see it, but I don't want to get ahead of myself. Aman wasn't there. He doesn't really know what's happening."

"Uh-oh. Aman is going to be pissed," Ari declares. She's immensely fond of Aman.

"Why would he be pissed?"

"Because he's always been protective of you."

"What makes you say that?" I ask, even though I know he has.

"Because of that douchebag who tore you apart." Suite 22. Ari always calls it as it is. "He saw how much it hurt you."

"Babe, I don't want to think about that guy." My voice is solemn. Even after all these months, that heartbreak still feels raw sometimes.

"Yeah, you can think about this new guy." She's giggling. "A non-Punjabi guy may be exactly what you need. What does he look like?"

"I don't have a picture of him." Then I remember. "Wait, we took a group picture last night." Amidst the drunkenness, I completely forgot until now. I show Ari the picture with Marcus when we're at a stoplight.

"Bub, he is cuuuuuuuuuuute. He has a mysteriousness about him. Look at those eyes! And his black curly hair!" She zooms in on the picture.

"Yes, he is. He's known as Hot Tea at school," I share, tittering.

Ari laughs out loud, impressed with the witty nickname. "That's clever."

I really look at the picture since I forgot we took it. Marcus and I are sitting next to each other, rather closely and both grinning exuberantly, and Mark is to my left with a smile that looks like he just finished laughing. About what, I don't remember. Sophia is on the other side of Marcus.

When I see his name in my text message list, I recall that Marcus and I exchanged phone numbers while at the bar. His number wasn't there before. I click on the message, and the same picture with him from yesterday is the single item in the chat box. He insisted I send it to him right then because he was certain that I'd forget, which I absolutely did. I forgot we even took it.

The ride from the station to my parents' house is fairly short. When Ari pulls into my parents' driveway, my dad opens the garage door, and our dog, Nala, comes sprinting out. She's crying, whimpering, and pacing around me in circles.

"Hiiiiiii bubby." My baby voice emerges whenever I pet or snuggle with her.

"We're standing here too." My dad speaks for himself and my mom, both smiling. Although we talk somewhat regularly, it's been a while since I've actually seen them.

"Where is the soon-to-be groom, by the way?" I study our garage, which has been taken over by Devan's wedding preparations.

"He's on a call," my mom answers. "Since he'll be taking a month off starting Friday, his work has been busy."

As soon as we transition from the garage into the house, I immediately smell the deliciousness of a home-cooked meal made with pungent Punjabi spices. I intentionally didn't eat breakfast prior to catching the train because my mom told me she was making *keema paronthe*, layered flatbread stuffed with spiced ground turkey. I don't eat Punjabi food regularly, but my mom's *keema paronthe* are an exception.

I quickly set my belongings down in my room upstairs. On the way downstairs, Devan's voice carries into the hallway while he's on the phone in my mom's home office. I resist the urge to pop in to say hello. He'll be done soon enough, and I can properly greet him then.

Ari is already seated at the table in the nook area, browsing through her phone, and my mom and dad prepare breakfast in the kitchen. I playfully flick Ari's phone, attempting to make her drop it. She looks at me, annoyed, and I snicker deviously.

"Not so great when it's done to you, is it?"

"Whatever, B."

"No fighting." My mom always thinks we're fighting when we're being mischievous.

"Mom, we're not fighting, we're joking!" Ari is still immersed in her phone.

"How's Aman enjoying home?" My dad brings a *parontha* over for me to indulge in.

"Last I spoke to him, he was having a great time," I tell my dad.

From the text exchange we had last night, I'm pretty certain Aman was annoyed, and then he irritated me. I remember him asking me to tell him when Mark and I got home, which I didn't. My irritation has diminished, but he must be livid.

Before texting him to gauge his mood toward me, I text Mark.

ME: HEY, DID AMAN TEXT YOU LAST NIGHT OR SAY ANYTHING?

Mark responds instantly.

MARK: YES, HE TEXTED LATE TO ASK IF WE WERE HOME. HE WAS PRETTY PISSED LOL.
ME: FUCK.
MARK: IT'S OKAY, BUNNY. HE WANTED TO MAKE SURE YOU WERE ALRIGHT. HE WASN'T TRIPPIN' TOO MUCH SINCE I WAS THERE.
ME: AND HE DOES THIS SHIT TO ME ALL THE TIME.

MARK: YES, AND YOU GET MAD AT HIM AND GET OVER IT. HE PROBABLY ALREADY HAS TOO.
ME: THANKS. WHAT'RE YOU UP TO?

I open my text box with Aman.

ME: HI. SORRY I DIDN'T TEXT WHEN HOME. I DIDN'T WANT TO WAKE YOU BECAUSE WE GOT BACK LATE.

He knows this is a lie because we both know timing doesn't make a difference to Aman. Aman doesn't respond as quickly as Mark does. He takes a few minutes.

AMAN: I WAS AWAKE, BUT MARK TOLD ME WHEN YOU GUYS GOT BACK.

I can't tell if he is annoyed with me or not. From those few words, it's hard to decipher.

ME: HOW'S HOME? MY DAD ASKED ABOUT YOU.
AMAN: IS THAT WHY YOU REMEMBERED ME ALL OF A SUDDEN?

I can't help but smirk because now I know he's pissed. Lightheartedly pissed.

ME: LOL, NO. I'M A LITTLE HUNGOVER AND MY BRAIN ISN'T FUNCTIONING PROPERLY.
AMAN: DRINK MORE THEN!

What a brat.

ME: I ASKED: HOW IS HOME, HIPPO?

I'm trying to lighten his mood. He must know that he's being a huge hypocrite right now.

AMAN: LOL. HOME IS GREAT. MY MOM IS HAPPY TO HAVE ALL OF US HERE TOGETHER.

ME: WELL, GOOD. SHE SHOULD ONLY BE HAPPY DURING HER BIRTHDAY WEEKEND.

AMAN: SHE'S AT THE SPA RIGHT NOW. WE'RE GOING TO SAN DIEGO WHEN SHE GETS BACK. SHE WANTS TO BAKE A PASTRY FROM THE BOOK YOU GOT HER, AND SHE'S MAKING ME HELP HER. THANKS A LOT LOL.

ME: WELCOME LOL.

Now that I know Aman is no longer peeved with me, I turn my attention toward my *parontha*, starving, but find my plate empty. I look at Ari's—she stole the *parontha* my dad brought over for me without my even noticing.

"Hey!"

She bursts out laughing as she's about to take a bite.

"You snooze, you lose, sucker."

"Mom, now we're going to argue. Ari stole my *parontha*!" I'm only slightly serious.

"That's okay! I am still making them. Don't argue!"

I have another text each from Aman and Mark, but my dad brings me my *parontha,* and I commence devouring before Ari takes this one too. When I'm halfway done, Devan comes downstairs.

"Ban!" he exclaims when he sees me. I give him a hug, careful not to touch him with my slightly greasy hands. Eating *paronthe* requires the use of your hands and can get messy.

I hurriedly swallow the bite. "Hi, mister groom!"

He chuckles. "Yeah, can't believe it's coming up so fast."

"How's Alina?" I ask.

"She's good. She's nervous about a lot of her family members' flights. There have been a lot of delays on the East Coast."

"I heard about that." Ari sets her phone down, finally joining the conversation.

"I think it'll be fine, though. The weather should clear up by the time their flights are scheduled to take off." Devan is realistically hopeful.

"Yes, I think it'll definitely be okay by then." My dad joins us at the table.

"*That's it?*" My mom calls my dad out on suddenly ceasing to help her. We all laugh at how my dad finessed his way out of helping my mom once it was his turn to eat.

This is exactly what I wanted. To spend quality time with my family before things got hectic with the wedding. Most of our out-of-town relatives will stay in the hotels close to the wedding venue, where Devan and Alina blocked off a number of rooms, but the house will be full during the events.

"What wedding prep do we need to do today?" I ask Devan. We've attended countless weddings, but it's a new and interesting feeling to host one.

Devan confidently shares that the wedding preparations are nearly complete, which is shocking for a Punjabi wedding. The wedding planner they hired is taking care of the majority of the responsibilities and planning.

There's some cooking that remains, but I don't think either Ari or I will be much help with that. Plenty of local relatives and family friends will come that week to help my mom with the cooking. In Punjabi weddings, it's customary for both the bride's and groom's families to prepare homemade sweets for their guests as a sort of *shagun*, or offering.

Among Punjabi families, the marriage order is usually, but not always, in the order of the ages of the children. During Devan's wedding week, I'm absolutely certain that I'll be asked questions or hear comments like, "You're next. Have you found someone? It's your turn now." I'm not looking forward to it in the slightest.

I'm also certain that plenty of people will think that Aman is my boyfriend, specifically those who don't know who he is. When they see us together at the wedding events, arriving and leaving together, it will inevitably draw attention. I won't be surprised if they directly approach and question him. I think it's a good idea to warn Aman of the high likelihood of that happening now so it doesn't come as a surprise then.

> **ME:** Btw, be prepared for a lot of aunties coming up to you during the wedding and asking if you and I are together.

His reply is instantaneous this time.

> **AMAN:** Lol. I'm going to say that we are, We'd look cute together.

chapter 20

It's rare that the entire family is together at the same time. The only plan we have for the remainder of the day is to go to dinner tonight at a new bistro that opened up in downtown Palo Alto. I've heard rumblings about it and seen the heavy interest it has drawn.

The bistro, Lampshade, is filled with different-shaped lamps, which provide a lovely ambiance throughout the restaurant. Each table is based on a specific type of lampshade displayed close to the tabletop.

My favorite bit, from what I can see in the pictures, is that there are two red rose lampshades at the entrance of the restaurant that give off a subtle red light over the hostess and waiting area.

While my parents search for parking, they request the kids to hop out of the car and check in for our reservation. The front of the restaurant is made up entirely of floor-to-ceiling windows. I'm in awe of the magnificent lighting reflecting throughout the restaurant from the outside. The pictures don't do the captivating atmosphere justice.

There's a musician playing soft jazz in the background, but the surrounding clanking of dishes and guest chatter are over-powering the background music.

"Hi, we have a reservation at eight," Devan says to the hostess.

"Under what name?" the hostess asks while looking over the list of reservations on her tablet.

"Naya." We always use my mom's name when we book a reservation.

A few minutes later, we hear, "Naya? Your table for five is ready." She politely grins, then escorts us to a table named "The Secretkeeper." The lampshade, like many, is in the shape of a bell and has a sheer black silk fabric with a lace design on it. It's beautiful yet mysterious, fully living up to its name.

"How's school?" My parents ask me about the topic I've been dreading.

"Well, the biggest news is about the TA who got into the ac-cident and died." The sick-to-my-stomach feeling creeps up each time I think of or talk about Gerald. I hadn't wanted to mention it at dinner, but I knew it would come up.

"Hmm." My dad is the only one who makes a sound. "You never know what can happen at any time," he adds in Punjabi, lowering his head.

"We have a new TA for evidence." I hope to simmer the mel-ancholy at our table.

Ari intentionally clears her throat. She avoids making eye con-tact with me, but covers a sheepish expression with her hand. I try to maintain a respectably neutral face.

"How is the new TA?" my mom asks, concerned. "This world is crazy."

"He just started this week, but he seems knowledgeable and smart."

Ari clears her throat again. Not knowing what she's reacting to, my mom hands her some water.

"The school's atmosphere has been depressing after this week's news." I don't tell anyone in my family about the after-the-gym incident I had. Their minds are already preoccupied with Devan's wedding, and I don't see a reason to make them worry.

"It's understandable. It's not something that you expect to happen to someone you know." Ari voices the thought that has occurred to me many times.

"Naya, didn't we see on the news that they brought someone in for questioning?" my dad adds. This is news to me.

"Oh, yes. The police said something about bringing an old girlfriend in for questioning. I haven't seen anything beyond that."

"Really?" I immediately reach for my phone to verify if what my parents are saying is true. Sure enough, it is.

An article I find online cites a recent discovery indicating problematic texts sent to Gerald from an ex-girlfriend a few days before the accident. It was posted on Friday, around the time Mark and I were out.

The article doesn't share details on the texts' content, but it must've been concerning if the police brought the girl in for questioning. The article adds that the police think she had a potential motive to want to hurt Gerald. It seems that he rejected her, but it doesn't share any details on who she is. Only that she is also affiliated with the university.

I forward the link to Aman and Mark, wondering if the school will comment on this on Monday.

"You have to take what the news reports lightly," Devan reminds us.

Desperate to stray from this topic and bring the merriment back to the table, I change the subject. "On a lighter note, I have an exam due on the Monday of Dev's wedding week. And I told you guys that Mark wouldn't be able to come to the wedding, right?"

"Yes. How is Mark?" my dad asks.

"He's been busy working."

"Hmm." He chews on a piece of the calamari we ordered as an appetizer.

"Don't worry, Dad. Aman will be at the wedding," I add to tease him, but also uplift his spirits.

"Such a good guy," he says in Punjabi and grins. Aman has a captivating presence even when he's not physically here. He has genuinely won my dad over.

At the end of our first year as law school students, Aman came home with me for the weekend, and he and my dad really bonded. They had a nightcap together and talked for hours. That's when my dad learned about Aman's history and family background, as well as about his dad. There were some things about Aman's history that I learned for the first time then as well, nearly a year after knowing him.

As we leave the bistro, I run into an old friend from high school, Tej. Although Tej and I were once close in high school, he isn't a close friend now, but he's a familiar enough face for me to briefly catch up with. He stops me to chat, and my family goes on to find where we will have dessert.

After high school, he went to college on the East Coast and worked there for a few years before coming back west for his master's in video production. He's studying at the same university where my dad is a professor.

"Wow, how's law school going?" he asks after I briefly update him on what I've been up to.

"It's extremely tough. But once you've been at it for a while, you get the hang of things."

"I don't doubt that. Bani, for someone who's in such an intensive curriculum, you look great!"

I have a puzzled look on my face, which he notices. I'm uncertain whether he means that as an insult or a compliment.

"No, no! I meant that as a good thing." I gather he feels foolish for not thinking twice about his delivery because he now seems nervous that he might have offended me.

"Listen, I have to get back to my group." He looks toward his circle of friends, who are already seated at a table and awkwardly yet intently watching our conversation. "But I'd love to properly catch up with you one-on-one. What's your phone number?"

I'm slightly alarmed at the blunt ask, but I exchange my phone number with Tej for old-time's sake, not expecting him to follow up.

"Speak to you soon." Tej gives me a quick hug, and then we part ways.

I text Ari to see where they decided to go for dessert.

ARI: AFFEZIONGELATO.

My family is waiting in line as I approach Affeziongelato. The line is wrapped around the corner of the building, but they've neared the front by the time I finished speaking with Tej.

"Who was that?" my dad asks me in Punjabi as I approach them. I assume he's referring to Tej.

"Someone I used to know. We went to high school together. He's been on the East Coast for a few years. I'm surprised I ran into him," I say matter-of-factly.

"He was cute, Bani. Why don't you consider something with him?" my mom says with a hopeful lilt in her voice.

"No, Mom. Right now, my focus is solely on school. I need to focus my attention on that and then the bar exam." The California bar exam is notoriously one of the most difficult bar exams in the country, if not *the* most difficult one.

"Yes, she needs to focus on school first," my dad adds, but then he gives the actual reason for his objection. "And she can't do that to Aman."

My dad winks at me, re-vocalizing his dreams of Aman and I ending up together.

"Dad, it's not happening."

"Why not?" he presses.

"Because we're friends, and I love it that way."

"Yes, Rumyn. Good friendships get ruined by romance. Let these kids stay friends if that's what they want," my mom adds. This is new. Usually, she's supportive of Aman and me dating.

Aman arrives later in the evening. In the meantime, I study at a coffee shop rather than at home. The café owner shuts the blinds and rearranges the outdoor furniture inside the premises. I consider that my cue to leave.

He sees me packing my belongings and says, "I'm sorry. Take your time. I'm preparing for closing, but there's still time."

"That's okay. I was planning on leaving ten minutes ago anyway."

He laughs at my lame joke.

Home is about five blocks away, but the sun has set, leaving me to walk alone in the dark. Poor planning on my end.

I approach a well-lit area a block away from home, but no one is around. The area is deserted.

Suddenly, a hand grabs my left shoulder, and an arm wraps around my body with such force that I'm unable to squeal in pain. The shock running through my body prohibits me from making a sound.

I imagine this is what a giant python wrapped around my entire body would feel like, restricting my ability to move or breathe. Another hand covers my mouth with what feels like a foul-smelling black leather glove.

I attempt to break free using all the force and power I can muster. But my attempts are futile.

Then, I notice a familiar bracelet on the hand holding my mouth. It's a black onyx beaded bracelet with a single gold bead.

The bracelet is barely visible, but I can make it out because I have seen this bracelet many times. It's the bracelet that used to belong to Aman's dad. The one Aman hasn't taken off since his death.

chapter 21

I'm panting, and my shirt is damp with my sweat. It's pitch dark all around me. My heart pounds inside my chest, and I'm uncontrollably shivering. For a moment, I'm confused about where I am.

When I gather myself, I realize that I'm still in my room at my parents' house in Palo Alto. I had yet another nightmare.

I attempt to recall the course of the day amidst my raging heart palpitations. I came home and spent time with my family. We went to dinner and had gelato. Once home, Ari and I briefly watched TV. I redlined Natalia's essay, and then I went upstairs to sleep. All are very simple and non-controversial things.

I often wake up in the middle of the night feeling parched and have a habit of keeping a water bottle around me when I sleep.

Tonight is a different situation. I gulp my water so vehemently that I have to gasp for air by the time I'm done drinking it.

It was just a bad dream.

What's most shocking was that Aman attacked me. Well, I assume it was Aman because the person was wearing Aman's dad's bracelet, and Aman always has it on, although I didn't see a face.

Aman is my protector. Why would I have a dream about him attacking me? I can't prevent my thoughts from getting the best of me. However, in the middle of the night and after a terrifying dream is not a logical time to analyze anything at all. It's not even light out.

Thirty minutes pass, and I'm unable to fall asleep again. Alina once recommended that I perform breathing exercises if I have trouble falling asleep. I need to inhale for four seconds, hold my breath for seven seconds, and then exhale for eight seconds. She advised me to perform this exercise three to four times in a row.

Grateful that I remembered this tip since it sounds both thera-peutic and exactly like what I need right now, I practice the exer-cise four times.

Moments later, I easily drift back to sleep.

The next day, and actually the next day, not a nightmare-next-day, I pace down the stairs when Ari screams at the top of her lungs that our ordered lunch has arrived, and if I don't come down in ten seconds, she'll eat it. Her threat is absolutely credible.

I'm going back to San Francisco today, but not until later. In the meantime, I plan on vegging out at home and doing absolutely noth-ing. I want to take advantage of what likely is the last day of relaxation I'll have before getting consumed with exam preparation and then wedding festivities. Everyone else is on board with this plan.

We each grab a plate full of food and eat in the living room, feeling supremely lazy this afternoon.

Devan suggests watching an older, classic Indian film. The next few hours pass, and around the time the movie is over, it's time for me to take a train back to San Francisco.

I admit that I've been avoiding Aman all day. He texted me to tell me when he was at the airport and then when he landed in San Francisco.

My nightmare isn't his fault, yet I feel incredibly uneasy toward Aman at the moment.

There's one person who can offer me advice and whose advice will help settle the feeling of uneasiness that's been in my stomach since I woke up.

> MARK: NIGHTMARES TEND TO LINGER. BUNNY, REMEMBER: AMAN CARES MORE ABOUT YOU THAN HE DOES HIMSELF. HE WILL NEVER, EVER DO ANYTHING TO HURT YOU.
>
> ME: I KNOW HE DOES. LIKE YOU SAID, THIS NIGHTMARE IS LINGERING. BUT WHAT I DON'T UNDERSTAND IS WHY I HAD THIS TYPE OF DREAM ABOUT AMAN TO BEGIN WITH.
>
> MARK: OUR DREAMS DON'T DICTATE OUR TRUE FEELINGS. THEY CAN BE A MIXTURE OF WHAT WE EXPERIENCE IN A DAY AND THE THINGS WE THINK ABOUT. DESPITE THAT, THEY CAN BE TOTALLY NONSENSICAL. HELL, I'VE HAD DREAMS ABOUT MYSELF GETTING SHOT BY A MAFIA MEMBER. HOW IS THAT ANY SORT OF RELEVANT TO MY REALITY? IT'S NOT.

Mark's right. Recent events have been unsettling me, but Aman is not at fault for that. Aman has been my protector throughout it all, and there's no legitimate reason for me to doubt him. I trust him completely. *My dream is not his fault.*

Guilt over ignoring him earlier overwhelms me, but I finally text him back.

ME: WELCOME BACK. SORRY, I'VE BEEN BUSY WITH FAMILY. THEY CAN'T WAIT TO SEE YOU NEXT WEEK. I'LL BE BACK BY EVENING. SEE YOU IN A FEW XX.

AMAN: YOU'RE TURNING INTO ME LOL. HOPE YOU'RE HAVING FUN. SEE YOU SOON.

A few minutes later, he sends another text message.

AMAN: DO YOU WANT ME TO PICK YOU UP FROM THE TRAIN STATION?

This—this is the real Aman. Always, always looking out for me and my safety. Not who I experienced in my ludicrous nightmare.

ME: THAT'S OKAY. I'M GOING TO GET A CAB DIRECTLY HOME. THANK YOU.

AMAN: HURRY UP AND COME BACK, IT'S LONELY WITHOUT YOU.

I add a smiley face at the end of the text.

This brief exchange alone made me feel a lot better. I reprimand myself for stupidly not replying to his message sooner.

"Are you nervous at all?" I ask Devan, referring to his upcoming nuptials. Devan is dropping both me and Ari off—me at the train station and Ari at the airport. I'm first.

"Not really. I don't think there's much to be nervous about." He's as confident as he's ever been.

"What a guy's response." Ari shakes her head.

"What's there to be nervous about?" I'm looking out the window, but I can hear the smile in Devan's voice.

"Getting married! Your life changing! Something going wrong at the wedding?" Ari exclaims.

Devan is quiet for a moment, probably contemplating potential nerve-wracking things per Ari's insistence. "Hmmm, nope. Not nervous."

"Wow." Ari sounds defeated.

"I'm excited, Ari. I'm not nervous."

"Aww, that's sweet." I smile at the unexpected response from my brother. He's been much more sensitive since he got engaged, not to say that he wasn't before.

"How's your guys' dating life going?" This is new. Devan typically maintains his distance from our personal lives unless it's something serious, thus proving my point.

"Okay, big guy. Just because you're getting married and are in a sappy mood doesn't mean we will talk about this," Ari jokes with a handful of seriousness.

Devan bursts out laughing. Ari's personality has no filter. She says what she's thinking and doesn't shy away from it. It's what I love most about her.

As we pull into the entrance of the train station, Devan and Ari each give me a hug, excited that the next time we will see each other will be for Devan's wedding.

Ari yells, "Don't forget to text when you're back!" from behind me. "You too!"

There's a decently long line to board the train. It's the last fast one departing for San Francisco tonight, and there's an incentive not to miss it.

For the fast train, the travel time to San Francisco is around thirty-five minutes. If I'm not on this train, the travel time to San Francisco would be close to an hour, and it will be late by the time it gets there. I want to avoid arriving in San Francisco when it's dark.

Listening to *bhangra* on the train not only makes the time go by faster but distracts me and puts me in a good mood. It's making me that much more pumped for the *bhangra* and dancing at Dev's wedding. The next thing I know, the train pulls into the San Francisco station, and I order a cab to take me home.

Once I am nearly there, I ask Aman to come down to help me with my belongings to avoid making multiple trips. I could carry everything in one trip if I tried, but I'd rather Aman be downstairs when I arrive. It's nearly fully dark outside.

The nightmare that was lingering a few hours ago has finally begun to fade. The anxiety-induced aftereffect of the dream is vaguely present, but it's no longer specific to Aman.

It doesn't feel like I saw him just two days ago. It feels longer. Aside from the terrible nightmare, I miss him.

As soon as the driver turns the corner onto the street of our apartment, I see Aman standing by the curb in the distance, waiting for me. He's rocking back and forth to keep himself warm despite wearing a hoodie. Even during the summer, San Francisco evenings tend to be chilly, and it's fall now.

He looks in the car's direction as we get closer, and he grins when he spots me in the backseat.

"Why are you waiting in the cold?" I say when I get out.

He chuckles. "I wanted to be outside when you got here."

I discretely sigh, wondering how I could ever have doubted him. "I'm not used to you being this sweet to me."

I turn toward him when I notice he's quiet, and he has a playful, annoyed expression on his face.

"Listen," he finally says. "I'm always sweet."

I purposely laugh loudly and exaggeratedly.

"You needed me to come down for this?" He's referring to the number of bags that I have with me, which is not a lot. "You made it sound like you had a mountain of bags you needed help with."

"Ha, ha." I thank the driver, and Aman and I stroll into our apartment building.

"How was home?" he asks while we wait for the elevator to come down.

"It was great. Much needed. They're all very excited to see you at the wedding."

He doesn't verbalize it, but I know Aman is happy. He always appreciates that my family regards him highly. He appreciates that they treat him as if he's also a family member. For all intents and purposes, he is.

"How was your weekend?" I ask him.

"Great! We made banoffee pie. It's actually pretty good." Aman mentioned that his mom wanted to try a recipe from the cookbook I got her.

"I'm glad that she liked it."

"She *loved* it," he reminds me. "She sent a little something for you as a thank you."

"What?"

"Banoffee pie." He laughs.

"Really? Please thank her for me. I've heard of it, but have never been able to try it."

"I already did," he teasingly murmurs.

As soon as we enter our apartment, I'm struck by the sweet, aromatic scent of a candle Aman lit. It's a crisp breeze scent. I'm guessing it's something related to the ocean. Aman loves the ocean.

"What do you mean you already did?"

"I told her you said *thank you* before you actually did."

"Wow." Now, I'm laughing.

"Are you hungry? I can make us dinner if you want," I suggest, recalling Aman's call out on Friday night when he said I don't cook for him.

"I'm going out for dinner today," he says so softly that I almost don't hear him.

"Where?" I ask.

"Probably an Italian spot." He's being evasive. I know what this means.

"With who?" I'm prying, but we are beyond the point of my feeling shy about it.

"I'm taking Sophia out for her birthday."

"Oh." I can hear the surprise in my voice, but I'm not sure if he can. "What happened to taking a break from girls?"

"She was grilling me for not being there for her birthday. I felt obligated to. It's just dinner."

"Interesting." I'm pensive even though he already told me on Friday that he was taking her. Something about this bothers me, but I can't pinpoint what or why.

"Do you not like Sophia? She's your friend." He sounds intrigued by my unsure expression, which likely speaks louder than any words I could formulate.

"Nothing like that." But what is it then?

"You're still my number-one girl." Aman winks and playfully nudges me.

"Oh, please." I lightheartedly scoff at his remark, but I smile to myself. "When are you going to go?"

"I'm meeting her in about an hour," he mutters. I eye him as he puts away the groceries that are on the counter. "Yes, I went grocery shopping today. I was bored after my flight."

I didn't say anything, but he knew what I was thinking.

"Why, thank you. You've been very domestic this weekend."

"Your pie is in the refrigerator."

"I'm excited to have it. It makes me want to bake too." I rub my chin. "And move to England."

"Ban, you don't know how to bake, and you can't leave me."

"I can bake if I try! I belong in England."

"No, you don't belong in England. You belong here. *With me.* You've tried, and you still can't bake." His voice is serious but full of amusement.

"Well, that's why I have you. I'll stay if you promise to always bake for me." Aman is a bit of a chef himself.

He smirks at me. "Gladly. *Anything* for you."

chapter 22

My phone buzzes on the kitchen counter as I lay cozily on the couch, watching my favorite weekly show. My laziness overcomes my desire to check it at first, but then I hear it buzz twice.

I sigh to myself but ultimately get up, partially to monitor the status of the food I ordered and partially so that it will stop buzzing annoyingly on the counter. I'm utterly, maybe pleasantly, surprised to find that I have two messages from Marcus.

I also have a message from Tej. His message is the usual friend-ly type you send after seeing someone after a long time, and he suggests catching up soon. I indicate my desire to do that, not thinking he's serious but simply being polite—the usual response to his type of message.

But then he suggests a few times and his willingness to come to San Francisco if that would be easier for me. Another surprise.

Quite frankly, I had a huge crush on Tej when we were in high school. I even felt nostalgic jitters when I first saw him yesterday. If this were ten years ago, I would have an enormous feeling of gratification that Tej has sought out a supposed "catch up" with me. We jokingly came up with a marriage agreement: if we were both thirty-five and unmarried, we would marry each other. Obviously, this was only high school banter. I doubt he remembers it.

Marcus' first message asks about my time at home, and the second asks when I'll make time for him. The second message is somewhat alarming, as the night at the bar was literally two days ago. I'm not even sure how to reply to his blunt message. He's an assertive flirt, and I'm not accustomed to it.

I screenshot the message to Mark, seeking his guidance on how best to respond to Marcus. He's unknowingly taken on the role of my advisor since Aman doesn't know about Marcus—not that there is anything to really know yet.

> MARK: HOMEBOY IS COMPLETELY INTO YOU.
>
> ME: YOU DON'T THINK THIS IS TOO MUCH?
>
> MARK: I GET WHY YOU'RE ASKING. BUT WE KNOW HE HAS A THING FOR YOU. IF YOU'RE NOT COMFORTABLE REPLYING WITH SOMETHING AS FORTHCOMING, WHY DON'T YOU SAY SOMETHING LIKE: 'LOL, I BARELY HAVE TIME FOR MYSELF! YOU, OF ALL PEOPLE, KNOW WHAT THAT'S LIKE, MR. LICENSED ATTORNEY.'
>
> ME: YEAH, THAT'S GOOD. THANKS, MARK. REMIND ME TO TELL YOU ABOUT THIS OTHER PERSON.
>
> MARK: DAMN, BUNNY! LOOK AT YOU. AMAN WOULD BE PROUD.

I highly doubt that.

> **ME:** LOL, NO NOTHING LIKE THAT. I RAN INTO SOMEONE THAT I USED TO KNOW.
> **MARK:** OKAY. DO YOU LIKE HIM?
> **ME:** WHO? THE OTHER PERSON OR MARCUS?
> **MARK:** MARCUS.
> **ME:** I'M INTERESTED IN SPENDING TIME WITH HIM. I THINK, MAYBE I'M CURIOUS?

Mark responds back with a teasing face, and I switch to my chat box with Marcus.

> **ME:** EASIER FOR YOU TO SAY, MR. ALREADY LICENSED ATTORNEY. ARE YOU FREE TOMORROW NIGHT FOR A LITTLE? I HAVE AN EXAM THIS WEEKEND SO TOMORROW IS THE BEST DAY.

He responds almost instantly.

> **MARCUS:** LOL, TOUCHÉ. I DO KNOW HOW YOU FEEL. YES, TOMORROW WORKS GREAT FOR ME. I CAN PICK YOU UP.

I think it's a little too soon for Marcus to know where I live, and instead, I propose meeting directly at a bar for a quick drink.

> **MARCUS:** YOU THINK I'M GOING TO STALK YOU?

How strange of him to say. That's not what I was initially thinking.

> **ME:** LOL, NO. I HAVE TO GO DOWNTOWN AFTER CLASS TOMORROW TO RETURN SOMETHING AT THE MALL. I THINK IT'LL BE EASIER.

I'm blatantly lying to him. I don't have anything to return, but this helps keep up the pretense.

MARCUS: OKAY, SOUNDS GOOD. KNOW OF ANY SPOTS?

It's nearing midnight, and Aman still isn't home. I text him to ask when he will be, and almost an hour passes before he responds. That can only mean one thing—he's not near his phone because he's probably getting physical with Sophia. I'm jumping to conclusions, but what other explanation can there be? He said they were just going to dinner.

AMAN: I'M ALMOST HOME. YOU'RE STILL UP?

I toss my phone on my bed without responding, incredibly irritated with him.

Sophia is my 3L mentor, and the fact that Aman is putting me in such an uncomfortable position, knowing that he doesn't intend to pursue anything meaningful with her, infuriates me.

I close my bedroom door, leaving a light on in the living room for him to navigate around once he's home.

I crawl into bed, but I'm not tired at all. Instead, I brush up on the case readings for both lectures tomorrow.

Aman and I don't argue often, but if I interact with him at all for the remainder of the night, we'll inevitably get into an argument. I won't shy away from expressing how upset I am.

I'm startled when I hear a knock on my door. I was engrossed in the case summary and didn't hear the front door open and close. How long was I in my study hypnosis?

Aman must've seen my bedroom light on through the small crack at the bottom. I can't immediately decide if I want him to come in or not. He knocks again.

"Yeah?" I finally say with a smidgen of attitude.

As soon as he opens the door, I can tell from his reddened eyes that he's had a bit to drink.

"Not sleepy?" Aman asks.

"No," I say pointedly, almost knifelike. If he was completely sober, my tone would be a dead giveaway that I'm upset.

"You sound mad." I'm surprised he picked up on it. He must not be as drunk as I was thinking. Maybe his eyes are red because he's just tired.

"No, I'm fine." Then I resume reading my case summary. Without looking up, I hear him walk toward me. There's a sudden jolt at my bedside as he plops down to face me, my mattress briefly springing up and down.

I glance up at him. "What?" I ask.

"I know you're mad. What's wrong?"

"I'm not mad. I'm focusing."

I resume reviewing my case summary. When I don't feel or hear Aman rise from my bed, I look back up at him again. He's waiting for me to spill.

I sigh out of exasperation and instinctively place my hand to my face. He's able to read me exceptionally well.

"How was your night?" I ask.

Aman's expression shifts from one of concern to one of surprise. "It was okay. Why don't you tell me what's on your mind?"

"Did something happen between you and Sophia?" I'm taken aback by my forward delivery, but I want straightforward answers.

Aman slowly starts to smirk. "Yes. We went to dinner, and we ate." He's purposely acting like he doesn't know what I'm referring to, even though it's evident.

"Aman." I want to know, despite our unspoken rule of never overtly bringing up or discussing this topic.

"Okay, relax. I'm trying to lighten the mood. But no, of course not."

Now I have a look of bewilderment. "What do you mean by, *of course not?*"

"Ban, she's your friend. Yes, she likes me, but that would put you in such an awkward position if something were to happen. I made it clear to her that the dinner was just friendly on my end. I don't want anything serious, and any girl that I talk to or date can't have a pre-existing relationship with you. Sophia does, and I'm not about to change that."

"Wow." I'm dumbfounded by his affection for me. He's never openly told me that he considers me a factor in who he dates.

"Why are you so amazed? He looks jokingly insulted. I'm not amazed. I'm actually quite touched.

"I...I don't know. You didn't respond for over an hour, and that usually means you're not around your phone."

"It can also mean that we went to a comedy club show, and they made everyone put their phones away to stop people from recording anything. The comedy club was a last-minute addition."

"Shit. I'm sorry. I didn't even realize that was a thing," I say, slightly lowering my head in shame. I assumed and convinced myself it was the truth. I'm disappointed in myself for being rash and immature. This is the second time I have done that today—and with Aman.

"Ban." He scoots closer to me, putting me at ease with that simple move. "Sophia is cool, but nothing is going to happen with her because, one, as you know, I'm not about that whole relationship thing. Two, I don't look at her like that. And three, because of you. Mainly because of you." He may not be as intoxicated as I thought he was, but he gets sappy with me when he's not completely sober.

He has a huge smile on his face, and he can tell that I'm at a loss for words. "You always think the worst of me."

That's not entirely true, but I did think that he disregarded me in this instance. "You talk a lot when you drink." I have a smile in my voice as I lower my gaze.

This makes him laugh out loud, literally.

"Okay, as long as we have that cleared up." He rises from my bed to go to his room. He's nearly at my bedroom door when I get the sudden urge to tell him about my dream last night.

"Aman."

"Hmm?" He turns around.

"I had another bad dream last night."

Because he's always been able to perceive my mood, Aman understands we've now transitioned to a serious conversation.

He stares at me intently as he leans against my door frame. He frowns, creating wrinkles on his forehead, and folds his arms across his chest. This position highlights his bulging muscles, and I'm momentarily in a trance. My best friend is so damn handsome.

"In my dream, I was almost home from the coffee shop on Feltham Boulevard when someone grabbed me and covered my mouth. I felt a sharp object against my back." I suddenly recall this detail as I repeat the story to him, not entirely sure what the sharp object was.

He's quiet and continues to listen to what comes next in my dream. To why I'm bringing it up to him at all.

"Well, I don't really remember how it ended or what happened next." I lose the intense eye contact I'm holding with him when I look down, but I sense his eyes are still focused on me. "But I saw your dad's bracelet on the wrist of that person." I eye the bracelet that is currently wrapped perfectly around his wrist.

He understands now. Aside from a slight flinch upon mention of his dad, his demeanor remains unchanged. His expression, his stance—nothing has changed, but I know he understands.

He maintains his posture for another few seconds and keeps his eyes locked on me, still expressionless. Then he slowly walks in my direction. I feel uncertain and wish I knew exactly what's running through his mind right now. Is he mad? Hurt? Upset?

This time he doesn't sit on my bed but remains standing. Given that I'm sitting on my bed, I have to tilt my head up to at least a forty-five-degree angle to look him in his eyes. He looks intimidating as I look up at him.

"Are you mad?" I eventually ask, trying to avoid eye contact with him but unable to.

Finally, a few seconds later, he says, "Do you honestly believe that I would ever do that to you?"

"What?" His question is unexpected but expected.

"Do you honestly believe that I could ever do that to you?" he repeats, slightly altering his words.

"No." I stupidly take a second longer than I should've to answer.

"Then that's all that matters."

With those simple words, and without elaborating more, he turns around and leaves my bedroom.

"Good night, Ban," he calls as he closes my door.

"Good night," I say.

I'm heartbroken. Even though his face didn't explicitly show it, he was hurt.

He knew I had a moment of doubt.

chapter 23

The next morning, Aman is sitting in his boxers on the couch, watching TV and eating a bowl of cereal. Today, however, he's not watching the news but a cartoon show. I highly suspect that this has to do with what I told him last night about my nightmare. Especially since it involved him.

"I used to watch this show growing up. Takes me back," he says when he notices me out of his peripheral vision. He looks fully enthralled with the show, but the cheer is missing from his voice.

"Good morning." I pivot toward the kitchen to grab some breakfast before school. "Hey." He's distracted by the cartoon and doesn't react immediately. "Aman?" I repeat.

"Hmm?" He briefly looks in my direction and turns his attention back to the TV. "Yeah?"

"Are we good?"

"Always." He doesn't look at me when he responds but takes another bite of his cereal. I don't feel fully settled with his answer, but I don't press him.

"Can we go to the gym tonight? And the rest of this week?" Mentioning the gym grabs his attention, as expected.

"Yes. That's a good idea. Ate too much this weekend, huh?" he teases in Punjabi.

"Just a tad." I smile at him. "And I think it'll be good stress relief."

Since I made plans with Marcus for tonight, I wonder what the vibe will be during class this morning. Will it be awkward when I see him, knowing that we're going on a pseudo-date tonight? I hope it's not noticeable.

"I'm going out tonight, by the way. Maybe we can go to the gym earlier?"

This captures Aman's attention entirely as he comes to the kitchen to set his almost-empty cereal bowl down into the sink.

"Oh, yeah?" He adds water to our coffee machine. "Where to?"

"Somewhere downtown. Can you make me a cup too, please?" I ask, knowing that this request will not change the subject.

"Who are you going with?"

I don't want to lie to him, but I think it will be infinitely more awkward if I tell him the truth immediately before we go to our Monday classes, which include evidence and Marcus.

"A friend."

He doesn't prod more, but I can tell that he remains curious. My answer is one he's familiar with. He's given it to me countless times when I've pried for details, and he doesn't want to share. He may very well know this is a romantic encounter without me explicitly telling him, but I don't want to make a big deal out of it.

Aman was there when I met Suite 22, and he was there during my healing following Suite 22. He was supportive and availed himself to me if I needed him. He was around even if I didn't say I needed him. If memory serves, there were several weeks during which the only places Aman went were school and the gym. Other times, he stayed at home with me even if we weren't physically in the same room.

When I first met him, Suite 22 initially didn't want to approach me because he thought that I was with Aman. But he opted to take a chance and further engage in a conversation with me after he saw Aman talking with another girl.

I don't like hiding things from Aman. I don't blame him for wanting to know details, so he can know where I am. It's understandable as my roommate and as my best friend. And as my protector.

It's even more understandable now, given the recent experiences and vivid dreams I've been having. He's worried about me.

Out of respect for him, I tell Aman which bar I'm going to. At least he'll know where I'll be. "The bar downtown is Nimbledom."

"Okay. I'm going to shower. Meet you out here in about twenty minutes?" He doesn't ask any more questions about tonight.

"Yeah, sounds good."

While I wait for him, I search for any updates on the police's questioning of Gerald's ex-girlfriend, but I don't see any news channels reporting on it. I imagine there will be reporters at school, but I highly doubt that the school will comment on this information due to its personal nature and to avoid any gossip that might result from the topic.

A different ongoing and highly publicized criminal trial has caught the public's attention, and it has become a conversation piece during our criminal law class with Professor Erikson.

Two friends went to a party together, drank booze, and left together. The next day, one turned up dead, and the other was sound asleep in his room. The two friends were apparently publicly arguing over a girl at the party, the defendant's DNA was on the victim, and the victim was last seen with the defendant. The defendant has maintained his innocence the entire time.

Based on how the prosecutor and the defense counsel have presented their cases, I can't determine what my personal stance is on the defendant's guilt. Both parties' arguments are extremely compelling, which exemplifies good lawyering.

"Please tell me you're almost ready to go." I glance up at Aman when he returns from his shower. His hair is damp, and he usually styles it.

"Yes, five minutes. What are you doing?"

"Watching the Madison trial."

"Why are you watching that?" he asks.

"Because if Professor Erikson chooses to discuss it today, I want to know what's happening."

"Good save." He looks ready to scold me for watching something he knows could trouble me later.

I'm certain Aman is caught up on the latest updates concerning the trial because he not only watches the news daily but also reads it daily. He probably didn't watch the broadcast this morning to spare me, but must've read about the latest on the trial online.

If Professor Erikson asks for Aman's opinion on the Madison trial, Aman's response will be informed by an appropriate—but brief—case analysis since the case is still ongoing. He always knows the answer, but never raises his hand. Whether or not Professor Erikson will actually ask him is a separate issue. Professor Erikson palpably dislikes Aman as well.

Aman told me that during office hours, Professor Erikson shared that Aman reminds him of a younger version of himself. Aman wasn't pleased with this comparison because he regards Professor Erikson as a heartless sociopath.

"Let's go," Aman says in Punjabi once he gathers his backpack from the sofa. I'm lost in thought.

"Thinking about me?" He smiles and then winks at me.

"You wish." I've gotten used to these comments from Aman. He isn't wrong, though. Technically, I was thinking about him.

"Thanks for sending me that outline, by the way." Aman refers to the one Marcus gave me on Friday at the library.

"It was great, wasn't it?"

"Yeah, it was helpful. Where did you get it?"

All signs in the universe point toward this being a good time to tell Aman about my recent interactions with Marcus. Yet I can't muster the courage to do it. Without getting into details, I downplay it.

"I ran into our new TA for evidence at the library on Friday, and he shared it with me."

"Oh, yeah. You were saying something about him on Friday night, weren't you? He was with you guys at the bar. How did that happen?" He sounds nonchalant, simply inquisitive.

"After I ran into him in the library, we left at the same time, and he mentioned that he hasn't explored San Francisco as much as he'd like since he doesn't know people. To be polite, I asked if he wanted to join."

"Hmm." Then, Aman is quiet.

"What?" I know there's more to his thoughts than a simple "Hmm."

"Is he who you're going to meet up with tonight?" I'm astonished, as I wasn't expecting him to deduce that so quickly. But then again, I was marveling at his intelligence not ten minutes ago.

I don't respond immediately, but I ultimately say, "Yes."

He's quiet again.

"Aman, what?" I sense he isn't too thrilled to hear about Marcus.

He holds on to his backpack straps and tightens them closer to his chest, sighing exhaustedly. "Just be careful. You don't know him, and I don't want what happened with that jackass to happen again." Suite 22.

"How did you know?" I'm curious.

"Are you kidding? You haven't talked to anyone since that prick—" *Suite 22 again.* "And the first guy you've mentioned since him is this guy."

I didn't know I was that transparent. Marcus is our TA—not someone I randomly met somewhere. Maybe I'm just transparent to Aman.

"How do you know I haven't talked to anyone?" I say somewhat defensively. My encounter with Tej was recent, but Aman isn't aware of that run-in.

He looks at me incredulously.

"*What?* I have ways of keeping things a secret." I attempt to paint myself to be more mysterious than we both know I actually am.

"Okay, Ban. We're roommates. It's easy for me to know what's going on in your life. It goes both ways." Aman always has a response to everything, but he's right. Since we live together, it's not hard for us to decipher each other's dating status.

I'm certain that evidence class will be awkward now that he knows, kind of. I hope Marcus doesn't approach me at any point.

Once we arrive, the lack of news trucks outside of the law school flabbergasts me, especially given the latest news about Gerald's ex-girlfriend. I was really expecting there to be at least a few. I wonder if Aman heard anything about this development.

"Sophia told me last night that the texts his ex sent to him were apparently stalkerish. They used to go on daily runs together, which I think is what pushed the police in her direction. She knows his route."

"Do you know who she is?" I ask.

"That I don't know." The details seem incriminating, but they may not be dispositive of guilt.

Before we enter the lecture hall, there's a soft tap on my shoulder. I turn around, and Marcus is smiling at me. Aman instinctively turns around as well. Unlike Marcus, he isn't smiling.

"Hey." Marcus directs his greeting at me and then looks at Aman.

"Hey, Marcus. Aman, this is Marcus."

"Yeah, I heard. The new evidence TA." Aman's posture and demeanor are as straight as an arrow. He's not smiling, nor is he further engaging in any conversation with Marcus.

"Nice to meet you," Marcus says.

"Same." Aman's response is short, but at least he's being polite. Sort of.

As I dreaded, this run-in is very uncomfortable. Although he's clearly reluctant to leave, Aman walks into the lecture hall, leaving me alone with Marcus. I don't chat with Marcus for long after Aman leaves since I'm seeing him later this evening.

Aman isn't in his seat when I approach the edge of the row we sit in. I glance around the room and see him conversing with another student. Mark's here and fully focused on his notes for class.

"Mark, Natalia is coming in three weeks, right?"

"Two." Mark is excited to correct me, given the shortening in time.

"Oh, that's right. We're going to Alcatraz the weekend after Devan's wedding. Good timing."

"What's good timing?" Aman is back in his seat.

"Going to Alcatraz at night during Halloween time," Mark answers.

"Hell yeah!" Aman says enthusiastically. "Ban, I'll protect you if you get scared." He gives me a side squeeze.

I roll my eyes at him and turn my attention toward the front. Marcus just walked into the lecture hall and is looking at Aman, his eyes shooting daggers directly at him.

chapter 24

I ask to shower first after the gym since I'm going out tonight, and Aman makes a fuss about it. "What if I was going somewhere too?" he asks.

"You're not."

"You don't know that."

"Okay, are you going somewhere?"

He is quiet and then smirks. "No." The one-word answer is filled with deviousness.

"Aman, you're a clown."

He laughs a fake laugh.

"What are you doing tonight, by the way?" I'm curious.

"Nothing. Hanging out at home and relaxing."

"Sounds perfect."

"You can do it too if you stay here with me."

I chuckle. "Maybe once I get back."

Since it's chilly outside, I select a light gray sweater dress with tan knee-high boots and a tan-colored coat as my outfit for my pseudo-date with Marcus. I keep my makeup fairly neutral and light. I don't want it to appear I dressed specially for the occasion. It's casual, so it makes sense to keep my outfit casual.

Following a glance through my jewelry collection, I conclude the smartwatch Aman bought me for my birthday is plenty. It's always on my wrist, partially because it monitors my daily physical activity and keeps me accountable.

Aman forced me to link my phone to the smartwatch to utilize the device tracker feature. I can find my phone or watch with either device. It's nifty and the primary reason he bought it for me. In fact, I use that feature now to locate my phone amidst the chaotic mess in my room.

"Wow," Aman breathlessly whispers as he watches me walk across the living room after I'm ready.

"Don't look at me like that," I say, lowering my gaze and feeling increasingly shy. I'm suddenly very cautious about how I look based on Aman's reaction. But I admit that I'm enjoying the moment of attention from him.

"You look amazing," he says plainly yet expressively.

"Thank you." There's a punch of awkwardness, and I shift toward the door before it escalates. "Okay, well, I'm going to go."

He nods and quickly turns his attention back to the TV, flipping through the channels aimlessly. "Okay, be safe," he murmurs.

"Thank you," I call out behind me, rushing to be outside.

On the other side of our closed front door, I exhale deeply and gather myself, my heart jittering inside my chest. The way Aman stared at me—it didn't last long at all, but what was that? I hate when I can't read him, and he can see through me like a glass.

Maybe it's pre-pseudo-date jitters with Marcus. Aman just made me more nervous about it. Yes, that's it, I decide. *Thanks, Aman.*

I ordered a car a few minutes ago, and I wait until it is already downstairs before taking the elevator down. I let Marcus know that I left the "mall" and am heading toward the bar. He replies back with his estimated time of arrival. We should get there around the same time.

I assume I'm the first to arrive because I don't see him in a quick glance around the room. The bar is busier than I expected it to be for a Monday evening. When I see the bar TV, I realize that a major football game is on, and fans are congregating to watch it.

I hurriedly go toward the restroom, hoping he'll arrive by the time I'm out.

There's a line to the restroom and a belligerent drunk girl on her phone, who is an aggressively speaking mess. I aim to avoid any sort of eye contact with her by fixating on my phone, fearing she might transfer that unwarranted aggression toward me if I do.

I unintentionally look in her direction once, not even *at* her, and only for a quick second. "What the fuck are you looking at?" She walks up to me, stumbling.

I maneuver my glance away from her, but she is physically too close to me.

"I asked you a question," she repeats.

"Bani!" I turn to my left and find Marcus approaching me. With him is the bouncer, who I assume will escort this toxic mess out.

"Ma'am, please come with me," he says with authority.

The girl transfers her attention to the bouncer, sparing me as a subject of her aggression. She resists him, but he eventually leads her out with the help of an even larger-bodied bouncer.

I didn't realize I had been holding my breath to the point that my chest feels compressed. As soon as she leaves, I breathe freely and deeply.

"Your timing is impeccable," I say to Marcus, truly relieved that he came at the perfect time.

He chuckles. "I got here when you were standing in line for the bathroom, and I heard this girl practically yelling. I went back to get the bouncer and then saw her approach you. Are you okay?"

"Yes. I really can't go out anymore."

"Don't say that. You're out with me." He smiles, and I relax a bit more, the rush of adrenaline I had slowly dissipating.

Marcus goes back to the bar seating area to find us seats while I use the restroom. When I return, he's saving a seat for me at the bar ledge. The bartender places a freshly made drink in the empty spot next to Marcus—an old-fashioned.

"Wow, you've already ordered my drink for me?" I'm impressed he remembers.

He lets out a cute little laugh. "This is one main thing that I've learned about you. It's pretty memorable for a girl to like an old-fashioned."

"I don't understand why it's shocking. When I first met Aman, he implied the same thing."

"So, what's going on with you guys?"

My expression of admiration for Marcus transitions to one of annoyed surprise. "What?"

"I saw you guys earlier today." I have no idea what he's referring to. He surely wasn't in our living room before I left.

"Okay, what did you see?" My voice is stern, alarming him.

"I, well…" He seems to be choosing his words carefully after seeing my negative reaction. "He flirts with you, and you don't seem to mind it."

"Aman is like that. If you knew him, you would understand. But you don't know him or my relationship dynamic with him."

He immediately recognizes that he's hit a sensitive button, and I'm not hiding it.

"Okay. I didn't mean to offend you. You look great, by the way."

"Thanks." His effort to change the subject is fruitless. My irritation is not going to subside that quickly. We silently sip our drinks for what feels like several minutes. What a horrible start to our first pseudo-date.

"Anything exciting planned?" he asks, nervously fidgeting with his napkin.

"There's a lot going on with school. And it's my brother's wedding next week."

"Really? I've been to an Indian wedding. They're a lot of fun. Very lively." The fidgeting stops, and Marcus positions his stance to face me.

"They're great. Punjabi weddings, especially. Very colorful, and there are many events leading up to the main events."

"Oh, yeah. I love the beat of Punjabi music. What's it called again?"

"*Bhangra.*"

"That's right. Do you have a favorite song?"

Marcus unintentionally and finally succeeds in changing the subject. Talking about *bhangra* undeniably puts me in a jolly mood.

The conversation continues, and I find he's curious about me but doesn't divulge much information about himself.

"What made you decide to pursue law?" I ask him.

"I like to correct wrongs."

"What a cryptic answer."

He laughs. "What about you?" he says, reverting the question back to me and, again, without divulging any more details.

"It's what best suits my personality. There aren't a lot of Punjabi lawyers. I like to be different."

"Different," he repeats. "I like that." His voice is flirtatious as he flashes a matching flirtatious smile.

"Do you want to stay in academics?"

"Bani, my interview for this job has already happened." I laugh at his implication that my questions resemble those of an interview.

"Sorry. I guess they do sound like that." I take a sip of my drink. This old-fashioned is good, but there's something different about it.

My phone lights up on the bar countertop. I have a text from Aman, but I don't read it yet because I don't want to open up another can of worms with Marcus.

"Do you want to get that?" Marcus asks.

"No, it's okay."

We spend nearly three hours together before I realize how late it is. Time flew by.

"Thanks for the drinks." Marcus doesn't let me pick up the bill.

"You're very welcome. Next, let me take you for a meal." He smiles at me.

"Yeah...sure."

I can't decide what I should do before we separate. *Hug or no hug?* A handshake would be too formal.

Then, Marcus decides for me when he takes a step toward me, gently reaching over my shoulder and pulling me in closer to him. The hug arguably lasts a tad bit longer than it should, long enough for me to decipher which cologne he has on. It wasn't exceptionally hard since I smell it every day. It's the same one as Aman's, but it's not quite the same. It smells different on Marcus. I've heard that— that the same cologne can smell different on different people.

I walk in the opposite direction of Marcus after we exchange goodbyes. I haven't thought about how I feel about him, but even if I had, I don't think that my answer to Marcus' dinner invitation would have been any different. Overall, it was fun.

It's past eleven, and I'm feeling nervous again. I call Aman to keep me company while I wait for my cab to arrive. It's a fairly busy street, even given the hour, but I'd feel more at ease talking to him.

The phone rings twice before he answers. "That long? You didn't even respond to my text."

"I actually haven't even opened it. What did you say?"

"I asked why you were taking so long." He chuckles, proud of his humor. "How was it?" Aman is chatty, and I'm relatively surprised that Aman is taking an interest in my outing with Marcus.

"It was good. He asked to take me out for a meal next time."

"Already? Guy needs to chill."

"Why?"

"You don't make plans with a girl when you're still with her. Have to keep her guessing and waiting."

"You realize that's really annoying when guys do that, right?"

"But it works."

It doesn't sound like he's at home because I hear odd noises in the background. "Where are you?"

"I went to the store."

"This late?"

"I was cleaning up my beard, and my trimmer broke." Aman is very particular about his beard. He maintains it very well, and I think that's part of what makes him look as handsome as he does.

Right as my car approaches, I tell Aman I'm heading home. I don't clearly hear what he says because an ambulance siren loudly passes by me.

Strangely at the same moment, I hear a siren on Aman's end of the phone as well.

chapter 25

It's an odd coincidence that there was a siren at the exact same time on Aman's end of the line, I think to myself on the car ride back.

But it can't be. There's no way that Aman was in the same area as me. It would be really weird for him to do that and completely out of character. He wouldn't lie to me.

The sirens were a coincidence, I decide. There are sirens all around San Francisco, and it's not unusual for one to pass by at the same time for both of us. There's also a hospital in the vicinity of our apartment.

Home is about twenty minutes away from where I am now. I use the rest of the car ride to gather my thoughts on the Marcus situation. I can definitively see that he's interested in me now. He's charismatic and cute, but not my usual type—looks-wise.

Maybe Marcus' being different from my usual taste is exactly what I need. Ari suggested that when I first told her about him too.

I'm getting ahead of myself. There's no need to rush anything. I can continue to spend time with him and keep an open mind. I'm not obligated to decide right now, and that's perfectly okay.

When the driver brings the car to a sudden halt, he also brings my mulling to a sudden halt. I was so lost in my thoughts that I didn't realize we'd arrived home.

I didn't ask Aman to come outside tonight because I didn't have a legitimate excuse like I did yesterday. And spending time with Marcus took my mind off recent events and fears.

I find Aman fast asleep on the couch once I enter our apartment. The TV is still on. I'm surprised he's asleep, having spoken to him only a short while ago. The ride took longer than expected because there was construction on the route the driver chose, but not by much.

I can't decide whether I should wake him. He looks peaceful.

He doesn't have a blanket on him, and since it's cold out, he'll eventually feel chilly. I'm going to wake him up. He'd do the same.

"Aman," I whisper softly.

He doesn't move.

I lightly nudge him. "Aman."

"Hmm," he mumbles.

"Aman, go to your room. Come on, let's go." I'm still whispering.

How did he fall asleep that quickly out here? We only spoke twenty-five minutes ago at most, and he knew I was on my way home. He wasn't even home at the time.

"No, I'm not tired," he mutters. Then I smell alcohol on his breath.

He didn't sound as if he'd been drinking when we talked. I suppose since we didn't speak for very long, I wouldn't have been able to tell.

I make a mental note to discuss this with him later. At the moment, my goal is for him to reach his bed.

"Aman, you're already sleeping. Come on. I'll help you."

"Ban? Ilrnaneu." He mumbles something that I can't really comprehend.

"What?" I ask.

His next sound is even more inarticulate than the prior.

"All right, big guy. Come on. Let's go."

"Okay," he says solemnly, finally opening his eyes. There's a sort of sadness or defeat in his voice when he says the simple word.

I help him up and walk him to his bedroom, easing him onto his bed. It's almost ineffective, considering our vastly different body sizes. Nonetheless, I attempt to hold him. He's already in his pajamas. All I need to do is tuck him in.

His room is clean and minimally decorated. It's primarily black and white and has very little furniture. It's simple, yet Aman.

As I finish and turn toward the door to go into my room, Aman murmurs something again. "Ilrnaneu." It sounds like the same sound he made earlier, but I still can't quite understand it.

"What?"

A sharp, deep sigh is all he manages again.

Knowing I won't receive any answers tonight, I say, "Good night, Aman," and leave his room.

I consider whether I should be worried about him or not. This is an odd occurrence because I've never had to take him to bed like this before. Drinking at home and alone is infrequent for Aman. Occasionally, we have a glass of wine with dinner, but that most certainly doesn't feel like the case right now. He's not as incoherent as he is today after a single glass of wine.

It's highly likely that I'm reading into this more than I need to. My only concern is because of the history with his dad.

Perhaps he wasn't alone.

The living room is empty the next morning, with no indication that anyone has been in it recently. The TV's off, the kitchen's clear, and there's no residual smell of freshly brewed coffee.

I head back toward the hallway of our apartment and knock on Aman's door. I don't hear any movement or receive any acknowledgement of my knock. I knock again but still don't hear anything. I don't think I need to panic just yet.

I hurriedly search for my phone to text Aman and ask if he's awake, but before I reach my own bedroom, the front door opens, startling me.

I don't recognize him initially because he's wearing a hooded sweatshirt that hides his face, but I'm relieved to see Aman at the door.

He doesn't see me at first and is similarly startled when he does.

"Morning," he says simply and goes into the kitchen to make his coffee.

"Good morning. Where are you coming from?"

"What?" He seems surprised that I'm asking him.

"You don't usually go anywhere in the morning."

"How do you know?" I'm taken aback by his defensive tone. What has gotten into him all of a sudden?

"Because we live together, and it's not hard to know if you go out early in the morning."

He quietly makes his coffee.

"Are you okay?" I ask.

"Yeah, why wouldn't I be?"

"You seem less like yourself this morning."

"I went on a run, Bani. No need to read into it."

What has gotten into him? His rare use of my full first name hints that he's definitely in a mood, but I don't probe him. Not now.

I don't bring last night up, and neither does he. Something is wrong with or bothering him, but I don't know what exactly. What's most alarming is his sudden and overnight mood change toward me. I can't recall the last time he has spoken to me like this. Or if he's *ever* spoken to me like this.

Without saying anything further, I turn around and go back into my room, more uncertain of Aman's mood with each step.

I leave for campus while he's showering and consider whether leaving without him will make matters worse. I wouldn't be stunned if it does, but I don't want to confront him at the moment. I tried that, and it got me nowhere.

He's in a mood, but I didn't personally do something to offend him—at least, I don't think I did. His behavior toward me is not justified unless he gives me a specific reason. Even if there is a reason, I don't need to pry it out of him. He should tell me without my having to ask him.

My phone vibrates in my pocket.

AMAN: WHERE ARE YOU?
ME: CAMPUS.

I don't expect him to respond to my message, but I don't want to be rude and ignore him. At the end of the day, no matter how Aman may behave toward me, I will always care deeply for him.

I'm currently in the library to print a document of helpful tips our professor provided for our legal writing exam. I print a set for Aman as well, expecting our legal writing class will be heavy on the preparation for the exam this coming weekend.

Aman is already at his seat, studying his notes when I walk into the classroom. He's focused and doesn't notice me walk in until I set my stuff down next to him.

"Here." I simultaneously slide the tips document toward him. Without saying anything, he reaches for the handout and studies it.

"Thanks," he says once he realizes what it is and returns his attention back to his notes.

There's tension between us, and it's become increasingly potent since I walked away from our conversation earlier this morning. We both quietly study the document directly in front of us until class begins, not speaking another word to each other.

Today's legal writing class calmed many students' nerves. Our professor briefed us on the exam, making it less stressful. She relayed that since we're 2Ls, the purpose of the exam is to promote team collaboration.

Aman didn't make a sound during the entire class. Even when the rest of the room responded with relief when the professor assured us the exam shouldn't be difficult, he said and did nothing.

Immediately once class is over, Aman darts toward our professor to discuss something with her without saying a word to me. He is indubitably hiding something from me, whether it's a piece of information or how he's feeling. There's a cause for this mood, related to me or not, and I'll find out what it is in due time.

I, on the other hand, go home to grab lunch. Midway through making my turkey sandwich, the front door opens. Aman walks in, his head lowered.

I immediately cut to the chase. "You want to tell me what's going on with you all of a sudden?"

He looks at me and away repeatedly, but stays silent for several seconds.

"Well?" I repeat myself.

"Why do you think something is wrong?" he pauses. "I could ask you the same thing. You left without me this morning."

"Yes, I had to print the sheet." I'm half-lying, and I know Aman will see through it.

"Really? And that couldn't wait until we went together?" He's not wrong.

"Aman, you practically pounced on me this morning." I exaggerate. "I asked you a simple question." It's unusual that he was entering the apartment when I barely woke up.

He opens his mouth, about to say something, and then closes it again.

"I'm worried about you." I finally admit.

His gaze softens. "Why?"

"One, you never talk to me like you did this morning, and two, when I came home yesterday and was helping you to bed, I smelled alcohol on your breath. You didn't mention going out or having someone over. It didn't sound like you'd been drinking when we were on the phone."

"There's nothing to worry about. It's as simple as having a few drinks at home because I wanted to."

"By yourself?"

"Yeah." He didn't have company. I didn't want to ask the question, and I can't quite comprehend why this is the answer I wanted to hear. But his admission to having more than one drink by himself concerns me.

Solo alcohol consumption is a sore subject for Aman, given what happened with his dad. He doesn't prefer it, but he succumbs to it at times, although not frequently at all. I wonder how much further I should push him, given the sensitivity of the topic.

"Okay, I'll accept that, but what about how you spoke to me when I asked you an understandable question?"

"Well, that was my bad, and I'm sorry. I was feeling hungover and lost in my thoughts." Lost in your thoughts? *Aman, I don't know what that means.*

This conversation isn't going anywhere. He's being both evasive and cryptic, but because he apologized for how he spoke to me, it would be unreasonable to drag it on. I hope he'll honestly tell me what's troubling him at some point.

"It's okay." I surrender, refocusing my attention on the contents immediately in front of me on our kitchen counter. "Do you want a sandwich?"

When I don't hear him say anything, I look back at him, and he's smiling.

"What?"

"Nothing. Yes, I want a sandwich."

"You're weird." I chuckle at him. "After lunch, I'm going to go to the library. Do you want to come?"

"Yes." He paces from where he's been standing at the entrance of our apartment to where I am. Unexpectedly, Aman gives me a side hug with a tight squeeze.

"Okay, big guy. No need to get emotional."

He laughs. "We need to always be good. Nothing can change that."

"Hm," I acknowledge. I don't want anything to change that either.

After lunch and an in-depth discussion on our thoughts on the exam following our legal writing class, Aman and I head back to campus together—normal this time.

Once we find a table in the law library, Aman and I agree to put our phones away after we message anyone who might worry that we'll be incommunicado for a few hours. Aman immediately puts his headphones on and dives into the reading, fully absorbed in it.

Then, on cue with terrible timing, Marcus enters the library. He hasn't seen us yet, and I avoid making eye contact with him by turning my attention to my backpack. I sincerely hope he doesn't come toward us, but in my peripheral vision, I see something moving in our direction.

Fuck. I have a feeling this won't go well.

"Hey!" he whispers enthusiastically.

"Hey," I say nervously. Aman notices him there but overtly ignores him.

"How's it going?"

"Good, just studying."

"I had a great time last night." His volume is not quite a whisper now.

"Yeah, me too," I fidget with my backpack zipper. "Um, we have a ton to get done before our exam this weekend. Can we catch up later?"

"Absolutely. When can we hang out again?"

"She's asking you to leave," Aman suddenly chimes in. He's loud enough to draw attention from our surroundings. I hear murmuring around us in response to Aman's sudden outburst. I turn to him, shocked at how loud he is.

Marcus raises his hands as if conceding and backs away. He winks at me and heads downstairs.

"What the fuck was that?" I whisper to Aman.

"We have to study, and I don't want anyone distracting me," he responds sternly.

"Yeah, it was heading in that direction."

He shrugs and puts his headphones back on.

Aman, what has gotten into you?

chapter 26

Exam weekend is here, and the atmosphere in 2L classes is tense. Our writing professor assured us that we'd be fine, and I believe her, but stress before a law school exam is inevitable.

Mark is one of the few 2Ls who isn't exam-stressed, but he's certainly preoccupied with his own schedule. The trial is over, but the workload is nonetheless keeping him busy along with his schoolwork. He's taking part of next week off for Natalia's sister's baby shower in Portland and is in a time crunch to complete all his work.

Even though Mark doesn't have to take the exam, he stayed over at our apartment last night because he was too tired to go all the way back to Oakland immediately after work. When he came to the door, he looked exhausted.

Later Saturday afternoon, Aman and I are immersed in our exam packet and are sitting on our counter stools since we technically don't have a dining table in our apartment.

"We need to get a table. Preparing for this exam would've been much easier with one."

"Yeah, sure." Aman is reading with such focus that I'm fairly certain he didn't hear what I said. I envy his brain sometimes. He won't need to reread the packet—he'll just understand the question.

Mark volunteers to make lunch for the three of us to save Aman and myself some time. Neither Aman nor I am at the point where we can commence writing.

When Mark says he is going to make his Portuguese seafood rice, Aman gets up from where he is sitting to exchange a pound-hug with him. "My man," he says.

"You never get this happy when I cook for you!" I exclaim.

He looks flabbergasted. "You barely ever cook for me!"

I gasp as if seriously offended, and both Mark and Aman laugh at me.

"What about lunch earlier this week?"

He's staring at me as if I just made the most ludicrous and nonsensical statement possible. "Making a sandwich is not cooking. Cooking requires some heat."

"I could've put it in the microwave for you."

"Ban, you're wildin'. You only cook when I'm not there," he adds, referring to the night I made dinner for Mark when Aman was in L.A.

"Ohhhhh, that was good!" Mark says. When he realizes Aman is making a pouty face, he adds, "Sorry, man. But it was."

Aman chuckles and then goes back to his reading. He's been so on edge and not like himself lately that this conversation is refreshing. He's talking to me normally. Even though we did make up that same day, things have felt off.

Mark announces our lunch is ready thirty minutes later, and Aman is the first to jump out of his chair to get his plateful. Even though he's fit and muscular, he has such an appetite for food.

The flavors of Mark's seafood rice burst in my mouth with each bite. It's a bit of a comfort food, which is appropriate for this weekend.

In between his mouthfuls, Aman convinces Mark to stay a little longer. Mark is initially hesitant, but he admits that he needs a strict, focused environment to ensure the completion of his own workload. With Aman around, he knows he will get that.

"But I'm going to leave tomorrow morning."

"That's fine," Aman assures. "All right, I'm going to go to the gym now."

"Right after eating?" I question if that's the best idea.

"I'll walk around a bit before I actually work out. It'll give you more time, slow poke." He winks at me.

"Whatever!" I scoff playfully.

He's laughing vibrantly as he walks to the kitchen sink to load his dishes in the dishwasher.

As soon as Aman changes into his workout clothes and leaves for the gym, Mark turns his attention to me. But before he asks me what I know he's going to ask me, I intervene with a question of my own.

"Have you noticed Aman's been acting weird recently?" I imagine his answer will be "no" because he's barely interacted with Aman as of late. Plus, Aman seems normal now.

As I expected, he looks confused. "No, why?"

"I don't know. He seems off and easily irritated these days. He snapped at me earlier in the week. He apologized, but it's so unlike him."

"Aman snapped at *you*?"

"Yeah. Early Tuesday morning, he was coming from somewhere. I asked where he went, and he was evasive. Then he said something like, 'I go places too,' or something. I can't remember. With hostility."

Mark listens intently.

"And he'd been drinking alone Monday evening when I wasn't home. He passed out on the couch. When I helped him up, I smelled alcohol on his breath. I'd spoken with him on the phone maybe twenty minutes earlier, and he sounded fine."

I exhale, and relief washes over me. I've been wanting to talk to someone about this. It feels like a load off my mind.

"Hmm, okay. Well, where were you coming from?" he asks.

"I went to have a drink with Marcus."

I immediately notice Mark's eyebrows rise with curiosity.

"Was he acting weird before that or after that?"

"After."

"And he knew where you were going and who you were going with?"

"Yes."

"Hmm," he says again, but I can tell he's thinking more. "He seemed fine to me today and yesterday." He pauses. "You know he loves you and is protective of you. Especially after what happened with that jackass."

"Yeah, that seems to be the consensus with that whole situation." Suite 22—he's coming up a bit too frequently lately.

"But it doesn't explain why he'd snap at you."

"Exactly. He said he was hungover and lost in his thoughts or something."

"Could be."

"Oh!" I recall what happened at the library. "Then, the same day we made up, we went to the library. Marcus approached us, and Aman essentially told him to leave."

"I think it's all coming from a place of love and protection," he says. "Have you tried talking to him?"

"Yeah, he just says 'it's nothing' or makes an excuse."

"Is he having girl problems?"

I look at Mark questioningly. "When is he ever invested enough to have problems?"

"Doesn't mean y'all don't cause problems."

I snicker. "I don't think he's talking to anyone. He was talking to that girl, Noor, but he ended things with her."

"Aman isn't talking to anyone? That's new. Well, I think Devan's wedding will put him in a good mood."

"Yeah."

I'm extremely appreciative of Mark's friendship. He considers both Aman and me as his closest friends, and his opinion is always objective. He doesn't choose sides. He advises based on what he can discern about what's in front of him and what he knows.

"Could be because school is getting stressful too."

It could very well be the stress of school that's bothering Aman, but it wasn't my first guess, given how smart he is and how he's been nonchalant about it. However, this is the toughest school has been thus far. For the time being, and unless told otherwise by Aman himself, I will assume that's it.

Mark gathers our dishes, and the sudden sound of silverware clanking together brings me back to reality.

"Tell me, how was the date with Marcus?"

"Pseudo-date," I correct him. "It was fine. He wants to take me to dinner."

Mark smirks. "Are you going to go?"

I audibly, exaggeratedly sigh. "I don't know. He's persistent, but I can't decide if I like him."

"Don't force yourself. If you don't like him, you don't like him."

"I don't think I'm at the point of *like* yet."

"It's still early. You're probably also scared to get hurt after what happened with that jackass."

"I am. You can't get hurt if you don't let anyone in." I shrug.

Mark looks at me as if I'm a sad puppy. "Bun..." He's at a loss for words. "Then you're closing yourself off from new experiences. What about that guy from your high school? At least you have history there."

I admit that I have a soft spot for Tej with our history, but I haven't fully assessed any potential current feelings toward him either. We hadn't spoken for years.

"He's been texting me almost daily, but it feels more like friends reconnecting. We're planning to hang out, possibly after Devan's wedding."

"Bunny, guys don't text girls every day unless they're interested. We just don't." He pauses. "Or if we're trying to get your attention."

"Is that what you did with Natalia?"

"She actually pursued me. She knew she wanted something and did what she had to do to get it. It was hot."

"Seriously? How did I not know this?" I'm surprised by this new discovery about Mark and Natalia's relationship.

"Probably because we've been together for ages. No one thinks back to the beginning."

Mark shares that he feels behind with his schoolwork because his externship work is taking up a lot of his time and energy. I offer to share Sophia's comprehensive evidence and criminal law outlines with him to help save time when he's in Portland.

He lifts his head, the look of panic transforming into a look of relief. Outlines are like gold to law students. They'll be an excellent starting point for him.

He gets up to give me a hug with a simple, "Thank you."

I giggle softly. "You're welcome."

"Come to think of it, I should send them to Aman too."

"When did she send them to you?"

"Last night."

"Didn't Aman hang out with her for a bit?"

"Yes."

"What happened with that?"

"He told her he considers her a friend, and nothing will happen between them because he doesn't want to put me in that position."

Mark shakes his head, grinning. "Sounds about right. He would do that."

"Really? I was surprised that he did."

"Why? He always puts close friends before that stuff."

This is true. I suppose I hadn't thought about it in the broader sense.

"How'd she take it?" he asks.

"I think she may have been pissed off, but ultimately understood. She's been fine with me."

"That's good. She gets it."

"I'm sure she resented me for a second, but we're good friends at the end of the day." I pause once I see the time. "All right, let's focus now. I won't hear the end of it if I haven't finished the reading packet by the time Aman gets home."

Mark laughs. "Okay, sounds good."

Slowly but surely, the issues are orchestrating within my brain. In preparation for my discussion with Aman, I briefly jot down all the issues and elements for each issue I've spotted as well.

Aman arrives back home right as I wrap up my final thoughts. I briefly look up at him when I notice he hasn't moved away from our apartment door. "Aman?"

"I just got stopped by the police," Aman reveals.

chapter 27

I jump to my feet. "What?"

"What are you talking about?" Mark says, shocked.

"Apparently, I was caught on camera near a crime scene the other day. The police stopped me to question me as I was about to come upstairs. They wanted to see if I saw anything."

What the fuck.

My thoughts are at a standstill.

"Well, did you?" Mark questions.

"No, man. I didn't see anything crazy or someone in trouble. I would remember if I did."

"It had to be serious enough for them to seek you out." Mark is pensive.

"When was it?" I finally say something.

"Tuesday morning, I think." That was when Aman said he went on a run early in the morning.

"Which area was it?" Mark asks.

"It was between Geary and Renton, near Fourth Ave."

What on earth was Aman doing over there that early in the morning? This makes absolutely no sense.

"What were you doing there? That's random." Mark calmly vocalizes my erratic thoughts.

"I went on a run." He doesn't sound very convincing right now, even though that's the reason he gave me then as well.

"What did you say to them?" Mark prods.

"I said I didn't see anything. They started the conversation by saying, 'You're not being detained.' This has never happened to me before."

"Fuck, man. That's crazy. Are you okay?" Mark adds.

I'm certain the look on my face is expressive of my emotions. To a certain extent, I may look like I'm doubting Aman. I'm not, but the timing and circumstances simply don't make sense. There has to be another explanation.

Aman turns his attention to me. "What are you thinking?" he says to me in Punjabi.

I open my mouth to speak but still can't form words. I'm confused and worried. Does it end here? Are the police going to come back again?

"What else did the police say?" I ask, aligning with my thoughts.

"Nothing, Ban. They asked me if I saw anything suspicious and said they've been questioning as many people as they can make out in the nearby surveillance camera. Apparently, it happened a few minutes after I passed by."

From what I can recall, Aman was wearing his hood on his head when he walked in. I don't understand how he was one of the individuals that the police were able to identify via surveillance cameras when I didn't initially recognize him in plain sight from only a few feet away.

"How did they know who you were and where to find you?" Mark asks.

"They didn't say."

"How can they know who you are without any source of information?"

"I don't know. But they showed me footage of me walking. They had to have some sort of clue on how to find me."

"What was the crime?" Mark asks.

I make no additional contribution and merely listen to Mark and Aman's ping-pong conversation.

"Attempted kidnapping."

"Holy shit!" Mark exclaims.

"They didn't tell me who the victim was. They want all this information but refuse to share anything in return. I understand why, but if you're going to pull me aside and question me, at least tell me what it is you think I saw. Help jog my memory." Aman's frustration with the encounter is obvious.

San Francisco is magnificent, but like in any other city, crime is inevitable. The other day I saw a woman riding a scooter on the sidewalk near Market Street, and a man confronted her. He had a beer in his hand and was berating her for riding on the sidewalk. She yelled, "I'm pregnant!" to try to get him to stop. That didn't stop the man from continuing to verbally attack her.

No one said or did anything. Everyone kept walking, sadly, including myself. Granted, it didn't seem like the altercation was violent.

The attempted kidnapping could have looked like an altercation that a passerby, like Aman, would ignore. If he even saw it.

"How did the conversation end?" I eventually ask.

"They thanked me for my cooperation and jotted down my contact information in case they needed to contact me again."

"Oh," I say.

Although he looks nervous, Aman is more composed than me. I'm certain I would be far more nervous if a police officer suddenly approached me in relation to a crime that I may have witnessed. Even in a completely innocent scenario, especially following Gerald's accident.

Aman lets out a long sigh of relief when I give him a comforting hug. "Don't worry. You're fine," I say, rubbing his back to provide him some sort of consolation.

"Thanks." Oddly, his warm embrace as he squeezes me tight before he releases me gives me comfort instead. Comfort I didn't know I needed.

"You good?" Mark asks him.

"Yeah, I'm good. We should get back to this writing exam." Aman gestures to me, eager to change both the atmosphere and the subject.

"I finished reading too." Aman smirks when I update him on my exam status.

He's quiet, and I turn to see him staring at me. "What?" I ask with a hint of a smile in my voice.

"Nothing. I'm going to take a quick shower, and we can get back to it."

"Are you sure you don't want a break?" I want to double-check that he's in an okay state of mind to continue. My nerves are amplified, and the confrontation didn't even happen to me.

"I'm good as long as I have you." There's a brief fluttering in my stomach when Aman playfully grazes my cheek, and then he leaves.

I'm unable to take my eyes off him until my phone lights up as it rests on the counter.

MARCUS: HOPE YOUR EXAM WEEKEND IS PRODUCTIVE. LET
ME KNOW IF YOU NEED A CARE PACKAGE.
ME: THANK YOU. WORKING ON IT AND GETTING THROUGH
IT. HOW'S YOUR WEEKEND?

I hastily set my phone aside before Aman returns. Moving
it far enough away that I'm not tempted to look at it. He'll grill
me for being on my phone and not concentrating. The most
important factor in Aman's success is his discipline. He doesn't
appreciate distractions.

His shower really was a quick one because less than ten minutes
later, he rejoins Mark and me at the kitchen counter, where his stuff is
already laid out. His hair is still wet, and he's wearing loose, light gray
sweatpants and a loose, plain black t-shirt. He looks physically relaxed
compared to when he came home.

"Okay," he begins. "I think there are four main causes of action
that we can break down into the elements that are in the statute set.
Ban, what did you get?"

Aman fully engrosses himself in the exam, and it *seems* he's no
longer troubled by his encounter with the police. He's tough and
resilient.

Even if something was bothering him in a situation like this,
he wouldn't necessarily overtly tell me or even exhibit it. He has
surprised me before, however.

Come Saturday evening, both Aman and I nearly have our first
drafts written. We have the rest of tomorrow to fine-tune our papers for final submission Monday morning. I'm extremely pleased
with our progress and feel much more at ease. Aman alleviates any
underlying nervousness of having missed an issue significantly.

He hasn't told anyone aside from Mark and me, but last year he
finished at the top of our class. He refers to himself as the "silent

killer." He wants to dominate law school silently, without flaunting it or with anyone knowing.

"Okay, I think I'm done with this for the night," Aman says slowly as he finishes typing his last few words. Once he's actually done, he checks in with me. "How are you doing?" His expression is serious and focused.

I'm still typing, and I gesture for him to hold on.

"I think I have another thirty minutes left before I can feel comfortable and be at the point you're at," I say.

He smirks. "Aw, Ban. I can make you comfortable to be at the point I'm at." He lightly squeezes my shoulders before heading toward the bathroom.

"I don't even know what that means, big guy." I like calling him that.

"I'm taking the night off, having a beer, and either watching a movie or playing video games."

"Down," I agree, semi-distracted. "Mark, what's your status?"

"I'm just about done myself." He sounds relieved. "Hey, man?" Mark says to Aman.

"Yeah?" he yells back.

"You were right. I was much more productive here than I would've been at home."

"*You hear that, Ban*? I was right," Aman jokes, thoroughly enjoying the opportunity to flaunt to me. "Mark, you down for a movie or video games?"

"Hell yes!"

"Let's order a pizza too," I add.

"I'll pick it up, along with some beer." Aman plops himself down on the couch to order the pizza on his phone. He's quiet for a few minutes. "Okay, it'll be ready in about twenty minutes."

"Send me a Weevee for my share," Mark adds, as usual, without fail.

"No, man." Aman sounds defeated at Mark's persistence to always split the amount for the food.

"Did you send me a Weevee for the groceries you bought for the seafood rice earlier?" Aman makes a valid point, and Mark knows he did not send a similar request. He blushes, but doesn't answer Aman's rhetorical question.

"Pizza is on me," Aman states simply. He looks away as I hold my phone, preparing to send him the Weevee.

"You can at least split it with me."

Without saying anything or looking at me, he brings his index finger to his lips, telling me to hush.

"I'll get dessert, then. What do we want?"

"You're sweet enough to be dessert." He briefly lifts his glance, winking and grinning cheerily at me, and then turns his attention right back to his phone.

Mark laughs at Aman, shaking his head as he looks back and forth between the two of us.

"You're ridiculous," I say, rolling my eyes and shaking my head at Aman. I smile to myself. This guy.

Shortly after Aman leaves to pick up the food, I finish my first draft as well and retire to the couch to take the rest of the evening off, feeling much more relaxed. I wonder how a few of my other friends are doing in their preparation for the exam—those friends who don't have Aman.

When I realize that Aman has been gone much longer than expected, I text him to ask what's taking him so long. The pizza place is not far from home. A few minutes pass without a response from him. I call him, and the phone rings twice before it goes to voicemail.

A minute later, and before I fully activate my worry mode, the front door swings open, and Aman walks in. I leap up, exhaling in relief. "What took you so long?"

"That hungry, fatty?" he teases in Punjabi. He sets the boxes down on the counter and faces me and Mark.

"No! Well, yes. But you left a half hour ago. I was beginning to worry." I'm amazed at how quickly I panic at a minor issue as of late.

"I've been outside for nearly fifteen minutes."

My concerned expression turns into one of confusion. "What? Why?"

"Right when I got home with the food, Noor was waiting outside for me, and she stopped me to talk. Thanks for calling, Ban. That was my cue to say I had to go."

"Didn't you end that weeks ago? Why was she here?" Mark asks. He is intrigued, as am I.

"I'm not sure. She seemed really off. I wasn't talking as much— she was doing the bulk of the talking. Apparently, I'm a fucked-up guy who played her and treated her badly."

Aman is not someone who treats women badly. He has his fun, but he's honest about his intentions. It sounds like Noor is trying to put Aman in the same category as I placed Suite 22, but Aman is nothing close to Suite 22. Not in the slightest.

"What do you mean by 'she seemed really off?'" I ask, growing angry with the ludicrously incorrect and audacious assumptions she is making about my best friend.

"I don't know. Girls act weird when they get rejected, but this was different. She seemed unstable."

"As in obsessive and unpredictable?" I attempt to put my thoughts into words.

"Yeah, kind of."

This is potentially worrisome.

"Quite a weekend you've had," Mark says, reminding us about Aman's earlier encounter with the police.

"Shit, for real, huh?" Aman jokes and fake chuckles. He's taking it amazingly well under the already stressful circumstances.

At least the weekend is almost over.

chapter 28

Aman and I are ready to submit our exams well before the deadline at noon, with plenty of time to spare.

I can now focus on this week and the biggest event for my family thus far: my brother's wedding. I pushed any thoughts of the upcoming joys of this week to the corner of my mind because of my exam.

Allowing myself to be present in the moment, I can hardly believe it's finally here. Devan is getting married. Devan is getting *married*.

I briefly talked to my parents, and at the time, they were preparing for the welcome ceremony and the *mehndi* tomorrow. The *jaggo* is on Wednesday, and the *mayian* is on Thursday.

On Friday, we're taking a break to prepare for the wedding on Saturday, with the reception to follow.

Aman insists that we go to Palo Alto today and surprise my family. It takes me some effort to persuade him—and myself, if I'm being honest—that it would be a better idea to stay and complete our work so that we can fully enjoy all of the events. One would think that it would be the other way around.

My parents also encouraged me to use the remainder of Monday to complete my work for the week to ensure the rest of the week is worry-free, school-wise. Aman and I still have a lecture on evidence and criminal law to attend today, but the professors were advised to minimize the reading for Monday because of our exam.

Come late afternoon, I'm confident we made the right decision by staying in San Francisco to finish the week's reading. Aman finished a few hours before me and went to the gym. He's accepted that he will be eating a lot and won't be able to work out much until Sunday, aside from dancing *bhangra* at the events. Honestly, I think this is the one week where he would accept missing workouts. He's that excited.

I'm leaving the library later than expected, but I feel a tremendous sense of accomplishment. I stroll past several benches filled with law students chatting amongst each other at the entrance of the library. Just as I am about to turn onto the sidewalk to head home, I hear someone calling my name from behind me. Following the direction of the sound, I spot Marcus eagerly approaching me.

"You've been a hard one to catch lately," he says.

Have I really, considering I replied to his text over the weekend? "I've been mainly hibernating this weekend in my apartment, working on my exam." I decide not to dwell on it.

"How was it?"

"Went as expected."

"Usually how it is. What're you up to this week?" he asks.

"I'll mainly be going back and forth to Palo Alto. It's my brother's wedding."

"Oh, right!" He beams when I mention the wedding, like he will also be in attendance. But obviously not. "Are you excited?"

"Really excited."

"I have an event over the weekend too, but let me know when you're available."

"Okay. I have to go now. Aman and I will be going to Palo Alto fairly early tomorrow."

"Aman is going too?"

"Of course." Marcus is caught off guard by the look of surprise on my face, but I'm caught off guard by his question. He almost seems bothered that Aman is going too, the glimmer from a moment ago is gone.

Through my peripheral vision, I see a figure coming in our direction from around the corner. It's Professor Erikson, and he's walking straight toward us.

"Ms. Sethi." He has never once directly approached me outside of lecture or office hours. I didn't think he remembered my name without his seating chart in front of him.

Marcus must have gotten a call because he excuses himself immediately after he looks at his phone. I nod in response to his goodbye, wondering who it was or what was on his phone that caused him to leave abruptly. He appeared tense before he hurriedly walked away.

"Hello, Professor. How are you?"

"I'd like to speak with you and Mr. Wajla." I suppose we're skipping over the exchange of pleasantries. "Please send me an email of times that would work for you both sometime this week. The sooner, the better." There's urgency in his words.

"Oh." I'm surprised by his unprecedented request, and I can't fathom what he needs to talk to both of us about. "May I ask what this is regarding?"

"I would prefer not to discuss this here." With that simple yet cryptic message, he leaves before I have the opportunity to respond.

I immediately text Aman to inform him of the odd request from Professor Erikson and to ask him if he knows what he wants to talk to the both of us about.

> AMAN: I HAVE NO IDEA.
>
> ME: WELL, WE NEED TO MAKE SOME SORT OF APPEARANCE THIS WEEK. HE WANTS US TO EMAIL HIM A FEW TIMES THAT WORK FOR US.
>
> AMAN: HOW ARE WE GOING TO DO THAT WITH THE WEDDING?
>
> ME: I GUESS IT'LL HAVE TO BE IN BETWEEN EVIDENCE AND CRIMINAL LAW ON WEDNESDAY. WE CAN TELL HIM THAT WE HAVE PRIOR ENGAGEMENTS THAT DON'T ALLOW MUCH FLEXIBILITY IN OUR SCHEDULE FOR THIS WEEK.
>
> AMAN: OKAY.

I rack my brain for ideas that may explain why our criminal law professor wants to speak to both Aman and me away from the law school.

I send him an email immediately once I get home and request the time slot between evidence and criminal law on Wednesday.

His response is odder than the encounter. It is succinct and presumptive, which is not unlike him, but still very strange. "Your Wednesday evidence lecture is likely to be canceled. Please meet me at the café on Feltham Boulevard at nine-thirty that morning."

Why is our evidence lecture likely to be canceled? And how is this something that he knows? He's our criminal law professor. Why does he want to meet us off-campus? Is it something personal?

Question after question pops up in my mind. Professor Gatlin didn't mention anything about our lecture being canceled earlier this morning. Everything seemed fine. *She* seemed fine.

Aman finds the idea of evidence being canceled without any mention from Professor Gatlin to be odd, but he doesn't dwell on it like I do.

"We'll find out when we find out. Let's focus on Devan's wedding. Stop driving yourself crazy." Typical Aman response.

He's right. I should be more focused on Devan's wedding, and although this hasn't happened before, I have no reason to think that something is wrong. This doesn't mean it's like what happened with Gerald's accident. My mind automatically jumps to the negative lately, and I reprimand myself for it.

"Let's go early tomorrow morning. We can be with your parents throughout the day and help with the *mehndi* at least," Aman says to distract me from my thoughts.

"I think that's good. They're expecting us to come early."

"I'm going to go to the gym before we leave in the morning, and on my way back, I'll bring the car." Aman refers to the plan that we made weeks ago to rent a car for this week, easing our travel to and from Palo Alto.

"Sounds good," I respond.

"Are you going to get *mehndi* done?" Aman's efforts to distract me continue to work. I love henna, but I want to avoid having a lot of henna on my hands. At the same time, it is my brother's wedding, and I'll definitely get some to commemorate the occasion.

"Yeah, a little bit." It's basically a requirement as the sister of the groom. Ari's also getting a design.

"Get the letter A snuck in there." He pairs his gorgeous smirk with a wink, knowing full well that girls often get the first letter of their significant other's name added to their *mehndi* design. *Aman and his jokes*, I think to myself.

Guys don't get as elaborate designs as girls, but increasingly, more guys have been getting simple, often one-liner, *mehndi* done. A bride gets her fiancé's full first name drawn into her *mehndi* design, and the groom has to find it. The artists do phenomenal, intricate jobs hiding the groom's name.

"As long as you get a B." I can joke with him too. Aman dramatically places his hand on his heart with a look of surprise, and it makes me giggle.

"Weren't expecting that now were you?" I ask mockingly.

He laughs, his gorgeous smile still flashing, admitting that he indeed wasn't expecting that. It warms my heart to see him laughing like this. I know another thing I can do for him that will add to his jolly mood.

I suggest cooking something for the two of us for dinner since we don't have plans, taking him by surprise again, but he's not complaining. He looks at me appreciatively and responds as I hoped—happily.

"Do you want me to make something in particular?"

"Hmm, why don't we make *tari wala* chicken?" I commend his suggestion. I've only made it a few times, but Aman is a pro at it. *Tari wala* chicken is a chicken dish with a thick and spicy gravy. Luckily, we have all the ingredients that we need to make it.

"Are you going to help me?" I ask coyly, even though I offered to cook for him.

"Yes, we'll make it together," he says like he wouldn't have it any other way.

Cooking with Aman is one of my favorite things to do. He's endearing and patient with me, even when I mess up.

As he prepares the game-changing Punjabi spices and cuts the tomatoes to put in the food processor, I add in and sauté the already ground onions, ginger, and garlic in oil one at a time.

"It's funny that we're making Punjabi food when we'll be eating nothing but Punjabi food this week and weekend," he says.

"Homemade is different, though. The food we'll be eating will be catered food."

"True."

"And I'm pretty sure that Devan and Alina are mixing it up a bit and not sticking strictly to Punjabi food."

"Yeah? What are they planning?"

"A variety. I think a pizza station was a popular potential."

"Sweet." He pours the tomatoes into the pan. From here, he takes over the ladle, and I station myself on the counter. He knows the perfect amount of spices to add.

"Is that all the help I'm getting, baby girl?" His voice is deep and husky as he grins. He used to call me that all the time before I met Suite 22. I didn't realize until now that he hasn't called me that since.

Right when I'm about to ask him why he stopped, a new notification on my phone lights up my phone screen, indicating I have an email from the law school.

"They canceled evidence for this week, not just Wednesday," I summarize the gist of the email.

"Did they give a reason?" he asks as he stirs.

"No. What's happening?" It's atypical for the law school to cancel a core class lecture with this late notice.

"Ban, don't read into it. It's probably nothing." How is he calm about this?

"The last time they canceled evidence office hours was because of Gerald's accident. This is the actual lecture."

"Yes, it's strange, but why assume? We won't know until we know. I'm more concerned that they canceled two evidence classes this close to the end of the semester. Did they say anything about make-up lectures?" he asks.

I read directly from the email, "There will be make-up classes, and academics will not be affected by the sudden cancellations."

"Well, that's good then. At least we don't have to worry about that this week with the wedding. Look at the timing." Aman—the voice of reason.

"Hmm," I hesitantly mumble in agreement. The timing *is* opportune.

What I find strange is that Professor Gatlin wasn't the one to send the email; it came through the registrar's office. I force myself to drop the topic before my imagination gets the best of me because if I keep lingering on the subject, it will.

Aman finishes his preparation of the chicken and leaves it in the pot to simmer and cook. He retires to the couch until we're ready eat.

I've asked him previously where and when he learned to cook this well, and his response, as expected, was from his mom.

I've only met his mom a few times. She doesn't come to San Francisco often, but she's one of the sweetest people I've ever met. Out of respect, I never refer to her or address her by her name. I can't bring myself to do it.

Interestingly enough, my parents have never met Aman's mom or stepdad, but it doesn't seem that way. My parents invited Aman's family to Devan's wedding. Unfortunately, they're not able to come because Raman has a promotion-determining presentation on Monday, and Charan has a conference to attend.

While dinner is on the stove, I video call home to see what everyone is doing. My dad answers my mom's phone. "Hi, Banu."

I can see he's distracted as he moves a chair around the living room.

"What are you guys doing?" I ask.

"Your mom is making me move the furniture in the living room area because the decorators are coming for the *mehndi* tomorrow morning, and they need a clear pathway for the backyard setup. She's in the kitchen. Ari is helping me. Devan is in the garage."

"*When are you coming?*" Ari yells in the back.

"Aman is picking up a car in the morning tomorrow. I think we'll be there pretty early." I look toward Aman to get his nonverbal confirmation. He nods and reverts back to his phone.

"Where is Aman?" my dad inevitably asks.

Aman hears my dad say his name and looks up, grinning from ear to ear, and I switch the camera toward him. He briefly exchanges pleasantries with my dad, both mimicking their fondness for the other and excitement for the upcoming festivities in the process.

Aman is good about that—capturing hearts.

The next morning, Aman knocks on my door and rushes into my room, urging me to shower. As soon as we're ready, we can be on our way and finally partake in the wedding festivities. I have a strong hunch that he has also been having FOMO from all the fun.

Since I woke up abruptly, my vision is still blurry, and I can faintly see Aman walk back into the living room area. From what I can tell, he's already showered and ready to go.

I flip onto my back, groaning at the early wake-up call Aman gave me.

Staring at the ceiling, I force myself to be as awake as I can be and give myself a mental pep talk, telling myself to fully enjoy the next few days. Knowing me, melancholy will strike me as early as Sunday morning when all the events have passed. I've felt this before with cousins' weddings, and I can only imagine how much more amplified it will be for my own brother's wedding.

Aman quietly reemerges into my room again, slightly startling me. I gasp, but I am quiet enough that he doesn't hear.

"Can you get up?" He stations himself at my door, staring at me and waiting until I finally sit up in my bed.

My vision is no longer blurry. Aman is showered and ready to go.

"When did you wake up?" My voice is groggy.

"I've been up since five-thirty," he says energetically.

My eyes widen, both in surprise and in an effort to awaken myself further.

"Why?"

"Gym!" He excitedly marches back into the living room. "I'm basically ready to go!" His enthusiasm for my brother's wedding is enchanting.

I check my phone to see if Ari messaged me, but it's unlikely that she's awake at this hour.

My attention is immediately captured by a new notification I received in the middle of the night indicating that I have another email in my school account.

The email is again from our school registrar informing us that Professor Erikson has had to urgently attend to a matter, and criminal law is also canceled for this week.

chapter 29

"I guess that means we won't be meeting with him tomorrow." I don't understand how Aman is still unbothered.

I can't say the same for myself because I'm growing curiouser and curiouser with these recent developments and sudden cancelations. What are the odds that two of our core class professors both cancel their classes the same week, and they also happen to be seeing each other?

"I don't think either of them is so unprofessional to cancel class for personal reasons. Well, Professor Gatlin isn't," Aman adds—his dislike of Professor Erikson still running strong. But I agree. It's unlikely that they're canceling classes for personal reasons. Perhaps the timing is coincidental. Or perhaps the reasons they're canceling class are linked.

Aman pulls me from my thoughts and physically makes me rise from my bed by placing his hands under my arms and lifting me up with such ease. I giggle at his incredible strength.

"Okay, get ready now." Then he disappears outside again.

I should actually be grateful that the bulk of our classes were canceled this week, freeing up our time. If we want to, we can probably spend the night in Palo Alto tonight and drive back late tomorrow night after the *jaggo*.

"Aman?" I yell out from my bedroom.

"Yeah?" he says, amidst the closing and opening of cabinet doors and clanking of dishes.

"Come here." After a few seconds, the clanking stops, and he arrives at my door. "Do you think we should stay in Palo Alto tonight? Since evidence and criminal law are canceled?"

He's intrigued by the idea. "Do your parents have enough room?"

"I can ask them."

I reach for my phone to call them and then concretely decide that it might be easier and more comfortable for both of us to drive back to San Francisco. Especially since Aman went through the trouble of renting a car for that sole purpose.

He notices my pause. "What?" he asks.

"Maybe we should leave it. It'll be easier, and I don't want you to be uncomfortable."

"That worried about me?" he endearingly says in Punjabi.

I laugh. "It's going to be a long week. We need to rest when we can. Plus, the drive isn't too bad. The reception will be closer to us here anyway."

"Oceana Azul golf course on Treasure Island, right?" Treasure Island is the connecting point of the Bay Bridge, right in the middle of the two segments.

"Yes."

"That view is going to be insane."

I've seen it, and I wholeheartedly agree with him. Oceana is right along the edge of the water, overlooking the San Francisco skyline. When my family went to scope it out as a venue, it was in the afternoon, but the view was still incredible.

Devan and Alina's wedding reception will be in a partially sheer tent and is starting just before sunset. The guests will be able to enjoy the view of the Golden Gate Bridge and skyline with the sunset as a backdrop. The weather has been warm for October, and the forecast predicts a pleasant evening that day. Although, regardless of what the forecast says, an evening right along the bay will be chilly.

When Aman and I leave San Francisco for Palo Alto, he plays Punjabi music to pump us up for the wedding.

Here we go.

It occurs to me that neither Aman nor I have seen the other one in ethnic clothing. Ari and I bought brand-new outfits for each of the functions in Berkeley a few months ago.

"You're right," Aman says when I point this out. "This is the first Punjabi event we've gone to together."

From what he told me, he's wearing dress shirts for the *mehndi*, *jaggo*, and *mayaian*, a *sherwani* at the wedding, and a suit for the reception. A *sherwani* is a fancy pant and long coat-like garment for men that sometimes includes a long scarf. Ethnic attire isn't necessarily a requirement for men, except perhaps for the groom.

Listening to *bhangra* and talking about the wedding makes our drive fly by, and before we know it, Aman turns onto the street that my parents' house is on. Aman lowers the volume of the music since it can, without a doubt, be heard from the outside and is likely to disrupt the peace of the neighborhood.

I'm surprised he remembers where their house is. It's been months since the last time he was here. Although, at present, it's easy to discern which house is my parents' because it's the only house that is decorated on the outside with Punjabi wedding décor. It's impossible to miss.

Aman and I spot a group of people standing in my parents' driveway. I don't recognize anyone, and I don't see any of my family members within the group. Ari must know that we're here, though, because I hear her yelling my name and running toward me from the side of the house. She nearly runs into me as she sprints to us.

"Finally!" She hugs me and then hugs Aman. "Haven't seen you in ages!"

He's much taller and more substantial than her. When he hugs her, it looks like a bear hug.

"Blame this one." He gestures toward me.

I scoff at him in return. "I've asked you to come with me each time I come home. You're always doing something."

He mischievously laughs and then gathers our things from the trunk.

"Who are these people?" I whisper to Ari, indicating the group a few feet ahead of us on the driveway.

"They're from the wedding planner's company. They're doing the decorations this week." Most of the events will be in my parents' backyard, which will provide a beautiful canvas for the décor.

My mom was nervous about holding the events at home, as people will inevitably make a mess. Although it's not required, it's customary for the bride and groom to have certain events at their respective home. We're expecting up to two hundred people on our side. The wedding and reception will be both ours and Alina's families and friends, doubling the attendance, but luckily those are at separate venues.

Immediately when I open the garage door, Nala zooms to the door, her collar jingling the entire way.

She loses it as soon as she sees Aman. She whimpers and cries, jumping up at him and licking his hands as he holds her up and pets her. I should've walked in before Aman because I'm a nobody to her at this point.

"Bubby!" I exclaim, but she still pays no attention to me.

Aman is thoroughly amused by this and has a sheepish grin as he pets her and looks at me. "Gooood girl," he says to her.

I roll my eyes at him and sigh defeatedly, giving Nala a quick peck while Aman holds her.

Next, my dad paces down the hall in our direction. This is the moment he has been waiting for.

Once my dad hugs me, he immediately turns his attention toward Aman, shaking his hand and similarly giving him a hug. I continue to be amazed by how Aman has won everyone's heart in my family.

"How's it going, man?" my dad asks Aman in Punjabi.

"Good, sir. It's great to be here." There's no mistaking how happy Aman is to see my dad and that he means the words he says.

"Thank you for coming to our son's wedding," my dad says humbly.

"Wouldn't have missed it."

"Aman!" My mom cheers as soon as we turn the corner into the kitchen. She is fully occupied with wedding preparation and cooking. I avoid her flour-covered hands as I lean in to embrace her. Aman mimics me, also avoiding her hands.

"Something smells amazing," he says.

My mom laughs. "We're making *jalebis*." *Jalebis* are a deep-fried dessert coated with a sugary syrup. They resemble smaller pretzels in appearance but are crunchier in taste.

In the backyard, my mom has a kitchen station set up, and a group of her friends are already at work while vivaciously chanting Punjabi wedding songs.

With perfect timing, the man of the week graces us with his presence. Devan's beard has grown since last I saw him, and he's gotten a fresh haircut.

"There he is!" I exclaim as I admire how handsome my brother looks.

His smile widens, and he nervously chuckles. He gives me a tight hug, then exchanges a brotherly handshake with Aman.

"Congrats, Dev," Aman says.

"Thank you! It's good to see you," Devan replies.

"That seems to be the consensus," I say mockingly.

"Someone is feeling a little left out," Aman jokes, nudging my shoulder with his.

"No, I'm not!" I'm actually relishing how happy everyone is to see him.

"What's the plan between now and tonight?" I pose the question to everyone.

My dad is the first to answer. "I think we're all set for tonight. There's not much that we're going to do since the wedding planner is taking care of everything."

"Yeah. We had cleaning to do, but we did that yesterday. You guys came at the perfect time," Ari announces sarcastically.

"I'm the only one who's still busy," my mom adds.

"We can help you," Aman says.

"No, no. I'm covered." She gestures toward her group of friends outside. "You guys rest before guests start to arrive."

Helping Aman with our bags, I lead him upstairs to my room and then to a guest room, which is down the hall from mine. "You can get ready here." He nods in acknowledgement. We head back downstairs and find that everyone but my mom is seated in the living room with a movie on.

There's about an hour and a half left before guests start arriving, and Ari and I both want to take a shower to remove any unwelcome dirtiness we accumulated over the day.

I have butterflies, and it's not even my wedding. Before I shower, I check on Aman to see if he needs anything.

"Knock, knock." His door is open.

"Hey," he says graciously, beaming.

"Wanted to check in with you and see if you needed anything. Did you want to shower?"

He looks amused.

"What?" I ask.

"Very attentive today."

"Well, you don't know where everything is, and instead of watching you look for it and embarrass yourself, I thought I'd help out." I'm careful not to call him a guest because he wouldn't like that.

He laughs, removing an item of clothing from his bag. "Yes, I do want to shower."

"Be right back." I quickly grab a towel for Aman from the linen closet, handing it to him once I'm back in his room.

He seems solemn now, which is strange considering how excited he was for this week. "Is something wrong?"

"No, I'm fine. Why?"

"You went from being pumped to being quiet."

"No, no. I'm good." I don't believe him, but I turn to leave anyway to give him some privacy.

"Seeing you with your family makes me miss mine," he confesses.

The thought had crossed my mind.

I turn back around, and his smile is melancholy. I didn't think he could be more handsome than he already was, but he proves me wrong in this moment. His raw display of emotion shows me his vulnerability, which is a rare sighting with Aman. It's no coincidence that my dad is the one person in my family Aman bonded with the most.

"My family is yours too, big guy." I mean it, and I know he values the sentiment. "We're about to have a great week."

He nods silently.

"We deserve this after the shit few weeks we've had, and I'm pretty sure they love you more than me," I say, hoping this will make him laugh, at least slightly. And it does.

chapter 30

I hear guests arriving, and I'm only halfway done with my makeup. To amplify the stress, my mom repeatedly calls from downstairs.

How is she already ready for the functions? She began dressing after me and Ari and was done before us. What boggles my mind even more is that she always looks perfect.

My outfit is a simple and elegant Punjabi suit—a traditional *salwar kameez*. A *salwar kameez* is a long top with loose pants accompanied by a long scarf called a *chunni*. The top of my suit, the *kameez*, is forest green with gold embroidery along the side seams and an elegant design running from the front neckline to the bottom of the *kameez*. The pants of my suit, the *salwar*, are black and puffy, with gold polka dots spread evenly across the fabric. Lastly, my *chunni* is a combination of the designs from my *salwar* and *kameez*. I fold it vertically and place it on one shoulder, running it evenly down the front and back of my body.

For my makeup, I complete a neutral look since the colors of my *salwar kameez* are very noticeable. To make my eyes pop, I add a bit of green liner. I leave my hair down and part it to the side but add loose curls to give my hair a wavy and bouncy look. As a finishing touch, I place a gold *tikka*, a traditional jewelry ornament that is placed on the forehead, to contrast with my *salwar kameez* right where I have parted my hair.

In addition to the arriving guests, the DJ plays various Indian and Punjabi songs in the backyard for background music. The music is quieter compared to the increasing chatter between the guests, but loud enough for me to discern which song is playing.

My attention to the faint background noise and music is abruptly interrupted by my baby sister, who comes stomping into my room because she cannot get her *tikka* to stay on her head. I secure her *tikka,* and we're both ready to partake in the quickly escalating festivities downstairs.

Once Ari and I are among the crowd, we're immediately and energetically greeted by dozens of relatives and family friends. There's still lustrous sunlight out, and the weather is pleasant for an October evening.

I hear the inevitable "you're next" from so many people that I lose count. Out of respect, I smile and laugh at the recurring comment, but in actuality, I'm annoyed.

I've been in the backyard for about twenty minutes, but I'm unable to spot Aman through the fast-growing crowd. Aman called out to me before he went downstairs since it took him a third of the time to get dressed. He should be here somewhere.

As I pull out my phone to ask him about his whereabouts, I hear a familiar voice behind me, very close to my ear.

Aman's breath hits my neck as he whispers, "You look amazing." His voice is low enough for me to privately savor his compliment—no one else is able to hear it but me.

I compose myself before I slowly face him and eye what he's wearing. "Thank you. Your outfit is pretty dapper too." I almost choke on my words. Suddenly, I've forgotten how to swallow.

He laughs at my use of the word "dapper." His medium-gray, white polka-dotted dress shirt is fitted to a fault. He looks breathtakingly handsome.

"Thanks." The smile in his voice is more prominent than the chatter amongst the guests. "We're matching." He refers to the polka dots.

I chuckle, clearing my throat. "Where have you been?"

"I was helping your dad in the front. He asked me to help him move some things around for the *mehndi* artists."

I debate whether I should wait to get my *mehndi* until later in the night or whether I should go now. Aman got his design earlier, the letters A.W. on the back of his left hand.

"Your initials spell AW. Awwww." I giggle. "So cute." Ari poured a glass of champagne for all of us, and I am, under no uncertain terms, feeling the effects of it.

"Yours spell BS." We alarm the people standing and chatting immediately around us with our sudden bursts of laughter.

The wedding planner and her company did a wonderful job with the decorations because now that the sun has set, the radiant lighting and ambience in our backyard are magical. The beautiful décor resembles an enchanted forest.

The five *mehndi* designers are stationed under a wooden archway that's centered in the northern part of the backyard and covered with white flowers and greenery. There are cushions laid out on the ground to allow for comfortable seating while the artists work. The layout of the backyard centers around the *mehndi* archway like it's a stage, and the remainder of the backyard is the theater, so to speak.

There are twinkle lights spread all around, and my favorite touch is the dark wooden benches and tables for guests to sit on instead of the usual plastic tables with tablecloths. There are also dark wooden standing cocktail tables near the bar, where Aman, Ari, and I are standing. Fake trees are spread out around the backyard, which are covered with forest green leaves and small white flowers. The fence surrounding the backyard is adorned with hanging white flowers as well.

The DJ plays soft melodic music, adding to the romantic atmosphere, and I hear the rhythmic sound of the water drops hitting the smooth cement structure of the water fountain that's centered in the backyard. The space is so very elaborately decorated that I momentarily forget I'm in my parents' backyard.

Aman, Ari, and I have each had about two glasses of champagne on empty stomachs, although Aman managed to eat a few appetizers between drinks. Being the responsible one, he takes charge of ensuring we eat something substantial before we continue drinking.

Devan joins us after completing some of his compulsory mingling, saying he's desperate for a shot. "At least that will make this bearable until I'm done and can relax."

Unable to say no to the groom during his special week, Aman offers to go to the bar to get three single shots and one double shot for Devan. Devan joins him while Ari and I use their absence to devour the delicious food.

I glance around after I'm finished eating and spot Devan and Aman still at the bar. Devan makes eye contact with me and visibly waves some guests toward us, who likely halted Devan to congratulate him. They're speaking to two girls I haven't seen before, but they must be friends or colleagues of Devan's.

"I already knew this guy was going to be popular this week." Devan gestures toward Aman as he and Aman rejoin us, tequila shots in hand. Aman smiles but doesn't elaborate for Devan.

"What do you mean?" Ari asks before I'm able to.

"You know those two girls that we were talking to at the bar? One of them is a close client. She brought her sister as her plus one, and the sister was painfully obvious in showing her interest in Aman."

Like my brother, I'm not surprised. Neither is Aman, but he downplays the encounter.

"Happens." Aman changes the subject. "All right, Dev. Let's take this shot."

"Yes!" Ari exclaims. The four of us gather our individual shot glasses and cheer.

"To the groom!" Aman shouts, and some guests standing nearby clap and cheer with us.

We all make the funny face one makes when taking a shot of alcohol. It's smooth but slightly harsh toward the end. At least Devan and Aman brought lime wedges to soften the blow.

Devan spends a few more moments with us before he begrudgingly continues his rounds.

"You're almost done," I encourage him as he walks off. "When you are, come join us," I add, although I know that it's unlikely Devan will be able to spend much of the evening with us. He *is* the man of the hour.

One of our cousins, Jay, joins us, taking Devan's place in the group. Jay is between mine and Devan's age. In fact, I think he's closer to Aman's age, maybe slightly younger than him.

Jay is humble and charismatic, and I think that's why we gravitate toward each other. He's one of my favorite cousins. And he loves Ari because he enjoys her energy. Everyone does.

I'm holding a small Punjabi-style clutch that contains both my and Ari's phones. I feel one of the two phones vibrate. When

I undo the latch of the clutch, the phone screen on my phone is lit up. I'm not expecting a text from anyone.

MARCUS: HOW'S THE EVENT? I BET YOU LOOK STUNNING.

I suppose I'm vaguely smiling because Ari lightly pinches me to get my attention. She eyes my phone, but I gently shake my head, indicating that we can't discuss this now.

Tucking my phone away into my clutch, I turn my attention back toward the group. Jay is chatting away, Ari is listening to him, and Aman is studying me.

My smile fades, and I concentrate on his gaze. *"You okay?"* I mouth, my eyebrows furrowed with curiosity.

He nods, then returns his attention to what Jay is saying. "Their wide receiver is killing the game right now," Aman adds.

This sends a passionate Jay in another direction of the conversation. I completely missed that they were talking about football.

Judging by his reaction, I'm sure Aman can guess it was Marcus who texted me. Even though he hasn't admitted to it, and I've never explicitly asked him, it's obvious that Aman doesn't like Marcus. The *why* he doesn't like him has yet to be ascertained.

When I glimpse Devan walking to the *mehndi* arch to get his simple design, I politely excuse myself from the group to follow my brother. Now is the perfect time. I want to get my *mehndi* done when he gets his design.

"Hey!" I lightly nudge Devan.

"Are you joining me?" Devan gestures toward the designers.

"Yes!" I'm excited. "What are you going to get?"

"I'm going to get Alina's name, and that's it. We agreed that I would get something small."

"It's sweet that you're getting that."

He smiles. "I might have them add a little star at the end. What're you getting?" Devan asks in Punjabi.

"I want to get a rose design for one hand and something else for the other."

He snickers knowingly. "I should have also guessed that." It's no secret among those who are close to me that I love roses.

Feeling a sudden rush of affection for my brother, I lock him in a brief side hug.

"What's that for?" He chuckles, gently rubbing my arms in return.

"I'm so happy for you. I mean, you guys were obviously going to get married, but it's finally here."

"Yeah, it feels a little strange. For all intents and purposes, we're already married, but this solidifies it."

The *mehndi* designers summon us both to sit down to commence our respective designs. Devan's is very simple and doesn't take more than five minutes. My design has more intricate detail and takes longer. My first design is an aerial view of a rose, and my second is a peacock.

Once done, they instruct us to come back after it dries so they can dab it with a lemon water and sugar solution to darken the *mehndi*.

The guests seem to be thoroughly enjoying themselves. Aman, Ari, Jay, and I are especially having a great time together. Amidst our enjoyment, the sister of Devan's client stops by to chat and, according to her, "Introduce herself to the groom's sisters." Her name is Seera.

Devan was right. It's incredibly obvious that she's taken by Aman, and her desire to introduce herself to us is a pretense to chat with him. Ari and I exchange blatant glances with each other as we witness her and Aman's interactions. It's difficult to determine if Aman is interested in her too, but he's certainly being polite.

Seera has moved on from asking about law school to asking what Aman likes to do for fun. She keeps brazenly opening a window for Aman to suggest that they engage in an activity together, but he neglects to take the opportunity. I gleam with pride at my best friend's poker face.

"Do you want to get a drink?" she finally invites him.

"Sure. You guys want to get a drink?" Aman asks the rest of us. If Aman wanted to go alone with her, he would have just asked if we wanted something. Instead, he asked if we wanted to get a drink, implying that he wants us to come with him. Out of Jay, Ari, and me, I'm the only one who knows Aman well enough to catch this subtle hint.

"Yeah! That sounds great." I play along, overexaggerating my willingness.

Seera doesn't seem too pleased initially, but she doesn't dwell on it. What is she going to do?

"Are you going to the wedding?" She directs the question only toward Aman, as the answer for the rest of us must be obvious—to her.

"Yes, I am," he answers distractedly, handing our drinks to me and Ari, and without reciprocating the question.

I don't think Aman is interested in her, and I can't help but feel a strange satisfaction in his disinterest in her.

"Thank you," we say, and he briefly smiles.

"Are you coming to the events?" Jay asks Seera.

"I wasn't planning on it, but I may just." She not-so-discreetly eyes Aman, who's not paying the slightest bit of attention to her.

It seems that we have a developing love triangle. Jay may be interested in Seera, Seera is interested in Aman, and Aman is interested in his drink. I giggle to myself but apparently a bit too loudly.

Aman hears and looks at me, perplexed. "What is it?" he asks in Punjabi.

"Nothing." I avoid eye contact with him and erratically move my eyes around, which probably makes it blatantly obvious that I'm lying.

He peers at me but is distracted by Seera once again.

She cheers the group before taking a sip of her drink, starting with Aman and ending with me.

"To this week," Aman says.

chapter 31

After the drink we had with Seera, Aman stopped drinking to give himself plenty of time to sober up before driving us back to San Francisco. He chose to be the responsible one for this week since it's my brother's wedding.

But he told me, in no uncertain terms, that during the reception, he was going to fully enjoy himself. I didn't dare argue with him because I want him to savor the moments as well. He deserves it. Better yet, he *needs* it.

At the end of the *mehndi*, my parents try to convince us to stay the night, to which Aman almost gives in, but I remind him that we don't have any of our things for tomorrow's function. Eventually, my parents forfeited and let us go back to San Francisco with the promise to return as early as possible the next morning.

It's late enough in the night for there to be minimal traffic on the highway back to San Francisco. I make conversation with Aman to keep him alert and awake during the drive home. However, it's difficult for me to mask how tired I'm feeling, and Aman knows it.

"Did you enjoy the *mehndi*?" I ask him immediately after I yawn exhaustedly.

"It was amazing," he says reminiscently. "It bums me out that this week is only a few days, and then we have to go back to our normal lives."

Suddenly wide awake, I look at him in disbelief. "I was thinking the same thing earlier today."

He grins. "More of a reason to make the most of it."

I snicker in agreement. "What did you think of Seera?"

He doesn't answer. Instead, he increases his driving speed, and I study him curiously. Aman isn't paying attention to me but is repeatedly examining the rearview mirror. I turn back slightly but don't really notice anything.

"What happened?" I ask in Punjabi.

He's still quiet.

"Aman?"

"This car behind us is aggressively tailing us."

"Wait, what?" I ask, not fully comprehending what he's saying.

"Yeah." He sounds distracted as he maneuvers from one lane to the next.

I look back again and realize what's happening when I see a car immediately swerve behind us in the lane we just changed into.

Whoever is driving the car definitely isn't accidentally too close because he or she is clearly, even deliberately, on our tail.

Is this a mistake? This is a rental car with which we have no previous association. How can someone be following us? How does anyone even know that we're in this car? My mind races with questions.

"Should I call the police?" My voice mildly trembles.

"Hold on." His tone is calm and level as he focuses on driving as carefully as one can under the circumstances. Aman doesn't sound scared in the slightest. Instead, he sounds determined.

He quickly reaches over and squeezes my hand to pacify me before he returns his full attention to the wheel. You'd think he was a professional race car driver.

The driver behind us drives erratically. I wonder if he or she is drunk, but whoever it is seems to be fixated on our car. There aren't a lot of cars on the highway, but there are enough.

I'm panicking, and my chest feels heavy. Each attempt to breathe feels like a difficult task, as if some air refuses to come out of my lungs.

I peek over at Aman, and he's still concentrated on the wheel and road. We've both been silent for the past few minutes.

"Aman."

"Hold on." He looks back and forth between the rearview mirror and any traffic ahead of him.

"Aman, this isn't our car," is all I can manage to say. *How is that even relevant?* I ask myself.

I'm scared, and he can tell. Finally, he says something.

"Ban, don't worry. You're okay." He speaks as though he's in a hurry, which he is. Then, he adds, "I got you," now taking his time with and emphasizing the three words. *I got you.*

Silence fills the car once again, and it feels like an eternity before it's broken.

The driver suddenly changes lanes to the one immediately to our left—Aman's side—but maneuvers in such a way as to intimidate us.

"Can you see who it is?" I ask with urgency in my voice. My stomach is queasy with panic, the alcohol from the night exacerbating the feeling.

"No." His response is succinct.

Suddenly, my instincts direct me to tell Aman to take the next exit with a physical barricade at the last possible moment, where the erratic driver can't preempt or predict the sudden change in direction. This will compel him or her to continue on the highway to avoid a crash.

We're already in the lane that's second to the last on the right side of the highway. Aman speeds up and miraculously makes a successful transition from the current lane to the exit lane for the highway that leads to downtown San Francisco and the baseball stadium.

The erratic driver is unable to mimic our maneuver at the last minute and continues on the highway as we steer toward the exit.

I must've been holding my breath for the last few seconds. As soon as we lose the driver and transition to the second highway, I breathe deeply and freely, my nerves beginning to calm. Everything seems quiet, still. The road, the car's engine, our surroundings, us—everything.

"Are you okay?" Aman breaks the silence, his voice low.

"Yes." I pause. "Are you?"

"Yeah."

"You were great," he assures me.

No, Aman. I was useless until the absolute end.

I can't help looking around and behind us again out of paranoia.

"I think we should take an exit and then take side streets back in case that guy decides to come back and follow us," he says.

"You saw it was a guy?"

"Kind of. I'm not entirely sure."

"I don't understand it. Why would someone do that? We just rented this car. It doesn't make sense."

Aman doesn't answer my, albeit rhetorical questions with anything more than a profound sigh. He looks behind him and takes the next exit.

This new route will extend our driving time by about fifteen minutes since the impromptu route change sent us in the opposite direction of home.

I don't know what's going through Aman's head, but I am unnerved. The combination of the alcohol, the high energy of the *mehndi*, and the surge of adrenaline from the ride home has left me in a state of delirium, exhausted and drained. This isn't how I imagined my brother's wedding week starting.

Although it's highly unlikely, and my thoughts are primarily motivated by fear right now, I wonder if the same thing will happen when we go home from the *jaggo* tomorrow night.

Before I realize we're back, Aman parallel parks the car in a spot that is miraculously directly in front of our apartment. We didn't utter a word the rest of the ride home.

He removes the keys from the ignition and doesn't shift or speak. When I glance over at him, he's resting his hands on his thighs as he stares absently straight ahead, temporarily frozen.

"Aman?" I'm the first to say anything since we arrived.

Another few seconds pass before he mumbles, "Hm?" He's lost in thought.

"What are you thinking about?" He appears very serious.

"I..." He pauses.

"What?" I ask.

"What if you were hurt." He phrases it as a statement rather than a question.

"What? What do you mean? Why would something happen to me?" His comment both confuses and terrifies me.

He gazes at me with a blank expression. "Nothing. Let's get inside."

Now, I'm unable to move as he unbuckles his seatbelt and steps out of the car. When he notices this, he leans down toward the driver's seat window and gently knocks on it, startling me.

Although he can discern the fear in my expression, he smiles reassuringly.

As soon as I raise my hand toward the door handle, I suddenly see a car's headlights shining brightly on my face, approaching slowly in our direction. I reflexively squint at the approaching car. My heart jumps, and I feel that gut-wrenching feeling again.

This car has captured Aman's attention as well because he stands up straight, waiting for it to pass. We both know that, at this time of night, our neighborhood is fairly quiet.

It feels like a century before the car is close enough for us to decipher who the driver is. As soon as it passes, I see a middle-aged woman driving with two distracted, fighting children in the backseat.

I exhale softly in relief, and Aman returns his attention back to me. Before he says anything, I get out of the car, and we quietly head upstairs.

Aman opens the door to our apartment, and once we're both inside, he locks the door behind us, chaining it shut with dramatic effect.

This isn't abnormal. We always lock and chain the door, but the sound of the lock and chain tonight is much more obvious than it normally is to me.

He walks into the kitchen while I remain standing near the entryway, the door locked and chained behind me.

He places two chilled water bottles on our island countertop, well aware that drinking cold water helps calm me down.

"Ban," he says, and I look in his direction. He stands as still as a statue, holding his water bottle in his hand.

Somewhat in a trance, I look at him first and then at the countertop, where the water bottle for me rests. He slightly pushes the water bottle in my direction, which spurs me to walk toward the counter.

"Ban," he says again to get my attention. I chug the water as if I haven't had water in days, the dryness in my mouth evaporating. I didn't realize how parched I was.

I set the empty water bottle down on the counter immediately in front of me and turn toward Aman. The same vulnerability from earlier is plastered all over his face, except this time, there's also concern, care, and curiosity. He's all of those things, but he hardly ever displays all four emotions at the same time.

"Talk to me. Are you okay?" he asks.

In this moment, I can honestly feel his friendship, his protectiveness, and his love for me. But for the first time, he also appears frightened.

I avert my gaze to the center of the island counter, avoiding eye contact with Aman as I feel tears emerge. Experiencing the excitement of my brother's wedding event mere hours ago, concurrently with the experience of being chased by a lunatic in a car, makes me feel disoriented.

Aman has shown such concern towards me, but I, selfishly, haven't returned the sentiment. Right now, we're alone, and both of us are able to express ourselves. Openly.

I look up at him, ready, the tears no longer on the verge of falling. His expression of raw emotion, again, softens my own anxiety and fear. What is it about this particular look of his that mesmerizes me?

I place my hand on his arm to offer some sort of solace, and he keeps his dark, soulful eyes locked on me. "How are you feeling?" I finally, genuinely, ask him.

"I'm okay," he whispers.

"Aman, be real." I'm not convinced by his words when his face tells me a different story.

"Really. I'm okay. I'm just worried about you." *What if you were hurt,* is the main thought on his mind.

I wonder how he would feel if something did, in fact, actually happen to me. He'd blame himself. I immediately dismiss the thought.

"I'm good, Aman." I step closer to him, gently rubbing his arm and inhaling the vivid smell of his lingering cologne. The scent that has been a constant reminder of how cared for I am simply by Aman's presence. I marvel at how a scent can elicit so many emotions.

I try my hardest to smile reassuringly—I can at least do that for him. But I'm not sure if my smile appears forced. He nods silently without saying a word.

After realizing how close I'm standing to him, I feel incredibly self-conscious. Stepping away from Aman, I throw my water bottle away as a distraction from looking him in the eye. Aman doesn't move, but I still feel his eyes on me.

My glance catches the time on the microwave—it's now past midnight.

"It's really late. We should go to sleep. We have to be up early again tomorrow. Or today." I shift to face him. "I should have listened to you. We should've stayed with my parents tonight."

"No, Ban. Don't think that. We had to come home tonight," Aman reassures me.

"Let's forget about it. You're right. We should go to sleep," he says, disappearing into his room.

chapter 32

Day two of the wedding festivities has arrived. It's only seven in the morning, and we're already halfway to Palo Alto. We left earlier today than we did yesterday. Despite having coffee, I can't stop yawning, which makes Aman yawn as well.

Originally, we were going to leave midday after evidence and criminal law. Following the mysterious cancelation of both classes this week, we decided to go as soon as we woke up, as my parents made us promise. Plus, we couldn't sleep properly last night. For obvious reasons.

"We should try to nap once we're there," I say, thinking about how difficult it'll be to maintain energy during the *jaggo*, a very high-energy function, if we're as tired as we currently are.

"I'm going to sleep as soon as we get there." He pauses. "On your bed." He aims to induce a reaction out of me as he gives me a sidelong glance and a smile. He's returning to his normal, silly self.

"I'll push you off the bed," I reply with my own touch of wit, and he laughs.

I didn't tell my family when we left San Francisco, but I know for certain that my mom will be awake. I scan through my text messages, searching for Ari's name to text her and see if she is too.

When I see Marcus' name in my message list, I recall that I never responded to his text from last night. I meant to once we reached home, but the lunatic on the road completely threw me off.

> **ME:** HEY, SORRY FOR THE LATE REPLY. LAST NIGHT WAS CRAZY. WEDDING WEEK IS GOING REALLY WELL. HOW'S YOUR WEEK?

I'm tempted to ask him whether he knows why evidence lecture was canceled. Since he's also my TA, I want to be careful not to intertwine the friendship part with the TA part, making it more uncomfortable than it needs to be.

> **MARCUS:** FORGOT ABOUT ME, EH? I'M GLAD YOU'RE HAVING A GOOD TIME. SEND PICS OF THE EVENTS WHEN YOU CAN.

His message sounds passive-aggressive. I don't think we're at the point where I'm obligated to text him. Irritated by his tone, I ignore his message.

Before I know it, we arrive at the front of my parents' home. Unlike yesterday, the driveway to their house is empty. Given the early hour, the neighborhood is a ghost town. There's a slight fog letting out an eerie vibe, which will likely dissipate come late morning.

My parents' house is huge, but luckily, the front door is within a good range for me to notice it open.

Turning my entire attention to the movement at the front of their house, I notice my mom emptying a pot of water into the plant bed that runs along it. She hasn't noticed us yet and is captivated by her gardening.

Her watering of plants at such a busy time of the week can only mean one thing—she's stressed. Understandably so. She's doing the most out of all of us with the homemade preparations for the wedding.

For the *jaggo*, it's traditional for the families of the bride and groom to each pass out a bag of sweets when the guests depart. It's common for the sweets to be prepared by a restaurant, but my mom was set on making them herself. Devan tried to convince her that it wasn't necessary, but there was no talking her out of it. After all, it is her firstborn's wedding.

It must be a nostalgia thing. Her mom, my grandmother, made everything by hand when she married my dad. Back then, my grandparents couldn't afford a big, lavish wedding like my parents' can now for Devan. Hell, Devan can afford his big, lavish wedding without any sort of help from my parents.

Aman manages to squeeze the car into a parking spot relatively close by. We're both within sight and hearing distance of my parents' house, and when Aman closes the trunk of the car, the sound is loud enough to divert my mom's attention away from her plants.

"This early?" She hugs and kisses me with an exhausted smile. "We weren't expecting you guys until later." Then, she hugs Aman.

"We wanted to get here as soon as we could. The excitement of the week woke us up early." I feel bad for blatantly lying to my mom.

Aman knows exactly why we're here as early as we are. Since this is my family, he leaves it to me to decide whether I want to tell them about last night or not. I'm certain he understands that, given the circumstances, this isn't the best time to make my family worry about a potentially problematic lunatic and what was hopefully a one-off incident.

"Mom, do you want some help?" She glances toward her plants.

"No, baby. Aman, you guys go inside and get some rest. In a few hours, we'll be full speed for the *jaggo*."

My mom must have read my mind or seen it on my face because I felt the exhaustion hit as soon as I saw her watering the plants. Something about how peaceful and serene she looked as she watered them made me feel secure.

"How much did you sleep, Mom? Come inside and take a nap before Kiran Auntie and Nishu Auntie come, please." Although there will be others who will help my mom, these two are the most reliable.

"I'm writing this week off, honey."

"Where's Dad?"

"Sleeping."

"Mom, you of all people need to get sleep. At least rest. Come on."

It doesn't take convincing beyond that. She knows that she needs to be well-rested for the week to enjoy it.

Aman carries our bags upstairs to my room and the room that he was getting ready in yesterday.

"Thank you," I say as he sets my bag in my room, flashing his dashing smile before going across the hall.

Without further thought, I collapse onto my bed and immediately succumb to the peace and warmth of my comforter and mattress.

I idly glance around my room and study the way I decorated it—a snapshot of myself in high school. It's been nearly a decade since I've lived here.

A preserved, crystalized beach stone on the shelf in my room brings back a chemistry lab memory. Tej and I were lab partners the entire year. I was enthralled with how we were able to create crystal with a simple stone, and Tej let me keep it even though I could tell he really liked it.

We're supposed to meet up once the wedding festivities are over, but I wonder if it's a good idea. *Do I really want to go there?* He's someone that I used to know but don't anymore. Not really.

For a moment, we both thought he was attending Devan's wedding through a connection with Alina's parents, but it ended up being a different wedding, also near San Francisco.

It almost seemed like he was suggesting crashing Devan's events. He strangely kept asking for details about Devan's wedding without alluding to any details of the wedding he was attending.

I haven't mentioned Tej to Aman yet, only to Mark.

Mark is always in favor of me meeting and talking to new people. I wish he was also here to celebrate with me and my family. Having Aman here is wonderful, but having Mark would be the cherry on top.

My phone buzzes in my hand, interrupting my thoughts. I have two texts from Aman while he's literally across the hall. I almost drop my phone on my face, something he would've undoubtedly laughed at if he saw it.

> AMAN: ISN'T SOMEONE ELSE SUPPOSED TO STAY IN THE ROOM I'M IN?
>
> AMAN: WHAT IF THEY COME AND THEY SEE A BIG PUNJABI GUY SLEEPING? LOL

I chuckle. I know I'd be startled if I walked into my designated room and saw someone asleep on the bed.

> ME: LOL. THE PEOPLE WHO WERE SUPPOSED TO STAY IN YOUR ROOM AREN'T STAYING ANYMORE. AND YOUR FACE IS PRETTY SCARY.

He sends me an eye-rolling emoji in response. Thinking that's all he's going to say, I set my phone down on my chest.

AMAN: YOU KNOW YOU THINK I'M HANDSOME.

I smile shyly, suppressing the unexpected nervousness I feel when I daydream about how handsome I truly think he is.

ME: YOU ARE.
ME: NOT.

He laughs loud enough for me to be able to hear him from my room.

And then I drift into sleep, assuming he does too.

chapter 33

Aman is wearing a *kurta* at my brother's *jaggo*. I wasn't expecting that in the slightest. He said he wasn't wearing Punjabi attire at any of the home events. I didn't even know that he owned a *kurta*, the Punjabi version of a *sherwani*, except it's more modest in design. Unlike a *sherwani*, it doesn't include a scarf.

Aman's is a simple, black Punjabi *kurta*. Simple is more traditional.

He's also rocking a *kaintha*, a golden pendant that some Punjabi men usually wear as an accessory to the *kurta*. But what really completes his full Punjabi attire are his Punjabi *jutti*, flats decorated with a Punjabi flare.

I almost don't recognize him when I enter the backyard. His hair is parted to the side, and his beard is perfectly trimmed.

Aman's *kurta* hugs his body, and the way his sleeves are rolled up to his forearms highlights the indentation of his muscles. His dad's black onyx bracelet circles his wrist comfortably, as it does every day. He looks unfairly attractive.

I blatantly stare at him as he chats with Jay, unable to look away and taking advantage of the fact that his attention is elsewhere. There's something about a Punjabi guy in complete Punjabi attire, but Aman leaves me dazed.

He'd never let me live it down if he caught me looking at him the way I currently am. He would not stop teasing me and would grin the entire time, basking in the moment.

Come to think of it, *Bani, why are you staring at him that way?*

To my relief, Devan comes up behind me, forcing me to finally stop fixating on Aman.

Devan is also wearing a *kurta.* He had to fight Alina on that, but we all agreed that the groom is the one person who should be wearing one. His is much fancier than Aman's because he's the groom. It's a very unique rose gold color and has gold embroidery and patterns. He looks royal.

Into the night, the wedding party and close relatives will enter the venue with colorfully decorated, candlelit vessels set atop their heads and dance. These days, it's more common to use battery-powered candles.

There's a well-known song that's played during the dance at the *jaggo,* along with singing by the wedding party. The dance is the center of the event, and the main idea is to celebrate the upcoming nuptials. It's an event that is specific to Punjab.

My outfit was specifically planned to adhere to the theme of the evening. I'm wearing a tight, red-fitted *palazzo* suit. A *palazzo* suit's pants are loose and flare toward the bottom. The top of the suit is medium-length, skin-hugging, and has tight-fitting half sleeves with green and gold embroidery. My *chunni* is yellow with gold embroidery that resembles the embroidery on my top. It's not as fancy as the suit I wore yesterday, but I have accessorized it to be a truly Punjabi outfit, emphasizing the cultural appeal.

My hair is tied in a braid with a *paranda*, a hair ornament that most resembles a necklace for hair. The *paranda* elongates my hair like a dressed-up extension. Like Aman, I'm also wearing Punjabi *juttis* to complement my full Punjabi outfit.

I'm not one to toot my own horn, but my outfit, makeup, and accessories look lovely this evening. My makeup is neutral and gold, with red lipstick to perfectly complement the color of my suit. I wanted my lip color to make a statement.

Since Aman seems busy with Jay, I look for Ari amongst the fast-growing crowd in my parents' backyard. She left to come downstairs only a few minutes before me, but I'm unable to spot her.

I do spot Seera amidst the crowd, the brazen woman who was obviously interested in Aman from the night before. She's talking to someone I don't recognize, but shockingly enough, she's consistently looking in Aman's direction. Aman, of course, doesn't notice.

Continuing my search for my sister, I'm fascinated with how different the scenery and decorations are from the night before. My parents' massive backyard has transformed from an elegant and white flower fairy-tale forest to a bright, colorful, and vibrant set full of Punjabi decorations.

The decorators have emphasized bright colors such as blues, purples, yellows, greens, pinks, oranges, and reds, which is very normal for a *jaggo*. They've set up electric candles all along the fence, alternating between the seven colors. Between each of the candles are thin, sheer swaths of fabric that are intertwined and placed as garlands along the fence.

In the two rear corners of the yard, there are platforms for the women to sit on and sing. The platforms have colorful pillows and Punjabi musical instruments set atop them.

Four tall polls are set in the corners of the yard. From the top of each pole hangs a massive, sheer but sturdy yellow cloth, each meeting in the center of the yard at a pole near the water fountain. The cloth makes a sort of unofficial tent over the entire yard.

Ornamenting the yellow fabric are two multi-colored cloths, including green, pink, and orange, which are decorated with intricate gold embroidery. They sparkle as they wave from the fence to where they meet at the center pole, which has been entirely covered with yellow and red flowers.

Tons of guests take pictures in a beautifully decorated carriage that's stationed on the north side of the yard. The carriage is gold and white in color and adorned with multi-colored flowers.

The guest tables and chairs are all light gold with either a sheer royal blue or purple tablecloth, alternating from table to table. Each table has a centerpiece in either the decorative form of a vertical and skinny standing *tabla*, a Punjabi hand drum, or a *tumbi*, an instrument similar to a guitar but with a single string.

My favorite part is the bar, for less obvious reasons. The entire bar platform imitates a heavy-weight truck in Punjab. It's very colorfully adorned with a string of red roses on each side. The trucks in Punjab are similarly decorated, but not as glamorously.

There's writing in Punjabi on the truck that translates to "Devan and Alina." There's a delicate yet meticulous design of painted, colorful flowers across the hood and body of the truck. The bartenders are behind the part of the truck that would be the flatbed structure.

I've never seen anything like it.

As I make a second scan across the backyard, my eyes halt on a familiar face that is already observing me. Aman.

He studies me with a look of surprise before he gestures me over to him and Jay. Since I still have not spotted my sister, I oblige Aman's request, knowing Ari will find me once she's free.

My bangles and my anklets jingle with each step and movement. I've always loved this sound. It makes me feel like a true *Punjaban*, Punjabi woman.

Crossing to them, I'm startled by a sudden hand on my shoulder. Ari came rushing from the direction of the side entrance.

"*Where have you been?*" I ask her.

"I was in the front. There was some guy walking around the neighborhood, asking about Punjabi weddings and our family. He was a little weird and freaked me out a bit. Good thing there were tons of people outside."

"Did you recognize who it was?" I ask.

"He looked kind of familiar. Looked like a completely normal guy…maybe a new neighbor? I don't know. Something about him was sketchy."

"Well, I'm glad you left." *I wonder who it was.*

Ari and I are intentionally dressed similarly. The color of our suits is different, but their style and our hair match. As we walk together, side by side, tons of attendees look and smile at us with admiration. We probably look like twins.

"I didn't know you even owned a *kurta*," I say to Aman once we're closer to him and Jay.

"Yeah, A!" Ari calls him that sometimes. "You look *hot*! With your beard trimmed and everything."

Aman's blushing. I don't recall ever seeing him blush. I enjoy seeing this new side of his personality. He looks adorable.

"You both look beautiful," Aman says to the pair of us. His gaze pauses a tad longer when looking at me. I'm pretty sure I'm the one that's blushing now.

"Thank you," Ari and I say at the same time.

"I'm in awe of these decorations," Jay says, adding a much-needed distraction.

"That's the first thing I thought as soon as I came outside," I say wholeheartedly.

"Speaking of which, let's check this bar out," Aman adds, unsurprisingly.

As soon as we reach the bar, a group of girls gape at Aman and Jay. I lightly nudge Ari, turning her attention toward the group, and she chuckles out loud.

"Nothing, nothing," Ari says when the boys turn around in curiosity. "Who is that?" Ari whispers to me.

"I have no idea."

At the same time, Seera approaches on the opposite end. Aman, again, oblivious to it. Or maybe he notices it but doesn't react. If that's the case, then I'm amazed by his ability to hide it.

"Hey!" she says to the group, positioning herself closest to Aman. Aman responds with a respectable level of enthusiasm, although not nearly as energetically as Seera.

His indifference is slightly surprising because she does look very much like his type.

"Doesn't this place look sick?" Jay directs the question toward Seera, referring to the décor when he asks. I haven't forgotten the interest he showed her last night.

"Yeah, it's nice." But she doesn't seem impressed and comes across as relatively snobby as well.

"These are some of the best decorations I've ever seen. Whoever Devan and his family hired really nailed the décor for these events." Aman takes the opportunity to call her out on it in his own way. "Excuse me. I need to use the restroom."

He said *family* to remind her that two of Devan's family members are standing right there. With that, he takes his drink from the bar and walks away, leaving the rest of us behind. Evidently, he doesn't need to use the restroom because he goes to the buffet, not inside the house.

I applaud his boldness but am also astounded by it. He reacted as if she had personally offended him, which I'm certain wasn't her intention in the slightest.

"Well, that was awkward," Ari says immediately after Seera makes an excuse and walks away. She isn't afraid to articulate what I'm sure we're all thinking.

"She did sound kind of rude," Jay says. His interest seemingly diminished after witnessing Seera's condescending tone.

The rest of us join Aman at the buffet. He's laser-focused on the dishes and doesn't notice us approaching him as he hoards a mountain of food on his plate.

"Oye. Leave some for the rest of us." Ari's relationship with Aman is very endearing yet playful. Aman nearly giggles, making a funny face at Ari.

"Why'd you leave so abruptly?" I ask as I grab a plate, although I know the answer.

"Hmm?" He's distracted.

"Just now. When we were at the bar?"

"Ah. I was hungry, and the food smelled amazing."

Typical of Aman to avoid telling me, even though we both know the real reason why he left, but I want to hear him say it. I like hearing him say it.

As soon as we finish eating, my mom and dad come to get us for the *jaggo* dance, which is starting soon. Aman is the most excited of all of us. He is exuberant at the thought of dancing with the *khadaa*, the beautifully decorated vessel with the lights, on his head. Devan, Ari, Aman, and I will each have a *khadaa* to place on our heads. My parents will dance holding a *danda,* a long and decorated stick, while relatives hold other Punjabi *jaggo* props.

Devan hears the onset of the infamous *jaggo* song that's played at almost every Punjabi wedding, which is his cue to start walking and dancing from the side entrance of my parents' house. He leads us along the path to the center of the backyard and onto the dance floor. Ari is in front of me, and Aman is behind me. I struggle with the *khadaa* at first but slowly get the hang of it. Every now and then, Aman helps position the *khadaa* properly on my head when he notices it slipping.

Once at the center of the dance floor, we all congregate into a circle and continue dancing to the *jaggo* song. The energy in the backyard is unmistakably spirited and full of elation. There are smiling faces everywhere I look.

The merriment is very powerful and makes one forget any negativity. Just as I do.

chapter 34

Both wedding events we've had thus far have been major successes. The main events that are left are the *mayian*, the wedding, and the reception.

Around eleven last night, Aman and I left my parents' house to go back to San Francisco. We successfully made it home without a repeat of the prior night. I had to admonish myself when I was dwelling on something that was unlikely to repeat itself. And it didn't.

We make the trek down south early Thursday morning again since the *mayian* is a daytime event. The *mayian* is the part of the wedding where I always feel how imminent the actual wedding ceremony is. In exactly two days, my brother will be getting married.

During the *mayian*, family members and relatives gather to rub *haldi*, a turmeric and flour paste on the bride or groom, whichever group they're a part of, to make their skin glow. It's traditional—but also the simplest of all the functions, so to speak. As a result, my parents reserved this for very close relatives only.

I'd guesstimate not more than seventy people are at the *mayian*, whereas there were nearly triple in attendance at each of the other two events. It's not only the smallest event, guest-wise, but also the shortest.

Devan wanted at least one event to be intimate, and he happened to choose the one where he's going to look like he's received a yellow facial, except the facial will be all over his face, arms, and legs.

The *mayian* will be in the part of my parents' backyard that's immediately south of the water fountain, providing a beautiful backdrop. The designers created a five-foot-long *rangoli* on the floor, a colorful design made using colored powder. Devan will sit on a low stool while setting his feet at the northernmost part of the *rangoli*. The design is a circle of hearts with the letters "D" and "A" on both sides of the circle, an intricate design on the outer circle, and a light outline sketch of a lion in the center. The lion is the mascot of Devan and Alina's college, where they met.

There's a row of red and yellow rose petals starting from both sets of the deck stairs in the backyard that run to each side of the *rangoli*, forming an elongated pathway. Tall flower towers made of red and yellow daisies are set along each side of the rose pathway, separated a few feet apart from one another.

The weather is comfortable enough to tolerate standing outside while the festivities ensue. The October sun is bright and shining, but it's not unbearably hot. Sporadic gusts of wind help deter heat.

Right before guests begin arriving for the *mayian*, Devan shares that he planned a surprise for us, and he plans on telling us what it is once everyone leaves.

"It's your wedding week. We should be planning a surprise for you." My mom glimmers with pride.

"Mom, you've done everything and beyond. I can organize a little something for my family if I want to."

"What do you think it is?" I ask Aman.

He shrugs, laughing. "We'll find out in a few hours."

Unsatisfied with his response but acknowledging that he's right, I divert my mind toward preparation for the *mayian*.

My suit is as simple as the ceremony today—yellow with multi-colored flowers. My hair is in an unadorned side braid, and my makeup is very light. A little yellow flower hairclip my mom handed out for the girls to wear during the ceremony adds a cute touch.

One blunt auntie, who's acquainted with my family, rudely commented that I'm not dressed as if my brother is getting married. I responded by saying, "I've received many compliments on the simplicity yet elegance of my suit." This seemed to have sent the message, because she didn't make any subsequent remarks before I walked away.

There's only so much I could say to an elder without being regarded as insolent, reflecting poorly on my parents' upbringing.

Upon second thought, why is she even at the *mayian*? Her family isn't regarded as close relatives of my family.

"She heard Kiran Auntie talk about it yesterday and insisted on coming," my mom explains while I help her carry out items to the *rangoli* set up.

"She invited herself?"

My mom looks at me with a disapproving face but is also grinning.

"Ignore her. I'll send a subliminal message to her showing that I don't appreciate her inviting herself to the *mayian* and then making such a rude comment to my baby during the event she invited herself to. Especially when my baby looks so beautiful."

She softly pinches my cheeks as an act of love and conciliation. Her responses are always artfully and skillfully delivered.

"Honey, we need to fix that part of the design," my mom adds, pointing to a blended segment of the design caused by the intermittent breeze.

As I grab a handful of colored powder, a sudden shadow replaces the sun that was blazing on me a few moments ago. I look up and see Aman standing, watching us as we correct the design.

"This is where the party's at," he says, kneeling to help.

He fills in the gaps that the wind ruined, fully focused. He adds a little red rose after my mom encourages him to include his own personal touch. Aman knows I love roses. Even though it's small compared to the rest of the design, the vibrant red is striking.

Before today, I'd been oblivious to Aman's artsy side. My brother's wedding is bringing out an entirely new side of him that I've never seen before in all the time I've known him. He's been hiding more than I realized.

"Did I tell you about this auntie who came up to me and basically told me that I don't look good enough for my brother's wedding?"

"I think this is the best you've ever looked," Aman says as he finalizes his touches on the *rangoli*, keeping his eyes on the design. I blush timidly, but Aman isn't looking in my direction to notice.

Before I can thank him, my mom and dad bring Devan over to the stool he'll sit on for the *mayian*. Four of us stand and hold a beautifully decorated red *chunni* over his head, and the rituals begin.

Since we want to be able to place as much *haldi* as we can on him, Devan needs to wear something that exposes the most skin—and something he's not overly attached to. The light gray tank top and red basketball shorts he's wearing will get covered with the *haldi* from the ceremony and *haldi* stains.

In the background, a group of aunties sings and chants trad-itional Punjabi songs. Given the simplicity of the event, the aunties are the sole providers of any sort of musical sound. Even without a speaker, they fill the backyard with their semi-off-key yet melodic voices.

When it's my parents' turn to rub the *haldi* on Devan, a few guests clap, adding to the background noise. Slowly, more attendees join in, and there's nothing but womanly and man-made sounds filling the atmosphere of the backyard. Devan is smiling and laughing, with yellow paste remnants all over his skin.

My mom puts *haldi* in his hair as a loving gesture, gently pet-ting his head. My dad cracks a joke in Punjabi as he rubs some on Devan's cheeks, and the eruption of clapping translates into an eruption of laughter. "I'm glad it's these cheeks. He's too big a boy for it to be the other set," he says.

When Aman puts the *haldi* on Devan, he quietly whispers something to him, but I'm not within earshot to decipher what it is. Devan laughs freely, and Aman's smile broadens as they talk. The videographer and photographer record and capture the pic-ture-perfect moment as it happens.

Eventually, Aman realizes he's monopolizing Devan from guests that are waiting to put *haldi* on him. After whispering one last joke, he pats Devan's shoulder and comes to stand right next to me, not saying a word as the merriment continues.

A half-hour later, lunch is served. I haven't eaten a thing all morning and am famished. While I pile *pakore*, or fried dumplings, on my plate, Aman takes one and eats it. He grins at me as he chews, his mouth full.

"You're literally right behind me!" I exclaim.

"It tastes better when I take it off your plate." He may not realize it, but simple, loving words like these from Aman—words of closeness—bring me great joy and give me immense comfort.

Aman is unaware of his value to me, and it doesn't help that I don't communicate it to him much.

He leads us to the cement ledge at the bottom of the deck stairs. At the moment, it's just the two of us. Ari and Jay are still in line for food.

We eat in silence, but there's an abundance of noise coming from the guests' chatter and laughter, plus the clanking of dishes from the food line.

"What are you thinking about?" Aman breaks the silence. I sense he's been keeping an eye on me.

"Hm?" I respond distractedly. "Nothing at all."

"Then why do you look lost in your thoughts?"

"This week is going by so fast."

"I know what you mean."

Since I have Aman alone, I take the opportunity to ask and gauge his interest level in Seera again. Each time I remember the subject, I'm not alone with him, or a lunatic is chasing after us, like the other night.

"What are your thoughts about Seera?"

"What do you mean?" He doesn't seem surprised that I'm asking him. He also doesn't seem interested in the topic at all.

"You know what I mean, Aman."

"There are no thoughts." The lack of enthusiasm in his voice is unmistakable.

"She seems to really be into you."

"Okay, and that means I have to be interested in her too?" I know he doesn't intend to flatter himself when he asks me this somewhat rhetorical question, but he does have a point.

"I'm not here to meet girls. I'm here to chill with my homie and celebrate my other homie's wedding." I smile at him. He's been very sweet this week.

"And when I say homie, I mean Ari. You already know the other one is Dev." He's side-eyeing me again to watch my reaction, and then erupts into laughter when I scoff at his add-on comment.

"You're something else, Mr. Wajla," I say laughingly.

"No, you are, Ms. Sethi."

Once all the guests leave my parents' house following the *mayian*, Devan gathers us in the family room to reveal the surprise he's planned for us, as promised.

"Okay. So." He positions his hands as if about to make a speech.

"Bro, you aren't presenting to us," Ari jokes and the rest of us laugh in agreement, including Devan.

"Alina and I wanted to thank our parents and families for everything that you've done for us this week. I know she's enjoying herself at all of her events, and I couldn't imagine a more exhilarating wedding week. As a thank you, we arranged for both of our families to have dinner tonight on a yacht in San Francisco. Alina's family is meeting us there."

As soon as Devan says the word "yacht," everyone vocally exclaims in elation. A few are surprised by such a gesture right in the middle of their wedding week.

"Honey, why did you do that?" my mom inevitably says, but she looks ecstatic. Devan has been stepping it up with his surprise planning.

"Because you, especially, are working hard to make this a memorable week for me. You deserve to enjoy and relax too." My mom smiles at her eldest child.

"We're going to the dock that's right on the Embarcadero. The yacht will sail under the Bay Bridge and the Golden Gate Bridge, and then it'll bring us back. The whole trip will take around two and a half hours. Shout out to Aman for helping me plan this for tonight. I couldn't have done this without you, man."

Everyone, especially me, looks at Aman in surprise, and he humbly nods to Devan's declaration of his help.

Aman knew all along.

chapter 35

Aman and I get a headstart to San Francisco to go home and change into more appropriate clothing.

Although he knew about tonight, neither Aman nor I are wearing appropriate clothes for dinner on a yacht. Knowing Devan, the yacht will be elegant, and all of my fancy clothing is in San Francisco. I don't plan on wearing anything extraordinarily fancy, but certainly an outfit that's in line with the theme of the evening.

As I peruse my closet for the best outfit, I select my black pencil skirt to wear with a loose black sheer blouse and a strappy black tank top underneath. After applying very light and simple makeup, I collect my black stiletto heels before I walk back into the living room.

Surprisingly, Aman isn't in the living room yet. He must still be getting ready. I slowly crouch down on the couch to strap on my heels, being careful with my tight pencil skirt.

"Aman? Ari texted that they're about twenty away." I secure a strap on my heel.

"Almost done!" he yells from behind his closed door.

The quietness and stillness of our apartment are unsettling as I look around it, waiting for Aman to finish up. Our entire week has essentially been spent in Palo Alto, and we've only been home to sleep. Everything looks untouched. Except I notice a law book on the floor near a rear window. Aman must've dropped it while I was getting dressed.

Aman's bedroom door finally opens, and I momentarily cease strapping on my heels when he appears in the living room. I do a double-take, breathing deeply, in awe of how insanely handsome he looks.

He's wearing cream slacks and a sophisticated medium gray sports coat, leaving the coat unbuttoned and his muscular torso prominent under a well-fitted, dark gray hooded sweater. His gelled hair is parted slightly to the side, and his beard looks even better than it did yesterday.

A waft of his cologne makes my skin prickle right as he approaches me. My chest flutters—the scent eliciting a different reaction from me tonight than it usually does.

"Wow." I can't believe that I'm actually speechless. I should be accustomed to his looks by now. He smirks, tying my stomach into knots. He knows I'm blatantly ogling him, but what he, thankfully, doesn't know is that I was doing the same thing at the *jaggo* yesterday.

"You literally look dashing."

I say "dashing" to add a bit of humor and diffuse any tension I may have inadvertently caused.

"Do I?" he finally says, a hint of flirtatiousness in his voice as he eyes me curiously. "You sound and look even more surprised."

I look down, feeling flushed. "No, no. Sorry. Uh. I'm just, uh, really digging that outfit." I can't believe I'm actually stuttering. What's wrong with me? This is Aman.

"I'm a handsome guy, Ban," he says, opening the refrigerator, then approaching me with a water bottle in hand. "You look lovely." The admiration in his gaze is hypnotizing.

"I'm a lovely girl, Aman." I mimic his response, falling out of the trance Aman momentarily pulled me into.

"That you are." He smirks enticingly and rubs his neck, reeling me right back in.

I clear my throat to overthrow the quickly escalating sentiment in the room. *Bani, stop it.* "Let's get a car there rather than drive," I say, changing the subject.

I rise from the couch with my heels securely fastened, feeling tall, and straighten my skirt. It's been some time since I wore high heels.

I struggle to maintain my balance, and Aman steadies me. For a quick moment, he locks his eyes with me and looks at me in an inexplicable way, in a way he hasn't before.

"I can't believe you kept this a secret this entire time." I clear my throat again, coarsely this time. "When did you guys start planning this?"

He chuckles. "Three months ago. The idea first occurred to us at the BBQ at your parents' house over the summer."

"Since before school started? Wow."

Aman closes the door behind us, and the tension that was in the air a few minutes ago dissipates as if our apartment is an insulated bubble.

On our way to the dock Devan told us to meet at, we drive through a neighborhood that has a bustling nightlife. It's Thursday evening, and there are increasing crowds on the sidewalks. We've been so immersed in school, the wedding, and Punjabi traditions, that normal life feels distant.

Seeing the bars reminds me that I have, once again, been ignoring my phone and any incoming text messages unless they're from my family members. I never responded to Marcus' passive aggressive-message yesterday, but he reached out again earlier this morning. He's trying, I guess.

I message him back, and he responds instantaneously.

MARCUS: ARE YOU ABLE TO MAKE SOME TIME FOR ME ON SUNDAY?

It may be too soon after the wedding for me to revert back to *normal* life, but perhaps it's the distraction I need.

ME: MAYBE. NEED TO CHECK WITH MY PARENTS IF THERE IS ANYTHING PLANNED.

I'm grateful my brother organized the yacht dinner. It adds to an already amazing week, making it that much more special.

"You're quiet," I say. When in fact, I am the one who's so preoccupied with my phone, including replying to Marcus, that I don't realize we're nearly at the dock. That was fast.

"You're on your phone. I didn't want to bother you," Aman states matter-of-factly and with a vague touch of disappointment.

"I—" Before I can finish, the driver stops the car. I feel guilty for not noticing that more than ten minutes had passed without us speaking.

Being the gentleman, he is, Aman dashes to my side of the car and holds out his hand to help me get out, even though he seems upset. He gently yet firmly squeezes my hand when I place it in his, giving both me and my insides a jolt. I stumble slightly before I'm able to straighten my posture, but Aman steadies me again. I chuckle nervously, wondering whether my heels are not really what is affecting my balance.

"You good?" he checks, and a "hm" is all I can muster.

As we get closer to the group of Punjabi people at the dock, I don't recognize some faces—they must be Alina's friends or cousins.

I haven't seen Alina in months, and I hurriedly rush to give my soon-to-be sister-in-law a hug for the first time during her wedding week. She does the same as soon as she sees me.

"Hi!" We both squeal in excitement, exchanging a tight embrace. Once we part, I ask her the obligatory question everyone asks a bride—"How are you feeling?"

"Nervous but excited. This week has been something else, but I can't wait for the wedding and reception." She's glowing, smiling from ear to ear—she's the epitome of a beautiful, happy bride.

Alina notices Aman standing a little further behind me. "Well, hello, handsome." Aman grins, giving Alina a similar big hug.

"Oi, boy. That's my fiancée." Aman, Alina, and I turn around and see a smiling Devan, my parents, and Ari approaching.

"Hey, baby." Alina's voice automatically softens as she addresses my brother. Devan gives her an extended hug, the rest of us watching the couple in love.

This is the first time during the wedding week that we've seen them together. They're surrounded by their family but take a moment to talk to one another as if they're alone.

"This week has been everything we could've asked for." Now that everyone has arrived, Devan and Alina take the opportunity to address the group. "It's entirely because of the love everyone has showered us with," Alina says.

"It's a blessing to be able to spend time with our closest loved ones during a hectic week. Especially on a yacht. But we wanted to make it happen to relish the moments," Devan adds after Alina. The sun is shining on both of them, providing a natural spotlight.

"We love you!" Alina's sister screams, and we all cheer in agreement.

Devan and Alina lead us onto the boat they've reserved for our dinner and ride along the bay. There are about fifteen people in total, including our family and Alina's parents, her older sister, her brother-in-law, two cousins, and her best friend.

Her two cousins are sisters and visiting from Vancouver. They decided to tag along since they didn't have any other plans. Unsurprisingly, they're staring at Aman, but they're not as obvious as others have been this past week. At least not yet.

It doesn't help that Aman helps everyone get on the yacht before he does. He's someone who holds a lady's hand or a man's shoulder and helps them onto a steadily rocking yacht. That is who he is. Devan too.

I'm the last person in line to get on the yacht, immediately behind Alina. Aman whispers, "I got her," to Devan, then Devan steps onto the yacht with his bride.

Right when Aman is about to extend his hand for me, he feigns bypassing me and going inside. I sport a jokingly offended look, not serious at all, because *I know* he's not being serious. He snickers, then also helps me on. Ironically, right after I step onto the yacht, my heels cause me to trip. Aman swiftly catches my arms from behind me, once again steadying me and preventing me from actually falling. *Three times, Bani.*

"Very graceful today," he jokes as he supports me in regaining my standing. Despite the wind along the bay, my skin tingles with warmth.

"Oh, my goodness." I exhale, placing my hand to my forehead out of humiliation.

"It's okay. I'm the only one who saw," he says in Punjabi.

"This is why I hate heels."

"I think you look hot." I brace myself and smile appreciatively, flattered by Aman's forward compliment. He's never used the word *hot* when complimenting me. There are a lot of firsts with Aman this week.

When he places his hand on my lower back to direct me to the couple of stairs that lead to the dining room, my stomach dips along with the motion of the yacht. Luckily, I don't trip at his gentle touch for a fourth time.

The dining room has a large rectangular table in the center and windows on all four walls, allowing us a nearly three-sixty view while we sail.

Devan and Alina sit across from each other, and the rest of the table is seated according to family affiliation. Ari and my mom are sitting next to me, and Aman is sitting directly across from me. My dad and one of Alina's cousins are sitting next to him. I'm told her name is Sonia.

Sonia's posture is stiff, with occasional fidgeting in her seat. She keeps looking at Aman out of the corner of her eye. Aman politely introduces himself, holding out his hand for a handshake, and she nervously giggles before she says a quick "hello." His hand could be made of paper, considering how fragile she is with it when she shakes it. He chuckles softly at the gesture, flashing one of his charming side smiles, then turns his attention back to my dad.

Devan was absolutely right. Aman is the hit of the wedding without even intending to be.

Once the servers finish pouring champagne into the flutes at each place setting, Devan and Alina both stand up to propose a toast. "To each person in this room on this beautiful yacht. We love you."

Her hand raised, Ari yells out, "To the bride and groom!" There's a domino effect, and everyone else yells, "To the bride and groom!" with added clinks in the background before we take a sip of our champagne.

The evening starts off like a precisely orchestrated dance, and the servers quickly follow the toast with the first course. I glance over at Aman as he devours his salad as gallantly as possible.

Sonia seems to be enthralled by him as she listens to the conversation he's having with my dad in between mouthfuls. Every now and then, she talks to Alina's other cousin, whose name I learn is Priya.

My dad is naturally chatty, and he loves Aman, which makes him chattier than usual. He's talking in a lower voice, and I can't hear what he's saying from across the table, especially since Ari and Devan are jabbering away.

I feel like an utter creep, eating and listening to the conversations happening around me. I decide to tune into the one my siblings are having.

"The last time I was in San Francisco, I saw a yacht like this one, but it was going a lot faster than we are now. I remember thinking how long it would take them to travel the same distance we're going today. Probably half the time," Ari says before she takes a bite of her salad.

"I asked the captain to decrease the speed to accommodate the time we want to be on the water. I think Mom would feel seasick if we went any faster. Right now, it doesn't feel like we're even moving."

"We can go out on the deck, right?" I interject.

"Of course, Ban. We can do anything outside of anything illegal." Devan winks at me, and I smile exuberantly back at my brother.

"Bub, when was the last time you were in San Francisco?" I ask Ari. Had she not told me?

"Months ago. Remember when Rayshaan had his birthday night out, and we stayed at your apartment after?"

Rayshaan is Ari's Aman, except Rayshaan lives in Atlanta now. He's a year older than Ari and graduated from the same university a year ago. He couldn't come to Devan's wedding because his mom recently had knee surgery, and he needed to stay back to take care of her.

"Oh, right." I recall the occurrence. I'm a fan of Rayshaan's because he reminds me of Aman.

"Doesn't Ari refer to Rayshaan as her Aman?" Aman reads my mind as he looks at me.

This catches Sonia's attention, and I notice her body becomes rigid. I quickly glance in her direction, and she's overly focused on the empty plate in front of her—it's obvious she's listening to our conversation.

I hate these girls. They consider me a villain because Aman gives me more attention than them. That's not a fault, let alone *my* fault.

Aman notices that I am peeved and mouths, *"What's wrong?"* He's both curious and concerned. It's not his fault that he's popular with the ladies.

He frowns slightly when I shake my head in response, turning my attention back to Devan and Ari.

Sonia, of course, witnessed this interaction and is visibly more annoyed, if that's even possible. I peripherally notice her shift in her seat and then hear her not-so-subtly cough.

I don't usually get *this* upset over the attention Aman gets, and it happens all the time. *Why does it bother me now?*

Perhaps I'm overreacting because my emotions are running high this week. For different reasons.

After all, after this week, things will be different.

chapter 36

I'm impatient to finish our meal and stand on the balcony of the yacht. The view is gorgeous enough for me to lose my appetite. Ari is eager, but not nearly as much as I am.

The sun is setting, but it's still bright enough to assure me that I won't miss it. With the few clouds out, the sky will look phenomenal minutes after the sun has set. That's what I'm most looking forward to—the cotton candy sky.

Amidst my daydreaming of a cloudy sunset, I hear a light chuckle near me.

Searching for the source, my eyes automatically land on Aman. He strokes his chin and beard with his fingers as he smirks at me, tilting his head in thought. *Is he doing this on purpose?*

But I know what he's thinking. He's thinking that he knows me well because he knows exactly what my thoughts are. He knows I'm eagerly awaiting the sunset and how at ease I feel when I'm gazing at a sun-setting sky.

Once everyone finishes, the servers gather the plates, and I immediately step outside when the yacht is at the base of the Golden Gate Bridge. We have less than an hour left on board.

I inhale the saltwater air around me and instinctively smile as I exhale. The all-around windows in the dining room allowed for a view while eating, but the aesthetics are only authentic once outside.

I'm not the only one. Shortly after me, Sonia and Priya step onto a ledge on a different part of the yacht. Unknowingly, however, they're close enough that I'm able to hear them and their conversation.

"I have no words," one of them says, but I'm unable to discern which one. Then I hear giggling laughter. The voices are slightly muffled by the sound of the water hitting the sides of the yacht and the strong wind on this part of the bay.

"I don't think I've ever seen someone as sexy and good-looking as him."

I immediately know what they're talking about. Or *who* they're talking about.

I also hear them insinuate and articulate rather repugnant things about me. Vapid girls. *How old are they?* I think sarcastically to myself.

Their comments about me are distasteful but expected of girls who are infatuated with my best friend and consider me a threat. Aside from the brief introduction Aman initiated when they first sat down, Aman hasn't so much as looked at them, let alone spoken to them.

A few moments later, I feel a touch of warmth on my left side, which is noticeable in this cold. Aman stands close to me, exuding his body heat. The scent of his cologne is still strong. *How does he do that?*

"I saw you laughing at me, brat." I refer to Aman's earlier chuckle at the table, shaking my head of any unbecoming thoughts.

"I wasn't trying to hide it, Ban." He laughs when I cackle.

We're both staring in awe into the distance at the spectacular view surrounding us. The sun has set, and in just a few moments, the sky will change color to a light mixture of orange, pink, and yellow hues. Directly in front of us, there's nothing but water and the horizon. Even Aman is briefly speechless.

"This is incredible." He gazes at me, then focuses back on our surroundings.

"See what I mean?" He nods his head in agreement.

The captain takes us slightly further into the Pacific Ocean, beyond the Golden Gate Bridge, before turning the yacht back around toward the city.

"Ban," Aman mutters.

"Hmm?"

"This has got to be the best week of my life."

I turn to face him, secretly admiring my best friend's profile. "Same."

"And the two most important events are yet to come," he says, satisfied.

"I know," I say, about to lean in and rest my head on his side until I notice two figures approaching. Thinking that it's someone from my family, I turn toward them, smiling.

I'm mistaken. The two figures approaching are not members of my family, but are Sonia and Priya. *Did they follow Aman here?*

Instead of being polite and smiling back at me, they're looking at me as if I'm psychotic. My smile quickly fades, and I turn to face the view again.

Aman is looking in the opposite direction and doesn't notice them. I look at his profile again, his jawline strong and sharp. Well, I can't blame them entirely. He really is very handsome.

I'm unable to turn away in time, and he catches me gawking. "What are you looking at?" he asks.

Damnnit. I bashfully shake my head, my lips pursed.

He laughs. "Mmhmm."

Sonia and Priya move closer and stand next to Aman, and in my opinion, a bit too closely for someone they've just met. Moving closer to me, he briefly shifts his head and smiles to acknowledge their presence, then faces the view again.

I roll my eyes at Sonia because she's standing in a way that shows off her body.

"Beautiful view," she says, likely only to Aman.

Aman forcibly chuckles. "Yeah."

I admit that I take pleasure in their obvious display of attraction toward him and his obvious lack of interest. He looks like he doesn't want them to be there. I can sense it. He seemed more at ease before they showed up.

"So, who's Tej?" Aman catches me off guard.

"What?" Honestly, I forgot about him.

"Tej—who is that?"

"What do you mean?" I'm flabbergasted. How does Aman know about Tej? I haven't shared anything with him at all. I was particularly careful not to.

"Come on, Ban. You know who I'm talking about."

I'm suddenly very nervous, feeling his eyes on me as he waits for my response.

While I ponder what to say, Aman reveals how he knows. "I heard Ari talking about you and someone named Tej."

That explains it. Although it's unlike Ari to overtly speak of something of this nature. She knows I'm sensitive about these things.

"Oh. That Tej." I feign uncertainty, and I'm certain he clearly sees through it. "I went to high school with him. Why?"

"Heard a new name and wondered who it was." He's succinct and doesn't ask me for further details. Why does he choose this moment to bring this up?

To avoid a conversation on the topic, I don't ask him what he heard Ari say. I certainly don't want the two obsessed twins to hear about my personal life. But I wonder whether bringing it up later would make it seem like a bigger deal than it actually is. Probably.

Aman's leaning against the railing of the ledge as he looks over the bay. The most he does is clear his throat after Sonia makes another failed attempt to spark a conversation with him.

Shortly after the second attempt, he excuses himself and goes back inside. Unsurprisingly, the two obsessed twins go back inside only a few minutes after him.

I chuckle to myself when they're not within earshot and roll my eyes at them. They're not the first and certainly will not be the last.

I'm alone for a few moments before Ari darts toward me. "I thought Aman was here with you."

"He was. You didn't see him inside?"

"No, I was on the lower deck."

"Bub, did you say something about Tej to him?"

"No. Why would I?" I wasn't expecting Ari to sound surprised and instead was expecting her to respond affirmatively.

"Oh." I'm confused. Aman said he heard the name through Ari.

"Aman gets weird about these guys, and I don't want to say something that will tick him off." She laughs it off, but I'm still very curious. Perhaps he overheard her?

Ari will be interested to know about the happenings with the obsessed twins and their borderline stalker behavior toward Aman. But I only share a light version.

"Aman sounds like he's handling it well," she says. "There isn't much more he can do."

"Yeah."

"He must be more annoyed than any of us. It sounds tedious. Especially if it keeps happening, and he's just trying to enjoy himself."

I've never pondered the thought. No wonder he looked bothered by their presence earlier. We were having a great time on the ledge alone, and he probably would've stayed with me if the two obsessed twins hadn't shown up.

Ari's right. It must be so annoying for Aman. He's said multiple times that he merely wants to enjoy this week. Having to dodge repeated romantic advancements is an added nuisance that he didn't sign up for.

"What are we doing tomorrow?" I change the subject, noting this newfound perspective Ari brought to my attention. It's the day before the wedding—the calm before the chaos.

"Probably decorating inside for the before and after wedding rituals," Ari says, referring to the inside of our parents' home.

The day of the wedding will be full of tiny, unique rituals that are imperative parts of a Punjabi wedding. These traditions and rituals make Punjabi weddings a delight for all involved; they're colorful, both literally and figuratively.

We still have another fifteen minutes, and Ari and I stay on the balcony until we approach the dock we took off from.

Upon disembarking the yacht, I'm extra cautious not to repeat the humiliation I experienced while boarding. Aman stays behind me and observes me the entire time, grinning. He is, once again, teasing me but ready to save me if I do fall.

When the yacht part of the evening comes to an end, Aman suggests we walk home—an excuse to extend the night. That'd be quite a walk, but there's still some light out, and I have Aman with me.

When Sonia overheard him suggest the walk home, solidifying that we live together, she actually flinched and popped her eyes. *Flinched.* It's almost as if she *expects* Aman to find her attractive or be interested in her.

Unintentionally, Aman is making it clear that's not the case. Not even a little bit.

chapter 37

For our path home, Aman chooses the scenic route along the Embarcadero. The Embarcadero is a walkable roadway along San Francisco's eastern shoreline. It has many piers and waterfront restaurants. I commend his suggestion because, with the color of the sky still striking, the view of the Bay Bridge is breathtaking.

The Embarcadero is the most common area in this part of San Francisco to enjoy a walk or run, even when it's later in the evening. There's a slight fall breeze that gusts periodically, and seagulls chirp energetically around us.

A line of restaurants along the right side of the Embarcadero, with a ton of outdoor seating, are filled with diners and buzzing with laughter. There's a birthday party at one of the restaurants, which is where the majority of the laughter emanates from.

"We should come to this side of town more often," Aman says. I was about to say the same thing. "We should."

As we pass by the birthday group, a drunk person from the group declares Aman and myself the cutest couple alive, and then invites us to grab a shot from the tray the bartender just delivered. Aman and I exchange endearing glances, laughing at the comment we frequently receive. *I've been told worse things.*

We linger on the patio for a few minutes before we resume our walk home.

It's getting darker and chillier. Aman makes the executive decision to order a car for the rest of the distance. We walked from the dock to the San Francisco Ferry Building, which is an impressive distance for me to walk in heels.

Aman convinces me to stay at my parents' house tomorrow night, even though the wedding venue is in San Francisco. He suggests taking some board games to help with de-stressing. My parents could use another fun, light evening the night before the two main events.

As we wait for the car to arrive, we observe an individual playing upbeat and lively music on the sidewalk of the Embarcadero pathway, prompting a couple to spontaneously dance in the middle of it. Others admire the couple and cheer, while some join in. Aman and I are among those who cheer.

We absorb the joy surrounding us. It's been a while since I've seen Aman this expressive. Even though I know he's enjoying this week, he hasn't smiled and laughed as freely as he is now. He has been more vigilant in keeping his cool around my family. Now, it's candid happiness.

It hasn't been easy for me to stay as cool, however. Seera and Sonia, Aman's adoring fans, pop into my mind, and I can literally feel myself getting angry at the thought of them and their behavior. Since this is *my* brother's wedding, I've had to hold my true emotions in, keeping a civil face.

"What's wrong?" Aman must have noticed my mood drastically change when he opens the door of the car for me. I resist telling him the truth, and he doesn't press it—for now, at least.

During the car ride home, I listen to the music the driver plays, my head slightly facing the opposite direction of Aman. From my peripheral vision, I can tell he looks at me every now and then without saying anything. I'm sure he's wondering what happened to me in a matter of minutes. We were smiling and laughing when watching the couples dance, and then my mood completely changed.

It's only when our front door is closed behind us and I'm walking toward my room that he calls my name. Bani, not Ban. His tone is serious.

When I turn around, he's still standing by the front door, waiting for me to say something. When I don't, he softly sighs and quietly crosses to the couch. He gestures me over as he comfortably leans against the back of it.

"What?" I ask him, pretending not to know what he wants to talk about.

Unlike when he asked me at dinner and when we got in the car, it's just us now.

I can't bring myself to begin the topic without sounding incredibly possessive of my best friend. I'm not even sure how he'd react.

He'll probably find it funny and ridicule me for being affected by two people that I don't know.

But he's also a guy and approaches these situations nonchalantly. I don't think I've ever seen him nervous around a girl before. He's Aman.

I know he's waiting for me to say something, and he knows I will. Eventually.

"Well?" he prods. "Why did your mood change faster than the speed of light? One minute you're happy and smiling, and then the next, you're pissed." He's blunt when needed.

He's going to think I'm a lunatic. I feel like one because I'm fully aware of my drastic mood change.

"Um. Do you ever feel like you're having the best time, but then there's always something that ruins it?" I'm purposely cryptic.

"Okay. What best time are you referring to, and what ruined it?" He's unintentionally talking to me as if I'm a petulant child. I don't blame him. I feel like one.

"Nothing. It's not important."

"Clearly it's bothersome enough for your mood to change that quickly."

I avoid eye contact with him. "It's just these dumb girls."

"What dumb girls?"

"How do you not see it?"

"Bani, you need to help me out a little. You're being too cryptic. Just spit it out."

"These girls that always swoon over the sight of you." This is the point where I expect him to tease and ridicule me. I expect him to smile because he's enjoying this. He does no such thing.

"*That's* what's bothering you?" His volume is higher than before. I nod silently.

"Why does that bother you so much?" I've asked myself the same question.

He was expressive earlier, and he still is, but his expression is different now. He looks curious, hungry, and eager for the reason why I'm troubled.

"I don't know why. I feel crazy saying this out loud to you. They all look at me and treat me like I'm a villain."

"Why would they do that?"

"Because we're close. Because you're my roommate. Because you're my best friend. They all think I'm their competition."

Aman stands up tall like a pillar, close enough for me to instinctively move away, yet I don't. Nor do I want to.

"Even if that's true, why does it bother you so much?" he asks, his voice husky.

"I don't know," I stall, the tone of my voice mirroring his.

"I handle it, don't I?"

"What do you mean you 'handle it?'"

"I don't give them attention. You're acting like I solicit it."

I step back, feeling instantly defensive. "What? I never said that."

"I've told you so many times that I'm not going to do something that results in an awkward situation for you. If these girls show interest in me, I don't reciprocate it. You really think I'd pursue something with Devan's client's sister or one of Alina's closest cousins?"

He's right, and he knows precisely who I'm talking about. He's told me that before, and I remind myself of this each time.

"I tell you this all the time. That's more than you do." His statement is accusatory. I felt my anger subsiding until he said that.

"What does that mean?" I'm defensive again.

"Nothing. Never mind."

"No, you forced what I was feeling out of me. It's your turn."

"I *forced* it out of you?" His tone matches mine. This discussion will only escalate into an argument if we carry on. So, I cut it short.

"We should be ready to leave tomorrow morning." That's the last thing I say to him. I glimpse anger on his face as I abruptly end the conversation, leaving him alone in the living room.

He stays put a few more seconds before I hear his footsteps. As I close my bedroom door, my phone rings. I almost thought for a moment that it was Aman.

When I see my sister's name flashing on the screen, I realize that I forgot to inform her that we reached home. *Shit.*

"You sound weird. Are you okay?" Ari picks up on my mood.

"Yes. I'm just tired. My feet hurt." The heel excuse is always plausible, and Ari believes it without hesitation.

"Ohh, I bet. Okay, good night, bub. See you tomorrow."

"Good night." I plop onto my bed.

I got into a heated argument with Aman.

Well, there's always a first time for everything.

The next morning is awkward, especially during the drive to Palo Alto. Aman doesn't say anything to me, and I don't say anything to him. It feels like the longest ride ever.

Normally after an argument, he would playfully poke me to spark up a conversation and reduce any heat to a simmer. However, I don't think that he and I have ever had a resentment-filled argument like we did last night. It's contrary to Aman's normal disposition. When I sneak a peek at him and see his cold demeanor, the realness of the argument sets in.

The entire ride to Palo Alto, his comment from last night, *"That's more than you do,"* lingers in my thoughts. He asked me about Tej earlier. Is that what he was referring to? Is he referring to Marcus? No, he knows about Marcus. Albeit, he doesn't know the details. And with Tej, nothing is even happening. We text, but it's nothing substantial, and he's an old friend. I've known him for years.

Something has been bothering him for a few weeks, but I thought it might be a fluke until last night. The week he's supposed to be happy is the week he berates me for a reason I'm completely unaware of.

Despite our argument, he brought the board games, as he suggested the night before. I wonder if his demeanor will be obvious to everyone else. Board games are supposed to be collaborative and energetic. Will my family know that we're not speaking? They likely will not notice, as Aman has generally been on the serious and quiet side this week. Even Ari is timider this week than she normally is.

I open my mouth to speak, but words don't come out. He's too focused on driving to notice, and I certainly don't want to distract or irritate him more. Instead, I remain quiet until we arrive at my parents' house.

On the wedding day, there's a popular tradition, a game, where the family and friends of the bride steal the shoes of the groom. If they succeed, then the groom must pay each person involved a monetary "fee" to regain possession of his shoes. Similarly, it's the groom's side's duty to ensure that the shoes don't get stolen by the bride's side. This game is more often than not taken very seriously.

Ari, Aman, Jay, and I are part of the group in charge of guarding Devan's shoes. If Aman and I aren't speaking, it won't be the same.

Once we're in Palo Alto, my mom tells the kids to move the furniture back to the living room because we need room to sit. Ari, thankfully, is monopolizing the conversation and masking the tension between me and Aman. It helps that she also has music blaring in the background. There is no silence to fill.

After the wedding tomorrow, a number of people, including the newlywed couple, will come to our house to complete the rituals that occur after the wedding. This includes the *pani varna rasam*, which is a part of the bride's welcome, and a game.

The *Fish the Ring* game is when the bride and groom's wedding rings are placed in a large, deep bowl filled with an opaque liquid, usually milk and water, with rose petals mixed in. The couple fishes for the rings, and the partner who finds them first wins the game. It's one of the most enjoyable rituals during a Punjabi wedding. There's inevitable hand flirting between the couple, resulting in teasing from the onlooking crowd.

Aman told me a few days ago that he plans to blatantly flirt with his wife when they play it after they're married. He was grinning the entire time.

After we're done moving furniture, we receive instructions from my mom to decorate the living room. She wants the decorations for the rituals after the wedding to be simple and not extravagant or done by the wedding planner. I imagine there's another sentimental reason behind it, similar to the reason she wanted to hand-make certain foods for other events.

First, we set up the background against the wall where Devan and Alina will sit. I've been charged with handing Aman the pins whenever he needs them to pin the cloth on the wall since he's the tallest. He doesn't verbally tell me he needs a pin. Instead, he opens his hand to indicate he needs one.

He's not looking me in the eye. I don't believe I did something truly atrocious for him to not even look at me.

Ari takes over for me when I pretend I have to use the restroom. Instead, I go to my room to text Mark.

> **ME:** AMAN AND I GOT INTO THE WORST ARGUMENT.
> **MARK:** WHY??
> **ME:** IT'S OVER SOMETHING SO STUPID, BUT I THINK HE FEELS THAT I HIDE THINGS FROM HIM.
> **MARK:** WELL, DO YOU?
> **ME:** I DON'T *HIDE* THINGS FROM HIM. I DON'T TELL HIM THINGS UNLESS THEY ARE SUBSTANTIAL.
> **MARK:** WHAT DOES THAT MEAN? YOU DIDN'T USED TO DO THAT. MAYBE THAT'S WHY HE THINKS THAT YOU'RE HIDING THINGS FROM HIM.

Mark is right.

> **MARK:** WHAT DOES HE THINK YOU HID FROM HIM?

I briefly explain what happened with Sonia and then Aman's question about who Tej is. Mark, too, finds this interesting. Perhaps Aman is upset by the sudden shift in *my* behavior, all while I perceive the problem to be his.

When I return downstairs, Aman and Ari have hung up three decorative *saris* on the walls, covering them in their entirety. It looks very colorful.

"Aman suggested we set a patterned border of rose petals for Devan and Alina to sit in," Ari says as I wonder what to do next.

I look up at him, and he's staring at me blankly. He knows I love roses. It's the first time he's looked at me since last night. I wonder if this is his nonverbal way of communicating with me.

Before I have the opportunity to respond, my mom walks in to check on the progress. "You guys are doing a great job!" she exclaims in Punjabi.

"Munna, do we have more *saris*? I was thinking we could do these other two walls too." Aman calls my mom Munna, which is his hybrid of Auntie and Mom. Mark also calls her that.

"We have plenty. Do whatever you want, sweetheart. Bani, can you and Aman go get more saris from my closet?"

Aman looks in my direction. "Oh, okay." The hesitation in my voice must be obvious because Ari notices it and volunteers to go instead.

She'll certainly question Aman in the process, and she'll certainly question me once she's alone with me. Whether she'll have any luck extracting anything from Aman is a different story.

In the meantime, I fold the *saris* that Aman didn't use.

When Ari and Aman return, I can tell that they talked about something in the brief time they were gone. I'm curious what they talked about because now it seems like Ari is annoyed with me as well.

What did Aman say to her?

chapter 38

My mom asks Devan and me to pick up pizzas for lunch while Ari and Aman finish up in the living room. Frankly, they both make a great team because it looks beautifully decorated.

The errand gives me some alone time with my brother, which is a blessing. I didn't think I'd have more than ten minutes with him this week.

"How did you get all that time off?" he asks since both Aman and I essentially didn't go to classes this week except for Monday.

"We had our legal writing exam last weekend. For evidence and criminal law, our professors canceled our classes, but we have no idea why. We were just told that classes were canceled."

"That's strange. You guys are having a mysterious year. Especially with your TA. How does someone run over another person and then keep driving? Do you think it was intentional?"

"The police were questioning his ex-girlfriend. I don't know what happened with that."

"Hmm. Ban, *what* is the deal between you and Aman?"

I'm taken aback by his question. Can he sense that we had an argument?

"What?" I attempt to mask any sort of facial response or reaction. "What do you mean?"

"You're my baby sister, and I love you. You're so smart. But how do you not see that Aman is crazy about you?"

I'm speechless, unable to formulate any words in response to what Devan just said.

"What?" I finally say something. That's not what I was expecting. I thought he'd picked up on the vibe following our argument.

"He's had girls throwing themselves at him all week. He doesn't look at them or give them a second thought." He pauses, then continues, "You think Alina and I didn't notice that Sonia and Priya were both obsessed with him yesterday? Alina said that Sonia wouldn't stop asking about Aman last night."

"Dev, that doesn't mean that he's crazy about me. It just means that he's not interested in them."

While I look at my brother as he drives, he smirks but doesn't rebut my reasoning.

"Alina noticed that?" I ask.

"Of course, she did. They're my would-be in-laws, but that doesn't mean that I agree with what they do. Like Sonia—she was embarrassing herself after a certain point. Even Alina knows that Aman is crazy about you. She thought that Sonia was wasting her time."

"No. That doesn't mean anything." I don't tell Devan that Aman and I are having an argument at the moment, particularly the reason we're arguing. It could potentially sway Devan's opinion even more.

Devan doesn't look convinced. What flusters yet resonates with me most is that Devan is the one to say it. He's never been this blunt or said something as personal to me. Especially about Aman.

Aman and I have both been slightly different toward each other this week—more attentive—and, excluding our argument, I think it's made us closer. But in the grand scheme of things, I haven't received any romantic indications from him. At least, I don't think I have. He was dating not more than a month ago.

Devan is also in the middle of his wedding week. He's clouded by the surge of romantic emotions he may be naturally feeling. Alina, too. Their perceptions are skewed, I decide.

Devan doesn't mention Aman again on our ride home from the pizza parlor. But he has planted a seed in my mind. He was insistent, and he's never been that way before. Not about this subject. Not about Aman.

Once we arrive home, Aman comes out to help bring the food in, grabbing all the pizzas from me and gesturing for me to bring in the bag with the appetizers. He says nothing the entire time.

We're both headstrong and ignore the urge to say something. Aman usually succumbs to this urge shortly after a disagreement, but I knew from his expression last night that this discussion, this argument, was different.

He sets the pizzas down on the counter in my parents' kitchen. It's just us.

Aman wants to say something to me now. I can feel it. He's standing directly in front of the pizza, not opening a box, as if about to make a speech.

"We're dropping this. For now," he finally speaks, but it's not the speech I was expecting.

He says this without looking at me, and instead stares at a random spot on the counter. When he does, I try to smile at him to ease the tension, but he just looks at me, expressionless.

For now. This means that this isn't over. I don't expect it to be.

I ponder those two simple words as the kitchen fills with my family members who are eager to devour the pizza. My dad pauses my thoughts. He was calling my name for a few seconds before I realized he was.

"What are you thinking about?" he asks in Punjabi. I shake my head in response.

I wait for my dad's attention to be diverted before I look at Aman, noting his expressionless stare has changed to one of focused interest. He presses his lips together and squints his eyes. I don't think he realizes he's doing this.

I try and follow Aman's suggestion to drop it for now, but it's hard. I can't pretend to be normal with someone when I know things aren't normal. Aman, on the other hand, is better about it, although he is not entirely his usual self.

It's obvious to me that Ari knows something is up because I continuously find her glancing between us.

When I briefly whisper to her to ask what she and Aman talked about when they went to get *saris*, she brushes my question off. "Nothing, nothing," is all she says.

I don't believe her in the slightest. But I know my sister. She's not being truthful with me for a reason. I don't know what that reason is yet, but I'll find out in due time.

Plus, she's my sister. There's no way that her reason is in any way ill-intended. It has to be a timing issue, and the most obvious timing

issue is that we're amidst my brother's wedding. I understand why
Aman said, "For now."

That evening, we played various collaborative board games for
a few hours, and Aman was right. It helped everyone relax and
loosen up tremendously.

The time for Devan to surprise Alina at her *mehndi* function
quickly creeps up on us. My mom has instructed him to come
back early since we need to be up early to perform the pre-wedding
rituals.

Devan asks if Aman would like to join him, but Aman politely
rejects the invitation almost immediately. I can tell that Devan was
hoping for a different answer, but he accepts it nonetheless.

"Why didn't you want to go to Alina's?" I ask him now that we
are supposedly speaking, but I feel like I might be poking a bear.

He pretends he's distracted or doesn't understand the question.
"What?"

"When Devan asked you to go to Alina's house, why didn't
you want to go?"

"Munna was saying when you guys went to get pizza that
there's a lot to get done here. I'm not going to know anyone at her
house anyway."

Well, that's not true, Aman. You know your adoring fans. I
keep calling them that. I could remark with a snarky comment,
but I know that'll cause an uproar, and it'll take us right back to
where we were a few hours ago. If not, worse.

I'm still bothered by it, but I resist saying anything. Even
though we got into an argument because of this subject, I'm *still*
bothered by it.

Whenever I look at Aman, I feel a combination of guilt and anger. I'm feeling guilty for being angry at him for something that's

not his fault, and I'm angry with him for acting as if I intentionally did something wrong. I didn't, and *that* is his fault.

I do agree with him, however. He'd be bored, and despite his adoring fans being there, he wouldn't talk to them. Aman would just stand around while Devan was with Alina and her family. He'd be more productive here.

"What needs to be done?" I ask.

"Munna wants to set up a little area for the *sehra bandi* tomorrow morning. She was initially saying the patio, but I checked the weather, and it's supposed to be windy in the morning." The *sehra bandi* is a ritual completed with close relatives and family where the sisters of the groom place and tie a headdress on the groom's head prior to leaving for the wedding ceremony.

"Where are we going to do it then?" I ask.

"She wants to set it up between the stairs." My parents' house has a butterfly staircase. Between the two sets of stairs that lead to the upstairs portion of the house, there's a foyer. It's an excellent and unique spot to have the *sehra bandi.*

In Indian weddings, there's a part during the *baraat,* the groom's wedding procession, called the *kori.* The *kori* is a horse that the groom sits on with the youngest boy in the family, the *sarbala,* either a cousin or nephew of the groom, as the groom's wedding party goes to the wedding venue to get his bride.

To keep the tradition alive, we rented a majestic white horse named Darcy that will be decorated in Indian wedding attire and will take Devan and our youngest cousin, Nirav, to the wedding venue.

The owner allowed a test run with Darcy to see how he reacted to the adornments atop him. He has done Indian weddings before, but Devan wanted to be sure and see for himself.

There will also be a *dholi*, an individual that plays a large Punjabi drum, a *dhol*, as the groom's wedding party dances toward the wedding venue. Even non-Punjabi cultures utilize a *dholi* when the groom makes his grand entrance during a wedding. No matter what the culture may be, the *dholi's* vibe is unmistakable, and the *dholi* is able to add music and danceable energy with a single instrument.

In preparation for the *sehra bandi*, Aman starts off decorating the foyer by himself. He doesn't ask anyone for help, but Ari joins in anyway.

Ari has been sticking by Aman a lot this evening, and I find it particularly noteworthy. She looks as if she is empathizing with him. What could she possibly empathize with Aman about?

Before he and Ari supposedly talked, he was hellbent on not speaking to me. After their talk is when he initiated a conversation with me, lessening the fire between us.

What did they talk about? I have got to talk to Ari.

Her behavior toward Aman is different and *new*, and he is welcoming it, although hesitatingly.

It must've been something significant to suddenly bond them to this extent.

chapter 39

My anxiety has amplified since Gerald's death, but I haven't had any nightmares lately, despite what happened this week.

Just a few days ago, a psychopath was following me and Aman. Then Aman and I got into our biggest argument after one of the best evenings I've had in a long time. The likelihood of back-to-back nightmares is high, especially for me. I'm hoping it's because the excitement of my brother's wedding is overpowering.

Normally, I'd talk to Aman about this, but despite his initiating conversation with me, we both know that we're not all the way back to normal. It's like he said. We are dropping it *for now*.

Today is also Natalia's sister's baby shower, and I don't want to distract Mark from that.

The next person I think of talking with is Marcus. He may not be so willing to chat with me given my inconsistent texting with him. Nonetheless, I take my chances.

ME: HOW WAS YOUR WEEK?

He doesn't immediately respond. I hope that my messaging him will be an incentive for him to respond to me without being peeved. Even though I've been completely inattentive toward him, I do have a good reason.

During our last message exchange, he asked me again if I was available the Sunday after Devan's wedding reception since I didn't provide a firm answer before.

ME: ARE YOU STILL UP FOR HANGING OUT TOMORROW?

But my phone screen stays dark.

Accepting that Marcus may be too pissed to entertain my texts, I place my phone away in my clutch. When, or if, he responds, I'll be able to feel my phone. I refocus on the fact that today is Devan's wedding day.

I was unable to speak to Ari last night to figure out what happened between her and Aman. She got a mysterious phone call, likely from Rayshaan, which kept her in her room for the remainder of the evening.

Then, our mom woke us up fairly early this morning to get ready before the *sehra bandi*. We had to have our wedding outfits on and our makeup and hair done before the first ceremony of the wedding day.

My mom, Ari, and I are all wearing the same color outfit with the same color of embroidery but different styles. My mom's is conservative, but mine and Ari's are modern. Our suits are a beautiful mint green and baby pink. They are gentle colors, appropriate for a modest yet elegant wedding.

Our hair is secured in fancily styled buns with our sheer *chunnis* placed and pinned on our heads, to be kept on throughout the ceremony. Our makeup is light yet fully done. We have glamorous necklaces, earrings, *tikkas* on our heads, and bangles clinking against one another on our wrists.

My dad is in awe when we gather downstairs, and the first thing he says is how this is the first time he's seen us look like triplets. He's right—we do look very similar.

The photographer requests to take a picture of the three of us, admiring how great we look. We don't see Devan or realize that he's come into the room behind us, but the photographer manages to catch a cute picture of Devan photobombing us.

In my completely biased opinion, Devan is the best-looking groom I've ever seen. He's rocking his cream and gold *sherwani*, which has hints of blue and red.

A Punjabi groom's *sherwani* is traditionally cream and gold or cream and silver. Knowing my brother and knowing Alina, there's a reason behind these blue and red additions. I can guarantee without seeing Alina's bridal outfit that she'll also have blue in it. Red is the traditional color for Punjabi brides, although pastel and bright colors are becoming increasingly common.

Aman's mint green *sherwani* and my dad's light pink one match Ari, my mom, and me. The three men look dashingly handsome in their Punjabi formal wear.

My mom called Aman a few weeks ago, demanding his *sherwani* measurements, having already bought one for him that matched the wedding party. Aman couldn't stop floating about it afterward, even to me, and of course I would be wearing a matching color as well. That was a light-hearted and cheerful Aman. I miss him.

Putting us in a line, it's obvious that we're together. When we stand next to Devan, it's clear that we're on the groom's side, even though we don't match with Devan himself. Devan thought that would be too corny. He wants to match his bride.

When my mom notices Aman standing off to the side, she urges him to join us in one of the family pictures we're taking before we complete the *sehra bandi*. I briefly glance over and catch a glimpse of his smile when the photographer takes the picture. It's heartwarming.

The wedding ceremony will respect both Hindu and Sikh traditions, and for this reason, it won't be held at a religious temple. Both Devan and Alina wanted a non-religious venue to best incorporate traditions from both religions. The wedding will, instead, be at the San Francisco City Hall.

Devan arranged for a limousine to take the groom's party to San Francisco City Hall. There's champagne in the limo for us to enjoy. My parents requested we not consume alcohol prior to the wedding since the event will nonetheless be a religious function.

Out of respect, no one argues with my parents on this point. No matter how religious I may or may not be, they're right. Besides, there aren't any limitations once the ceremony is over.

The ride to city hall is spirited, and the consensus is that my big brother makes a stunning groom. Everyone is especially complimenting him on how much his growing beard suits him.

"Aman, is your beard hard to maintain?" Devan asks.

"It was when I first grew it out years ago, but you get used to it. I'd look unrecognizable if I didn't have one now." He laughs, shuddering at the thought.

"I don't think I've seen you without one either," I add to test his behavior toward me.

He genuinely smiles and shakes his head. "No, you haven't. I haven't been clean-shaven since college." That was ten years ago.

"I feel like you'd look much younger," Ari adds.

"Isn't that the case most of the time?" I ask.

"I'm a great test case. Until recently, I wasn't clean-shaven, but I had stubble. Did I look younger then?" Devan says.

"Not necessarily younger, but the beard makes you look more mature," my dad shares. Devan contemplates keeping it.

I look over at my mom every now and then and notice she has the expression she gets when she's about to cry. Devan catches her, and then she bottles it back up again, reminding her that this is a joyous occasion and tears aren't allowed.

"They're tears of happiness, dummy," she says in Punjabi. The Punjabi translation of *dummy* is an endearing, silly nickname that she has for my brother.

"Only smiles," he adds cheerfully.

Once we reach San Francisco, the driver doesn't take us directly to city hall, but rather to the pathway that leads directly to it. That's where Darcy and his owner are waiting for us.

The *dholi* will play his drum, and the rest of us will dance our way to the front steps of city hall, where Alina's family will greet us. The walk itself is very slow, as simultaneously dancing and walking slows down the process considerably.

Nearly every bystander pauses to watch us as we pass by. They all smile and look at us in admiration and interest. We're hard to miss with the crowd, the colors, and the music. My elder cousin encourages a bystander to dance with us, and she does. Her enthusiasm makes the rest of us clap with her.

I scan the rest of the crowd that's watching us, and I swear that I see Marcus or someone who looks remarkably like him. But as soon as I do, a group of my uncles dances directly in front of me, obstructing my view.

By the time my view clears, the person has already left. All I can see is his back, which isn't helpful in the slightest.

Thinking of Marcus prompts me toward my phone. I don't think I felt it amidst the dancing, but I can't be sure. I check to see if Marcus replied to my proposition to meet up the following day. Actually, my repeating of his initial proposition.

I do, in fact, have two messages from Marcus that were sent a few minutes ago.

MARCUS: YES.
MARCUS: I'LL FIND A SPOT.

And that's it. Although he's willing, his responses seem curt. I tuck my phone back away into my clutch, curious how tomorrow will go.

We are finally near the front of city hall, where Alina's family awaits Devan's *baraat* to begin the *milni*, meaning *coming together*. The *milni* is the first formal part of the wedding, where the two families symbolically unite and become one. It's also the bride's family's welcoming of the groom's family.

Family members from both sides meet in the middle to exchange garlands for the welcoming. The mom meets the mom, the dad meets the dad, the grandfather meets the grandfather, and so on. If there are no matching family members on one side, then any relative can step in to greet and welcome the other.

Ari and I go at the same time to meet Alina's older sister. Our greeting is timid and not as flamboyant as a lot of the other pairs, but it's nonetheless sincere. I notice Alina's sister well up, quietly sniffling when we part from an embrace. As an older sister, I understand, and I'm certain I'll also cry when Ari gets married.

Once the *milni* is complete, we are escorted to the room in city hall where snacks will be served. I'm certain that Alina is within the walls of the building with her closest friends, the bridesmaids, and family members.

Eager to visit her, Ari and I both venture out after we finish our snacks to see if we can find her and sneak a peek at her bridal dress.

Before leaving the room to search for Alina, I check up on Aman to see what he's doing—he's at one of the standing tables with Jay.

The tension has eased between me and Ari and me and Aman, but then I see Sonia and Priya standing at the table immediately behind them, not so discretely eyeing him. I laugh to myself before following Ari out, suppressing any buildup of irritation I may be feeling.

Alina is waiting in a room upstairs, down the hall from where the actual ceremony will take place. She's surrounded by an army of people. The photographer is taking many creative and artistic pictures of her, focusing on her shoes, her bangles, her *mehndi*, and a silhouette of her profile.

My favorite is the aerial shot the photographer takes of Alina sitting at the center of a "D" that her bridesmaids form. She's kneeling on the ground and holding her hands out, displaying her *mehndi* design while looking down and smiling slightly. She looks stunning.

As I expected, her bridal outfit matches Devan's *sherwani*. Alina's outfit is a *lengha choli*. Alina's *choli*, a glorified and Indianized crop top, shows very little of her midriff. She also has a *chunni* and a heavy *lengha,* a long skirt, that's predominantly red with subtle cream and blue more obviously displayed than Devan's.

As soon as she sees Ari and me, she exclaims with excitement, but since the photographer is still taking pictures, he doesn't let us greet her just yet. In between poses, she summons us toward her for a quick "hello" and picture. Before we return downstairs and before I miss the opportunity, I approach the photographer with a very important, small request of my own.

At the top of the stately staircase, Ari and I pass by the *mandap*, an altar for Hindu ceremonies that Devan and Alina will get married under.

The *mandap* is made of a cream-colored dome that is covered and surrounded with cream and pink roses, along with a few red roses thrown in for contrast. The inner circumference of the dome has a slightly lowered, draped red cloth. In the middle of the dome is a tasteful crystal chandelier.

It's a beautiful sight. I've never seen a *mandap* like this, and the ceremony location is in the best part of the building.

Since there will be both Hindu and Sikh wedding traditions, there's a small platform on the right side for when the Sikh wedding rituals will be performed. The ceremony will be longer than normal, but in between the ceremonies, my parents arranged for another smaller snack break with a complete lunch buffet following the completion of both.

"I think I'm going to walk around and admire the décor for a bit," I say to Ari, who goes back into the room where a majority of the guests are still mingling.

The staircase is similarly lined with cream and pink roses leading up to the *mandap*, but in this assortment, there is a green flower that I do not know the name of, adding more contrast. The roses consuming San Francisco City Hall make it look like a fairy-tale wedding venue.

There are chairs for guests placed all around the floor at the bottom of the staircase. Every single guest chair has either a white or pink rose framing it. There are tall pillars featuring garlands of the same green flower that I don't recognize.

I prance down the grand staircase holding my *lengha* up, careful not to trip on it, until I can turn around and look up at the *mandap*.

The hall looks majestic with the decorations and the natural colors that already encompass it.

Mesmerized by the decorations, I don't notice someone approaching me from behind, but the familiar scent instantly alerts me as to who it is. It's a unique, crisp, subtle-smelling cologne that I'm well acquainted with, and I've smelled it a lot—especially this week. It's the scent that I've grown to love.

chapter 40

I keep looking at Aman from the corner of my eye, and the continuous side glances cause a strain. Since he broke our "no speaking" streak, we have, ironically, not really spoken. Even though I should be the one to initiate this time, I can't think of a single thing to say. My mind is frozen.

"Are you thinking of something to say to me?" he says.

Turning quickly, I look at him, not at all surprised that he knows exactly what my thoughts are.

He's smiling. It's not his usual "Aman" smile, given our current state, but it's a smile nonetheless. I'll take it.

"I am." I return the gesture, but he frowns in response to my smile, which is probably blatantly displaying that I miss him. "Us not being normal is not how I imagined this week would go."

"Hm." He quietly considers what I said for a few moments, then stares decidedly back at me. "It could be normal."

He chuckles genuinely when he sees my furrowed eyebrows and inquisitive expression. "Come on, Ban. Don't look at me like that. Just because we got into a little disagreement doesn't mean that we're not going to make up." This time, my smile reflects relief when he playfully nudges me, easing the tension.

"Did you miss me?" Instead of answering my question outright, he gives me a side hug, squeezing me tightly. He did.

Contrary to yesterday, when his tone was still filled with resistance, this feels much more authentic. The sick feeling I've had since we first had the argument starts to dissipate.

"This is seriously tight." He lets go of me, gaping at the decorations.

We spot a collage of Alina and Devan's engagement pictures as well as pictures over the years. I've never seen a number of them before.

"How long have they been together?" Aman asks.

"Seriously, huh? They met in college, but these pictures make it look like they've known each other forever."

"It's amazing that they found each other, made it work, and are still crazy about each other after all this time."

"Makes me feel inadequate." I chuckle.

"You're anything but that. You'll get it."

With that simple utterance, he walks away, leaving me speechless.

Devan is seated at his designated stool at the *mandap*, ready to get married. My mom and dad are immediately near him, and Ari, Aman, and I are seated close by. There's limited seating at the top of the staircase, and only immediate family members sit up here. Even Jay is seated at ground level.

The guests are seated in their designated chairs, awaiting Alina and her bridesmaids. The priest summarizes the rituals that are performed for the wedding ceremony for Devan, who listens intently.

"Do you know when we're starting?" Ari asks me and Aman.

"I think any minute now," Aman responds for the both of us. Just as speculated by Aman, the pianist, who's been playing instrumental background music, announces that Alina is ready to join her future husband at the *mandap* and requests everyone to turn their attention to the walkway on the right side of the landing.

The gradual onset of a familiar romantic Punjabi song echoes beautifully throughout the hall, bringing my insides to a twist. I haven't heard it for months. The song is the one that reminded me of Suite 22. Surprisingly, it still elicits an emotional response from me, although not nearly as strong as it once used to.

I refocus my attention on my to-be sister-in-law, ignoring the old association with the song. This will be what I associate this song with from now on—my brother's wedding.

There's the inevitable chatter as soon as the guests see Alina walking with her parents, commenting on how marvelous she looks. The most prevalent things I hear are gasps and "Wows!" echoing through the large hall.

Devan also watches her as she approaches him. For a brief moment, I see them look at each other adoringly. Devan even chuckles slightly when he does so. Their love is so pure.

Once Alina arrives at the *mandap,* Devan takes her hand into his and kisses it. The entire hall erupts into oohs and aahs, resulting in subsequent laughter from the guests.

And just like that, my brother is getting married to one of the most beautiful people I've ever met in one of the most beautiful venues I've ever seen.

There's just enough time following the completion of all the post-wedding rituals to prepare for the reception. My family, including Devan and Alina, is staying the night at the famous British-themed Notting Hotel in San Francisco.

The Notting is about a ten-minute drive from the reception venue. Aman and I, obviously, opted out of the hotel since we'll be close to our apartment. I offered Ari to stay the night too, but she planned on hanging out with some of our cousins at the hotel following the reception. Something about an after-party.

Ari, my mom, and I are in Ari's reserved hotel room to get dressed for the reception. My dad and Aman are in the room my parents have, which is on the same floor as Ari's.

For the reception, I'm wearing a *lengha choli*. My *choli* is navy blue with minimal gold embroidery and slips off the shoulders on both sides. The *lengha* is also navy blue, covered with gold stars that are spread evenly across the entire skirt, and my *chunni* is made of navy-blue net with simple gold embroidery.

The three of us are getting our makeup and hair professionally done again for the reception. As of right now, it's just us in the room with our respective makeup and hair professionals.

"Banu, how is Aman enjoying the wedding?" my mom asks, positive I will know the answer.

"He's having a great time."

"I noticed he's been quiet this past day or two," she says, but then is distracted by the makeup artist.

I know why, but I hope that my mom doesn't know why. She often asks questions despite knowing the answer.

Right as I'm about to speak, Ari interjects, "I was talking to him yesterday, and he wishes his mom was here." I immediately look at her to determine if what she's saying is the truth. Usually, she glances toward me to affirm, but this time she doesn't. Instead, she avoids my glance.

My mom sighs. "Poor baby. It would've been nice if Harmeet-ji had been able to make it." That is Aman's mom's name, but my mom adds the *ji* out of respect.

"He's such a nice boy," she adds.

"He is," Ari agrees.

I glance at her again with a confused expression, but she still doesn't look at me. I wonder where this new-found generosity toward Aman is coming from. Part of me is certain the conversation they had the day before is contributing to her outpouring of empathy for him, and that conversation didn't solely consist of Aman saying he wishes his family was here. She wouldn't avoid me if that was the sole reason.

It's also probable that Ari has developed a particular soft spot for Aman since we've been spending a lot of time together. He's been incredibly invested in my family's happiness, as is evident from his actions. Not only is he being helpful, but his demeanor has changed from his usual carefree attitude to one of compassion. He's been more serious than the Aman I know well. I've witnessed a different side of himself this week that he kept hidden all this time.

"Bub, I know that you get asked this all the time, but have you ever looked at Aman as more than a friend?" Ari's bold question makes my eyes pop. The question also catches my mom's interest.

She's never overtly asked me this before. First Devan, now Ari?

Before I'm able to respond to her or even inquire why she is asking, there's a knock at the door, and Ari is the one who answers it. The door isn't visible to my mom and I, but we hear Ari yelp in excitement when she opens it.

"What happened?" my mom shouts in Punjabi.

Within seconds, an ecstatic Ari appears again, and alongside her is a smiling Rayshaan.

"Oh, my god!" I squeal, springing up from my chair. Rayshaan sets aside a rolling suitcase to give both my mom and me a hug. He must have come straight from the airport.

Apparently, no one knew he was coming except for Aman, who has known for weeks. He'd texted Aman once he landed to get our room number.

Although Rayshaan's mom did have knee surgery, she insisted that Rayshaan at least come for the reception. For Ari. He's taking a midafternoon flight back home on Sunday.

It warms my heart witnessing how happy Ari is to see her best friend. Her Aman.

Rayshaan's arrival created such a frenzy that both my mom and sister forgot about the question Ari asked me right before his arrival.

Have I ever looked at Aman as more than a friend?

It *has* crossed my mind.

chapter 41

My dad and Aman left for the reception long before we did. They're standing at the entrance of the partially sheer tent at Oceana when we arrive, purposely placed at the corner of the golf course. Aman is taking on my mom's role of welcoming guests.

He's wearing an all-black suit with a black shirt, black silk tie, and black loafers. His dark, sleekly trimmed beard and his neatly styled hair naturally complete his all-black ensemble. He did something new to his beard, and I don't know what it is, but he looks drop-dead gorgeous. I realize that I've checked out my best friend nearly every day this week.

Have I ever looked at Aman as more than a friend? Ari's question pings in the back of my mind.

Aman and Rayshaan's greeting to one another is a big, knowing, we-pulled-the-surprise-off-successfully kind. My dad is amazed that he came all this way just for the reception.

"You're full of surprises this week," I say to a grinning Aman.

"I know, A! The surprises have made this week that much more beautiful! And look at this tent," Ari exclaims, still over the moon that Rayshaan is here with her tonight.

The cream, silver, and gold-colored décor in the tent resembles a classy winter wonderland. There are white roses and white-stemmed trees everywhere. There is blue ambient lighting throughout, and the sides of the tent that aren't sheer are covered in twinkle lights. Some areas even have fake snow spread on the floor.

"You're right, Ari. I can't even say this tent is the most beautiful thing of this week," Aman says, drink in hand. I glimpse Ari squeeze his arm so quickly, I almost think I imagined it.

I notice him constantly looking in my direction. He's maintaining his newfound serious demeanor, but he doesn't say anything directly to me.

Just as I'm about to respond, Aman excuses himself to get another drink from the bar.

"Have you two realized that you're in love with each other?" I ask Rayshaan rather bluntly and more boldly than I intended. It's just the two of us as Ari excused herself to use the restroom. I suppose The Doctor's Cure, Alina's specialty cocktail, I'm having is stronger than I expected. Devan's is called Money Well Spent.

Rayshaan isn't offended by the question, though, and neither is he surprised by it. Instead, he's smiling sweetly, and it's adorable.

"That's so cute," I say, giggling.

"It's nice to see her happy," he says shyly, smiling and laughing, which provides as much of a response as if he were answering my question directly.

"I think your surprising her—I mean *us*—sent her over the moon."

He grins. "You know, Bani, Aman helped a lot. I wouldn't have been able to pull it off if he didn't help."

He gives me a sideways glance, and I immediately regret asking him the question about him and Ari, because now I know I have a similar one forthcoming.

"*Have you* two realized that you're in love with each other?"

"I've been hearing that a lot lately." I chuckle. "We're friends." I don't know what else to say or think.

"So were Ari and I. Be right back," Rayshaan says hurriedly as Ari pulls him to introduce him to some cousins.

I search the crowd for Aman, and find him conversing with my mom and a few guests near the bar. My mom introduces him to the guests that recently arrived. He graciously shakes their hands, smiling.

It has crossed my mind, particularly as of late. A lot, in fact. The butterflies I get when I see him at times, the longing way he's looked at me recently. But, if Aman liked me romantically, he would have said something after all this time. He's had plenty of opportunities to.

In desperate need of fresh air, I head outside for the skyline view of San Francisco. It's still light out, and the evening sunset has just begun.

There's a yacht with partygoers passing by in the distance. I mull over all of these thoughts about Aman, but the cheering from the yacht, the sound of the waves splashing energetically against the rocks of the island, and the DJ's music from inside the tent distract me.

"Ladies and gentlemen." The DJ tests his microphone.

I need to be present for my brother and sister-in-law. It's their day. The rest of this can wait, I decide, and then return to the tent.

"The Sethi and Bajwa families would like to thank you all for joining and celebrating the joyous occasion of Devan and Alina's wedding. The bride and groom are a few minutes away. When we announce that they've arrived, we ask that you take your seats and give them a warm welcome."

Both families will each have their own small entrance prior to the couple's. The announcement from the DJ was our signal to approach the entrance of the tent. Alina's family will enter first, then us.

Alina and Devan's limousine appears in the distance at the entrance of the parking lot. As soon as they exit the limousine, both families cheer for the lovely couple.

Devan's all-white tuxedo and Alina's full-sleeve white and silver *lengha* make them both look royal. A massive necklace adorns Alina's neck, which is our family heirloom that was given to her as a wedding gift. The red bridal bangles lay across her arms, adding a beautiful and natural contrast to her entire outfit.

During Alina's family's entrance, we hear an eruption of cheering through the tent. Ari is the first to enter from our side, and amongst the cheering, I can specifically hear Rayshaan.

When I hear the onset of my and Devan's favorite song, an American rap song, the drapes of the tent open for me. The spotlight is shining brightly, and I'm unable to properly see anyone. Had I not known where Aman, Rayshaan, Ari, and Jay were sitting, I wouldn't have known where to go.

Amidst the clapping and blaring music, I hear Aman whistling and cheering the loudest. I'm reveling in the moment, dancing to the upbeat song for the remaining time that it plays.

"The parents of the groom, ladies and gentlemen! Let's give them a big round of applause," the DJ announces next.

My parents adorably hold hands as they dance. Since they don't necessarily have a song with Devan, they chose their first dance song from their wedding reception.

Once my parents arrive at their respective seats, the DJ requests that everyone stand, and he makes the announcement that the entire crowd has been eagerly awaiting. When Devan and Alina pass by, the guests are to pop the individual confetti poppers placed at each seat toward them.

"Ladies and gentlemen, now for the moment we have all been waiting for. The couple of the hour, the newly married Mr. and Mrs. Sethi!"

Within seconds, the tent is flaring with cream, silver, and gold confetti, resembling a winter snowfall. There is an endless sea of smiles all around the tent. So many people are partaking in my brother and sister-in-law's happiness. It's a testament to how loved they are.

Alina and Devan decided against any sort of speeches or dance performances. Instead, they opted for any words from close family or friends to be added to the wedding video, which the videographer completed within the last half hour. Guests watch the various moments of Devan and Alina from this week and from the years of their relationship in wonderment.

In between scenes, there's a clip of Aman, which must have been taken earlier today at the wedding. In the clip, Aman congratulations the couple and specifically mentions me as being the reason he's able to be here and celebrate Devan and Alina. In the video, for everyone to see, he refers to me as his best friend. *Friend.* More proof that Aman doesn't have feelings for me.

"Come on, young man. Let's have that drink I've been waiting to have with you," my dad says in Punjabi, promptly pulling Aman away once the video is over. I didn't get a minute to acknowledge Aman's words from the video.

Ari jokes about how Aman is his favorite of the three of us because he didn't summon either Ari or me to join.

As I glance around, my eyes land on my dad and Aman, who are standing close to the bar, drinks in hand. From my vantage point, they appear to be having a meaningful conversation, although I can only see Aman's face. He nods his head with an intense, concentrated stare.

My dad changes his positioning, and I can now see his profile. He's actively and consistently using his hands when speaking. He does this when he's trying to make a point, but I don't understand what he'd be trying to make a point about to Aman.

The entire time I've been observing, which is for a while, I haven't seen Aman speak. He doesn't even open his mouth to try to get a word in. He just nods his head, sips his drink, or smiles. I plan to ask him later what my dad is talking to him this passionately about—what has Aman so enthralled.

But for now, I immediately position my chair toward the dance floor when the DJ announces that it's time for Devan and Alina's first dance. It is my favorite part of a wedding, and I need to be able to see it perfectly—the *just-married, incandescently happy* glow.

Specifically, I'm impatient to hear which song they're going to dance to because it's usually a song that has meaningful significance.

Before Devan and Alina take to the dance floor, Devan makes an announcement of his own. Unbeknownst to any of the family members or guests, both Devan and Alina arranged for a famous singer to sing during the first dance at their wedding.

"Why don't we make an already special week and evening even more special?" Devan exclaims.

The entire tent goes into a fantastic frenzy as soon as they see the singer appear following Devan's announcement. No one was expecting a surprise of this caliber.

The singer breaks out into a melodic tone of one of his famous upbeat songs. I watch as my brother leads my sister-in-law to the center of the dance floor. As they begin their dance, Alina laughs at something Devan says, and they both grin happily.

I'm enraptured, but I briefly look down, unintentionally staring into space. Despite this being a joyous moment for my brother, I can't help feeling a sudden moment of sadness for myself—confusion over what everyone is saying about my best friend. I was better off not knowing about any of their thoughts.

Feeling selfish, I look back up to re-focus on Devan and Alina, who have danced their way directly in front of me on the dance floor. Further in the background and to the left, I see a familiar figure standing close to the bar and facing my direction. I instinctively turn my head to the figure and see it's Aman. He's already looking narrowly at me.

He slightly smiles, putting a brief pause on his fixed, serious expression. He's simultaneously squinting his eyes and pressing his lips together with an expression of speculation and interest. The same one he doesn't realize he makes.

Aman can't know about all of these thoughts and opinions of Rayshaan and my family. We're barely getting over a huge argument.

I need to do my best to be normal with Aman, I think to myself.

I mouth the word "favorite" to him with what I'm sure is a love-sick face as I point to my brother and his wife engaging in their first slow dance. His smile grows only a bit.

Nodding in acknowledgement, he takes a sip of his drink. He knows this is my favorite part of a wedding. I don't need to tell him.

Alina and Devan's first dance lasts a few more minutes before the DJ invites all the couples to the floor for a slow dance.

chapter 42

Aman

"You love her, don't you?" She had asked me the day before the wedding.

"Who?" I'd said, avoiding eye contact with her, but knowing she wouldn't fall for my pretense in the slightest.

I pretended to be distracted by my phone. *She'll know if she sees my expression*, I thought. I couldn't falsify indifference at that moment.

But she kept pressing.

Accepting that she wouldn't give up until I gave her the answer she knew was the truth, I responded simply, "I'm crazy about her." That was the first time I'd ever said it out loud—to anyone.

She looked at me with both pity and hope, assuring me that she'd maintain my confession in confidence.

I have to admit, it was immensely satisfying to finally reveal my feelings for Bani to *someone*.

Since then, Ari has been by my side. She caught on to the lack of normalcy between us and suggested that I take the initiative to rectify it before it became obvious to others, not just to her.

Ari is adamant about determining whether the feelings are reciprocated and is convinced that they are.

"I know my sister. She *may* not realize it herself yet, but I know her," she repeatedly declared, providing me with a glimmer of hope each time.

I have kept this to myself for nearly a year, and the only way Bani will find out is directly through me. This has been a long time coming, and she *should* only find out through me.

Multiple girls at her brother's wedding are giving me their undivided attention. I'm fully aware of it, but it's bothersome. Contrary to what I told her, I didn't stop dating because I was taking a break from girls. I stopped dating because they weren't—aren't—*her*. She's the one I want and have wanted.

It initially developed months ago, when I saw her fully focused and studying in the law library. She was mesmerizing.

I'm not sure what it was about that particular moment, but I couldn't take my eyes off her. It may have been a combination of her messy bun and the blue highlighter she'd unknowingly streaked across her face. She was focused, natural, and unbothered.

When that feeling didn't go away weeks later, I decided it was time to do something about it and tell her how I felt.

She was in a particularly good mood that night and wanted to celebrate. We'd gotten our civil procedure write-ups back, and she'd done superbly.

We'd gone to Suite 22, the bar, and at some point that evening, I was going to confess my feelings to her—tell her that I didn't want to be with anyone who wasn't her. Right when I was about to do it, I lost my nerve, pausing before I was close enough, and went down the hall.

I was embarrassed that I needed to gather myself first. But as cliché as it may sound, I knew she was different. I *know* she is different. For the first time ever, I felt nervous to tell a girl how I felt. Me, Aman Wajla.

She still doesn't know the real reason I hate that place—Suite 22. The night I almost told her is the same night she met that...I feel myself growing both angry and hurt. Aware that I'm clenching my jaw, I take a deep breath and then take a sip of my drink, letting the ice-cold bourbon have a similar chilling effect on my quickly boiling blood.

The same night she met that jackass.

I know she still thinks about and wonders about him. Earlier today, when Alina was walking out for the wedding ceremony, she was thinking about him then. It was the song.

Mark was also there that night, but he didn't know how I felt toward her. He still doesn't. If he did, he would've done something to help. He did corner me once, when I first met Bani, to ask me whether I felt the emotion I feel now. At that time, I didn't. Or at least I didn't realize I did. So, my honest response at the time was "no."

That night at Suite 22, I was only gone for a second. Right when I was coming back to the bar, I saw a tall, scrawny guy talking to her. She's really good at looking disinterested when talking to a random guy, but this time I didn't see that. She was interested.

She was *interested*? In *that* guy? He looked like a fuckboy.

Then he turned out to be one. And I couldn't do anything to protect her. She wouldn't have believed me. He was good at hiding it until the very end, and frankly, it wasn't my concern. At least not in her eyes.

I know her. She's feisty, but at the same time, she's incredibly sweet and thoughtful. She has a pull that hasn't stopped reeling me in one way or the other since the day I met her. The hold she has on me—and she doesn't even know it.

Eventually, I must have stopped fighting it for my feelings to bring me here.

To this day, I wonder how that jackass could have possibly looked at this beautiful woman and even thought to treat her that way.

I clearly and unequivocally communicate my intentions up front whenever I date a woman. Bani knows this and respects this about me.

But this guy. He made it look like he was *actually* interested in her and wanted to be with her. Then he left her. As if it was the easiest thing he'd ever done. Never looked back once. She was wrecked for months. That son of a bitch took a piece of her, and she's been scrambling to get it back since.

Suite 22. That's what she calls him. If I *ever* see that guy, I won't stop myself from beating the shit out of him.

I'm growing angry once again as I tightly grasp the empty glass I was drinking from. There's no bourbon in it to calm me down. I gesture to the bartender to prepare another drink for me before I shatter this glass.

He only wanted to fuck her, and once he did, he took the easy way out. She's never told me they slept together, but I know they did. She wouldn't have been as hurt as she was if they hadn't.

I thought my feelings were gone. I thought I was safe. But now that I'm looking at this girl right in front of me, she's still as mesmerizing as the day I saw the blue highlighter on her cheek. As the day she told me her favorite drink was an old-fashioned.

Under the pretense of getting a celebratory drink, her dad took me aside after Devan and Alina's wedding video to emphasize to me how strongly he felt about us being together. I assume the cocktails he'd already consumed were impacting his blunt delivery, but regardless of the alcohol, I know her entire family agrees.

If I didn't already feel what he was urging me to feel, I would've thought that he was impressively persuasive. I was aching to say to her dad, "I'm not the one who needs this talk. Your daughter does." But I couldn't say that to him. All I did was listen to him, nodding my head and maintaining composure as he energetically preached to me. Because I agree with him. *One hundred percent.*

Thursday night, Bani and I got into the most serious and vehement argument we have ever had, and not speaking to her was intolerable. I can only fake it so much.

Initially, I was hopeful when I saw how bothered she was by Alina's cousins' interest in me. Why would it bother her to the point she felt she needed to bring it up to me? The attention had happened plenty of times before, but this time, she sounded jealous.

There are moments where I believe Ari when she says that Bani has feelings for me too. She's been different lately. I seem to be affecting her in a way that's more than just a friend. She's looked at me differently. She notices me differently.

Despite the argument, this week has probably been the best week of my life. She's given me a second family without even intending to. She is my family.

It's the first time I've seen her in Punjabi clothes. A girl in Punjabi clothes is hot, but Bani in Punjabi clothes isn't something I was mentally or emotionally prepared for. Both are my weakness.

When the DJ announced that Devan and Alina would head to the dance floor for their first dance, I instinctively looked at her. It's her favorite part, the slow dance, and I couldn't stop staring at her. Her reaction is always enchanting.

I felt somewhat protected because while everyone was look-ing at Devan and Alina, including Bani, I was the only one who wasn't. I was looking at Bani. It was less obvious this way.

My concentration was momentarily interrupted when Devan announced that he had a surprise for the guests. He introduced a famous singer who sang the song for their first dance here live to-night. I wasn't at all surprised that Devan managed to arrange this.

As soon as the singer came out, the entire crowd erupted into cheers and clapping. We weren't expecting this, and Devan con-clusively made this the best wedding I've ever attended.

He and Alina smiled uncontrollably at the crowd's reaction to their announcement, as did the singer. The singer congratulated the couple and began crooning his famous song, but an acoustic version of it.

I turned my attention back to Bani, who watched her brother and sister-in-law engage in their first dance as a married couple. Her hands were propped under her chin for support, and she sport-ed a love-sick expression. I quite literally wanted to grab her and take her with me to dance right alongside the newlywed couple. But I couldn't.

She suddenly shifted her gaze from her brother and sister-in-law and briefly looked down. She almost looked sad. When she finally looked back up, her gaze briefly returned to the couple, then came directly for me. *Me.*

My face was expressionless, if not serious. I may have smiled slightly unknowingly.

She returned the smile, but it was sweet—solemn.

That's the thing about this girl. I know what she's feeling without her intending to show it to me—or anyone for that mat-ter. She craves love.

Then, she mouthed something to me. I fully comprehended what she said without having to think twice. Because right after she mouthed it, she pointed to her brother and sister-in-law. She mouthed "favorite," meaning the first dance is her favorite part of a wedding.

Bani, I know.

I gave a faint smile and then nodded, acknowledging what she conveyed to me without speaking out loud. I sipped my drink, hoping it would soothe the aching sensation in my throat. It didn't. I suppose it only helps with calming any growing anger.

She diverted her attention back toward her brother and sister-in-law. But I couldn't look at anything, or anyone, else.

It was all very blatant of me, but I didn't care. Not tonight.

When the DJ welcomes other couples on the dance floor for the second slow song, I quickly contemplate whether it'd be uncomfortable if I walked over to her and asked her to dance with me. We're not a couple, but it wouldn't be weird, would it?

No, it wouldn't, I decide. Fuck it. I'm doing it.

I hurriedly gulp the rest of my drink, partially for liquid courage so I don't get nervous again this time. Seera approaches me with an annoyingly huge grin, but before she's able to say anything, I excuse myself.

Unnoticed by Bani, I hurry to the table. Ari, on the other hand, is facing my direction and sees me approaching. She may have been watching me because when I make eye contact with her, she's already smiling.

Bani's profile is facing me, but she's fully engrossed with the dancing and doesn't notice me approaching. Without saying a word, I hold my hand out to her, waiting for her to grab it so I can lead the two of us to the dance floor.

Her eyes flare momentarily with surprise. Except the perception and circumstances have changed after this week. There's more to our relationship now. I sense it.

As the surprise dissipates, a blank expression appears across her beautiful face. It takes her what feels like an eternity to reach out for my hand and accept my invitation. But she does. There are still remnants of tension between us, and I hope this gesture will alleviate that and maybe allude to something more. I'm hoping for the latter.

Our hands remain locked as I lead the way to the increasingly crowded dance floor. Her hands are incredibly soft, and I feel heat rushing through me. Her bangles gently tap against my palm as we walk. The nervous feeling I had the night I almost told her returns. But I'm not backing out this time.

Devan spots me while dancing with Alina, whose back is toward us. His smile toward Alina translates to a smile toward me, winking at me as I bring his sister to the floor. He whispers something to Alina, who discreetly turns around to face us, but Bani doesn't see this because I'm blocking her view.

Once we're on the dance floor, I turn around, and she's looking up at me. I clasp her hand and wrap my other hand around her waist as we begin slow dancing. She follows.

She looks confused and concerned. Since this is a somewhat new facet of our relationship, her response is understandable. I'm careful to initially maintain the normalcy that she's used to from me. I don't want to alarm her.

"What happened?" I say in Punjabi, acting like we do this all the time, when in fact it's the first time.

She is momentarily astounded.

"Oi," I repeat myself when she doesn't say anything.

"Since when do you slow dance?" she asks.

I laugh, glad she's not upset. "Ban, there's more to me than this pretty face." I mockingly stroke my beard. This is the Aman she's used to.

She laughs, sending me on cloud nine. I can sense that she feels more at ease than she did at first. The uncertainty in her demeanor is evaporating. My impromptu gesture was a wild card in terms of how she'd react, but I'm relieved she responded favorably.

Alleviating the pressure, Ari and Rayshaan also join us on the dance floor. Unlike Bani and me, they both *know* they have feelings for each other and evidently are more comfortable.

"What were you and my dad talking about?" Bani breaks the few moments of silence between us. I didn't know she'd witnessed the interaction with her dad.

"When?" I feign ignorance, not sure if it's convincing or not.

"Earlier, at the bar."

I don't know if I should truthfully tell her the topic of our conversation. Now is not the time to tell her, I decide. If I tell her now, it could potentially bring about a surge of awkwardness, and that's not a risk I'm willing to take. Not when we're amidst her brother's wedding reception, thoroughly enjoying ourselves.

"He was telling me how happy he is that I'm here," I say, which is not a lie, because he did say that. That's just not all that he said.

"Really?" She doesn't sound convinced.

I hoist an eyebrow at her dubious look. "Yes. Why is that so hard to believe?"

She laughs again.

God, she's gorgeous. I stare down at her when she looks in her parents' direction. Even with her heels, our difference in height is enough for me to continue to look at her without her noticing. But I need to remain cognizant of our surroundings because now the physical dynamic has changed. I can't look at her unnoticed.

"I think my dad said more than that. He was energetically waving his hands all over the place."

"He was energetically telling me how happy he is that I'm here." We both laugh this time. She's trying to pull it out of me, but I don't give in.

I relish this moment because right now, I have an acceptable pretense to hold her. We're not intimately close, as the actual couples are, but this is the closest we've ever been for an extended period of time.

When I realize I'm still gazing at her for too long, I gesture in the singer's direction. "Did you know about this?" He continues to give his amazing live and intimate performance, singing lyrics that exemplify my feelings for her to the dot as I hold her.

"No, I didn't! Isn't that insane? They both keep surprising us this week when it's their celebration."

"I'm not surprised. Your brother is a badass."

"He is." She grins.

Once the singer dramatically yet marvelously wraps up the second slow song for all the couples, the DJ automatically begins playing *bhangra*. The pairs that are already on the floor convert their energy to the more upbeat dance, and the dance floor slowly fills up.

Bani is glowing with zealous energy. Before I get caught up in the moment and inadvertently reveal anything to her, I excuse myself, leaving her with her family on the dance floor.

She has been extra cautious and resilient since Suite 22. But I think I've made some progress.

Then, earlier this week, when we were getting trailed by that car after Devan's *mehndi*...How do I tell her? How do I tell her that I *think* I know who it was?

She may think I'm completely out of line since I have no proof. If I tell her without being sure, I could potentially lose her friendship. But if I don't tell her, it could put her in danger.

No, I have to *at least* warn her.

Drink in hand and ready to sip, I turn back to face her, exhaling sharply. The things I've done to protect her.

chapter 43

Bani

Amidst some obligatory socializing, I glance over at Aman and find him standing at the bar talking to a girl I don't recognize. She's flirting with him by grabbing his arm every chance she gets. I can tell by his obvious demeanor that he's merely being polite. His body language is standoffish.

Thinking back to the second slow song, I was initially surprised when Aman asked me to join him. One, I've never seen him slow dance, and two, it didn't occur to me that he'd ask me.

I considered whether this new and unexplored aspect of our relationship would make things awkward, especially on top of our recent argument and after all I've heard. But it didn't. It was extremely comfortable and didn't feel like it was the first time we'd danced together. I was completely normal and didn't give him any indication of my turbulent thoughts. I'm proud of myself.

Immediately following the slow dance, there was a transition to a booming Punjabi song, drastically altering the serene atmosphere to a thunderous one. The base was strong enough to be felt throughout the entire tent.

Aman let go of my hand and disappeared from the dance floor. After dancing to a bit of *bhangra*, I returned to my seat, and that's when I noticed he was at the bar.

As I'm observing him, the DJ plays an extremely familiar song—Aman's and my favorite song. We make eye contact at the onset of the first beat and beam with excitement. He immediately gestures to me to head to the dance floor, disregarding the girl he's talking to. He hurriedly mouths to her, "I have to go," and leaves before she has the opportunity to respond to his abrupt departure. I briefly notice her appalled expression.

The gist of the song is about a guy who breaks up with a girl and is happy at first, but then begins missing the girl over the next few weeks. This artist came up with an upbeat song about a break-up, which is truly impressive but not atypical with Punjabi music.

Aman grabs me and pulls me toward the dance floor. I don't think I've ever seen him dance as happily and energetically as he is now. *Bhangra* is naturally an upbeat dance, but Aman is taking over the dance floor with his inherent enthusiasm. The entire audience is surrounding us and cheering. All eyes are on Aman primarily and on me secondarily as he dances and sings the lyrics of the song to me.

I first heard this song when I was dating Suite 22. He'd gone home to San Diego, and he posted a video on social media of him dancing to it with his family to celebrate the birth of his nephew. It was during this trip that he ended things with me. He wasn't communicating with me at all, and the minute I voiced that to him, he bolted, figuratively.

For a while, the song only reminded me of him. But then, Aman converted a song that I loathed to one that I love by distracting me from the original source and creating happy memories with it. Now it's my favorite *bhangra* song because Aman made it *our* song.

He's done so much to help me cope with that horrible experience. He's done so much for me, period.

Our energy calms down enormously when the song is over, and Aman reaches over to give me a short but tight hug. There's an echoed "aww" and whistling from the audience in response to his embrace.

"How much did you drink?" I ask rhetorically over the blaring music.

He's unable to hear me. "What?"

"How much did you drink?" I repeat myself louder than before.

"You know how I get when that song comes on." He laughs, panting as he speaks, reflecting the level of energy he set forth when dancing to it.

It's true. When that song comes on, he may very well be hypnotized by it because he's always in his own world.

Midway through the next song, my mom and dad summon me over to where they are.

"This is our eldest daughter, Bani. You met the youngest already," my dad introduces me to an elderly couple in Punjabi.

"How are you?" the aunt asks in Punjabi.

My response is brief and polite. I stand there, nodding my head and smiling, as my parents converse with the couple. Then I hear the aunt say, "Now it's your turn."

The inevitable comment strikes again, resulting in a fake laugh from not only me but my parents as well. They're not ready for me to get married yet. Neither am I.

Once the conversation veers away from me, I subtly excuse myself.

When I turn my attention back to the dance floor, Aman, Ari, Rayshaan, and Jay are no longer there. I meander around the crowded tent to find at least one of them, and eventually make my way to the main entrance of the tent that leads to the parking lot. There are tons of guests swarming in and out.

It's dark outside, making it difficult to see beyond the bright lights of Oceana. I'm careful not to venture too far away from the crowd and into the nearly pitch-black lot since I'm alone.

Still unable to locate Aman, Ari, Rayshaan, or Jay, I turn for the tent until I see a familiar face walking toward a car.

It's Marcus.

Impacted by the alcohol, I'm confused for a split second about where I am and how Marcus could possibly be at my brother's wedding reception. I yell his name to get his attention, but he doesn't hear me at first. I yell again, and he hears me this time.

When he finally sees me, his expression is full of surprise, similar to mine. Except mine is also mixed with confusion. I don't recall telling him where the reception was. How is he here?

He's staring at me as I approach him. I ponder a subtle way to ask what he's doing here, but nothing comes to mind. "What are you doing here?"

He's dressed in casual clothing, not wedding attire, and looks me up and down before smiling. "Holy crap, Bani," he comments on my appearance, but my facial expression remains unchanged.

"What are you doing here?" I repeat.

"My friend was invited to this wedding, and he asked me to pick him up because he was too drunk to drive." He's still smiling nonchalantly. "I had no idea this wedding was *your brother's* wedding," he adds in response to my silence.

"Which side is your friend attending the wedding for?"

"The bride. His sister is friends with the bride."

"What's his name? Maybe I know him too." Frankly, beyond Alina's immediate family members and a few close relatives, I don't know the majority of the individuals in attendance on her behalf.

"Neel." The name doesn't ring a bell.

"Why? Do you think I followed you here?" He grins, leaning against the car.

The thought did cross my mind, but I didn't tell Marcus about the reception location, and he would have no other way of getting this information. I don't think he knows Devan or Alina by name in order to make the association on his own.

"No, I'm just really surprised to see you here." I sound more nervous than I intend to.

"Me too. Small world." He remains leaning against the car with his arms crossed, staring inquisitively at me.

I don't remain with him for long because I'm certain that my absence will be noticed if I'm gone from the reception for too long. Marcus reminds me of our drinks date the next day before I walk away.

Because of the run-in with Marcus, I've drifted farther from the tent than I intended.

That wasn't an encounter I was expecting in the slightest, I think to myself. Although seeing Marcus at my brother's wedding was strange, the whole week has been a weird kismet of events.

I'm almost at the entrance when I see a figure approach me from my right. It's Aman, and his expression is grim.

"Hey, I was looking for you," I say.

"Were you?" He actually looks peeved, which I wasn't expecting.

"Yes. Where were you?"

"Nowhere. I was just around." He's being cryptic and avoiding eye contact with me.

A few seconds later, I spot the same girl that he was talking to earlier emerge from the same direction he came from, fixing her clothes and sneaking back into the tent.

chapter 44

I'm livid, but I keep my feelings hidden.

This was the core of our argument on Thursday, from which we're still recovering. Yet he has the audacity to secretly disappear with some random girl that he's never met and doesn't know—that I don't even know—at my *brother's* wedding reception? What were they possibly doing? I'd been looking for him for nearly twenty minutes.

And to think that my family thinks he's *crazy* about me. I shake my head in disappointment.

I make a serious, genuine effort to focus on the remainder of the reception and not be affected by Aman and his typical antics. We haven't spoken since the encounter outside. I've been mainly successful because I've been hanging out with Jay. Ari has been understandably exploiting the limited time that she has with Rayshaan.

Aman has now caught on to the fact that there's a residual, lingering issue. However, he looks confused as to why. But the timing was too perfect for me to misconstrue the situation.

At this point, I wish that instead of deciding to go to our apartment, I was going to a hotel room so I wouldn't have to go home with Aman. The option to stay with Ari in her hotel room exists, but since Rayshaan is here, I don't want to impose. Plus, if I suddenly decide to join them, it'll raise suspicion.

Instead, I feign exhaustion.

My parents ask whether we're coming to their house tomorrow evening for more post-wedding rituals. Since we've been completely disregarding our course load since earlier this week, we both determine how difficult it will be to neglect our workload the day before we return to classes.

Aman opens the car door for me and helps me in the car as I struggle with my puffy and enormous *lengha*. By the time he comes around and sits opposite me in the backseat, I position my head against the windowsill. Closing my eyes, I pretend to rest during the ride. I'm not in a confrontational mood at the moment.

Despite my eyes being closed, I can sense Aman fidgeting. I must be truly tired, because as I'm mentally running through the evening, I fall asleep.

The next thing I know, Aman is gently nudging me. "Hey, hey." His voice is low and soft, careful not to startle me. "We're home."

"Hm?" I respond sleepily, opening my eyes. I look around and recognize our neighborhood. For a moment, I feel disoriented because I can't seem to recall which direction our apartment building is in. Aman appears to my left, opening my door to once again help me out of the car.

I stand by the door of the car while Aman removes our bags from the trunk. As soon as he closes it, he looks immediately past me toward a familiar face in front of our building. Noor.

Aman looks exhausted and exasperated. *What is she doing here?* He must be wondering the same thing. One thing is evident from his facial expression: he definitely doesn't *want* Noor to be here.

This night keeps getting better and better, I think to myself sarcastically. I'm too drained from the week to stay awake to hear about what happens between Aman and Noor. In fact, this is great timing because otherwise, he was going to inevitably confront me once upstairs to understand the reason for my attitude toward him. This way, I will be able to quickly change into my pajamas and go to bed.

I do empathize with him, though. He must be equally tired, if not more so, than me. I overheard him telling Ari that even though this has been the best week, he's looking forward to the comfort of his bed. Now, before he can do that, he has to deal with why Noor showed up here this late. Even though he blocked her.

When I pass by her, Noor doesn't make eye contact with me and instead looks like she's holding back her obvious dislike of me. She's fixated on Aman.

"I'll be right back," Aman says to Noor. I don't see or hear her response.

Her behavior has been alarming, and her unexpectedly appearing at our home in the middle of the night just takes it another step further. But I'm sure Aman will manage the situation in his own way.

During our walk up the stairs, Aman doesn't say a word to me. Once we're in our apartment, he sets the bags down and says, "I'll be right back."

Before I have the opportunity to respond, he's out the door.

I look around our apartment. Even though we were here recently, it feels lonelier than it did then.

To minimize my time in the common space of the apartment, I remove my makeup and complete my bathroom rituals before I change into my pajamas in my room.

I'm relieved to have altered my normal routine because I hear our apartment door open only a few moments after I get into bed. Aman enters our apartment shortly after I turned the light off in my bedroom.

According to him, I'm already in bed and asleep, and there's no reason for him to interrupt me. Nonetheless, I hear a gentle knock on my door.

Despite the fact that I'm awake, I don't indicate that I am. I stay quiet.

I hear footsteps walking away from my door, but instead of hearing Aman's bedroom door open and close, I hear a more distant sound. The front door of our apartment opens and closes again. *Where is Aman going at this hour?*

The next morning, our living room is empty. It's difficult to determine whether Aman is asleep or not at home. I must've been in a deep sleep because I don't recall waking up when Aman came back after he went outside again. Actually, I don't believe I heard him at all this morning.

His bedroom door is closed, and I don't have a text from him, which isn't unusual, but recently he's gotten better about communicating with me when he leaves home for longer than normal. I wonder if this is because of the uncomfortable vibes from last night. We've hardly spoken since I ran into him after spotting Marcus.

Marcus.

My memory has been so fogged, I forgot that I'll be meeting him in a few hours. I forgot that I ran into him last night at Devan's reception.

We have yet to receive any sort of correspondence from our school staff regarding the cancellation of last week's classes. I continued to check my email, even during the week, but didn't receive anything for either evidence or criminal law. Since we haven't received an email from either the professor or the registrar by now saying anything to the contrary, I assume class is not canceled, and I decide to go to the library to refresh my memory on the assigned cases from the prior week.

To avoid an encounter with Aman, I gather my laptop and books. I tiptoe around our apartment while getting ready, being careful not to make any loud noises in case he's at home.

He will nonetheless want to know where I am, and I can't avoid saying anything. No matter how I may feel toward him at the moment, I know he'll be concerned if I disappear without a word. I would be if the situation were reversed.

Instead of texting him and allowing room for a conversation, I quickly scribble,

At the library
-B

And leave the note on the counter where I know he'll see it.

Aman and I both agreed that, without compulsion, Professor Gatlin wouldn't cancel class for personal reasons. Without compulsion, that is.

It's interesting that even when I come home from the library, Aman is still nowhere to be found.

Well, I'm not completely clueless about his whereabouts. In response to my note, he added, "Me too," but I have no idea what time this was written. I certainly didn't see Aman at the law library, but given the vast size of it, that's not unsurprising. When he studies alone, he normally goes to the second floor, where he wouldn't have crossed paths with me.

There's no mistaking that our relationship is tumultuous. Again. Instead of texting Aman, I add to the note, "Getting a quick drink with a friend," without divulging any details of where I'm going or who I'm going with. Contrary to what I normally do.

Marcus texts me that he's five minutes away from the bar we're meeting at when I leave home. Not that I'm late, but he alluded to not wanting me to wait alone because of the aggressive drunk girl from last time.

Once I arrive at the bar, Marcus is waiting outside for me and positions himself on the sidewalk to open my door. Similar to Aman's gesture last night when we got back from the party, Marcus holds out his hand to help me out of the car.

The bar is surprisingly busy for a Sunday afternoon. It must be because of the summer-like weather this late in the year and the desire to soak every bit in.

Marcus has apparently prearranged a table for our date because we're immediately seated upon entrance into the bar.

Despite the coincidence of running into Marcus last night, he hasn't mentioned the encounter. He's discussing everything but the wedding, which I find odd.

"You know I like you, right?" I nearly choke on my drink in response to the blunt, rhetorical question. My throat feels hoarse as I clear it.

"What?" The surprise is audible in my voice.

He laughs in response. "Yes, I like you."

"Thank you." I don't know what else to say. I nervously chuckle, avoiding eye contact with him.

This is something that I already guessed. I was thinking about it on the drive here. What I wasn't expecting was for him to openly express it right now. Not in the slightest.

I wait for the awkwardness to pass, which it doesn't for several moments. To my relief, Marcus excuses himself and goes to the restroom.

I'm certain his need to leave the table is genuine because he doesn't strike me as someone who avoids awkward situations. Deep down, I'm flattered, but I can't say that I *like* Marcus per se. I am curious about him, though.

Bani, relax. I give myself a mental pep talk in the meantime, convincing myself to loosen up more. My awkwardness isn't Marcus' fault. No one has ever openly professed their feelings for me before. It's refreshing, and I should embrace it.

As he's returning to our table, he's stopped by a man standing at the bar who seems to recognize him. I'm unable to hear their conversation, but the man appears assertive, and Marcus appears both bothered and evasive. They're interacting as if they know each other. Marcus mouths something to the gentleman with a stern expression before he returns to the table.

"Want to get out of here?" he asks me unexpectedly.

We've only been here for twenty minutes. I was expecting a short date with him, but not this short. His mood seems put off, and I assume that our precipitous exit is due to his interaction with the man at the bar.

Who was this man who caused Marcus to want to leave suddenly?

chapter 45

Drifting from precedent, I invite Marcus upstairs for a drink since our time at the bar was interrupted. It takes some mild convincing, but Marcus eventually accepts my offer. Given my reaction to his overt statement earlier, I feel this is the least I can do.

"How did you know this was it?" I'm surprised when Marcus knows which apartment door is mine since it's the first time he's been to my apartment.

"Oh, you mentioned you live next to a market." It's possible I did. In all honesty, everything before this week feels like a distant memory.

Marcus seats himself on one of the stools in the kitchen while I make each of us a margarita, sparking a discussion on where we'd most like to travel—a random subject, but it provides conversation for a while.

His mood has considerably altered since we left the bar, and he seems to be enjoying himself now.

Nearing an hour since we arrived, the front door opens, and I presume Aman is home. The moment I was hoping to avoid has inevitably arrived with an added layer of complexity caused by Marcus' presence.

I'm feeling rebellious, however. If I truly wanted to avoid Aman, I wouldn't be in the kitchen, let alone *with* Marcus, knowing that he could walk in at any moment.

Aman must not have gone anywhere particularly formal because he's wearing a light pink and peach fitted hoodie with comfortably fitted black sweats. His ensemble isn't appropriate for either the gym or a restaurant.

The disdain between these two guys is palpable. They don't greet or acknowledge each other. It parallels the interaction between me and Noor. In fact, Aman doesn't greet me either.

"I should head out now. I have to meet friends for dinner." Marcus takes Aman's entrance as a signal to leave without hugging or physically touching me. I know he's not meeting anyone because he said that his evening was free earlier.

Marcus briefly pauses when passing by Aman on his way out the door. Again, neither party acknowledges the other.

Aman's face is inscrutable. "Why was he here?" he asks as soon as the door closes.

I look at him, confused. "What do you mean? We went on a date." My response is forthcoming, bold really. I hop on top of the counter, now sitting on it.

"Why was he *here*?" Aman asks me again.

"I wasn't going to sleep with him, if that's what you're asking," I proclaim, taking a sip of my ice-cold margarita.

For a second, I swear I almost see a look of relief on Aman's face when I say this. Except for that one second, he remains expressionless.

"He's not good for you."

I'm instantly defensive. "What? Why not?"

"Ban, you need to be careful with this guy. Please." His plead catches me off guard, but he still hasn't given me a reason. It must be because of Suite 22.

"Aman, every single girl that you talk to isn't good. Do I ever say anything to you?" There is immense attitude in my tone from the residual anger I still feel toward him.

Aman doesn't appear offended by either my remark or demeanor. Nor does he answer my question. Instead, he walks into the kitchen and stands directly in front of me.

Without saying a word, Aman places both his hands on either side of me atop the counter. As he traps me between his arms, I follow his movements, the effects of the margarita slowing my reaction. He leans into the counter, closer to me, and instead of moving back, I gaze at him, struck by his expression and ridiculously handsome face.

There's something different about the way he's looking at me. He looks concerned, almost yearning. The way he's looking at me makes me think of what Devan said to me the other evening about Aman's supposed feelings for me. What Rayshaan said. What Ari asked. Is it true? Was I wrong?

Aman takes one hand away from the countertop and presses it against my left cheek, gently stroking it, and my stomach churns at his touch. He pushes a strand of my hair off my face and behind my ear, then brushes my cheek with his thumb, cupping the side of my face with his hand.

Unable to move, I'm at a loss for words and momentarily forget that I'm angry with him. What's happening? This is Aman, my best friend.

He strokes my left arm and places soft kisses on my hand, slowly moving up toward my shoulder. I shiver with each kiss.

My dry throat is accompanied by a quickly rising heart rate, and words aren't coming out even when I try. I feel dizzy.

Finally, I manage to clear my throat and whisper, "Aman, what are you doing?"

He doesn't respond. He makes brief eye contact with me but then continues kissing me. He goes from kissing my neck to my jawline. My heart is now pounding inside my chest. But I'm not stopping him because I'm loving it.

Suddenly, Aman picks me up, and I jolt up into his arms. I knew he was strong, but this is the first time I've witnessed his strength firsthand. My legs instinctively wrap around his waist, and my arms circle his neck. This is the most intimately he's ever touched or held me. Even more than when he asked me to slow dance last night.

We stare at each other without saying a word for several seconds. I don't smell his usual cologne as he holds me. Instead, he smells like fresh soap. It's so irresistible that I can't help myself from burying my head into his warm neck, taking this new scent all in. The heat from his neck is now pressed against my cool lips, and Aman squeezes my waist, exhaling at my touch.

Aman then gently places his hand on the back of my head, laying me on the couch. He maneuvers me with such ease.

Once Aman sets me down, he strategically uses his leg to create a gap between mine and rests his between them, being careful not to put his body weight completely on me. Aman leans into me again to kiss my forehead, and then he softly kisses my lips.

Aman and I are kissing. My mind is going wild and racing with thoughts. *What's happening? This is Aman.*

This is Aman!

I'm relishing the feel of him, taking it all in as he deepens the kiss between us. I'm not even aware of how long we've been kissing.

One of his hands remains on the side of my face, and the other caresses my side. My memory and instincts feel incredibly fogged by this new encounter with Aman. What's most surprising to me is how much I'm enjoying it. I don't want him to stop.

As soon as he places his hand to undo the first button on my shirt, I suddenly come to my senses, pushing him away and jumping off the couch. He sits up, and I stare down at him with a confused, angry look. He slowly stands upright, and I'm now looking up at him. Our eyes are locked, and I can feel the tears well up inside my eyes. "What are you doing?"

Aman stares at me intently, appearing slightly alarmed. He lets out a heavy sigh as he briefly looks down on the ground. "I...I'm sorry."

"What?" I demand. "Do you think I'm one of your random girls that you can just have your fun with or sleep with?"

I think of the girl from last night, her clothes askew. Only last night, he was with someone else, and now he's kissing me.

His attention returns to me, and his intent look transitions into an offended stare as his eyebrows furrow. He wasn't expecting me to say *that*.

Hell, I wasn't expecting me to say that.

"How the fuck can you even think that?" His voice is not as loud as my question.

I ignore him. "I'm not an option, Aman. Just because things ended with Noor or whatever you had going on with Sophia or that random girl you met at Devan's wedding, you thought, 'Let me go to the next girl I see. Oh, there's Bani at home.'" Some of my words are completely nonsensical and not warranted, and I know it.

He looks both hurt and angry. "Is that what you think?"

"Yes," I lie.

Actually, I don't know what to think. This is all too new to me, and I didn't have time to process my feelings before I started spitting out the first thing that came to mind. Reflex. There's also lingering anger mixed with confusion about what I saw last night.

"I'm finally dating someone," I continue, referring to Marcus even though I don't believe I'm dating him yet. "And I'm sorry that it means I'm no longer an option for you."

He seems to know who I'm talking about, and yet his anger starts to subside. "Bani, you're not an *option*." His voice is solemn and quiet. "He's not good for you. You don't know."

"What don't I know? What I *want* to know is how, *coincidentally*, some random girl turned up from the exact area you were coming from last night when you found me in the parking lot. That wasn't enough for you, Aman?" I feel myself spinning out of control.

I liked kissing him. It felt good. It felt right. But I can't bear the thought of him treating me like all his other girls, as though I'm expendable. No matter how irrational that thought may be.

"What are you talking about?" Aman both sounds and looks perplexed.

"The girl you were talking to last night. When I said I was looking for you, she emerged from the same place you came from with her clothes all fucked up." I'm exaggerating.

He takes a moment to recall the events from the night before he responds. After an instant of silence, he still has a blank expression on his face.

"I literally have no idea what you're talking about."

I'm not sure whether I should believe him or not. I take this moment to abruptly and somewhat dramatically leave. "Whatever."

"Hey, hey," he says softly, clasping my elbow and turning me toward him. He squeezes my elbow and gently softens his grip. We're close again.

He doesn't say anything else, and neither do I. I'm avoiding eye contact with him and forcing an angry expression.

When I finally look up at him, he's looking at me in the most indescribable way. It reminds me of last night when we were dancing to the couples' dance. Except now, he has some anger toward me.

"Let go," I say sternly as I maintain eye contact with him, tears emerging once again. He doesn't so much as flinch, keeping hold of my elbow.

"Let go of my elbow, Aman." I maneuver to shift out of his grip. He hesitates, then eventually releases it.

Once free, I leave him standing alone in the living room.

I contemplate whether I should take the fast train home to Palo Alto and have Ari drop me back off in the evening. It's still early. I can go and still get a respectable amount of sleep before resuming classes tomorrow.

Ari wouldn't hesitate to pick me up. She's been texting me throughout the day, randomly wondering what I'm doing. I know my sister. She's messaging me frequently because she misses having me there.

At this moment, more than ever, I miss her too. The energy at my parents' house must be the polar opposite of what it is in this apartment, and I need that. I feel lonelier than ever.

As I sit on my bed, staring off into space, I hear my phone vibrate.

ARI: TAKE THE NEXT TRAIN. I'LL BE THERE.

I quickly stuff my purse with any necessities, order a car to the train station, and quietly leave without saying a word to Aman.

Ari is already at the train station by the time I arrive, and I'm grateful for her promptness. I'm certain she picked up on the sense of urgency, even if it was a conversation through a text message.

I haven't thought about what happened between me and Aman, and I've been on the move since. I have no idea what this means. I blurted out a lot to him, but I didn't mean any of it. I know Aman, and he would never do something that would jeopardize our relationship. He values it too much.

But one thing I knew immediately is that I've been wanting that to happen for a while now.

Ari immediately realizes that something is wrong. I attempt to convince her that I'm simply nostalgic about the week and wanted to partake in all the events, but the mere fact that Aman isn't with me without an explanation tells her I'm not being truthful. She knows he'd come in a heartbeat if asked. *If* asked.

"Why have you guys been off this week?"

"What do you mean?" I pretend to be ignorant, knowing that my act isn't believable in the slightest.

"It feels like you've been bickering this whole week."

"No, nothing more than usual." I pause. "How's everything at home?" I'm desperate to change the subject, careful not to inadvertently disclose anything to Ari.

"It's been low-key for the most part, but I know that you'd want to be part of it. Daddy is super happy you decided to come." I knew he would be.

I feel my phone ringing in my purse. Aman's name, along with a photo of him with a gorgeous carefree smile, flashes on it. It's strange to look at this older picture of him the same way. Things are different now.

I don't answer, but I also don't ignore the call. I let it ring. He calls me a second time, and when I don't answer the second call, he texts me.

Aman: Where are you??

I don't respond, knowing full well that he'll worry. I'm still confused and uncertain about what I should say to him. If I answer and tell him where I am, he'll probably show up at my parents' house, which is a confrontation that I want to avoid. I don't need to broadcast to everyone in my parent's house that something is going on.

I feel my phone buzz again, but it's not Aman.

> **MARK:** WHAT'S GOING ON? AMAN JUST CALLED ME FREAKING OUT BECAUSE HE CAN'T FIGURE OUT WHERE YOU ARE.

Although it feels incredibly petty to respond to Mark and not to Aman, there's no good reason for me to not respond to Mark, whereas with Aman, there is, and he knows it.

> **ME:** I'M GOING TO MY PARENTS' FOR THE AFTER-WEDDING FESTIVITIES. I WAS HAVING MAJOR FOMO.
> **MARK:** ARE YOU NOT SPEAKING TO AMAN?
> **ME:** LONG STORY BUT YOU CAN TELL HIM WHERE I AM IF YOU WANT.

The fact that I tell Mark to relay the message to Aman instead of texting myself is incontrovertible proof for Mark that Aman and I are not normal.

> **MARK:** OKAY…

I hate that Mark is in the middle. I'm sure he's uncomfortable, especially since he has absolutely no idea what's going on.

Moments pass, and I don't receive a subsequent message from Aman. Mark tells me that Aman didn't message him again either once Mark told him where I was.

My lack of response will make things exponentially worse since I'll eventually see Aman, whether that's later today or tomorrow. But I'm confused and unsure of what to say and how to initiate the conversation with him. Until I know exactly what to say without spiraling out of control, I can't talk to him.

Aman has been my closest friend for a long time, and I don't want to lose that. But Aman *kissed* me, and I *liked* it. The dynamic of our friendship has shifted. There's no way around it.

I need time to process everything without making any rash decisions concerning Aman right now.

Eventually, I also need to talk with him to specifically understand what he's thinking, maybe even feeling. To understand if this was the result of the slow buildup of something more, like everyone thinks, or a sudden reaction.

Did this happen because he really is *crazy* about me? If yes, why didn't he ever say anything to me? I need to understand *where* this came from.

Unsurprisingly, everyone asks me where Aman is and why he didn't come once I'm at my parents' house. As I'm making an excuse, I feel Ari's eyes on me, and I'm suddenly very conscious of my choice of words.

My white lie may have been believable to everyone but her. I wouldn't be surprised if she texts Aman, but I sincerely hope she doesn't.

During the festivities, I stand in a corner of the room, not far from where Alina and Devan are sitting, and listen in on their conversation. Every now and then, I chime in when spoken to.

I remind Ari that she needs to drop me off in San Francisco in the next half hour, and she distractedly agrees. Devan and Alina are also coming, as they decided to extend their stay at their hotel for another day.

Still not fully ready to face him, I hope that Aman is either sleeping or in his room by the time I'm home. Nonetheless, I prepare myself on the drive back in case I do see him.

When I get home, Aman is neither sleeping nor in his room. Instead, as soon as I open the door, he's the first thing I see sprawled out on the couch, watching TV.

He briefly looks toward the door, locking eyes with me for a few seconds, and then turns his attention back to the TV. He stiffens. I can't decipher whether he's angry or hurt. Maybe both.

I set my purse down on the kitchen counter and instantly recall what happened here only a few hours ago when Aman started kissing me.

I may be blushing at the recollection, but I clear my throat and walk toward the back of the couch, where I rest my hands. I gently graze the fabric as a distraction from the discomfort filling the room.

Aman still hasn't shifted his attention toward me. He's blankly, yet obviously, fake-fixating his attention on the TV.

"Aman?"

He repositions but doesn't respond immediately.

I continue as if he isn't ignoring me. "I—"

"You want to know the real reason why I don't like going to Suite 22 anymore?"

Now I'm confused. "What?"

He looks directly at me. "I hate Suite 22."

I'm uncertain whether he's referring to the person or the place. I already know he hates the person.

A muscle ticks in his jaw. "I hate Suite 22 because the night that you met that jackass, I was going to tell you how crazy I am about you."

I'm speechless. My mouth lightly gapes with shock and surprise.

"When I got back to the bar, I was going to tell you, but then I saw you talking to him. And then you started dating him, so I shoved my feelings aside. Then that son of a bitch hurt you." He rakes his fingers through his hair.

"I thought you were still healing from that, and I didn't want to push you. But then, this week, Bani. This week was the best week of my life. I realized that my feelings for you are very much alive. Actually, not even just this week. You're the reason I ended things with Noor. You're not like any other girl to me, Bani. You're not just an *option*." He says this with a touch of insult in his voice, like it was ridiculous for me to even think it, let alone speak it.

This is the most serious that I've ever seen him.

"You are the one I want." He pauses and takes a deep breath. "Bani, I love you."

He waits a few seconds for a reaction from me, but I remain speechless, unable to swallow, let alone speak. Then he leaves the room, leaving me completely bewildered.

I was given a warning that this is the truth, but it feels completely different, having actually heard him say it. I always denied it. I thought it was impossible for Aman to feel that way about me.

But Aman Wajla told me that he *loves* me.

I remain standing, unable to move, in the same position for several minutes. All of the little things Aman has said or done for me in the past race through my mind, along with how I completely missed the true sentiment behind them. They all came from a place of love, but I misconstrued the *type* of love.

I don't recall which direction Aman went in. He either left the apartment or went into his room. I only remember hearing a door close.

While professing his feelings to me, Aman didn't ask me if I felt the same way about him. If he had, I would have told him the truth. The truth is that it's crossed my mind many times if my feelings for him might be deeper than friendship each time anyone brought it up, but I never let the idea linger or develop any further.

Until recently.

Recently, any time he came close to me, anytime he'd touch me, when I'd feel a change in the way he looked at me, when I couldn't take my eyes off of him, when he'd simply be his silly, adorable self, I had to suppress my bubbling feelings. I had to remind myself that *this was Aman*, my best friend. But then it would happen again and again.

I've been resisting falling in love with Aman for so long, I don't know how to unlock my feelings.

This week—and how I reacted to the girls showing Aman attention. I reacted that way because I was actually jealous.

Aman said that he was planning on confessing his deeper affection for me over nine months ago, on the night I met Suite 22. That means he's had feelings for me even longer than that. All this time, I never suspected a single thing. He was very careful not to allude to more than friendship. *Why didn't he just tell me?*

I suddenly realize how practiced he is at keeping secrets from me.

The next morning, a persistent knock on the door jolts me awake. I sleepily walk to the door, but Aman is nowhere in sight. I don't think he's home—the door is unchained.

I look through the peephole and see two men I don't recognize. Once I open the door, peeking through the small gap with the door chain re-secured, the two men are standing with extremely serious expressions on their faces. Before I'm able to say anything, the man to the left speaks.

"Good morning, miss. My name is Matthew Shepherd, and this is my partner, Curtis Blake. We're detectives from the San Francisco Police Department. Does Mr. Aman Wajla live here?" They both flash their badges as evidence that they are indeed officers.

Detective Shepherd looks vaguely familiar now that I've opened the door. "What is this concerning?" I blurt out, knowing very well that they won't tell me anything.

"We would like to speak with Mr. Aman Wajla. Is this his place of residence?" Detective Shepherd speaks while Detective Blake remains quiet. I alternate glances between the two.

"Yes, but I don't believe he's home," I say, even though I don't know for certain if he is or not. I hope that he's actually not home because if he were to pop out of his bedroom right now, that would look suspicious.

To my left, we all hear footsteps coming up the stairs, and I see Aman's familiar black hoodie. He looks in my direction with a confused look. I stare at him blankly.

"Hello. Is something the matter?" Aman asks casually. From his reaction, I can tell that he isn't aware this visit relates to him.

"We're looking to speak with Mr. Aman Wajla. Is that you?"

"Yes. What is this regarding?" He genuinely looks perplexed.

The detectives introduce themselves again to Aman. "We'd like to ask you a few questions about Mr. Gerald Lambino's death and the disappearance of Ms. Sarah Gatlin."

chapter 46

Professor Gatlin is missing. *Professor Gatlin is missing?* Why hasn't the law school communicated this to the students? How long has she been missing? Why would Aman know about both Gerald's death and Professor Gatlin's disappearance?

Once the detectives are inside our apartment, they explain to Aman that they're not arresting him, but they are requesting he undergo voluntary questioning.

Aman was pulled over by the police just a week ago. The police sought him out then for information on an attempted kidnapping, information which he said he didn't have. The detectives haven't shared whether this incident is related to that one.

I imagine Aman only agrees to the questioning in order to get some insight into what's going on. As a law student, Aman knows that if the questions are too probing, he can invoke his right to have a lawyer present, which will compel the detectives to stop immediately.

My thoughts are jumping from point to point. It's all very confusing, but some of it begins to make sense. This is why class was canceled the previous week. This is also probably why Professor Erikson canceled criminal law and his request for a meeting with us, although it seemed urgent initially. What I can't understand is how Aman factors into all of this.

Detective Blake begins his questioning. "Mr. Wajla, can you please explain your whereabouts this past Monday?" He's interrogating Aman as if he's directly related to Professor Gatlin's disappearance.

"I'm sorry, what?" Aman asks the officer in disbelief.

"A source has informed us that you were seen in the vicinity of where Sarah Gatlin is presumed to have disappeared."

I have no words. I'm attempting to recall what happened on Monday. I wasn't with Aman all day, but I remember assuming he was either at home, the gym, or the library.

"Who is this source?" he asks.

"We can't divulge that information."

"I want to know who's trying to screw with me." Aman is getting angry.

"Sir, we're simply trying to get more information," Detective Shepherd says. "If you can calmly answer our questions, it will greatly assist with our investigation."

"I had school! It was a Monday!" Aman's tone is defensive. "This is now the second time you guys have sought me out to ask me questions about something I have no information on. First an attempted kidnapping, and now this?"

"Sir, we've confirmed with other witnesses, and these witnesses recall seeing you in the vicinity on Monday around two in the afternoon."

"What vicinity is that?"

"The northeast entrance of Golden Gate Park."

That's not far from here. Aman seems pensive, trying to recollect what he was doing in that area that day. That was the day we submitted our papers for the legal writing exam.

"Sir?" the detective asks when Aman takes too long to respond.

"I'm in that area often. That's one of the ways to get to our school gym."

"Do you usually also linger in the area?"

"Okay, detectives. This is the only information I have to offer, and I'm not answering any further questions without a lawyer present. Please leave." Aman puts the voluntary questioning to an immediate stop.

They get up to leave, taking the hint that Aman will no longer be proceeding with any sort of voluntary questioning. Before the door closes behind them, they tell Aman they'll be in touch.

Aman is visibly livid and rushes to the kitchen to pour himself a glass of cold water. I don't think I've ever seen him as stressed before. He looks genuinely worried.

"Aman, what's going on?" I finally manage to speak, although with hesitation. I haven't uttered a sound to him since he confessed his feelings to me, but everything from yesterday seems inconsequential compared to this.

He chugs another glass of water down so quickly that I'm afraid he will choke on it.

"I don't fucking know." He's not looking at me but is instead staring at a spot on the counter.

Before I can speak further, Aman dashes into his bedroom without saying a word. We have our evidence lecture in thirty minutes, but I'm not sure if Aman will go. He doesn't seem to be in a mental state to sit through a lecture. Nonetheless, I text him from the living room.

ME: I'M GOING TO LECTURE. WILL YOU BE COMING TOO?
AMAN: NO.

My phone vibrates again.

AMAN: PLEASE DON'T MENTION THIS TO ANYONE.
ME: OF COURSE NOT.

I know Aman well enough to guarantee that there's been some sort of misunderstanding. He's not someone who'd ever intentionally hurt someone, let alone commit a criminal offense, especially not against our law professor or TA.

At the same time, I can't help but wonder why there are so many coincidences and factors against Aman. What's the likelihood that he was seen in the same neighborhood at the same time that Professor Gatlin was last seen? Aman has used that route to go to the gym before, but that was because there was construction on the normal path. Presently, the faster route to get to the gym has no such obstructions. Is someone screwing with him?

By the time I arrive in the lecture hall, the room is steadily filling, but I don't see anyone at the head of the classroom yet. It doesn't seem like anyone knows what's happening with Aman. Plenty of people exchange a friendly wave with me without approaching me to probe me for information.

Mark walks into the room, and I'm relieved to see my friend, not only because I haven't seen him all week but because of all that has happened. I don't bring up Aman's confession last night, given that something bigger is happening, but seeing him provides me with enormous solace.

"Hey!" He's smiling ear-to-ear as he approaches me, completely unaware of his two friends' realities, more so Aman's than mine.

"Where's pretty boy?" Mark scoots his way behind me to his seat.

"He can't make it today."

Mark immediately finds this strange, especially considering our text exchange last night. It's unusual for Aman to skip class unless he absolutely has to, no matter how rebellious he may seem. But Mark doesn't dig any further.

Within the next few minutes, the professor who is teaching the other section of evidence walks in and introduces himself, stating that he's filling in for Professor Gatlin without any further explanation.

Class passes slowly because I'm only intermittently paying attention while primarily thinking about Aman. Unfortunately, given the short period of time between the end of evidence and the start of criminal law, there's not much I can do.

When the criminal law lecture begins, the TA of our section is standing in for the lecture without any mention of where Professor Erikson is.

Then, it dawns on me. The day that Professor Gatlin was allegedly kidnapped was the same day Professor Erikson sought us out for a meeting. Given his personal relationship with Professor Gatlin, that meeting must have been concerning her disappearance.

As the lecture is ending, I rush to open a text that was just delivered from Aman.

AMAN: I NEED TO FIGURE THINGS OUT.

I've never received a message as cryptic as this from Aman, and I don't understand what it means. I imagine he's saying he needs time, but it's unclear. All I manage in response is a bunch of question marks, to which he doesn't respond.

I'm hoping that since his message was sent recently, I still have time to catch Aman at home before he does anything stupid. I hurriedly gather my belongings and tell Mark that I have to go, leaving him dumbfounded.

I'm walking so fast that I'm sweating. My heart rate is uncomfortably fast as agonizing nausea rises within me. Our apartment is close to school, but it feels like an eternity before I actually get there. I take the stairs instead of the elevator and run up the four stories to our apartment as fast as I can, dramatically opening the door and yelling out Aman's name.

There's no response.

I rush over to his bedroom door. It's wide open. None of his stuff has been touched or moved. If all of his stuff is still here, where did he go? He can't be far. Perhaps I'm dramatizing the situation much more than needed.

I go to my room and lie on my bed, brainstorming where Aman may have gone, but my thoughts are interrupted by the ringing of our doorbell. I rush to the door, feeding myself false hope that it's Aman because I know that he has a key. Unless he forgot it?

When I see Marcus standing at the door, disappointment washes over me. I'm certainly not expecting him. I look at him inquisitively, wondering what he's doing here.

"I saw you leave campus hurriedly and wanted to make sure you were okay." He pauses. "You look pale." He brushes my cheek with the back of his hand, and I flinch at the unexpected gesture.

"I'm fine," I say, which is completely unconvincing because I sound and likely appear distracted.

"Can I come in?" he asks, furrowing his brows. I allow it since he came all the way here to check on me.

Marcus tries to converse with me, but since my attention is elsewhere, I keep missing what he's saying.

"Bani. Are you sure you're okay?" he asks again when I don't respond.

"What? Sorry, what did you say?"

I can't mention Professor Gatlin's disappearance to Marcus or ask if he knows about it. Aman asked me not to divulge any information to anyone, let alone someone that he clearly doesn't like.

It's evident that Bheau doesn't want anyone to learn of the disappearance and has kept this completely confidential. The professor who was lecturing for Professor Gatlin today wasn't behaving abnormally in the slightest. If Bheau didn't inform the professor why he was teaching for Professor Gatlin, I'm certain they opted not to disclose any information to her TAs.

"How do you feel about the professor that replaced Professor Gatlin?" he asks again.

A certain word he says catches my attention when Marcus asks this time. "Replaced? She's being replaced?"

"I mean standing in for," he corrects himself.

"I thought his lecture was fine, but I definitely prefer Professor Gatlin's style. I'm used to hers."

"Yes, they most definitely have a different style," he responds matter-of-factly.

I consider messaging Mark to help me find Aman, or at least to confirm whether he has any indication of where Aman might be. However, I'm torn between my eagerness to know where Aman is and his clear instructions to not tell anyone about his situation.

I barged into our apartment in such a frenzy that I don't even recall where I put my phone.

Taking a glance around the room and my immediate surroundings, I don't see it, but my smartwatch will be able to track its location for me. It must be in my bedroom.

A light-hearted and worry-free Aman set up my smartwatch for me to begin with. I wish that Aman was here with me.

"What are you looking for?" Marcus eyes me with peculiarity.

"Nothing."

He taps on the countertop as he stares at me with a strange smile smeared across his face.

His expression reminds me of the first time I ever saw him—in the hallway at school. Like he has a right to be focusing on me. He was blatant about it then too.

"What did the police say to Aman this morning?"

I immediately glare back at him. "How do you know about that?"

All he does is smile. This time, his smile is not remotely friendly.

chapter 47

Bani then Aman.

Bani

My heart rate increases again. I feel anxiety and fear growing within me at an exponential rate. The smile hasn't gone from Marcus' face, and he's still tapping on the counter like he owns it.

He laughs out loud, then sighs both heavily and dramatically.

"Bani, why are you looking at me like that?" he asks.

"How do you know the police came to talk to Aman this morning?" I sense his reason for knowing isn't a good one.

He's standing close enough to incite a level of fear within me. There's something chilling about him.

Only a minute ago, his expression was calm and thoughtful. Now it's frightful and vindictive, and he's laughing.

He strolls back and forth immediately in front of me. My eyes are fixated on him as he's about to speak.

"There are so many things I've wanted to tell you." Marcus shakes his head, scratching behind his ear. His behavior is quickly transitioning from normal to erratic.

I immensely regret not having my phone nearby. Praying and hoping that Aman somehow miraculously walks through the door, I glance over my shoulder toward the door.

"What have you wanted to tell me?" I attempt to soften my expression from fear to compassion, likely failing miserably. I keep the conversation going to distract Marcus as best I can.

He pauses his pacing and faces me.

"One thing for sure is that when I started all of this, I had no idea that I'd meet you. I had no idea that I'd walk down the hall and run into you." He continues as if in a dream. "You looked beautiful that day. What's most miraculous is that I never thought I'd be able to feel that way again. Especially not after what happened."

"What happened? What did you start?" I ask, ignoring everything else that he's rambling about.

This isn't the Marcus I'm used to interacting with, but seeing his behavior now, I realize that the Marcus I was interacting with wasn't who Marcus is at all. This man before me, right now, is the real Marcus.

"Do you think that I showed up here by chance, Bani? I mean, look at the timing. How is it that I'm named the TA to replace that other guy." He pauses to recollect the name. "Gerald. I made it so that I was there."

"What do you mean? I don't understand what you're trying to say!" I yell out in frustration. His roundabout way of telling me a story is prolonging my anxiety.

"I'll let you in on a few secrets, but I'm not going to give them all away yet. There are a few things I didn't reveal about myself. My name *is* Marcus, and I *am* a lawyer." He chuckles, his tone swarming with haughtiness. "I needed to get access to someone at this school. Before I could come, I needed to make sure that it was for an extended duration. I didn't apply for this job because I came across an open position. I *created* the position for me to take."

He looks at me again for my reaction, but I'm still at a loss. Then he states a truth that leaves me in complete shock. "He wasn't supposed to die."

I now know exactly what he's referring to.

"The hit-and-run wasn't an accident. I hit Gerald so that I could be Gatlin's TA."

I press my hands to my face and repeatedly shake my head in disbelief. Marcus is the one who killed Gerald. It wasn't an accident—it was intentional. And now he's in my apartment, directly in front of me.

Aman has understood Marcus' true nature from the moment they met. He told me just last night, immediately after Marcus left, that Marcus wasn't good, but I glossed over it because so much more happened between us after. I completely forgot that Aman told me I needed to be *careful* with Marcus.

Then with the detectives this morning…. the detectives.

The reason Detective Shepherd looked familiar to me was because he was the same person Marcus was talking to at the bar yesterday. The only way Marcus could've known that the detectives came to see Aman today would be because he was the one who led them to Aman. Marcus must've been the one to say something to the police, to imply that Aman was involved.

Tears are welling up inside me, but I try my damnedest to stay strong and not let them fall.

This is my fault. Aman is in trouble because of me. Remorse grows inside me as I ridicule myself for putting the one person who has remained true to me and protected me in harm's way. For wondering why there were so many coincidences against him instead of just trusting him.

"See. You're getting it now." Marcus' nonchalant tone makes me want to vomit. And he's laughing at my reaction.

The tears I'm holding inevitably come pouring down my cheeks. All the moments I felt uneasy and scared weren't because I was paranoid.

"Bani, don't cry."

When he attempts to touch me, I push him with as much force as I can muster. This angers him.

"Don't do that," he says, eerily calm, restraining himself from lashing out at me.

"Why are you bringing Aman into this?" I scream at him, shivering with fear.

"Come on. You know the answer to that."

"No, I don't!" I exclaim.

He furrows his eyebrows at my statement. "Bani, he's getting in my way."

"In your way of what?"

"*You*. I don't think you see it. He's in love with you."

The truth of his words, which I learned of last night, compels me to sob achingly and miserably. My crying is now uncontrollable, and my eyes are so blurry that I can't see Marcus anymore. Whether he's smiling or angry, everything is a blur. A rush of emotions strikes me like a tidal wave, making it difficult for me to breathe and prompting a pounding headache.

"Aman wouldn't go away. I tried to subliminally persuade him to leave you alone, but that guy is tenacious. I have to hand it to him, though. He's a really smart guy. I think he was always suspicious of me. It probably didn't help when he saw me at your brother's wedding reception Saturday night and came looking for me."

"What? You said you were picking your friend up." Marcus came to the reception not because of a friend but because of an ulterior motive.

That's why Aman disappeared, and I couldn't find him. He was looking for Marcus. And I thought it was because he was with some random girl.

I can't stop crying.

"Babe, why are you still so surprised? I've been eyeing you from the moment I saw you. Our running into each other repeatedly in such a big city wasn't a coincidence." He winks at me, and I'm repulsed.

Aman, please walk through that door. Please, please.

"I wanted to take you Tuesday night on the freeway." *What does that mean?*

It takes me a few moments to understand what he's referring to.

The person who was following us on the freeway Tuesday night was Marcus? If he was following us the entire time, then he knows where my parents live.

"Why are you doing this?" I plead for an answer.

"Again, I wasn't planning on meeting you. But once I did, I couldn't turn the other way. I had to have you. You've yet to see my initial plan, and that one is a *big* surprise. You won't believe me unless you see it for yourself. I'll take you there."

"I'm not going anywhere with you." I'm surprised by my confident tone, although there's a hint of shakiness.

"You don't have a choice," he says matter-of-factly, making it sound like he's going to take me against my will.

I instinctively look around the room for any sort of escape or object I can use in my defense, but there's none. At least nothing that I can get to quickly.

"I really wanted to see how you looked dressed up for the pre-wedding festivities. You and your sister look so much alike." He immediately distracts me from my search.

I tremble with fright. "What? What do you mean?" *When the fuck did he see Ari?*

"Well, I walked up to your parents' house the day of a very vibrant and colorful event and saw someone who looked similar to you. I assumed she was your sister. I started asking her about the party. I think she already likes me." He seems satisfied with himself.

Ari told me about this encounter the same day. Contrary to Marcus' perception of his interaction with Ari, Ari said he was creepy. *He* was the one who made Ari feel that uncomfortable?

Fuck, I think to myself. If only I knew who it was at that time. Ari said that he looked familiar. He looked familiar to her because she'd seen a picture of him on my phone—the picture I showed her weeks ago.

Fearing for my sister's safety, panic fills my entire body. I'm having trouble breathing.

Marcus notices this and walks over to me. His proximity to me freezes me. I'm afraid to even breathe.

"You look so much like her," he whispers so quietly that I can barely hear him. He's eyeing me with an odd sort of admiration.

"Who?" I ask nervously, gathering myself and praying he's not referring to Ari.

He doesn't say anything but continues to stare at me. Tears well up in his eyes.

"Who do I look like?" I repeat sternly.

"My fiancée," he responds simply.

"Where is she?"

"She's dead."

Aman

As much as I hate to admit it, there's only one person who can help me. He's also the one person who'll be the least willing to help me if what Bani said about him and Professor Gatlin is true and if he has discussed anything with the police. But I have to make him listen to me.

At least he's willing to meet with me even though I'm sure he's going to want to physically hurt me, and that's probably the only reason he agreed. I don't blame him. He thinks I have something to do with this. If someone took Bani, I'd beat the shit out of them with my bare hands.

As I approach the coffee shop, I see him sitting at an isolated table immediately outside. I suggested we meet in a public place, but not public enough that others would be able to hear our conversation.

He eyes me with intense hatred as I approach. The dislike we share is mutual, but he has answers to my questions, and I have answers to his.

"Professor Erikson," I say simply and remain standing next to the table.

"Aman." I don't let the cold look on his face affect me. He looks to be in pretty bad shape, like he hasn't slept. I sit down once he gestures for me to have a seat.

He leans in and whispers, "Give me one good reason why I shouldn't kick your ass right now."

"I know you're in contact with the detectives who came by my apartment, but I didn't do anything. I have no idea where Professor Gatlin is. Look, man," I plead with him. He could be my peer versus my professor. "I'm not someone who could hurt someone else, no matter what anyone thinks about me."

I don't expect him to believe me simply by saying that I'm innocent.

He reaches into his pocket and places a folded piece of paper on the tabletop. I read the note aloud, "You took mine, so I took yours."

"Does the handwriting look familiar?" he asks.

The handwriting looks like mine. "Shit." He's seen my handwriting countless times during office hours.

"I got this right after she went missing. Matt... Detective Shepherd... told me yesterday that you were reportedly seen in the same area that she was in. They're looking at video surveillance as we speak. It won't be long before your pathetic ass gets put away." He doesn't sound as professional as he does in lectures. Of course he doesn't. This is personal.

"Someone is trying to set me up, and I know who it is." My suggestion seems to interest him, as he waits for me to continue. "Marcus Hendricks."

Professor Erikson scoffs at me in disbelief. "You're going to try to blame this on Sarah's new TA? He's only just met her. Why would he kidnap her?"

"Why would *I*?" My voice is louder than I intended, and I remind myself to be cognizant of my surroundings. "If you received a note that sounds like this has to do with revenge, and someone needs you to know how it feels, then this isn't about Professor Gatlin. It's about you. What reason do I have to want that from you?"

He considers what I'm saying.

"Marcus is a creep and a stalker. This past week was Bani's brother's wedding. On our way home on Tuesday night from Palo Alto, Bani and I were being aggressively followed by someone in a car. Right when we were about to dodge the driver, I briefly caught a glimpse of who it was, and it looked like Marcus. I was the only one who was able to see him. Then, on Saturday night, I saw him lurking at Bani's brother's wedding reception venue. When I went to look for him, I couldn't find him." I pause.

Although it may seem minor, I remember one more point. "I think he's hiding his real name. When he first introduced himself to the class, he wrote his email on the board, and his last name in the email was *Hendricks*. Bani and I ran into him at the library once, and I saw 'M. Hendrix' written on one of the papers he was holding. Why would he misspell his own last name?"

"Did you tell Matt this?" I can tell he's still ambivalent about believing me.

"No, because I have absolutely no proof of any of it. It's only what I saw."

"That's convenient." He pauses. "Even if it is him, how does this relate to me or Sarah? How are you sure that Marcus is trying to set you up when more than one person saw you in the same location Sarah last was, and there was no report of anyone seeing Marcus?"

I sigh, defeated, because I don't have actual proof of that either. "That's why I wanted to talk to you. Did you have any interactions with Marcus before he became Professor Gatlin's TA?"

"No, there's no report of him ever working for the university before."

"What about during your law practice?"

He gives my question some thought. "I don't know, but he never worked for me. I'd need to search through my hard drive. There are cases that I haven't thought about in years."

"Can we at least look through your hard drive to see if his name comes up at all?"

He studies me and evaluates the sense of urgency with which I'm asking him to review his files. From his demeanor, it seems that he's entertaining the thought and potentially starting to believe that I had nothing to do with Professor Gatlin's disappearance or Gerald's death.

He rises from his seat and gestures for me to follow him, leading us to his car. Once he's driving, he goes in the direction of Bheau. The entire ride, we sit in the car in complete silence. I prefer it that way.

The law school looks deserted in this part of the building, the part that has the professors' offices. We pass by Professor Gatlin's office, and the door is closed, but you can see the complete darkness inside from the small window atop the door.

Professor Erikson closes the door behind him and locks it once we're in his office. He eagerly turns his computer on as we both wait for it to load.

While it's loading, I text Bani, urging her to stay away from Marcus until I have more information. She's likely unhappy with the plethora of cryptic texts I'm sending her, but this is for her safety.

The software finally loads. At first, he incorrectly enters *Hendricks,* and the search yields no result. Professor Erikson asks me for the spelling of Marcus' last name, which I saw on the paper. The second time around, the software takes several seconds to provide its search result, giving me hope that there's something there.

Sure enough, there's only one result listed, and there's a hyperlink attached. Professor Erikson clicks the result, and a criminal case from years ago, where Professor Erikson served as the lead defense attorney and Gerald Lambino served as a case analyst, pops up on the screen.

"Holy shit," he whispers in disbelief as we both read through several trial documents and newspaper clippings on the case.

And Bani hasn't responded to my messages.

chapter 48

Aman then Bani.

Aman

I try calling her repeatedly, but she's not answering. Something is wrong. There's no way she would ignore me to this extent, even given our current situation.

I ask Professor Erikson to drive me to our apartment to ensure that Bani is safe. He agrees because after seeing the documents on his computer, he believes that I have nothing to do with Professor Gatlin's disappearance.

It doesn't take long for us to get there. I immediately jump out of his car before it comes to a halt and sprint faster than I ever have up the stairs to our apartment. Panting in exhaustion and fear, I open the door to a fully lit but empty apartment.

"Bani?" I yell out. There's no response.

Professor Erikson enters our apartment several seconds after me.

"She's not here." My voice is solemn and insanely low.

"You've looked everywhere?" Professor Erikson glances about the room.

"No. I know she's not here."

"How?"

"Because she never leaves her book bag or purse messily on the ground." I point to the items scattered across the living room floor. There are clear signs of some sort of struggle.

"Try calling her again," he suggests while he looks around.

"I've called her tons of times!" I yell out in frustration. *Where the fuck is she?*

I pull my phone out to try to call her yet again. I'm not surprised that she doesn't answer, yet I'm hopeful each time I try. I hear something making noise along with the ringing of the dial tone. Pulling the phone away from my ear, I still hear the same sound. It's a vibration.

"Do you hear that?" I ask Professor Erikson.

"Yeah."

We search the apartment to determine the source of the sound. It leads me to Bani's bedroom. Her phone is ringing on her nightstand, and my name and a picture of me are lighting up the screen. Once I disconnect the call, there are eleven missed calls from me on the screen as well as the text I sent earlier. It's still marked as unread.

I bury my head in my hands and curse myself for not warning her or saying something beforehand. Even if she didn't believe me then, it would've been in the back of her mind. Especially since that son of a bitch knows where we live.

"He took her too."

"How do you know?"

"I don't know." I really don't know precisely how I know. "He was here last night, and there was something about him that didn't feel right. It's a feeling."

"Fuck." Professor Erikson combs his hair with his fingers.

"But I think I know how to find her. And I'm hoping that we'll find Professor Gatlin too."

"How?"

"Her phone. I made her sync her phone with her smartwatch. She never takes it off. Odds are that she's wearing it, and the app will show exactly where she is."

"We need to call Matt and tell him as soon as we know."

"I'm not waiting for them before we go to her. We need to leave now." Honestly, I don't know how long it's been since she's been gone. I can only guess.

Then, I get a gut-wrenching feeling when I see her phone is locked. I don't know her phone's passcode. Bani's phone passcode is a four-digit code. I try her name, her birthday, her mom's name, her favorite color, and her dog's name—none of them work.

Frustration grows inside me. This is the best way to find out where she is, but I need access to her phone to do that. Plus, I only have two more tries before the phone locks itself.

"It's always what you least expect," she'd teasingly said to me when I tried to hack her phone once.

It hadn't occurred to me at the time, but the last thing I would expect her passcode to be was something related to me.

I type in "Aman," and the phone opens immediately. I'm momentarily frozen as I stare at her unlocked screen.

Her background picture is from the wedding—right before the *sehra bandi* when her mom told me to come in for the photo. She's looking at me, smiling, while her family and I smile at the camera.

I'm no longer feeling melancholy or fear. The only thing I'm feeling right now is intense rage.

That psychotic bastard has her. I'm going to find him, and then I'm going to kill him.

Bani

The last thing I remember is being in the apartment, listening to Marcus confess to atrocious things. Gerald's death. Marcus' intentional following and stalking of me since the moment he saw me. He admitted to trying to get Aman out of his way.

All of it is vividly coming back to me as I run through each of his words again and again. It all feels unreal. And Marcus said there's more that he has to tell me. Or show me.

I search my immediate surroundings and discover I'm no longer in my apartment. I'm in a large, dark warehouse-like room that only has light coming from two dimly lit lamps.

I remember now that I impulsively tried to make a run for it when Marcus' attention was diverted, but he attacked before I succeeded. I feel a developing bump on the side of my head. He must have knocked me unconscious before bringing me here.

I can't move to touch it because my hands are tied to the chair I'm sitting in. The pressure against my wrists makes me feel woozy.

I don't know how he was able to bring me here without drawing attention, given that it's still light out. Or maybe it isn't. I don't remember what time it was when he knocked me out, and I haven't the slightest idea what time it is now. By habit, I rotate my wrist to read the time on my watch.

My watch!

Hope fills me. Aman will figure out that something is wrong when I'm not home but my phone is. The state of our living room wasn't typical of how we normally keep it. It was unkempt.

He knows I wouldn't intentionally leave home without at least my phone, especially considering how fearful I've been. He'll see my phone in my bedroom and will definitely remember that the watch he bought me is linked to my phone.

He can send officers to my location. *I know he will, I know he will*, I repeatedly chant to myself like a prayer.

Then I remember my phone is locked. I shake my head in disbelief and cry. The hope I was feeling a moment ago dissipates as rapidly as my pounding heartbeat.

Aman doesn't know my passcode, and he'll never guess that it's his name.

The police may take too long to unlock my phone. By the time they'll be able to view my location on the app, I don't know what will happen, where I'll be, or if my watch will have died because I haven't charged it.

If he sees my smartwatch, Marcus will recognize it. I try to cover my wrist with my sleeve using one hand, but it's difficult to do with tightly bonded hands.

My helplessness is only contributing to the dread. I'm imagining the worst and thinking that I'll never see my family again. I'll never see Aman again.

I groan, as if physically in pain. "No, no, no," I say between sobs.

Immediately, I hear a sound in the room. A soft and subtle noise.

The sound could not have come from more than thirty feet ahead of me.

"H-Hello?" My voice is shaky.

I hear the same sound again. It sounds like a weak cry or moan.

"Hello? I repeat. "Is someone there?"

I hear a familiar eruption of laughter. The same unnerving laugh I heard back at my apartment.

A bright light shines directly on me, almost blinding me and exacerbating the throbbing pain in my head.

"How are you feeling, babe?" Marcus asks.

I'm tied to a chair. How the fuck do you think I'm feeling, you psycho?

He continues, "I hated doing this to you, just so you know. But you were trying to leave me after all I've done and gone through." He can't honestly paint himself to be a victim here.

Marcus walks directly to me with a glass of water, holding it to my lips. I instinctively turn my head with disgust and anger, not trusting anything this man is capable of.

"Drink it," he says with force, but I still look away from him.

I hear the same soft cry as before.

"*Shut up!*" Marcus yells out, startling me. My heart races inside my chest. I wouldn't be surprised if he is able to hear it.

"W-What is that?" I nervously ask him.

There's something incredibly unsettling about the way he laughs. He sounds unremorseful.

"I think it's time for me to tell you my next secret." He walks over to the wall, and I hear a click.

A second bright light shines in the direction that I heard the cry come from. While I regain my vision from the sudden, intense lighting, I eventually recognize the second person sitting and physically bound in the exact same way as I am.

It's Professor Gatlin.

More tears stream down my face. I've been crying so much that my face is stinging with pain.

Professor Gatlin looks at me with hopeful yet terrified eyes. The only difference in her restraints is that her mouth is covered, and mine is not. Her appearance is completely disheveled and drastically different from the confident aura that usually emanates from her.

"Give her some water right now!" I demand and attempt to shake free from my chair, ultimately unsuccessfully. I notice her eyes glisten with tears.

This psychotic man has not only kidnapped my law school professor but is attempting to frame Aman for it.

"All right, all right. I'll give her some water. She probably is thirsty." He thinks he's being compassionate.

There's no mistaking that Professor Gatlin is severely dehydrated, and Marcus is the cause of her current state. He's torturing her.

"Give her some food too!" I try not to push my luck, but I can't look at her this way.

He develops a look of surprise. "Bani, you're being a little demanding there, aren't you?" he says with a disapproving tone. "Besides, it's not time for her to eat yet. Her food is on the way."

He's monitoring and controlling her like an animal. Is this how he will keep me too?

If Professor Gatlin has been missing since last Monday, she's been enduring this treatment for a week. Her current state looks as if she can't take much more of this.

"Why are you doing this to her?" I plead for an answer.

"I need her to teach someone a lesson." His response is nonchalant and simple. "He took mine, so I took his. He needs to know how it feels."

"What are you talking about?" I'm sobbing again. Professor Gatlin yelps in pain, and I pray that Marcus doesn't yell at her or do anything worse. From this distance and in this lighting, I can't be sure, but I think I see faded bruises on her neck and face. Since he physically struck me, I'm nearly certain that they're bruises.

"You know how I told you that I had to be here for an extended duration? Well, ask her why. She knows." He gestures toward Professor Gatlin, who closes her eyes tightly out of desperation. Tears fall from her eyes.

"Oh, wait. She can't." Marcus cackles evilly. "She knows why. I talk to her about it every day. Every day, I ask her if he'll find her before it's too late."

"If who will find her?"

"Er-ik-son," he stiffly exaggerates each syllable, fury in his eyes. "What do you have against Professor Erikson?"

The wounded look now on Marcus' face is by far the most dangerous I have seen throughout his psychosis. He looks as if he's capable of doing anything to anyone. Professor Gatlin violently shakes her head at me as Marcus' back is turned toward her.

Realizing I've struck a triggering nerve with Marcus, I avoid eye contact with him.

"HE TOOK EVERYTHING FROM ME!" he screams, slamming the wall with his hand. His reaction causes an echo in the building. I wonder how secluded this building is and whether someone could hear his scream.

"He thinks he's such a hotshot lawyer and that he's invincible. As long as he gets his money, he gets murderers off and lets guilty men run free." Marcus takes a deep breath. "My fiancée was walking to meet me for dinner. *For dinner.* And then some rich kid thought it would be funny to attack her and pull her into an alley." He doesn't hold back his emerging tears. "You want to know what the sick, pathetic excuse of a man did?" he asks rhetorically. "Erikson knew that his client was guilty, but he destroyed the evidence that incriminated his client. She was my everything, and he let her killer run free. That evidence would have convicted him." He wipes the falling tears from his eyes.

I remember him talking about his fiancée at my apartment. He said that I looked like her.

He stares at me for several seconds before he walks closer to me. When he's about to brush my cheek, I turn away. This angers him—he seems like he's restraining himself from striking me again. I flinch, and he immediately takes a few steps backward.

"I knew something was wrong. She was never late. Ever. If I was more than fifteen minutes late, she wouldn't stop teasing me about it. She'd always say stuff like, 'A baby can be born in fifteen minutes during the second stage of labor.' She was in medical school at the time and was in her OBGYN rotation." Marcus appears to be in a daze or trance as he remembers her. Then, there's a knock on the door.

I'm the only one who's startled. Neither Marcus nor Professor Gatlin look as if they're surprised by the knock, which tells me that this visitor, whoever it is, is expected and not someone who can help me or Professor Gatlin.

Marcus sighs loudly, as if the visitor's timing has interrupted his story. Nonetheless, he quietly walks toward the door. I'm eager to see who it is.

As soon as he opens the door, and even though it's dark and the person is wearing a hooded sweatshirt, I can make out who it is. I glare in shock.

Noor is standing at the door, holding a bag. I'm speechless, not realizing until several moments later that my mouth is still gaping with surprise. Marcus makes a note of this and chuckles.

"Babe, I think you two have already met." He gestures toward Noor, who, unlike Marcus, is not smiling at me. Neither Noor nor I say anything to each other. I knew she was low, but I never thought she was *this* low.

"You know what makes a trustworthy accomplice?" he asks me, again rhetorically. "Someone who desperately wants the same thing as you. I recruited her in my efforts once I figured out that we both wanted you and Aman away from each other. Once I take you away, Aman will be able to focus on her."

"You both are crazy!" I scream out. Marcus laughs, and Noor's expression doesn't change.

"Not crazy. We are…" He pauses. "Equally enthralled."

Since she got here, Noor hasn't said a word, nor has she taken her eyes off of me.

I have the urge to yell and curse at both of them, but I refrain because I'm nervous one of them, mainly Noor, will lash out. She looks like she's waiting for me to say something. Like she's expecting it. The only thing that's probably stopping her from attacking me right now is Marcus.

Coming closer to me, he whispers something so neither Noor nor Professor Gatlin is able to hear. "Between me and you, I don't really care what happens between her and Aman. I tacked her on for my own benefit. She's delusional." He winks and turns back toward the center of the room.

Noor moves for the first time since she arrived and carries the bag over to Professor Gatlin, which presumably holds her food.

Marcus seems to enjoy hearing himself talk because he reminds himself that he is in the middle of a story and continues, "Naomi wasn't answering my calls. He left my Naomi there to die. I was only able to find her because I always had her share her location with me on her ph—" He stops abruptly and looks directly at me.

"Where is your phone?" he roars.

chapter 49

Marcus momentarily looks frantic. When I was unconscious and before he brought me here, he must have forgotten to check that I didn't have my phone on me since it could pinpoint my location.

"Where is your phone?" He repeats worriedly.

"I...I don't have it." I'm telling the truth, but given how shaky my voice sounds, even I wouldn't believe it.

He quickly pats the pockets in my pants to ensure that I'm not lying. Relief washes over him when he doesn't discover a phone on me.

I discreetly tug on the end of my sleeve with my fingers and hold the material to block the view of my watch. With the darkness in the room, hopefully the indentation across my wrist won't draw attention. I want to keep it on me as long as I possibly can. The longer it's on my wrist, the higher the probability of Aman finding us, as minuscule as that probability may be.

Aman, please somehow figure out how to open my phone and find me, I recite repeatedly to myself, not sure if it's wishful thinking.

As Marcus is about to continue with his story, Noor whispers something to him that angers him. I hope that he doesn't leave the room because I would be powerless before Noor. Instead, they both go, leaving me and Professor Gatlin in the room.

It's eerily silent in the room. The silence is intermittently broken by water droplets falling into a puddle nearby. There's something peaceful about the sound. It's faint, but I focus my attention on it, counting how many seconds pass between each drop to keep myself awake and alert. Seven seconds.

I look over at Professor Gatlin again, and she's hungrily eating her food. Her arms are still restrained, but Noor adjusted them to allow Professor Gatlin to raise her hands to her mouth to eat. I wonder what she's thinking and how she's feeling. She looks numb and lost, almost childlike.

Professor Gatlin has been in this state since last week, I think to myself over and over again. That's enough time to break someone. In all this time, no one has been able to locate her.

I have zero knowledge of which part of San Francisco we're in or whether we're still in San Francisco at all. I try to listen closely for any sounds that I may recognize outside, but I'm unable to hear anything.

As quietly as I possibly can, I attempt to loosen the restraints around my right wrist while firmly maintaining my hold on my sleeve with my left hand.

Professor Gatlin notices my rather futile attempts amidst her mouthfuls and shakes her head aggressively toward me. She's indicating I should stop, and her eyes are filled with fear. She's alternating glances between me and the door that Marcus and Noor exited through.

Right when I turn to look at it, the door opens, and Noor and Marcus reenter the dimly lit room. I immediately freeze.

Then I see it. Marcus is holding a gun. I've never seen a gun in my life. It looks bulkier than I imagined. There must be a table that I can't see because I hear him place the gun on a solid surface not far from where he's standing now.

Marcus walks toward me and places both his hands on either side of me, reminding me of Aman and what happened yesterday on our kitchen counter. The only difference is that with Aman, I felt protected. With Marcus, I wince in anticipation of pain and prolonged fear.

I need him here, I finally admit to myself. *I need Aman here.*

"Sorry to leave you. She needed to talk to me about something urgent," he whispers, disinterested. "You know, I don't blame Aman for ending things with her. She really is obsessed."

If I had the courage to laugh in his face at the irony, I would. I wish I had the courage.

"Bani, can you imagine how scarring it was for me to look for Naomi, fearing that something was wrong but hoping I was only being paranoid and then finding her lying in a puddle of her own blood on the cold cement in an alley?" He shakes his head at the thought. "The guy had blood on his shirt, and Erikson was able to get him off."

Despite how arrogant and pompous Professor Erikson presents himself, he's never struck me as an immoral attorney who would fabricate or destroy evidence to protect his client. His reputation is as renowned as it is because of the artful strategy he implements when he handles a case. His cases have never alluded to or reeked of malfeasance, only skill. Even Aman would agree with me despite his dislike of him.

"Erikson needs to know how it feels to love someone, never see her again, and then see her killer walking around freely, right in front of his pathetic face. Not only will I get that, but I'll get you now too."

The word "killer" makes Professor Gatlin groan. He's going to *kill* Professor Gatlin.

I challenge his statement. "You're not going to kill anyone," I say, feeling sudden courage and some confidence.

He gives me a curious look. "And what makes you so sure of that?"

"You would have done it already."

He chuckles in a way that sends goosebumps all throughout my body. "I *have* done it already." His tone is mocking. "Bani, didn't I tell you that I was the one who ran over what's-his-name? You know what's funny? I didn't realize this until recently, but that guy *helped* Erikson during the trial. Yeah, he was a case analyst. He worked for that bastard and helped my Naomi's killer run free. It wasn't until I saw more and more pictures of him on the news that I realized it was the same man. Turned out well for me in the end. He got what he deserved too."

For as long as I have known him, Gerald has been an evidence TA. I had no idea that he used to work for Professor Erikson and practiced criminal defense. Not once have I ever seen them interact at school.

"Bani, it turns out that meeting you saved Gatlin's life for a few more days since you weren't part of the original plan. When I met you, I met Aman. You can't have a murder without a killer." He's basking in the self-perceived brilliance of his plan. "Seeing that Tuesday didn't work out, I wanted to take you Saturday night," he continues.

"What?" I nearly choke.

"Not at the party," he says as if he'd done me a favor. "There were too many witnesses. When you came back from the party Saturday

377

night, she wanted to talk to Aman." He points to Noor. I recall Noor standing outside of our apartment when Aman and I returned from Devan and Alina's wedding reception. "When they were outside talking, I went into your apartment and knocked on your door."

Horror strikes me. I remember the incident clearly. At the time, I thought that it was Aman knocking on my door to talk to me, but I didn't respond when I heard the knock. I remember being confused when the front door opened and closed again, wondering why Aman was leaving at that hour when he'd just returned.

It wasn't Aman. It was Marcus. He was able to come into our apartment despite the door being locked. I can't bring myself to ask how many times he's done that before and how he's able to enter our locked apartment. I don't want to know the answer.

But the fact that he only acts when Aman isn't around makes me think there's a part of him that's afraid of Aman. Aman rarely left me alone at that time of night. I don't understand how Marcus thinks he can keep me without eventually being discovered.

Then, it hits me. He plans on implicating Aman not only for Professor Gatlin's murder but for my disappearance as well.

"I thought that it was too risky to take you that night with Aman just outside. Plus, I thought it would be more strategic if it happened after the detectives came to talk to Aman. If you disappeared on Saturday and Aman has an alibi and a witness, they won't think that he was involved." He says this quietly, as if it's a secret. "Aman would have been collateral damage had I not thought of a better use for him. Your roommate was the cherry on top of an otherwise perfect plan."

"What?" Noor speaks for the first time, enraged. The look of shock and anger across her face is unmistakable. "This wasn't our agreement! You get her. I get him—that's what we agreed."

"You can go to jail with him if you want." The nonchalance in his voice is unreal. "Do you think he gives a shit about you? He loves her!" He points directly at me.

Noor is visibly filled with seething anger.

"You're so stupid that you don't see it. I'm actually doing you a favor."

Shut up, Marcus. He's only making this worse.

"He doesn't love you." Noor glares at me, searching for some sort of acknowledgement and agreement with her statement. I don't provide it, and this only angers her more. "I'm going to kill this bitch. She's literally getting in the way of everything." Although her face is furious, her voice is oddly calm.

Marcus grows livid, and his face turns red.

Noor jolts toward the table where the gun is but stops midway. Her furious expression quickly transitions into one of complete terror. I can't see what she sees, but there's definitely something there. She looks as if she's seen a ghost. Her face drains of color.

Marcus eyes her, but since his point of view is similar to mine, he also can't see what she does. A hooded figure silently emerges from the darkness of the room.

Aman.

I breathe so freely that it feels like I've come up for air after being underwater. Unlike Marcus' and Noor's reaction to seeing Aman, I begin bawling like I never have before. I aggressively try to maneuver out of the chair now that I no longer need to hide my watch.

Despite me calling and crying his name, he hasn't yet made eye contact with me or even looked in my direction. His entire attention is focused directly on Marcus and Noor. He's glaring at both of them with such monstrous intensity that I don't even recognize him.

Aman approaches Marcus first as if Aman is a predator and Marcus is his prey. The size difference between the two is obvious. Marcus is big, but Aman is much bigger. My theory that Marcus is afraid of Aman is decidedly confirmed, despite Marcus' efforts to feign strength when he sees Aman.

Neither says anything to the other, but Aman maintains his stride toward Marcus.

In the back, Professor Erikson quietly unties Professor Gatlin as fast as he can.

As soon as he reaches Marcus, Aman punches him uncontrollably. Marcus tries to fight back, but Aman's rage blinds him, not providing Marcus with an opportunity to strike back. Aman is overpowering Marcus to the extent that Marcus begins bleeding with the second punch. Aman's hand is also bleeding, but he's not stopping.

I cry at Aman to stop, but he doesn't even flinch in my direction.

"Aman! Stop, stop!" Professor Erikson also calls out to Aman.

But Aman does not stop. Even when Marcus struggles and attempts to crawl away from Aman, he follows and continues striking him.

Aman pushes Professor Erikson away when he attempts to take Aman off of Marcus. Between Professor Erikson and me, the yelling echoes through the building.

Over the commotion, a sudden loud popping sound, like an amplified firecracker, brings the yelling to a screeching halt.

I look for the source of the sound, and Noor is holding the gun in Aman's direction. She turns and aims it toward me, and I wince in my chair, helpless. There's another extremely loud popping sound.

Noor falls to the ground, blood oozing out of the open wound on her arm. She writhes on the ground, yelping in pain.

Behind her, Detective Shepherd points his gun directly at her before he secures it in his holster when he sees Noor is no longer a threat. He rushes to help me, directing Detective Blake to check on Aman and to call an ambulance immediately.

Marcus is lying on the ground, breathing heavily and holding his ribs, struggling to move.

Aman is lying on the ground unconscious, surrounded by a pool of his own blood.

chapter 50

There's a persistent ringing in my ears. I hear shouting, but it's muffled. Everything around me is a blur, and the only thing I see is Aman, immobile on the ground. He's not getting up. I don't even know if he's still breathing.

I remain still, solely focused on Aman, and don't immediately realize that Detective Shepherd has undone my restraints.

When the medics arrive and gather around Aman, I finally escape the temporary paralysis I'm experiencing.

I jump up and attempt to run toward Aman, but Detective Shepherd holds me back. Despite my efforts to fight and escape him, his strength overpowers mine. All I can do is watch the medics tend to Aman. *Aman can't die*, I repeat to myself. *Aman can't die.*

"Maintain pressure on the wound. His pulse is faint." I hear one medic say. *He's alive.*

"The bullet is still inside." I hear another say.

"On the count of three, we're going to pick him up and place him on the stretcher," the first medic says. "One, two, three."

"I have to go with him!" I scream at the detective as the medics rush outside to transport Aman to the hospital.

"Ms. Sethi, you can't go with him, but I can take you to the hospital that he's being transported to," Detective Shepherd says reassuringly.

Professor Erikson interjects, "I'll take her to the hospital."

Professor Gatlin is standing alongside him, still trembling. Up close, her injuries are worse than they seemed from a distance. Two more ambulances arrive to take Professor Gatlin and then Marcus and Noor separately to the hospital.

I feel anger boiling up inside me, seeing both Marcus and Noor awake and fine. I can't look at them without wanting to beat the shit out of them myself. They did this to Aman.

Professor Erikson senses my urgency to leave and follows behind me, eventually leading us to where his car is parked.

"Where are we?" I ask Professor Erikson, my voice glum.

"Mission Bay. The hospital is a seven-minute drive." We're still in San Francisco, about twenty minutes away from our apartment. I must have been unconscious for a considerable period of time if Marcus was able to transport me from my apartment, drive to Mission Bay, and then tie me up in the abandoned building we were in. That would require at least an hour total.

"We should get you checked out too," Professor Erikson advises once we're in his car. I nod in response.

"Is there anyone you want me to call for you?" he asks again.

"Who's Naomi?" I ask without responding to his question.

He sighs heavily and remains silent for a few moments.

"I know all that Marcus may have told you, and I know what you may be thinking, Bani." He's never called me by my first name before. "But that guy is highly delusional and completely off about what happened to his fiancée."

"He said that you fabricated or destroyed evidence and let his fiancée's killer run free."

"I was doing my job. Without breaking attorney-client privilege, I will tell you what I argued during the trial. There was enough evidence to place my client at the scene and arrest him, but there was not enough evidence to convict him of the murder."

"Aman was shot because of a technicality? None of this would have happened had it not been for that," I wail.

"You're not listening to me." His voice remains calm. "My client saw a girl in the alley and walked over to see what was going on. He was afraid when the girl wasn't moving and fell right near the puddle of her blood. He called the police to report the crime. All throughout the trial, he maintained his innocence. Marcus refused to believe that he was innocent only because there were no other leads. Instead, he thought that I was defending a truly guilty man. He didn't get his closure. It was a tragic ending to a heartbreaking case, but that's unfortunately how it is sometimes. My client was acquitted because the evidence was not enough to prove guilt beyond a reasonable doubt. There's the presumption of innocence."

Innocent until proven guilty.

He pauses, waiting for me to say something. When I don't, he continues, "About a year later, the same thing happened to another girl a few blocks from where Naomi was murdered. The police connected the two crimes because of how they were committed. It was the same technique. Fortunately, the police were able to identify and locate the person the second time. The man was charged and convicted of the second murder, but the police needed more information to connect and charge him with Naomi's murder." He pauses at a stop sign.

"I know the officer who was the lead on Naomi's case. The police contacted Naomi's family. They were able to get in touch with her family, but Marcus had lost contact with everyone after the trial. Marcus is completely unaware of any of this, and even if he knew it, I'm not sure he would believe it."

I agree with Professor Erikson. Had all this been explained to Marcus, I doubt that he would have believed it. He seems well beyond the truth at this point. He would have probably thought that Professor Erikson was behind the second arrest in some way. Maybe that he'd offered an innocent man as a scapegoat.

Professor Erikson continues driving toward the hospital in silence. I take in his story, but I'm mostly distracted and focused on Aman. I can't shake the thought that Aman...*no!*

Bani, stop. I literally shake my head to remove the thought from my mind. *He is fine,* I repeat over and over to myself. *He will be fine.*

The rest of the drive to the hospital is the longest five minutes ever. I ask Professor Erikson to drop me off at the emergency room entrance before parking his car. I'm too restless to wait.

I run to the nurse that's standing at the nurse's station in the E.R. "I'm looking for Aman Wajla. He was brought in by an ambulance."

"Are you family?"

I shake my head.

"I can't discuss patient details with someone who's not a family member, miss."

"But I'm his roommate." After seeing the look of immense concern on my face, she reviews his chart on a tablet, wrinkling her eyebrows.

"What's your name?"

"Bani Sethi." *Hurry up and tell me, please.* I'm feeling more and more anxious with each passing second.

"You're listed as Mr. Wajla's emergency contact." I try to maintain my composure as the nurse tells me this.

"Mr. Wajla has a bullet in his lung. The medics indicated to the doctor that Mr. Wajla coded on the way here, but they were able to stabilize him. He's been taken into emergency surgery. A doctor will periodically come outside to update you." I'm no longer able to compose myself. Tears come streaming down my face, and the nurse looks at me with empathy.

"If the doctor doesn't come out for a while, that's usually a good sign." She smiles reassuringly. "You can have a seat right over there." She points toward a group of seats in the waiting room, not too far from the station.

I take a seat and gaze at a specific spot on the floor. Within a few minutes, Professor Erikson walks in.

"What did they say?" he asks.

"He's in surgery."

"Okay. Try to relax. I'm going to see how Sarah is doing. Did you see a doctor?"

"For what?"

"To get yourself checked out."

"No."

"I'll ask someone to stop by."

Aside from the scrapes and cuts, the doctor determined that I had a mild concussion, likely from the blow to my head Marcus inflicted at my apartment. He advised me of what symptoms to monitor during the next twenty-four hours and asked me to report back if anything worsens or changes.

For a brief time, the examination took my mind off of Aman, and I welcomed it. I'm going insane sitting here and waiting.

Reality slaps me in the face when I remind myself that Aman's mom deserves to know what's happening. I pull out my phone to call her and tell her what happened, but I can barely muster the courage to speak with her.

When she answers my call, she immediately knows that something is wrong, because I never call her. My voice chokes as I formulate the words. Her son is in this situation because of me, and instead of being angry with me, she thanks me for being there and says that she and Charan will fly to San Francisco tonight.

Hours and hours have passed now. As the fatigue and exhaustion consume me, I see the restricted doors near the E.R. open. Two doctors in operating gowns walk out, rather slowly, with their operating caps removed. Even they look exhausted.

Even though there are tons of people waiting in the waiting room, I can sense that they are the ones that operated on Aman. My feeling is confirmed when they make eye contact with me and head in my direction. I shoot up from my seat, nervously awaiting what they're going to say.

"Are you here for Mr. Wajla?"

"Yes."

"The bullet was lodged in his lung cavity. Although it did not hit a major artery, there was still a lot of bleeding, and since he coded en route, it was touch and go for a long time. We were barely able to get him stable for more than five minutes."

I'm frozen like a statue, but a tear manages to escape.

"I wish I had better news for you, ma'am." I feel a gut-wrenching pain upon hearing these words.

"He's stable now, but given the fluctuations, we'll be monitoring him closely." Relief washes over me as I hear these simple words. He's stable. He's alive.

"The next forty-eight hours are critical. We will only be able to say he's out of the woods if he remains stable during this time. He's a fighter," the doctor continues. "Once he's able to breathe on his own, that will be a great sign."

He's alive. Aman is alive. I cry tears of relief and hug the doctor delivering the news, realizing how inappropriate it may be. But I don't care.

"Where is he now?" I ask.

"He's in the ICU, but you're allowed to stay with him if you like."

I nod eagerly before the doctor finishes speaking, and he leads me to where Aman is. I don't know what to expect when I see him. I'm grateful and solely focused on the fact that he's alive.

He's in a corner room of the ICU. When I reach the door, I stop fast in my tracks as I overlook his bed. He's hooked up to so many wires and tubes, with machines all around him, and his right hand is completely bandaged. If the doctor hadn't directed me to his room, I wouldn't have known that it was him. The tube in his mouth, which I assume is helping him breathe, obscures his face entirely.

It breaks me to see the Aman I know and love like this. The Aman who dominates and energizes any room he walks into is now lying in a hospital bed in the ICU.

The doctors leave me alone with him. As I walk closer to him, I pout to prevent more tears, but they come rolling down despite my efforts. The upward and downward breathing movement of Aman's chest, facilitated by the ventilator, gives me hope.

His eyes are closed. Barring the tubes, he looks like he's sleeping. I wonder if he knows I'm here.

I scoot the chair over next to his bedside, then rest my head near his left hand and immediately fall asleep holding his hand.

chapter 51

I feel someone continuously yet gently nudging me. Although I'm waking up, I'm unable to move. It must be a combination of exhaustion and the effects of the mild concussion. I feel paralyzed.

I recognize the voice of the person. The person who's nudging me is Aman's mom.

"Bani." I'm awake enough to hear the pain in her voice. "Wake up, sweetheart."

"Hm?" I was in a dreamless sleep. It was empty time that gave me the illusion that none of the events of the past day actually happened.

Waking up to Aman still in his bed in the ICU brings me back to what I was hoping was solely my imagination or a really, really terrible nightmare. Like the ones I've had before. The realization is painful.

My head is still resting on Aman's bed, and I'm still holding his hand, although loosely now. The only thing that takes me out of my temporary paralysis is the need to confirm that he's breathing through the respirator. I jolt upright, startling Aman's mom.

I look directly at him, and it takes a few moments for my brain to register that his chest is moving steadily upwards and downwards.

I look at his mom with tearful eyes. Charan is standing in the corner with an intense look of concern. His mom hugs me and holds on to me extra tight. I haven't touched anyone, aside from Aman, since we left the abandoned building. I hold on to her tighter than she's holding me.

"Are you okay?" Her son is lying in a hospital bed in the ICU and her few words to me are to ensure that *I* am okay. My heart aches with guilt, and all I manage is a brief nod.

She walks to Aman and grabs the same hand I fell asleep holding. "What did the doctor say?" she asks as she gazes at Aman, delicately grazing his hand.

"He had a rough surgery, and the next forty-eight hours are critical. If he remains stable throughout, he should be okay." She doesn't ask me for details about what happened. I can tell she's not ready to hear them.

She gently nods, taking a seat on the chair I vacated. Needing to do something to distract myself from the anticipation, I offer to get something for them from the hospital cafeteria.

Aman's mom shakes her head, but when I turn to ask Charan, he mouths to get her some water and some tea for him. Although I don't want to leave Aman, they need a moment alone with him.

I purchase three water bottles and one English breakfast tea for Charan. The doctor recommended that I stay hydrated at all times, which will help combat any dizziness.

From the corner of my eye, I see a figure approaching me. When I look up, Detective Shepherd walks toward me with a look of concern. There's a blood stain on his shirt and I wonder whose it is.

"Ms. Sethi, may I speak with you for a moment?" he asks politely.

I nod and follow him as he leads us to a table in the cafeteria. He pulls a chair out for me before he takes a seat himself.

"I apologize for the timing of this, but I really need to get a formal statement from you. We find that it's best to get a statement from a witness when it's still, excuse my words, *fresh*."

Now is the best time to share as much information as I can to fully help in prosecuting both Marcus and Noor for what they've done to Aman. That's the only reason I agree.

"I'm going to ask you some questions to stimulate your memory flow. You'll find that as I ask more questions, you will recall more and more details that will aid in the cases against both individuals. We'll need to start from the beginning."

He leans in a little closer and speaks in a low, hushed tone, "Just so you know, as soon as the doctors discharge Marcus and Noor from their care, which should be soon, they're both going straight to the county jail. They're both currently handcuffed to their beds."

I nod at him appreciatively, and before he begins, he gives me a reassuring smile.

"How did you first come into contact with both Marcus Hendrix and Noor Roshan?"

In order to move on from the worst period of my life, I have to relive it and recite it in detail. But since it's for Aman, I answer each of Detective Shepherd's questions with as much detail and specificity as I possibly can.

Detective Blake visits Detective Shepherd for a separate inquiry during our meeting, and offers to take the water bottles and tea to Aman's room. I accept his offer, considering this may take a long time with Detective Shepherd.

The questions take around forty minutes. Before Detective Shepherd gets up to escort me to Aman's room, he seems hesitant to mention something to me but finally does.

"Bani—" I encouraged him to call me by my first name during the questioning—"Marcus is repeatedly asking to see you."

I physically cringe and chills run down my spine. "I won't waste another second with him."

He nods in agreement. As important and inevitable as that session with him was, I'm glad that it is over.

Within a few minutes of my return, one of Aman's monitors begins beeping rapidly, prompting a nurse and doctor to rush into the room. Aman's mom, Charan, and I are panicking, but the staff urge us to move out of the way.

"What's happening?" Aman's mom and I ask simultaneously. She doesn't need the trauma of seeing her son's condition worsen before her eyes. She's been through enough.

No one responds, as they focus on Aman and chatter medical jargon amongst themselves. Several snail-speed minutes pass before the doctor turns her attention to us.

"This is actually a great improvement." She's smiling. "He's fighting the tube and is showing signs of breathing on his own. We'll start to wean him off the ventilator in an effort to remove the tube."

Aman's mom was already crying from fear, but now tears of joy run down her pretty face. She thanks the doctor, wiping the tears from her eyes. As soon as the doctor leaves, Aman's mom turns to hug me again and then hugs her husband.

"Thank you, God," she says over and over again in Punjabi.

Now that I feel like my lungs have received fresh air after struggling to breathe for hours, I urge Aman's mom and Charan to eat something. They've been here for a while and haven't eaten a thing. She looks at Aman with uncertainty.

"Don't worry, I'm here. You need to eat," Charan assures her in Punjabi. I make a mental note to bring something back for him.

"Okay," she says reluctantly.

Aman's mom asks me how the wedding was when we're in the cafeteria, presumably to think of anything but her son in a hospital bed. I can't believe the wedding was only two days ago.

Understanding that she needs a distraction, I think back to the wonderful time we had at the wedding. Specifically at the reception, when the whole wedding party on Devan's side was dancing to a popular older song in pairs. Aman and I were paired together for a part of the song. He sang the lyrics to me as we danced.

Aman's mom responds well to this. The distraction is working.

There are moments of silence while we eat. Once she finishes, she gazes at me until I'm done. I can tell that she now wants to know how her son ended up in a hospital with a gunshot wound to his chest.

"Bani, I don't want to know what happened—with the gunshot. I can't hear that. But I do want to know why it happened. Why my Aman? The police said that you were in an isolated building?" I nod in response. "What were you both doing there?"

I look away, but I still feel her eyes fixed on me.

Taking a deep breath, I muster the courage to tell her the truth, only giving her the highlights from the beginning.

"The guy who did this, Marcus, replaced the TA who died a few months ago. Our original TA was hit by a car during his morning jog. Since it was a remote area, the police weren't able to determine who did it. There were no cameras or anything." I pause briefly to gauge her reaction. She seems okay, presumably because this isn't the part that relates directly to Aman.

"Once he started working as the TA, I guess he became interested in me and considered Aman a threat. I don't know." I hesitate. "Today, after class, I went home to check on Aman." I pause again, not explaining why Aman didn't go to class or why I needed to check on him.

"Marcus must have followed me home, knowing that Aman wouldn't be there. He started spilling everything to me. He was the one who hit our TA with a car, which killed him. I don't remember how I got to the building, but Marcus knocked me unconscious and took me there. Next thing I know, I woke up in the building, and our evidence professor who went missing was also there."

She still seems okay. But the heartbreaking part comes next. "He wanted to entrap Aman, so it seemed that Aman was responsible for the kidnapping of our professor and me, and I think the hit-and-run of our TA. Aman knew something was wrong and came to find me, and that's when it all happened..." I allude to the events that occurred without explicitly stating them. I don't mention Noor at all, even though she was the one who pulled the trigger. She was just a pawn.

Aman's mom closes her eyes, and several tears fall down her cheeks.

I did not want to lie to her. The truth is that Aman is where he is now because of Marcus' obsession with me. By proximate cause, I'm the reason Aman was shot.

I'm nervous to hear her next words.

She wipes her tears and straightens her body posture. "I'm proud of him and his bravery. He did the right thing."

Her words crush me.

"He always protects those he loves," she says as her tears continue to fall.

She knows. She knows that Aman loves me.

"He didn't tell me, but I already knew. I'm his mom. We always know."

Now that Aman's mom knows, I need to tell my own family what happened. The longer I wait to tell them, the angrier they'll be.

"What are you doing?" my dad says as he answers my call. The calm in my dad's voice slowly breaks my heart because, even though I'm okay, I'm about to tell him something that will frighten him regardless.

When I speak, he figures out that something is wrong because my voice is initially shaky. Him saying, "What's wrong?" prompts my mom to immediately speak up.

"Put her on speaker," she says. There's a brief pause.

I ask them not to worry, knowing very well that I'm a fool for making this request. They will drop everything and come to the hospital once they hear of Aman's condition. They love him just as much as I do.

I don't give them as many details as I did to Aman's mom, but I do say what Marcus did to me and what he did to Aman. I tell them that he wanted Aman out of his way because of me, and he fabricated a story with the police to entrap Aman.

The urge to fight back my tears is the hardest when I hear them in my mom's voice. My dad hasn't spoken.

My dad finally says, "We're on our way," then disconnects the phone once he provides me with their approximate arrival time. As difficult as that was, I feel a sense of immense relief now that I have told them.

I linger around the hallways before I go back to Aman's room in the ICU. Amidst my lingering, I see a familiar and welcomed face wandering the hallways. *Mark.*

He's maneuvering his way around the hospital but is obviously lost. I walk directly toward him as he looks at his phone. Once he sees that it's me, he rushes to me with his arms extended for a hug.

Mark doesn't barrage me with questions. Although I can tell he's anxious to ask me what happened, I'm extremely grateful that he doesn't.

As Mark and I near Aman's room, Aman's mom runs into the room sobbing like I've never seen her sob before. There's a lot of commotion coming from inside it.

My heart sinks to the bottom of my stomach. Both Mark and I sprint toward his room as fast as we can.

No, no, no, I repeat to myself as I run, fearing the worst. We finally reach the entrance of his room and stop fast in our tracks.

There's Aman. He's awake. Hazily, but he's awake.

I've already cried so much that I didn't think I had any more tears left in me, but I do. For this moment, right here, I do.

He hasn't seen me yet. He repeatedly opens and closes his eyes, not looking in the direction of the doorway. He understandably appears to be in pain. As he softly grunts and moans, his mom rubs his arm to alleviate any pain with her mother's touch. Tears stream down her face, but she's smiling.

Something turns Aman's attention to the door because he looks directly at me. He doesn't move at all, but I know he wants me to come closer to him, and I instinctively do so.

He keeps his eyes on me, and I keep mine on him.

When I'm within his reaching distance, he weakly chuckles, and slowly grabs my hand, squeezing it. I fiddle with his dad's black onyx bracelet, the bracelet fully intact despite the struggle from before.

I bend down, first kissing his forehead and then planting a soft kiss on his lips. I lean closer to his ear and whisper, "I love you, too."

Aman places my hand on his chest and closes his eyes, smiling.

Aman. Never did I ever expect him to be the one.

chapter 52

Aman was discharged from the hospital about two weeks ago. The doctor ordered regular check-up visits and is confident he will feel fully normal in a few more weeks.

Our Alcatraz night trip was inevitably delayed following the incident. Mark was able to reschedule it closer to Thanksgiving break when Natalia is visiting again. Not quite the scary Halloween-time tour we had planned on, but both Aman and I have experienced enough scary things to last us a while. Besides, I'm more thankful than anything.

Marcus and Noor were both charged for their heinous crimes. They were in the hospital but were taken straight to the county jail after their respective doctors discharged them, as Detective Shepherd promised. The lengths that the both of them went to in order to achieve their twisted purpose is incomprehensible.

There are moments when it still feels new to hold Aman's hand, but they're brief moments. Right now, we're wandering around the Alcatraz penitentiary with the audio guides speaking in our ears.

There's a part of the tour where we end up outside and can see the San Francisco skyline. It's not quite the same view as from Devan's wedding reception—Alcatraz Island isn't part of the view since we're currently on it. It's a nice break from the immensely interesting, but depressing, stories of the island.

I was expecting the tour to be a good time, but I didn't imagine it would be this entertaining. Aman is thoroughly enjoying himself. He hasn't let go of my hand the entire time we've been here. Midway through, we lose track of Mark and Natalia, but I don't think they're too far behind. Right now, it's just Aman, me, and this remarkable view.

Amidst my marveling at the view, I don't realize that Aman has been staring at me while we've been out here.

"Stop it, you creep," I say to him. He still makes me feel incredibly shy at times, but I love it.

He smiles and strokes my cheek. "What?" he responds innocently.

"You're staring at me."

"Well, yes. Because now I can do that without any hesitation."

He's right on that front. Although it was an adjustment from our previous relationship dynamic, this feels much more natural. We are right where we should be.

I'm facing the water when he comes up behind me, wrapping his arms on either side of me to keep me warm. I instinctively lean back to rest the back of my head on his chest. Happiness rushes through me to the point that I feel butterflies in my stomach.

"It's still a little weird to see you like this, but you're so damn cute." Both Mark and Natalia smile at us with lovesick admiration. Aman is smiling from ear to ear.

"Long time coming, my man. Long time coming." Aman squeezes my hand. Mark chuckles, but Aman means what he says.

"What's your favorite part of the tour?" Natalia asks both me and Aman.

"This part," we answer simultaneously, referring to the outside where we can see the back of the penitentiary and the view of the bay.

"What about you?" I reciprocate the question.

"The dining hall was pretty cool. They have postcards there to write to some prisoners in other penitentiaries."

"Really? We haven't gotten to that part yet." Aman gestures for us to go.

"Yes, go check it out!" We let them enjoy private time in front of the breathtaking view we spent a good twenty minutes in front of.

Aman wanted to save the dining hall for later, but neither of us realized that there were postcards to send to different prisoners from other prisons. In fact, one of the postcards is to an inmate located at San Quentin, which is a prison right across the bay.

One inmate was accused and convicted of brutally beating his pregnant girlfriend in an alley in San Leandro, where she later died in the hospital. It reminded me of how Marcus' fiancée was killed, but this inmate's trial happened decades ago.

Since the incident with Marcus, Professor Erikson and Aman have taken a liking to each other. They have a "mutual acceptance," as Aman calls it. I'm relieved, because his dislike of Professor Erikson was exhausting. The experience understandably bonded them.

He spends a few moments writing the postcard before he's ready to go. He has a tremendous look of concentration as he's scribbling away, but I don't ask him what he writes.

Finals for the fall semester are over, and Christmas break has begun. It took a few weeks for the school to get over the frenzy of our incident, but the professors worked hard to ensure academics were not compromised.

We're going on a small outing tonight with a few of our friends to kick off celebrations. Before that, Professor Erikson and Professor Gatlin invited us out for a drink nearby and are meeting us here—at home. Aman wanted to keep it easy, but also celebratory enough for the season.

"Remember when we went to Alcatraz, and I sent that inmate a postcard?" Aman asks.

"Um, yes," I respond distractedly.

"The inmate responded to me."

"You gave him our address? Why would you do that?" Suddenly, I am no longer distracted. The man is on death row.

"I gave him a P.O. box. Before I lived here, I had all my mail sent to a P.O. box and never got rid of it."

"Oh." This is something about Aman that I didn't know. "You never told me what you wrote to him."

"I told him in broad strokes about what happened. I told him about how it was all because of some psychopath who thought something was true when it wasn't. There's only so much you can write on a small postcard."

"Why'd you do that?"

"What do you mean?"

"Well, he was found guilty of the crime he was charged with. Here, Marcus was mistaken about the whole situation. What did he say?"

"I haven't read it yet. I picked it up earlier today and thought we could read it together."

Growing increasingly curious, I sit down next to Aman. He looks to be holding a stack of three or four pieces of paper; the inmate was extensive in his response. Upon glancing at the letter from a distance, the writing is very neat.

SIR. I THANK YOU FOR WRITING TO ME. IT WAS REFRESHING TO HAVE A PIECE OF MAIL DELIVERED TO ME AFTER NEARLY 30 YEARS. MY FAMILY HAS ABANDONED ME. I HAVE NO FRIENDS. ANY TIME I LEAVE MY CELL, AN INMATE'S ATTEMPT TO ATTACK ME IS INEVITABLE. THEY VEHEMENTLY BELIEVE I COMMITTED SUCH A HEINOUS CRIME BY KILLING MY PREGNANT FIANCÉE. NEVER MIND THE THINGS THEY DID, BUT I WILL NOT DIGRESS. YOUR STORY DOES REMIND ME OF MINE. IT'S NICE TO READ THAT YOU ARE ALIVE AND WELL. I CANNOT SAY THAT ABOUT MY MELANIE. WE DIDN'T KNOW WHETHER OUR BABY WAS A BOY OR GIRL. WE JUST CALLED IT 'BUN.' NOT SHORT FOR 'BUN IN THE OVEN' BUT SHORT FOR 'BUNNY.' BUNNY MIRACULOUSLY LIVED BUT WAS TAKEN AWAY, AND SINCE I WAS NOT LEGALLY MARRIED TO MELANIE, I WAS NOT INFORMED OF MY BABY'S WHEREABOUTS. NEVER MIND THAT I WAS BUNNY'S FATHER. TO THIS DAY, I'M NOT CERTAIN IF I HAVE A SON OR DAUGHTER, BUT I DID HEAR THROUGH THE GRAPEVINE THAT I HAD A SON AND MY MELANIE'S SISTER AND SISTER'S HUSBAND TOOK CUSTODY.

Aman looks at me, and I understand what the look is for. Mark calls me "Bunny." He continues reading.

I MAINTAIN MY INNOCENCE TO THIS DAY. I COULD NEVER DO SUCH A THING TO MY FAMILY. I

WAS NOT EVEN THE INITIAL SUSPECT. THERE WAS AN ENTIRELY SEPARATE TRIAL THAT HAPPENED PRIOR TO THE PROSECUTOR CONVICTING ME. THE DEFENSE ATTORNEY FROM THE TRIAL INSTEAD PRESENTED EVIDENCE TO IMPLICATE ME AND TO ACQUIT HIS CLIENT, WHO WAS SOME RICH KID FROM THE SUBURBS.

I HAVE TRIED TALKING TO LAWYERS ABOUT THIS, BUT NO ONE LISTENED TO ME. I SIT HERE, AN INNOCENT MAN IN THIS HOLE, CONDEMNED FOR LIFE.

IN THIS HOLE, I READ A LOT. I HAVE BEEN READING EVERY PIECE OF NEWS THAT I CAN ABOUT THE WITNESSES, DEFENSE ATTORNEYS, AND PROSECUTORS IN MY CASE TO SEE IF THEY CRIMINALIZE ANOTHER INNOCENT.

I MUST TELL YOU, SIR, THAT I READ OF A VERY SIMILAR INCIDENT HAPPENING TO ANOTHER YOUNG GIRL. THEN, NEARLY A YEAR LATER, ANOTHER YOUNG GIRL WAS MURDERED IN THE SAME WAY. SIMILAR TO MY TRIAL, THERE WAS AN INITIAL TRIAL WITH A RICH KID FROM THE SUBURBS WHO WAS ACQUITTED. THE PECULIAR ASPECT IS THAT THE ATTORNEY WHO DEFENDED THE FIRST BOY IN MY CASE IS THE FATHER OF THE LAWYER WHO WORKED ON THE TWO RECENT CASES.

I PRESUME NO ONE LINKED THE CASES AND THE RELATIONSHIP BETWEEN THE LAWYERS BECAUSE THEY HAVE DIFFERENT LAST NAMES. THE SON IS NOW A CRIMINAL LAW PROFESSOR AT THE MOST PRESTIGIOUS SCHOOL IN SAN FRANCISCO. A MR. ERIKSON.

SINCE I HAVE BEEN FOLLOWING MR. ERIKSON, I HAVE READ OF A YOUNG MAN WHO WORKED AT THE SAME LAW SCHOOL AND WAS KILLED IN A HIT-AND-RUN. IF I AM QUITE FRANK, THE YOUNG MAN WHO DIED REMINDED ME OF ME. HE LOOKED LIKE ME WHEN I FIRST CAME TO THIS PRISON. AT FIRST, I THOUGHT THAT HE MIGHT BE MY BUN, BUT I REFUSE TO THINK THAT MY OWN CHILD MET THE FATE OF THAT YOUNG MAN.

THE UNCERTAINTY OF NOT KNOWING IS BOTH A BLESSING AND A CURSE, BUT ONE THING I KNOW FOR CERTAIN IS THAT MR. ERIKSON CANNOT BE TRUSTED.

Before Aman and I have the opportunity to react, there's a knock at the door.

acknowledgements

To my family (Dad, Mom, Bhaji, and Moni)—my support system. This was new for us, but you believed in it. Love you always.

Thank you, Sav and Jasleen. Your love for literature and excitement for rbw made me that much more passionate about this novel.

To my editor, Sherri Shackelford. You made me a better writer, and I am forever grateful to you for that. Thank you for your advice, encouragement, and attention to detail.

Dr. Patel and Dr. Sachdev, thank you. You acted not only as my cheerleaders, but you managed to help me whenever I needed it, in addition to saving lives for a living.

Kenisha Day, Esq. Law school was one of the best times of my life, and that is where we became friends. Your selflessness and willing to help me meant more to me than you know. Thank you, my friend.

Kelly Lawton-Abbott, Esq. You cheered me on as a friend, fellow professional, and an avid reader. Thank you for helping me navigate such confusing topics and giving me solace with your guidance.

SSN's papa, you believed in this novel since the day I met you. Thank you.

Nicole, love you forever. Miss you every day.

Finally—thank you, dear reader. However my novel may have come to your attention, I am immensely thankful that you gave it a chance, and I thoroughly hope you enjoyed it.